ERICA JAMES

SWALLOWTAIL SUMMER

Complete and Unabridged

CHARNWOOD
Leicester

First published in Great Britain in 2019 by
Orion Fiction
an imprint of The Orion Publishing Group Ltd
London

First Charnwood Edition
published 2020
by arrangement with
The Orion Publishing Group Ltd
An Hachette UK company
London

A catalogue record for this book is available
from the British Library.

ISBN 978–1–4448–4548–8

Published by
Ulverscroft Limited
Anstey, Leicestershire
Set by Words & Graphics Ltd.
Anstey, Leicestershire
Printed and bound in Great Britain by
T. J. International Ltd., Padstow, Cornwall

This book is printed on acid-free paper

SWALLOWTAIL SUMMER

For many years, Alastair and his best friends Danny and Simon have spent summers together with their families at his gorgeous holiday home, Linston End, against the idyllic backdrop of the Norfolk Broads. The memories are ingrained in their hearts: picnics on the river, gin and tonics in the pavilion at dusk, hours spent seeking out the local swallowtail butterflies. There's no reason to believe the good times won't continue down the generations, though there are surprises in store for them all . . . After Alastair's wife Orla passes away in a tragic accident, he goes travelling — and when he returns, it's not just adventures and memories he brings back, but Valentina, his new love interest. Is this just a holiday romance? What will Alastair's decisions mean for the long-time friends?

Books by Erica James
Published by Ulverscroft:

A SENSE OF BELONGING
ACT OF FAITH
THE HOLIDAY
PRECIOUS TIME
HIDDEN TALENTS
PARADISE HOUSE
LOVE AND DEVOTION
GARDENS OF DELIGHT
TELL IT TO THE SKIES
THE QUEEN OF NEW BEGINNINGS
COMING HOME TO ISLAND HOUSE
SONG OF THE SKYLARK

This book is for my sons Edward and Samuel, Ally and Rebecca, and my grandson. But it's also in memory of Jane Wheelhouse, a dear friend who was such a great inspiration to all who knew her.

There is no greater sorrow than to recall in misery the time when we were happy.

Dante Alighieri

1

The taxi trundled along at a leisurely speed, as though the driver had all the time in the world to cover the short distance from the station to the riverside village of Linston.

In the passenger seat, his stomach churning with anticipation, Alastair Lucas was on edge, a state of mind that was not helped by the annoying rattle in the door panel beside him. He was tempted to ram his elbow hard against the panel to see if that would silence the noise, but he didn't think the taxi driver would appreciate him doing that.

To ease his anxiety, he focused his attention on looking out of the windscreen, at the sky that was littered with puffy white clouds and the sun that was already shining brightly. Rain must have fallen in the night, making the wet road glisten in the early morning sunlight. The passing scenery was wholly familiar to him, yet he was seeing it through new eyes, comparing it to the rich and varied landscapes that had been home to him since he'd gone away nine months ago.

'Where did you say you wanted me to drop you off?' the driver asked.

'Linston End,' said Alastair, 'it's on Linston Lower Road.'

'That'll be one of those exclusive places along the river, then, lawns right down to the water's edge. Some lovely old houses there. I like those traditional properties, especially the thatched ones. Must be a nightmare to maintain though. Are you visiting?' The man was probably thinking of the large backpack and scruffy holdall in the boot of the car.

'No; I'm coming home.'

'Been away have you? Somewhere nice?'

With no apparent expectation of a reply from Alastair, which was something of a relief to him, the man continued on with his chatter. 'But I doubt you could find anywhere better than here. As my wife is always telling me, and she's a local girl through and through, there's nowhere in the world better than the Norfolk Broads. Okee-smokey, here's Linston Lower Road, what number are we looking for?'

'No number,' said Alastair, suddenly wanting to have this last part of his journey over with. 'I'll tell you when to slow down.'

'Right you are. Bet you're looking forward to a decent cuppa, aren't you? Doesn't matter where you go in the world, there's nothing like coming home to a nice cup of tea.'

'It's just around the bend after the beech hedge and the sign for Grebe House,' said Alastair, thinking that a nice cup of tea couldn't be further from his thoughts. The churning in his stomach had increased and his mouth was now dry. 'You can drop me off at the gate if you like,' he said, when the driver spotted the sign for Grebe House and slowed the car yet more, then began to turn the steering wheel.

'No, no, if a job's worth doing, it's worth doing properly or not at all.'

2

Alastair's first glimpse of the thatched house as the car travelled the length of the hedge-lined drive filled him with irrational dread, had him wanting to tell the driver to turn the car around and take him back to the station.

But that would be the coward's way out. He was home to face his demons and put the past to rest. Pulling himself together, he cast his mind back to when Linston End had been a place of great happiness for him, when it was the only place he wanted to be.

Thirty years ago his great Aunt Cora had left him the house in her will. Her generosity had not come as a surprise; Cora had repeatedly voiced her desire for him to inherit Linston End, knowing that ever since spending most of his childhood holidays with her, he loved it like a close friend.

It was Cora who had taught him to sail, and Cora who had shared her love of the Broads and its fascinating but threatened wildlife. It was Cora who had insisted, when he became a teenager, that he should bring with him a couple of friends for the summer holidays, not wanting him to be bored of her company.

Dear old Cora, she had given him so much, and now he was about to betray her, or so it felt. Would she be spinning in her grave at the thought of what he was about to put in play? He hoped not. He wanted her to understand that this was important to him, that to be happy he had to take this drastic step.

★ ★ ★

3

When the taxi driver had driven away, Alastair stood on the doorstep, his luggage at his feet. He was visited by a memory from a long time ago — the memory of his seven-year-old self arriving for the summer holidays. It was the first time he was to spend the holiday without his parents who, as actors, were starring together in a play touring the country. Normally they tried to avoid this happening, but in this instance there had been no avoiding their being away at the same time and so Cora, a woman not known for her love of children, having none of her own, was approached to take care of Alastair. Initially she had been unwilling, but had capitulated so long as her great nephew would not interfere with her bird watching, or any of her other pursuits and daily routines. His behaviour must have met her high standards, for from then on she invited him to stay every summer, and always without his parents. 'They're busy people and need time to themselves,' she would say.

Alastair pushed the key into the lock of the front door and in a further attempt to distract himself, he recalled the knee-trembling apprehension he had experienced as a boy that day when the taxi driver had dropped him off that first time. Cora had originally intended to collect him from the station herself, but for whatever reason she had changed her mind at the last minute. She had greeted his cautious ring of the doorbell with a pair of binoculars hanging around her neck and the words: 'Ah, so you're here, are you? Good. Now then, stow your suitcase over there, go to the lavatory if you

4

must, and then come with me. We haven't a moment to lose. We're off to Ranworth Broad to see some swallowtail butterflies.' No sooner had he done as he'd been told, than he was being hustled outside and down the sweep of lawn to the boathouse, running at breakneck speed as though their lives depended upon it.

That was how life was with Cora: time was of the essence, not a second was to be lost. Life was to be lived to the fullest; otherwise, as she often said, what was the point? She had been one of the most spontaneous and passionate people he had known and it was how Alastair had wanted to live his own life. It had not always worked out that way, but now he was determined to follow Cora's advice to the letter.

He opened the door and stepped into the large octagonal hall. The spacious and airy entrance always took visitors by surprise, but then the whole house was a clever blend of quirky and traditional Broadland architecture. Closing the door behind him, his heart — his treacherous heart, forever prone to nostalgic sentiment — gave a small, but unmistakable lurch at the prospect of what he planned to set in motion.

Thousands of miles away, his decision had been an act of much-needed liberation. Now though, as the familiar embrace of the house welcomed him home, and reminded him how good it had been to his wellbeing over the years, that it had always had the power to lift his spirits, even when life had felt more than he could cope with, he experienced a shadow of doubt.

He dumped his luggage at the foot of the stairs

and walked through to the kitchen at the back of the house. He stood at the French doors to look out over the lawn and to Linston Mill on the other side of the river. The three-storey mill was privately owned, and one of the most photographed landmarks along this stretch of the River Bure. Artists flocked to it, too.

Originally built as a drainage mill for the surrounding marshland, it had a sense of isolation to it, in that to reach it one had to use a boat from this side of the river. There was the more inconvenient option by which it could be approached, and that was the long way round by road, but that entailed having to leave your car three hundred yards away from the mill and take the footpath that snaked its way through a dense copse of trees.

As a child, and when Cora had deemed him old enough to do it alone without coming to grief, he had often rowed over to visit the owner of the mill, an eccentric old boy who had been Cora's closest friend. Back then Alastair never once considered they might be anything other than friends with a mutual interest in birdwatching, but as an adult he suspected there had been more to it than that.

For the last ten years the mill had been a second home for a couple of architects from London who had modernised it and occasionally let it out to friends. Linston End had been a second home for Alastair also, until two years ago, and shortly before his sixtieth birthday, when he and Orla had taken the step of moving here permanently from London. Something they had always planned to do once he retired from a longstanding career in banking and asset management. Risk assessment had been his particular forte, which was ironic, given the risk he was now about to take at the age of sixty-two.

With that thought, he turned away from the garden and view of the river and mill, and looked at the central island unit where, next to a glass vase filled with flowers, there was a note.

Welcome home!

I've filled the fridge and made you your favourite shepherd's pie — after all that foreign food you've been eating, I thought you'd like something simple and English!

Your bed's made up and I've put all your mail in a cupboard in your study. I reckon it'll take you until Christmas to work your way through it!

Best wishes,
Sylvia.

P.S. Neil plans to cut the grass in a couple of days if that suits you. Oh, and he had to get the hedge trimmer fixed, the motor packed up on him.

Sylvia and Neil Finney had worked at Linston End for many years and from what Alastair could see, they had kept the house and garden in good order while he'd been away. Again he felt a stab of guilty betrayal at what he would have to

7

share with them in the coming days. But who knew, maybe they would welcome a change.

But telling Sylvia and Neil of his plans was the least of his concerns. Explaining to his friends would be a far harder sell. He wanted to believe they would be happy for him, but he feared they might well think he was mad, that grief had tipped him over the edge. Just one of the things he had to tell them was bad enough, but the combination of the two — two bombshells — would quite possibly feel like the ultimate disloyalty to them.

He took off his leather jacket, hooked it over the back of a chair, and after filling the coffee machine with water, he retraced his steps out to the hall. He thought briefly about taking his luggage through to the utility room and the washing machine, but instead found himself drifting around the ground floor of the house, as if reacquainting himself with the rooms and their contents. With each step he took, he experienced the haunting sensation that he wasn't alone, that Orla was here, that any minute he would turn and there she would be. *Surprise!*

Nowhere did this sensation hit him more forcibly than when he came to a stop in the conservatory, which he and Orla had built on to the house after Cora's death. Apart from her studio in the garden, where she had spent so much of her time, this had been his wife's favourite room. It had been very much her space rather than his.

Abruptly he turned on his heel and went back to the kitchen.

He poured himself a mug of black coffee, and took out his mobile phone from his jacket pocket.

Who to ring first, Simon or Danny?

2

'He's back, then?' remarked Sorrel Wyatt, when Simon came off the phone. She was finishing the job of emptying the dishwasher, paying particular attention to lining up the handles of the mugs in the cupboard, arranging the plates so that the pattern of each one was in the same position as the one beneath it, and placing the cutlery in the drawer in neat organised piles. She hated to open the cutlery drawer and find it in disarray.

'He flew in at the crack of dawn and is already home,' said Simon, grinning happily. 'He says he wants us all to go up for the weekend.'

Poor old Simon, thought Sorrel, these nine long months he'd missed Alastair like a dog misses its owner, and now that his oldest friend was home he was practically wagging his tail and running around in circles ready to go walkies.

Joined at the hip didn't come close when it came to describing the relationship between Simon and Alastair, and Danny too. They had been friends since being at school together and such was the strength of their friendship Sorrel, Orla and Frankie had accepted that in marrying into this trio of best buddies they had to recognise that the three men more or less came as one, a sort of BOGOF, except in this instance, it was a case of buy one, get two free, plus wives.

Even on their honeymoon, Simon had sneaked away to phone Alastair, despite promising he wouldn't. That broken promise, as absurd as it had been for Sorrel to expect Simon to keep, had always rankled with her. It had been foolish of her, but it had been a test on her part. A test that Simon had failed.

'I thought he wasn't due home for another month,' she said, going over to where her husband was leaning against the table, on which the remains of breakfast still lay, along with that morning's partially read newspaper. Her hands moving automatically, Sorrel began tidying things away, and with an irritation that she found difficult to hide.

She would never have thought she would become one of those awful wives who complained of her husband getting under her feet when he retired, or nagged that the bulk of the domestic chores always seemed to fall to her, but she had indeed turned into that very wife.

Retirement for her had come a year before Simon's and, after saying goodbye to her colleagues at the sixth-form college in Cambridge where she had been an administrator, she had had a full twelve months to establish herself at home, stamping her mark on the days by carving out a new routine to follow. She joined the local tennis club and threw herself into 'local good causes', including helping as a volunteer at Chelstead Hall, a local National Trust property. It was the kind of work women of her ilk were destined to do. Simon had not felt any such compulsion when he retired; instead he mooched about the house like a bored teenager. Alastair going off when he did had not helped matters.

'Change of plan apparently. He wants us all there,' Simon repeated, rubbing his hands together, and with what Sorrel imagined unkindly as another wag of his tail.

'Yes,' she said, 'I heard you the first time.'

'I'll give Rachel a ring, shall I? Then Callum.' He was effervescent with eager excitement. That's what came of having so little to do with his time, she thought.

'Why?' The question was disingenuous of her. She knew exactly why.

'Because Alastair wants to see us all; the whole gang. He has something important to tell us.'

Sorrel considered this last statement, taking her time to tease it out. 'Is there something you're not sharing with me?' she asked. Was it possible that this summons to Linston End was more than just a get-together to welcome the conquering hero home? A man who was home much earlier than planned. 'He's not ill, is he?'

Simon gave her a startled look. 'Why would you think that?'

'No reason,' she said, putting away the jars of honey and marmalade in the cupboard, turning the pots so that the labels all faced outward in the same way. She then went over to straighten the tea towels on the chrome rail of the cooker. She'd swear that behind her back Simon deliberately made them lop-sided just to annoy her.

'You never say anything without a reason,' he said. 'What made you think Alastair might be ill?'

'I don't know,' she said, 'it just popped into my head.' Her husband was right though; rarely did things pop into her head. She was not a spontaneous woman. Not anymore. Spontaneity, in her experience came with a cost; it led to regret and she'd had quite enough of that. Enough to last two lifetimes over.

God forgive her, but the reason behind her suggestion that Alastair had returned home early because he might be ill — terminally ill — was that if he died it might actually mean that at long last they — she — would be free.

It was not the first time such a thought had occurred to her, and as before, the extent of her malice pained her. There was, of course, a much more likely scenario for Alastair's returning home earlier than planned. 'Maybe he's met a woman and wants to tell us all about her?' she said.

Simon looked scandalised. 'A woman? He wouldn't! Not . . . not so soon.'

'There's no such thing as too soon for a man,' she said, matter of factly.

⋆   ⋆   ⋆

Out in the garden, and as she hung the washing on the clothesline in the bright sunshine, Sorrel hated herself for as good as wishing a man dead, but also for intentionally alarming Simon, for wanting to burst the balloon of his happiness that Alastair was home. It had been unnecessarily vindictive of her.

Jealousy was a cruel and indiscriminate master and countless times over the years she had sworn she would not allow it to get the better of her, but she was defenceless against such a powerful emotion. In that, she was like a puppet with a superior force than her own pulling on her strings.

Those strings were being pulled now as she observed Simon circling a flowerbed as he chatted on his mobile to Rachel, telling her about Alastair being back and his desire to have them all to stay for the weekend. It was one of Simon's many habits, pacing while speaking on the telephone. He claimed it aided his thought process.

'You are free, aren't you?' Sorrel heard him ask, a note of pleading in his voice. 'You are? That's great! Uncle Alastair will be so chuffed. I know it's a busy time for your brother, but fingers crossed Callum will be able to join us.'

For weeks now Sorrel had been trying to persuade their daughter to come home for a weekend, but without any luck. If she were to be believed, Rachel led an action-packed life with something always going on that took priority over seeing her parents. Was it too much to ask for her to spare the time to visit them in Suffolk? To make it easier, Sorrel had often suggested she and Simon go to London to take Rachel out for lunch, her boyfriend too, and whom they had yet to meet, but invariably the idea would come to nothing; always at the last minute something would come up.

Yet lo and behold, here was Rachel telling her father that she was free this coming weekend. Well, of course she was, this was no ordinary invitation from a boring old parent; this was Alastair and such was his popularity, everybody always did what he asked.

There she went again, thought Sorrel peevishly, pinching the waistband of a pair of Simon's boxer shorts to the line with a peg. Could she not think of anything positive to say about Alastair? He'd been a good friend to them over the years; generous to a fault, especially with the many holidays and long weekends they'd spent at Linston End. No summer would have been complete without their annual pilgrimage to the Broads. As children, Rachel and Callum couldn't wait for the end of term to come so they could pack their things into the car and escape to Linston.

One year, desperate for change — desperate in so many ways — Sorrel had rebelled and insisted they ring the changes and hire a gîte in Brittany. It had been a disaster. They'd arrived to find a house that was cold, damp and about as inviting as Bates Motel. The weather conspired to do its worst by raining almost every day, making the longed-for days on the nearby beach an impossibility. Simon had wanted to pack up and drive home to join the rest of the gang at Linston End, but then they all went down with food poisoning after eating at the one and only restaurant in the village where they were staying. Just as soon as they were well enough to travel, they piled their belongings into the car and headed for the ferry at St Malo. Rachel and Callum moaned the entire way home that they'd had the worst holiday ever and never wanted to go anywhere else but Linston End, to stay with Uncle Alastair and Auntie Orla.

Nobody actually blamed Sorrel for the disastrous holiday, not in so many words, but it

15

became the family horror story that was given a regular airing at the slightest provocation. Usually by the children who adored Alastair and Orla, which often happens with couples who have no children of their own, especially if they can offer maximum fun and adventure. If they can do that, they take on an almost mystical persona that no parent can ever hope to emulate.

'I expect you're pleased Alastair's home,' Simon had said in the kitchen, when she'd been wiping down the table, rounding up the toast crumbs and refolding the newspaper.

'Why's that?' she'd asked, taken aback at his remark.

He'd laughed. 'Well, it'll be like old times again with him being around, except even better now that Danny and I are retired as well; us boys will be able to spend more time together.' He'd given another short laugh. 'It means that I'll be out from under your feet.'

'I hadn't thought of that,' she'd said, wringing out the dish-cloth at the sink. Although of course she had.

In common with Simon and the others, Sorrel had been surprised when, a few weeks after Orla's funeral, Alastair had announced his intention to go travelling, to find some space in which he could recover from the trauma of losing Orla so tragically. 'I need to make sense of it,' he'd said. Wouldn't we all want to walk away and go travelling to make sense of our lives? thought Sorrel, jamming a peg onto the washing line and snapping it in two.

To add yet more shine to Alastair's already

sparkling golden halo, his travelling had involved helping to build houses for the homeless in the Gambia, as well as a new orphanage in Sri Lanka. He'd also thrown himself into attempting a range of challenging exploits, such as white-water rafting and extreme cycling trips around Kenya and Tanzania. What had he been trying to prove, that at sixty-two he still had 'it'?

And where did that leave Simon and Danny?

Trailing hopelessly behind in his wake — no doubt his now tanned, fit and lean wake — just as they'd always been, that was where.

Oh, it was so maddening, this endless adulation of Alastair bloody Lucas! One day, if there was any justice in the world, he'd trip himself up on his own perfection.

3

'The thing is,' said Danny Fielding, clasping his hands together on his lap, and staring through the open window at the garden in the bright July sunlight, 'I'm scared of time running out for me. Well, I suppose if I'm honest, I'm scared of the actual moment when I know it's game over. But then, don't we all worry about that, that final moment of no return?'

There was no answer from dear old Mrs Maudsley, although he hadn't expected a response from her. She was fast asleep, and had been so since Danny had exchanged a few brief words with her on his arrival. Talking to the old lady like this, with such honesty, as inappropriate as it might be for a woman who was so close to death, was his way of saying out loud the unthinkable, of uttering what he couldn't possibly say to anybody else, and without the risk of any comeback. It was what he called his 'thinking aloud' time. Certainly he couldn't burden poor Frankie with his concerns, or their daughter, Jenna. So here he came and poured forth his fears in the hope of getting everything off his chest.

Now, after saying goodbye to Mrs Maudsley and then chatting to Tess Moran, a volunteer at Woodside Care Home, he signed out in the visitor's book by the main entrance door and set off for the car park.

With each recent visit he'd made, and seeing how fast Mrs Maudsley's health had deteriorated, he'd wondered if it would be his last. But somehow she hung on. Bedridden, with her sight failing, and her body painfully crippled by arthritis, there seemed so little for her to live for, and yet she kept on going. Apart from Danny, she had no other visitors and he had promised himself that for as long as the poor woman drew breath, he would make the effort to spend time with her.

Originally his visits to Woodside were to see his mother, a woman who, along with her husband, had come into Danny's life when he was ten years of age. After years of bouncing from one foster home to another, he landed with Rosamunde and Michael Fielding, a childless couple in their forties. He assumed that history would repeat itself and he wouldn't be staying with them for long, but he was wrong and proved to be their first and only foster child. They were both teachers at a small prep school for boys — Michael Fielding taught classics and his wife, English. Following several months of intensive tuition at home, they persuaded the headmaster of the school to allow Danny to take up a place. Which was where he met Alastair and Simon, both also relatively new to the school.

When Michael and Rosamunde decided they wanted to make things more permanent by adopting Danny, he had never known such happiness. Finally he would have a place he could call home, a forever home. They were kind and loving parents and it was a great sadness to him when Michael died fifteen years ago. With the passing of time, Rosamunde's own health started to deteriorate and Danny and Frankie suggested she move in with them, but she was an independent soul and wouldn't hear of it. But then last year, following a fall, Rosamunde took the decision to become a resident at Woodside Care Home, and so began Danny's regular visits, during which he got to know Mrs Maudsley. Her room was next to Rosamunde's and the two women hit it off when they discovered they had known each other many moons ago at university. It cheered Danny to know that Rosamunde wasn't lonely when he left her to go home. Her time at Woodside was short however; she died within three months of moving there.

Since retiring Danny had the time to visit Mrs Maudsley more often, but after a while he stopped telling Frankie where he was going. Irrationally he worried that his caring for Mrs Maudsley might show a weakness in him, as if he were unable to let go of that last remaining connection — as vague as it was — to an extraordinary couple who had changed his life so dramatically. Had Rosamunde and Michael not fostered and then adopted him, who knew what would have become of him?

He surely wouldn't have been given the opportunities he had. He wouldn't have met Alastair and Simon, or gone to university and met the woman who became his wife, and then there would have been no Jenna, their precious and most beautiful daughter.

He was a lucky man, no question.

But as if to remind him that the Grim Reaper could take that luck away at any moment he chose, Danny's chest tightened and his heart gave a painful thud — *Hah, I'll give you luck, sonny!*

Behind the wheel of his car, and concentrating hard on keeping his breath steady — *in, out, in, out* — he drove through the gates of Woodside and headed for home, where he would arm himself with a pair of secateurs and the wheelbarrow and pretend he'd been busy — not too busy, of course — in the garden for the last hour or so. He was banned from using the lawnmower; Frankie had seen to that.

This afternoon Frankie was at the Sewing Bee in Chelstead where she ran quilting workshops twice a week. It was during those sessions that Danny slipped away to Woodside. The fact that he had kept quiet about his visits for as long as he had made it all the more difficult to admit what he'd been doing. Better to keep things as they were, he reasoned, and wait for nature to intervene, when his 'secret' would die with Mrs Maudsley.

He would have to find something else to do with his time when that day came. For the most part he enjoyed pottering around at home, fixing things that had been waiting since forever to be fixed, and being with Frankie, but at the same time being careful not to get in her way. According to Frankie, Simon drove Sorrel mad by not having enough to do. Whenever Danny mentioned to Frankie that maybe he ought to do some kind of voluntary work, she urged him not to rush into anything and put his health at risk.

It was early days, was what he told himself whenever he and Frankie had this kind of discussion. In the circumstances it was understandable that she should be protective of him. For now he was still finding his feet in this new world of retirement, when the day stretched out ahead of him and was entirely his own with nobody making demands of his time.

Despite being at an age when retirement was clearly on the horizon, it had actually happened sooner than he thought it would. With no real specific plan in place he had foreseen going on with running the partnership of Wyatt Fielding Solicitors with Simon for some years yet, but fate had other ideas and put a stop to that when, out of the blue, he had collapsed in the office.

He'd been feeling vaguely out of sorts all that week, conscious of a hint of breathlessness combined with a spacey sense of not being quite with it. He'd put it down to tiredness, having had a run of nights when he hadn't slept well, worrying over a client's abusive husband who had taken to showing up at the office to harangue him. Twice the man had terrified Joan, their receptionist, by barging through to Danny's office and threatening violence unless he stopped acting on behalf of his wife who wanted to divorce him.

It had been the first time anything like that had happened to Danny and had caused his heart to pound ferociously fast, at the same time feeling as though a strong hand had wrapped itself around that vital organ and squeezed it painfully hard. It seemed obvious now that he had ignored the blatant warning signs that something was seriously wrong, but he'd convinced himself that it was nothing to worry about.

The next day, when everybody but the cleaner had left the office for home, he had collapsed while on his way up the stairs to use the toilet. He'd been halfway up when he'd felt as though that iron grip of a hand had seized hold of his heart and suddenly the air was gone from his lungs and his legs gave way beneath him, and down the stairs he tumbled, banging his head as he went. When he came to, he was on a stretcher and being lifted into the back of an ambulance, which the cleaner, who had found him — God bless her! — had rung for.

He was kept in hospital for several days with numerous tests carried out on him, but then allowed home under strict orders that he was not to return to work for at least three weeks. 'Treat this as a warning shot,' he was told by a cardiologist who looked so young he should have been preparing for his A-levels, never mind qualified to perform heart surgery.

At home Frankie watched over him constantly; Jenna too, having caught the first available train home to Chelstead when her mother had phoned her. The concern in their faces filled him with anguish that he had caused them so much distress, and so he had made light of what had happened.

'A lot of fuss about nothing,' he'd said with more bravado than he felt, but Frankie was having none of it and laid down the law that he was not to work the long hours he had been used to doing. That was when the word 'retirement' was mentioned, not in an abstract sometime-in-the-future kind of way, but as hard indisputable fact.

Funnily enough it was Simon who seized the bull by the horns and declared Danny's heart attack a sign that it was time to sell the business to the firm of lawyers from Chelmsford who had been sniffing around them for the last sixteen months. 'Look,' Simon had said, 'Alastair threw in the towel, why don't we? I mean, come on, let's have some fun while — '

'Don't you dare say *while we still can*,' Danny had interrupted him. 'And it wasn't a heart attack I had, it was just a . . . '

'A what?' Simon had said.

'A glitch. A small bump in the road brought on by that aggressive man putting the mockers on me.'

'Call it what you bloody well want,' Simon had said with a shake of his head. 'I for one don't want to have your death on my conscience because you wouldn't retire. Come on, let's sell up and take it easy. Who knows, we might follow Alastair's example and chuck a few things into a rucksack and go travelling.'

'Would that be with or without our wives?' The thought of Sorrel roughing it with the bare essentials contained in a back-pack was laughable to Danny. Frankie might consider it for a few days, combined with a walking holiday and a comfortable bed to fall into after a decent meal, but months on end away from home not seeing Jenna would be out of the question. As it would be for him.

The surprise to Danny was that Simon was ready to retire, having shown no previous indication that he'd been giving it any serious thought. He claimed he'd been mulling it over ever since Alastair had taken the plunge.

Orla's death had also played its part in the decision they reached. Frankie said it had made them grow up, that they couldn't kid themselves they were immortal anymore. Within their close-knit group, Orla was the first of their number to fall, which underscored the realisation that at any moment one of them could be next, and with that 'bump in the road' that Danny's heart had given him, retirement — a chance to take it easy — seemed a sensible option.

All this had taken place in February and March of this year, while Alastair was in Sri Lanka. Danny had insisted that his 'bump in the road' be kept from Alastair, knowing that had he heard of it, he would have been sufficiently alarmed to cut short his travels and return home. It was what Danny would have done, had the boot been on the other foot.

He had been tempted to tell his old friend yesterday when Alastair had called with the news that he was back, but he hadn't been able to bring himself to do it. Besides, there was plenty of time to bring Alastair up to date. When Danny did, he would make light of it, shrug it off as just one of those things. Not a word would he say of his deep-seated fear that he felt as though every day was a day that could be snatched from him, that he might not live to see Jenna marry, to walk her proudly up the aisle, or have the chance to play with any grandchildren.

He slowed the car and turning the steering wheel, he pulled onto the drive and surveyed the house before him with its prettily painted yellow walls and front garden planted with a combination of box hedge and lavender. Walnut Tree Cottage had been their home — their very happy home — since Jenna was a toddler, and once more he told himself that he was a lucky man. The words had become a mantra to him, and maybe if he said them enough Lady Luck would continue to bestow her generous favours upon him and fend off the Grim Reaper.

He was getting maudlin, he muttered under his breath while letting himself in at the back door. That's what came of spending too much time at Woodside with the elderly and the dying. Thank goodness he had the weekend to look forward to, when they'd all be together at Linston End. Except, of course, there would be no Orla. It still took some getting used to.

But there would be Alastair, he forced himself to focus on. He had missed his old friend while he'd been away. Never had they been apart for so long. Initially there had been regular updates from Alastair, but then the informative emails tailed off until it was only an occasional photo accompanied by a wise crack of a comment.

'I have something to tell you all,' Alastair had told Danny on the phone yesterday.

'He's met a woman,' Frankie had said when

26

Danny had repeated this to her.

'A woman?'

'You know, one of those superior creatures with soft curvy bits that drive men wild.'

'But so soon after Orla?'

'There wouldn't be an easier time for it to happen, when he's vulnerable and at the mercy of his emotions. What better way to recover from his grief than to fall in love? Or to fall in lust for that matter?'

'Do you think that's what I would do?' Danny had asked, shocked. 'Find myself a replacement for you?' Frankie never failed to surprise him with her pragmatism.

'I'm not saying you'd seek a replacement straightaway, but your subconscious would be on the look out for a likely candidate.'

'Is that what you'd do?' As he'd asked the question, the grasping hand he imagined taking hold of his heart made its presence felt and he'd sat down.

Frankie had stopped what she was doing, laying out squares of fabric on her work table and stared at him. 'Are you all right?'

'I'm fine,' he'd lied, suddenly feeling clammy, his pulse beginning to race.

She'd come over to him then, knelt on the floor, her hands resting on his knees. 'Danny,' she'd said, in that gentle voice of hers, 'you have to stop worrying about everything. You care too much, that's your trouble. You always take things so personally.'

Did he? Did he really care too much? Was such a thing possible? If it was, was that what had caused him to collapse in the first place?

And why should it bother him that Alastair might have met somebody and fallen in love again? Didn't he want his closest friend to be happy?

Not if it meant things would have to change any more than they had already in the last year — first Orla, then his mother, and then his 'bump in the road', followed by retirement.

He wasn't a fan of change; he'd experienced too much of it as a young child. He liked things to stay the same. Rarely did it happen, but if there was the faintest of chances that Frankie was wrong, that Alastair hadn't met a woman, what else could it be that he was so keen to share with them?

4

Friday morning and the prospect of getting out of London for the weekend and escaping to Norfolk brightened Jenna's day considerably. It would be great to see Uncle Alastair again and to hear all about his time away. After the charity projects he'd been involved with, she imagined it might take some readjustment to being back at Linston End.

For her part, she couldn't wait to be there, to spend two days relaxing by the river with friends and family. She had no complaints about her life in London, and her new job at Heart-to-Heart, but never far from her thoughts was the hope that one day she would gravitate back to Suffolk, or maybe even Norfolk, just as Callum had. She envied the life he'd carved out for himself, but she especially envied his cosy little cottage right on the river, the shortest of walks from where he worked. It was a far cry from the cramped studio flat she rented in Hackney and her tedious, jam-packed commute. A temporary arrangement, she regularly told herself. One day her life would be how she wanted it to be.

For now, she was fortunate to have a job she loved and a fun team to work with. She had been at Heart-to-Heart for three months, her decision to leave the goliath of a law firm where she'd previously worked coming shortly after her father's heart attack. She had grown bored of her then situation, having also made the mistake of forming a relationship with a colleague. Boredom was anathema to her, as were bad manners, and when she realised that Giles thought nothing of humiliating a waiter who made a mistake over their drinks order, she told him exactly what she thought of his behaviour. For good measure, just in case he needed it spelling out, she'd said, 'I think we can safely say this relationship is over.'

From then on he made life awkward for her in the office, freezing her out of conversations, or worse, trying to make her look incompetent by deliberately not keeping her informed about a case they were assigned to. She was about to go to HR and lodge an official complaint, when Dad suffered his heart attack and suddenly Giles and his pettiness was the least of her concerns.

To be sure that Dad was receiving the correct treatment and care, she took to the Internet. As the leading charity in the country for research into heart disease, Heart-to-Heart figured largely in her online trawl for information, and when she came across a link for employment opportunities, she delved a little further and discovered an interesting job working in the legacy department. It appealed straightaway and following several rounds of interviews, she was taken on. Her team, including herself, numbered eight — six women and two men — all roughly in their mid-thirties, the same age as she was. She found the work enormously satisfying, and was astounded at the generosity of donors who bequeathed hundreds of thousands of pounds to the charity, their homes as well. The downside to these incredible acts of generosity was that occasionally there were disgruntled relatives who contested the will.

There was a great sense of camaraderie within the team, something that had been markedly absent from her previous place of work; there it had been a testosterone-fuelled bear pit of competitive aggression. But as well as she got on with everyone in the office, she had vowed never to become romantically involved with any of her colleagues. Which meant, given how much time she spent at work, there was little opportunity to meet anybody new. She had been unattached for nine months now, and in Rachel's opinion — given that Jenna was thirty-five years old — this was a very unsatisfactory state of affairs.

She smiled at the thought of Rachel and her bizarre eagerness to be married, and to anyone, or so it seemed to Jenna. For reasons which Jenna couldn't fathom, her friend had been planning her wedding since the age of six. Back then she had forced her brother Callum to pretend to be her bridegroom and Jenna her bridesmaid. Sometimes their roles were reversed, but Rachel was always the bride. The part of vicar alternated between one of their teddy bears and Callum's precious Darth Vader action figure.

It felt like ages since all three of them had been together, with their parents too, and Jenna couldn't wait to finish work and make a dash for Liverpool Street Station. She was meeting Rachel there and they were travelling up together. She hoped Rachel wouldn't be late; punctuality had never been part of her skill set.

To be on the safe side, Jenna sent her a text, then returned her attention to the matter she had volunteered to take on, that of constructing a Punch and Judy booth.

The charity was often left strange items in wills, but this one from a Mr Jim Percival of Basildon had drawn a mixed reaction on its arrival. Some had backed away when they caught sight of one of the puppets, others had smiled and adopted Punch's well-known catchphrase — *That's the way to do it!* — before drifting back to their desks.

The bequest had been delivered to the office that morning in a large wooden chest, not unlike a coffin, the courier having left it downstairs in the shared foyer of the building. Not knowing exactly what to expect, Jenna had gone down for it on her own and with a bit of help from the receptionist, together they had carried it into the lift by the rope handles at each end. It was surprisingly heavy and awkward in size, and the only way they could get it inside the lift was to stand it upright, which made it seem even more like a coffin.

The letter from Mr Percival's solicitor, advising them of the donation and its arrival, explained that puppets were traditionally burned or buried with their owner — or professor, to use the correct terminology — but in this case Mr Percival had wanted his collection, and the booth, to go to Heart-to-Heart, being all he had left to donate to the charity. The solicitor's letter further explained that Mrs Percival had died of heart disease and her husband had wanted to give something in her memory to help others. Apparently they had performed their Punch and Judy shows on Margate beach during the 1960s and then when the vogue for British seaside holidays had fallen out of fashion, they had taken their act on the road, performing at village fetes, country shows and birthday parties.

The faded red and white booth now constructed, Jenna unwrapped the rest of the puppets, carefully removing their cloth bags and setting them out on her desk. Most were made of papier mâché, while the others were of carved wood. In all there was quite an array, each one a variation on the usual suspects — Mr Punch, Judy, the baby, the policeman, the doctor, the crocodile, the hangman and the devil. There was a dog with a string of sausages, and a few characters Jenna didn't know.

Unable to resist it, and checking nobody was about, Jenna slipped her hand inside a particularly old-looking Mr Punch. She found the lever on the wooden grip and moved it with her thumb to open Mr Punch's mouth. She smiled and snapped the mouth open and shut. 'That's the way to do it!' she said.

'Is it really?'

She spun round, and like a guilty child caught stealing a biscuit, she hid Mr Punch behind her back.

The cause of her embarrassment laughed, clearly amused. Jenna didn't have a clue who he was and could feel her cheeks reddening. He approached the booth and, tall enough to do so, he leaned over the edge of the opening and peered inside. 'There's not much room in there, is there?' he observed.

He was about the same age as she was, maybe a little younger, and dressed in a pair of dark indigo jeans with rips at the knees, and a charcoal coloured T-shirt that declared him to be 'built for speed'. It was pretty much the standard uniform for most male co-workers at Heart-to-Heart. Not that there were many male employees, they were far outnumbered by women. That was the charity sector for you, as she was told when she came for her interview.

'No,' she said in answer to the question. 'Not much room at all.'

He eyed the puppets on her desk. 'Can I have a go?'

Jenna hesitated, suddenly feeling protective of Mr Percival's bequest. The puppets had very likely represented a life's work; they weren't toys to be played with for the benefit of a cheap laugh.

'I promise I won't break anything,' he said. 'You know, when I was a child I was once chased by a giant-sized Mr Punch on the pier at Brighton and I still suffer nightmares from the experience.' He picked up one of the wooden puppets, a Mr Punch with a gruesomely large and pointed chin. 'You see,' he said solemnly, finding where to put his hand, 'this might be a way to exorcise the memory.'

Jenna stared at him. His brows were drawn in an expression of intense seriousness. 'A giant-sized Mr Punch,' she murmured, 'that must have been awful. How old were you?'

A slow smile worked its way across his grave features, and then he laughed. 'I was joking. But a full-size Mr Punch would be bloody scary, wouldn't it, especially if it was chasing you? I have to say, your face was a picture.'

Annoyed that he had played her for a fool, or more specifically that she had been gullible enough to be taken in, she removed the puppet from her own hand and laid it carefully on the desk. 'Were you looking for somebody in particular to annoy, or was I your intended victim?' she asked.

'I heard about the puppets and was curious to have a look,' he said. 'We haven't met before, have we? I'm Blake Darnell. I work upstairs in the brand and marketing team. You must be new. I'm sure I would have remembered your prickliness had I encountered you before.'

'I've been here three months actually,' she bristled, but then realised she was only endorsing his criticism of her. And had she really just said *actually* in that absurdly prissy voice? She tried to change tack, to offer some sort of apology. 'And — '

'And what?' he interrupted her, before she could get the words out.

'I'm sorry I was short with you.'

'There, that wasn't so difficult, was it?'

'What wasn't?'

'Being nice.'

'I'll have you know, I'm always nice,' she retorted. 'I'm known for my niceness, you could say I'm legendary for it.'

Still holding the puppet, he raised it so it was

level with his face. 'Do we believe her, Mr Punch, that she's known for her niceness? I want to believe her, but I have my doubts.'

Mr Punch's mouth clacked open and then closed with another clack.

'What's that you say, Mr Punch? I should ask for her name? Oh, I couldn't. She might bite my head off.'

'Okay,' said Jenna, 'you've made your point. But you know, it's not often anybody from Brand and Marketing deigns to visit us lowly types down here.' She should have known which department he was from. With his boyishly grinning face and collar-length curly hair, he had the look of having been ordered straight from central casting to fulfil the role of creative geek.

'Lowly types?' he repeated. 'You have to be kidding; we live in fear of you lawyers, you're all so scarily smart and grown-up. And we know what you think of us, that we're nothing but a bunch of hyperactive toddlers let loose with a box of Sharpies.'

'In that case, I hope I haven't disabused you of our reputation.'

'Quite the contrary, your reputation remains fully intact, if not further venerated. I shall report back to the others, who, when I left them, were scribbling on the walls while waiting for a responsible adult to read them their home-time story.' He paused, then directed his words to the puppet in his hand. 'What's that, Mr Punch, I still haven't asked for her name? Do you think I should risk it? It could be dangerous. There again, I'm inclined to think her name might be

Mrs Tiggy-Winkle, what with all the prickliness.'

The puppet nodded and unnervingly swivelled its head to look at Jenna, its large unblinking eyes as direct as those of Blake Darnell.

'Mr Punch, tell your friend my name is Jenna Fielding,' she said, and with a meaningful tap of a finger against her watch, added, 'and I'd be obliged if he went about his business, as I have a train to catch.'

5

Her dignity entirely abandoned, Rachel had to run like the wind to make it to the platform, and after making her way through a string of crowded carriages she eventually found the one in which Jenna was sitting.

'Made it,' she gasped, just as the train began to pull out of the station.

'Yes, and by the skin of your . . . ' — Jenna did a double take — 'of your amazingly white teeth.'

Shoving her weekend bag into the rack above their seat, Rachel flopped breathlessly into the seat beside her friend. She smiled exaggeratedly, giving Jenna a proud flash of her teeth. 'I had them done this afternoon,' she said, 'that's why I was late. I thought I'd never get out of that dentist's chair. Nearly two hours I was there with nothing to do but have a laser blasting away at my teeth. It was insanely boring!'

'I expect that's the longest you've ever been quiet, isn't it?'

'Oh, hello, Little Miss Snappy, what's got into you? Bad day?'

'Not especially.'

'What then? Come on, I could do with a good laugh after being bored out of my mind.'

'You're killing me with your concern.'

Rachel laughed, and knowing that everyone jammed into the packed carriage would be deaf to their conversation — either they were talking on their mobiles or they had their ears plugged with headphones — she urged her friend to say what was bothering her. Because no amount of denial from Jenna would persuade her that nothing was wrong; she could see it in the set of her face, and hear it in the terseness of her voice.

Having known each other since forever, and with only a year's difference in age — Jenna was thirty-five and Rachel was thirty-four — they were as close as sisters, which meant they knew each other's moods through and through, as well as their likes and their dislikes, and what irritated them. They could also be completely honest with one another without ever causing offence. Jenna was definitely the more sensible and measured of the two of them, and hated not to be taken seriously, whereas Rachel was wildly impulsive and unguarded, and rarely took anything seriously, least of all herself.

'Did somebody at work annoy you today?' she pressed.

'Kind of,' said Jenna. 'But it's not important.'

'If you don't tell me, I won't tell you why I had my teeth whitened. And don't lie to me that you couldn't care less, I can see you can barely contain yourself.'

Jenna smiled. 'Whatever the reason, I'm sure it's a lot more interesting than me making an idiot of myself this afternoon.'

'Ooh, made a Charlie of yourself, did you? Sounds good.' Rachel wrestled a bag of Haribo Tangfastics out of the jumble of her handbag on her lap. 'I love nothing better than hearing about someone else making a fool of themselves.

Makes me feel so much better about my own shortcomings.' She shook the bag under Jenna's nose.

'He called me Mrs Tiggy-Winkle,' Jenna said, after Rachel had listened to Jenna's account of embarrassing herself. 'I mean, come on, me, Mrs Tiggy-Winkle! Can you believe the cheek of him?'

'Yes, I can. Jenna, you're the prickliest person I know.'

'I am *not*!'

'There you go, defensive prickles out with hardly a prod from me. You do it all the time. But what annoyed you most about the guy? Was he hot? Was that it?'

Jenna helped herself to another sweet. 'I didn't notice what he looked like.'

'You *so* did. That's why you're annoyed. You failed to make a good impression on him. That's the rub of it, isn't it?'

'I had no intention of making a good impression on him. Anyway, haven't you forgotten, I took a vow of no more office relationships after Giles?'

'Well, if you ask me — '

'Something I'd never do,' Jenna cut in.

Rachel tutted. 'But if you did, I'd put to you the question — why are you so bothered by what he called you?'

'I'm cross because I behaved like such a cliche, like one of those pathetic girls in rom coms who meets an attractive man, takes a dislike to him and then surprise, surprise, falls for him. It's the plot of far too many books or films.'

Rachel laughed. 'I've heard you say some crass things over the years, but that's award-winning. I notice you used the word *attractive*, so using our unfailingly accurate hot-ometer, and assuming Kit Harington and Tygh Runyan are still scoring an outright ten, what does this guy score?'

'I don't know.'

Rachel gave the bag of Haribos a shake. 'No more sweeties until you've rated him.'

'If it'll make you leave me alone — a seven.'

'Are you sure?'

Jenna rolled her eyes. 'At a pinch an eight. And I mean, a pinch.' She indicated just how small a pinch with her thumb and forefinger.

'Which coming from you is a generous ten in my book. What's his name?'

'Blake Darnell.'

'*Nooo!* That's a made-up name if ever it was. Oh, my sparkling white teeth! This gets better by the second. Tell me more.'

'No, it stops right now. And since you've extracted every last mortifying detail out of me, explain about your teeth. Should you be consuming sugary sweets so soon after having them done?'

Rachel shrugged and popped another one in her mouth. 'A girl's gotta eat.'

'Hmmm . . . and the reason for this act of vanity, which doubtless cost a middling-sized fortune, would be what exactly?'

'In readiness for meeting my in-laws.'

Her hand poised over the bag of Haribos, Jenna looked at Rachel, her face wearing a satisfying expression of surprise. 'In-laws? Have you gone off and got married in secret?'

'You know as well as I do, that's never going to happen. When I marry you'll know all about it because you'll be helping to organise it, as well as being my chief bridesmaid.'

'Yeah, that's right, I'll be in charge of half a dozen bridesmaids following you up the aisle and we'll all be forced to wear hideous claret-coloured dresses with emerald green sashes.'

Rachel grimaced. 'I think you're describing your own distasteful wedding day. But to anwer your question, I'm meeting Paul's parents for the first time next weekend.'

'For that you've had your teeth whitened?'

'I want to make a good impression.' She saw the disapproving expression on Jenna's face. 'There's nothing wrong in wanting to look my best.'

'Rachel, you always look your best. You couldn't look anything *but* your best. Are you nervous about meeting them?'

'Not at all. Well, maybe a little. But only because it's important.'

'How important?'

'I think it's a sign that Paul is getting serious, that, you know, he's finally over his ex and isn't worried that our relationship is a rebound thing. It's a step in the right direction, and after I've met his parents, I'll take him home to meet Mum and Dad. Mum's been on at me for ages to meet him.'

Jenna's expression had switched from disapproving to dubious. 'Remind me,' she said, 'you've been a couple for what, six months, or is it longer?'

'Six months and twenty-one days.'

'Not that you're counting. So it's taken him this long to figure out you're easily the greatest thing to come into his life?'

'Are you going to be like this all weekend, putting a downer on everything? No wonder that bloke in the office called you prickly!'

'I'm sorry. And I seem to be saying that a lot today. I don't know what's the matter with me.'

Rachel sniggered. 'I do. You're not getting any sex, that's your problem.'

'Oh, tell everyone on the train why don't you?' hissed Jenna, looking around the carriage to see if anyone had heard.

Her voice low, Rachel said, 'It's true though, isn't it?'

'I'd sooner put up with celibacy than be stuck with the wrong man,' responded Jenna, turning to look out of the window.

Rachel took it as her cue to keep quiet, which she'd be the first to say wasn't easy for her. Nor was letting somebody else have the last word. She pulled out the paperback she'd brought with her; it was one of her mother's book club choices and so far she was finding it heavy going. Secretly she preferred the type of book Jenna had earlier dismissed. She liked to be entertained, not lectured or preached at.

Some time later, when the train stopped at Manningtree and the carriage emptied by half, and she'd read the same page several times over, Rachel gave up on the book. Next to her Jenna had her laptop out and appeared to be working. Rachel rarely worked outside of the office if she could help it. Or even inside the office if she could get away with it. She wasn't a dedicated career girl like Jenna; her job in the HR department of an insurance firm was a means to an end; it paid the bills and enabled her to indulge in her favourite pastime, that of online shopping.

Recently work interested her less and less; she was, to put it bluntly, waiting for the next stage in her life to begin. She wanted a husband — or a committed partner — and a family, and not necessarily in that order. Without realising it was happening, she had reached an age when she desperately wanted a baby. Her treacherous hormones screamed out for one, made her do crazy things like look longingly at toddlers in pushchairs, or had her staring gooey-eyed at tiny babies strapped to their fathers' chests. She had even started browsing baby clothes online, which had to be a browse too far. Not a word of this had she dared so much as hint at to Paul. If he knew how fast and loudly her body clock was ticking, he'd probably run a mile.

She closed her eyes and thinking of Paul and the all-important meeting with his parents next weekend, she gave herself up to the familiar fantasy of her wedding — of the pretty church at Linston decked out with flowers, and the boat to take her along the river to Linston End where there would be a fabulous marquee on the lawn.

The sun always shone in her wedding dream, nothing ever went wrong or was overlooked. There were no last-minute nerves, no bride jilted at the altar, no hung-over groom who could barely stand, no bickering amongst the guests, no best man getting drunk and throwing up in the shrubbery or getting off with the bridesmaids in the bushes.

At the centre of this wedding perfection would be Rachel and the love of her life shimmying elegantly across the dance floor, fairy lights twinkling, music playing, her friends and family looking on with indulgent tears in their eyes as they watched the happy couple perform their first dance — the first dance of the rest of their lives together.

Over the years the shape and style of the wedding dress in the dream might have altered with the change in taste and fashion, along with the groom — Leonardo DiCaprio had been her long-standing fantasy husband, followed by Keanu Reeves and Jude Law — but the one essential ingredient that was always the same was Linston End. It had started as a joke with Alastair and Orla that that was where she would one day have her wedding reception, but now she couldn't imagine her big day taking place anywhere else.

'What do you suppose it is that Uncle Alastair wants to tell us?'

At Jenna's question, Rachel opened her eyes. 'I don't know, but Mum reckons he might have met somebody while he was away.'

'Mine said the same.'

'Do you believe it?'

Jenna shook her head. 'He and Orla were such an amazing couple together, I can't picture him with anybody else, can you?'

'No more than I could imagine my dad with

another woman, or yours.'

They both winced at the thought.

'Then what else could it be that he wants to share with us all this weekend? What couldn't he just say on the phone to our parents for instance?' asked Jenna.

With a shrug of her shoulders, Rachel said, 'You're the one with the brains; I'll leave it to you to come up with something. I have more important things to do.'

'Such as?'

For answer, Rachel held up her mobile in front of her face, and instead of sucking in her cheeks as she normally did for a selfie, she smiled the biggest smile she could. 'I'm going to send this to Paul and see if he notices my lovely shiny white teeth.'

'What's he up to this weekend while you're away?' Jenna enquired, after Rachel had shown her the photo and hit send.

'Wishing he was with me, of course.'

'Of course,' said Jenna, 'how could he not?'

Seconds later Rachel's mobile pinged with a text. But it wasn't from Paul; it was from her brother, Callum.

6

Twenty minutes after Callum had texted his sister, he was at the station waiting for Rachel and Jenna's train to arrive.

Rachel would hate him coming for her in this beaten-up old van from the boatyard, but it was the best he could do in the circumstances. His Porsche Boxter, which was nearly as old as the van, and with almost as many miles on the clock, wouldn't have accommodated the three of them, so Rachel would just have to grin and bear it.

With time to kill, he began idly to tidy the worst of the mess in the van, shoving what he could in the glove compartment. What he had left over — old newspapers and angling magazines, a broken Maglite, a collection of tools that should be in the tool-box in the back, a number of ropes, which he coiled, a pair of gloves, and the shrivelled remains of an apple core — he dumped into a dusty bin bag he'd unearthed from under the junk.

With a grubby bit of cloth he gave the bench seat and the dashboard a wipe, acknowledging that he was doing it not for his sister's benefit, but for Jenna's. The stupid thing was, Jenna probably wouldn't object to a bit of mess, and if she did mind, she wouldn't say anything. Unlike Rachel, Jenna had a filtering system and didn't go out of her way to cause offence. She could be direct when she chose, very direct, but never offensive.

As young children they'd been the best of friends, but as is often the way, once they'd hit adolescence things changed between them, mainly because Callum found himself in the awkward position of wanting to be more than just friends.

He'd once kissed her, having spent days meticulously planning how to go about it. They'd gone out sailing together, just the two of them, and after suggesting they moor up and eat the picnic they'd brought with them, he'd summoned his courage. Thinking it better to kiss her before they'd eaten their cheese and pickle sandwiches, he hastily pressed his mouth against hers and kept it there for a couple of seconds, not really sure what to do next. Very calmly she had pushed him away and set about unwrapping their sandwiches, telling him she didn't think it would be a very good idea for him to do that again.

It was an example of how direct she could be, but perfectly pleasant at the same time. Even so, his embarrassment had been acute — he'd been all of fourteen years old and Jenna a year younger. He was suddenly concerned that she might tell Rachel, knowing that if she did, he'd never hear the last of it. But Jenna kept his first clumsy attempt at seduction to herself, and for that he was forever grateful.

Her discretion became the bedrock of their friendship; he knew that whatever he told her, she would keep to herself, and vice versa. He regarded the trust between them as an echo of the mutual and lifelong trust that existed between their fathers and Alastair.

A lot of water had passed under the bridge since he was that fumbling gauche boy; a fair number of girls too had come and gone. His track record was impressive if one judged these things on quantity, but he scored no points for longevity. In that he was an abject failure.

He'd be thirty-six in the autumn and that seemed to be a critical age in the eyes of many — his mother for one — who regarded it as an age when 'settling down' should have kicked in by now.

Girlfriends had accused him of being afraid of commitment, an accusation he refuted. What he was far more afraid of was being stuck with the wrong girl, a girl who wasn't prepared to accept him as he was, flaws and all. Was it possible though? Could two people genuinely coexist without the urge to change the other?

His parents' marriage was hardly an advertisement for marital harmony, not with Dad's lack of sensitivity and Mum permanently finding fault with him, but then from what he could see, even those relationships that gave the appearance of being perfect were no such thing. One marriage in particular, one that he had always thought was perfectly balanced and set the benchmark of what he aspired to, had turned out to be anything but. He had been shocked when he'd discovered that, and it still troubled him now.

In comparison, throwing himself into his work was a whole lot more straightforward than trying to find the ideal relationship. He wouldn't go so far as to say it was more satisfying or rewarding, but it won hands down in all other respects. But then he was lucky to be doing something he loved.

He'd moved to the Broads part-way through his time at Loughborough University, having gone there to do a degree in Commercial Management and Quantity Surveying. When he'd admitted to Mum and Dad that he felt like a round peg in a square hole, they'd given him the chance to re-apply and do something that might suit him better. Unable to think of any course that really appealed to him, and while taking time out to decide what to do with his life, Alastair suggested he spend the summer at Linston End and see what casual work he could get. He'd fluked a job at Snazzell's Boatyard in Linston, probably after Alastair had put in a word for him, just doing odd jobs here and there. At the end of the summer, Bob Snazzell declared Callum a quick learner and offered him a permanent job, effectively as an apprentice to learn the craft of boat building. Callum didn't think twice; he leapt at the chance. He moved out of Linston End, where he'd been staying with Alastair and Orla, and moved into the loft space above the boatyard office. In exchange for being on-site more or less 24/7, there was no rent to pay, which suited Callum perfectly.

With its reputation as a traditional Broads boatyard, Snazzell's specialised in repairing and restoring old cruisers, and it was restoration work that Callum particularly took to. He loved the smell of wood and varnish and glue. The modern boats built of fibreglass were all well and good, but they didn't have the soul of the classic old craft.

Thirteen years on and Callum still could not quite believe that he now owned the boatyard. Five years ago, Bob Snazzell, who had never married or had children of his own, had left him the boatyard in his will; a will he'd had drawn up some weeks after he'd been diagnosed with pancreatic cancer and with only a couple of months to live. Not a word of his illness, nor his intentions, did he mention to Callum, or any of the others at the boatyard, and it was only on his death that Callum learned of the contents of Bob's will. He was stunned, but also determined to do his best by a man who had put his trust in him.

It had not been easy, what with the financial crisis that had dragged on and on, but somehow they'd kept going. Callum had long since accepted that it would always be a precarious way to earn a living, but there wasn't anything else he'd rather be doing. As a sideline, Snazzell's — Callum had kept the original name in honour of Bob — now owned a modest hire fleet of boats, just run-of-the-mill picnic boats that punters took out for the day. Callum was considering extending the fleet to include a few larger cruisers, but his first love would always be boat-building.

He checked his watch. Another two minutes and the Norwich train should be here.

He wondered what latest relationship drama Rachel would be bringing with her. The opposite to him, she seemed determined to throw herself into a full-on relationship with one goal in mind:

to be married. Every time a new boyfriend came along, she was convinced he was husband material and devoted herself to the task of falling in love. It was hardly surprising when the boyfriend would disappear into the distance faster than Usain Bolt making for the finishing line.

Whatever latest drama his sister brought with her, he was looking forward to the weekend ahead, of them all being together again, and under happier circumstances. The last occasion when they'd been brought together was for Orla's funeral.

This was their first summer without her. For as long as Callum could remember, his childhood summers had revolved around Linston End and Alastair and Orla. How would everyone feel being back here, but without Orla when she had been such an integral part of the tradition that had been set in place so many years ago?

Only once had the tradition of the whole gang staying at Linston End been broken, and that had been when Mum had insisted on that fateful trip to France. It had been the worst holiday ever and since then no one had ever broken rank again and opted out.

Another Linston End tradition to be upheld was for him to pick up fish and chips for their supper that evening. He couldn't remember a time when they hadn't done that on their first evening together, whether it was for the start of their summer holiday, or for a weekend like this one. When it wasn't warm enough to be outside in the garden, they would gather around the table in the large kitchen, not bothering with plates or cutlery, eating the fish and chips with their fingers straight from the paper — much to Mum's censure, but at Orla's insistence.

Orla always had to do things differently; it wasn't in her nature to conform. As a young boy Callum had been fascinated by her, and the sculptures she produced. He had often spent time watching her at work in her studio. Normally she hated being watched, but she had granted him special permission to join her so long as he promised to sit absolutely still and keep quiet. She could be quite stern when she wanted to be, and he had grown up being a little in awe of her. She was the kind of woman who could turn her hand to most things without a second thought and assumed others could do the same.

She had also been something of a practical joker who loved to play pranks on them as children. She once made a birthday cake for Rachel that was flavoured with mustard and chilli powder. Pranks can sometimes have an unplanned element of cruelty to them, and Rachel hadn't seen the funny side of the cake that had looked so delicious, but which had tasted so awful. She had cried great crocodile tears until Orla had presented her with the proper cake she had made for her.

Orla's treasure hunts in the garden had been one of the many highlights of any stay at Linston End, along with being allowed to camp out at night. It was a freedom their mother — always mindful of the terrible what-ifs of life — had never permitted back at home in Suffolk.

This weekend gathering hadn't come as any

surprise to Callum. Of course Alastair would want to see his old friends the moment he was back from his travels. Everyone would be so pleased to see him again.

Linston really hadn't felt the same without Alastair around. Or Orla for that matter. But then, for Callum, it wasn't just their absence that had felt like the flow of the river had been disrupted; it was what kept going round inside his head.

He spotted Jenna first and thought how well she looked. Better than when he had last seen her. But that was understandable; it had been at the time when her father had been taken into hospital. As soon as the news had reached them, they had all, apart from Alastair who had been away and deliberately kept in ignorance of events, rushed to visit Danny, to reassure themselves they weren't about to lose another of their number.

Behind Jenna came Rachel. At the sight of the predictable eye-rolling expression of disapproval on her face when she caught sight of the van, Callum smiled and went to greet them.

7

The gin and tonics and wine had flowed freely for the evening as Alastair, breathless with chatter, filled them in on what had to be just a fraction of all that he'd got up to while he'd been away. Simon, although not given to fantastical flights of fancy, would swear that Orla's presence was here with them. It really was as if he could feel her hovering amongst them in the flickering candlelight, shooting those clever sidelong glances of hers when something amused her.

Was he the only one to feel it?

Was he also the only one to detect, beneath the surface of Alastair's conversation, a few false notes, a strain to his manner, a wary watchfulness in his eyes? Eyes that never quite settled or met theirs?

Looking around him where they were seated in the pavilion at the end of the garden — the wood and brick pavilion that he and Danny had helped Alastair design and build one summer many years ago — Simon thought of the countless meals they'd eaten here. He thought of the laughter shared, the teasing, and the differences of opinion, usually between Orla and Sorrel, and settled by Frankie. Maybe it was maudlin of him, but he couldn't help but feel there had been a smugness to their happiness back then, a careless belief that they'd cracked it, had life thoroughly sewn up. Invincible, that was how they'd seen themselves.

Until Orla's death.

Until Danny's heart scare.

The last of the evening light had given way now to a smoky dusk that had yet to form into complete darkness. Facing out towards the river and Linston Mill, their wineglasses refreshed and the fish and chip wrappers tidied away, a hush had fallen on the group. It was the first time it had all evening.

In the deepening quiet, Simon glanced at Danny, and then at Alastair, his two oldest and closest friends, neither of whom he could contemplate not having in his life. Danny's heart attack had frightened the living daylights out of him. It had forced him to face up to his own mortality, and to the one inescapable clichéd truth: they only had one shot at life and there was nothing else for it but to make the most of it.

It was strange that Orla's death had not induced the same reaction in him. No sooner had he thought this, than once again he could have sworn he felt her presence moving amongst them. He had to be imagining it, but he could even smell the perfume she used to wear.

What nonsense! It was nothing more than psychosomatic, a case of one thought leading to another. Nonetheless, he found himself gazing around the assembled gathering, as if searching for Orla in the shadows cast from the flickering candles on the table, and as he did so, a memory crystallised in his head, a memory that had no right to come to him.

Not now, he told himself. Not after all these years.

But the memory of Orla would not be chased away so easily. And as he had so many times since her tragic death last year, he thought how it still didn't seem possible that she could have drowned. All these months on, and he couldn't bear to think of her life ending that cruel way.

To stop himself from getting upset, he took a gulp of his wine and asked the question he'd wanted to ask since arriving. Or rather since Alastair had called to say he was home early.

'Well then, Alastair,' he said, 'you've kept us in suspense for long enough. Out with it, what momentous thing is it you want to tell us?'

'Yes,' joined in Danny, 'you have to admire our display of self-restraint in not tying you to a chair and shining an interrogation light into your eyes. I must say, it's not like you to be so secretive, or more accurately, so mysterious.'

'That's rich coming from you, Danny,' replied Alastair, 'when you kept your heart attack from me. I don't think I'll ever forgive you for that.'

'I've explained why we did that,' replied Danny with a frown. 'We didn't want anything to spoil your time away.'

'And if you'd died?'

Simon winced. He noticed Frankie and Jenna did too. It wasn't like their old friend to be so blunt. 'Come on, Al,' he placated, 'let it go. The important thing is, we're all here now and hanging on your every word.'

'Yes,' said Rachel, 'we're all desperate to know your big news. The hot money is on you having met somebody.'

Awkward laughter rippled around the group.

Trust Rachel to say out loud what they were all thinking. To Simon it was inconceivable that Alastair would find somebody to replace Orla, and so soon. Surely Alastair knew that it would be nigh on impossible for anyone new to fit into their close-knit circle? They were far too well-established a group of friends for a stranger to be able to find their place within their number; that person would always feel an outsider, no matter how hard they tried to welcome her into the fold.

With everybody now waiting for Alastair to speak, Simon watched his friend's sun-tanned face break into a smile, the lines around his eyes crinkling.

'You're absolutely right, Rachel,' Alastair said. 'I did meet somebody while I was away. It was the last thing I expected to happen, but to my surprise, and delight, I suddenly realised I was happy again. Really happy. And it was all down to this incredible woman!' He shook his head. 'Just listen to me; I sound like a teenager explaining his first crush.'

'Well,' said Frankie, in the pin-drop silence that followed Alastair's words. 'How wonderful for you.'

'Yes,' agreed Danny, 'you deserve to be happy.'

'Where did you meet her?'

'What's her name, and when do we meet her?'

'Where does she live?'

'How old is she and what's she like?'

Alastair laughed and raised a hand. 'One question at a time!'

Interestingly, the questions had all come from the children, mostly Rachel. Simon wanted to feel happy for his old friend, but he couldn't summon that one vital emotion. All he felt, and he couldn't really say why, was that this was a betrayal of their friendship.

Irritation was lurking there as well, for hadn't Sorrel predicted that this would be the case, and hadn't he said that Alastair would never get involved with anyone, that Orla was irreplaceable? Next to him, her expression unreadable, Sorrel sat with her arms folded across her chest. She was probably thinking, *Told you so.* He reached for the bottle of wine on the table in front of him to refill his glass.

'Her name's Valentina,' Alastair said, 'and we met while I was scuba diving in Sri Lanka. She lives in Paris for now; before that she was in St Petersburg.'

'She gets about, doesn't she?' remarked Callum.

'What do you mean by *for now?*' asked Sorrel.

Oh God, thought Simon. '*For now*' means until she comes here to Linston End.

'I'll get to that in a moment,' said Alastair. 'Any chance of anybody else having some of that wine, Simon?'

Simon passed him the bottle, his gaze lowered. He couldn't bring himself to look at his old friend, didn't trust his face not to give him away, that he hated the sound of Valentina and all her cosmopolitan gallivanting. She was a threat; he just knew it. With her in the picture nothing would ever be the same again between them. This was the end of all that had gone before. It was the end of an era. He downed the wine in his glass with one angry gulp.

Bloody hell, he then thought, he was over-reacting big time! What had got into him? Give the guy a break, he told himself. Let him be happy. Was that too much to ask? Who knew, odds on this Valentina would be no more than a brief holiday fling. A means for Alastair to put Orla's death behind him.

'So how old is she?' This was from Sorrel, her tone feather-light, as though she were asking something as insignificant as what the time was.

Simon wasn't fooled. His wife might be pleased that she'd been right with her prediction that Alastair had met somebody, but she would be no happier about accepting a girlfriend into their midst than Simon. Almost holding his breath, he waited for Alastair's answer, willing his friend not to embarrass himself, or them.

'Valentina's forty-six,' Alastair said, adding with a chuckle, 'so a very respectable age, which I hope puts your minds at rest that I haven't made a fool of myself over some scandalously young girl.'

'As if we'd ever think that.'

'You're such a liar, Danny, of course that was exactly what you were thinking. I can't say I blame you; it happens all the time to vulnerable old fools like us.'

'Hey, speak for yourself about being an old fool,' said Simon, making an effort to lift his mood and to look directly at Alastair.

Alastair smiled, but didn't return Simon's gaze. 'In answer to the question about when you'll get to meet Valentina, she's hoping to join us in a few weeks. She's looking forward to meeting you; I've told her so much about you all.'

'Is it serious between you two, Uncle Al? I mean, are you going to get married?'

'Don't be ridiculous, Rachel,' said Simon with a loud guffaw of laughter. 'They've only just met.' Immediately he regretted his words, and his dismissive tone.

Alastair raised his glass to his lips and looked straight at Simon, and for the first time that evening, their eyes met head on. 'It's not that ridiculous,' he said quietly. 'People often fall in love at first sight.'

'Well yes,' said Simon, back-pedalling, 'but not at our age, not when we know a bit more about life. It's not as if we're at the mercy of our emotions now, not like when we were young and foolish.'

'Dad, I think you'd better be quiet,' said Callum, 'you're digging yourself a massive hole there.'

Alastair laughed. He'd done that a lot this evening, thought Simon bitterly, and not once had it sounded genuine to him.

'Actually,' said Alastair, 'and I know you might find this hard to believe, but Rachel's question is perfectly valid. It is serious between Valentina and me.' He paused, as if needing to summon the courage to continue. He cleared his throat and swallowed. Simon knew him well enough to know that was a sign he was nervous. 'So serious, in fact,' he continued, 'that I've taken the decision that it's time to make some big changes in my life. I've decided to sell Linston End. Valentina and I are going to buy somewhere else and build a new life together.'

His words threw them all into a stunned silence.

Rachel was the one to break it. 'But you can't!'
Everyone turned to look at her.

'You can't sell Linston End,' she said. 'It's just
not . . . ' her voice trailed away. 'It's your home.
It's part of you. Part of Orla too. Part of all of us.
You can't sell it!'

Every word was true to Simon's ears. There
was a collective history here, of lives combined,
lives shared. How could Alastair think of selling
this beautiful house? Had he lost his mind while
he'd been away?

Simon watched his friend look at Rachel with
the sort of kindly patience he'd always reserved
for her when she was upset. 'I know all that,' he
said softly, 'and believe me, Rachel, this wasn't
an easy decision for me to make. But I know it's
the right one. I need to make a clean break of it,
create a new home and a new life for myself.'

'But what about us?' she persisted. 'You can't
just forget about us, surely? And what about my
wedding? You promised me that we'd have the
reception here. You and Orla made that promise.'

As selfish and as childishly trivial as her
protests sounded, his daughter's obvious distress
touched Simon, caused him to feel an illogical
hatred towards this Valentina woman, a woman
who hadn't yet set a physical foot into their lives,
but who was already a divisive influence. Was
that why he had felt Orla's presence, Simon
wondered?

Shocked that he could even consider such a
thing, he blinked hard. Since when had he
started to believe in ghosts? But was it possible?
Could it be that Orla's spirit had known this

conversation was about to take place and wanted to be here with them? Did she want them to stop Alastair from going ahead with this reckless plan?

It was then, while Simon was contemplating the irrational state of his mind, that Danny spoke.

'From what you're saying, it sounds as if this will be our last summer together here at Linston End?'

'Yes,' said Alastair. 'It will be.'

8

Frankie lay in the darkness waiting for Danny to come back to bed. He was in the bathroom. He'd been there for some time, longer than his usual nocturnal visits went on for. But then they had all drunk rather a lot — before, during and after Alastair was delivering his bombshell.

It was absurd to think of his news in those terms, but there was no getting around the hard irrefutable fact that it really had come as a huge shock. Certainly Frankie and Sorrel had both pondered the strong possibility of Alastair meeting somebody while he was away, but to come back and announce he was selling his beloved home, that absolutely had not figured in their second-guessing.

For a charming and attractive man like Alastair — a man who had always taken great care over his appearance — it was almost guaranteed that women would be drawn to him. Frankie wouldn't go so far as to say he was an excessively vain man, but he'd always been driven by the kind of pride Danny and Simon had never really possessed. He probably only weighed a stone more than he had when he'd been in his twenties; neither Danny nor Simon could say the same, but then they had settled for playing golf rather than running on a regular basis. And unlike Simon who had lost a good deal of his hair, Alastair had kept his, with only minimal grey at the temples. Danny could also boast a full head of hair, but the pepper was shot through with a lot more salt these days.

Equally, Frankie and Sorrel had not escaped the ravages of time completely unscathed. There would be no chance of Frankie squeezing into the dress she had worn on her wedding day, that's if she still had it; she was definitely a size 12 now, as opposed to the size 8 of then. Her light brown hair had long since been given a helping hand by a clever hairdresser, and the same was true for Sorrel in maintaining the striking ice-blonde look she had always favoured.

Frankie suspected that Sorrel had secretly experimented with Botox, not that she needed to in Frankie's opinion, but then Sorrel had always been more conscious of her appearance than Frankie ever had. Their different attitudes had obviously rubbed off onto their daughters, for Rachel was much more interested in fashion and shopping than Jenna. Jenna loathed clothes shopping; she had as a child, and back then she had always been happy to throw any old thing on.

Of them all that evening in the garden, when Alastair had revealed his plans, Jenna had been the least vocal, but then that was so typical of her — *think first, speak later*, was her creed. Rachel, on the other hand, had jumped straight in with both feet and said exactly what she thought.

Of course Alastair had a perfect right to do as he wanted, but their shocked reaction to his plans rather went to show just how much they had taken Alastair — and Linston End — for granted. It implied ownership of something they had no right to think they owned, just as they couldn't own their friendship with Alastair. Yet they had, and it was counter to everything Frankie believed in. But the uncomfortable truth was that she was as guilty as the others in assuming something was theirs because it had always been available to them. Over the years they had come to think of Linston End as their second home, knowing they were always welcome, knowing too that it would always be there for them.

Alastair had joked many a time that the only way he'd ever leave Linston End would be when he was carried out to be put in his final resting place. He'd called the house his sanctuary, and in turn it had become a sanctuary for his closest friends and their children.

Now here he was, excitedly making plans to sell up so he could embark on a new life. Poor Danny and Simon, the expressions on their glum faces had made them look like a couple of abandoned toys, tossed into the toy box by a child who had outgrown them.

Hearing the sound of the toilet being flushed in the en suite bathroom, then the tap running, followed by the creak of the door opening and light spilling out, Frankie turned over.

'Everything all right?' she asked. Ever since she had picked up the phone that cold winter's evening nearly six months ago and had been told her husband had suffered a heart attack, she watched over him, constantly on her guard, constantly fearing the worst. She was vigilant to the point of madness, her relentlessly watchful eye noting the slightest twitch or grimace of pain he made. She monitored what he ate and drank, particularly alcohol and coffee. She had got him used to decaffeinated tea and coffee, but it had taken some doing and he didn't always stick to her advice.

She worried about him all the time, especially when they were apart. She very nearly gave up teaching her quilting classes at the Sewing Bee so she could be at home with him, but Jenna had warned against doing that. 'You'll suffocate each other if you don't spend any time apart.'

Wise words from their daughter, ever the voice of common sense. As a consequence Frankie forced herself to hide the worst of her anxiety, accepting that the last thing Danny needed was her fussing over him.

'I'm fine,' he answered, sliding into the bed beside her, his body cool against hers as he moved in close. 'Just a bit more wide awake than I'd like to be. My own fault, I shouldn't have had that espresso; I should have stuck to the decaf as you suggested.' He gave a small tut. ' 'Wise after the event', that'll be on my gravestone.'

Frankie raised her head and looked at him in the darkness. 'Jokes like that aren't allowed,' she said sharply.

'Sorry. A slip of the tongue and in poor taste. So what do you think this Valentina will be like?'

'I've no idea,' Frankie said, 'but for Alastair's sake we're going to have to keep an open mind.'

'He's clearly besotted. Bit like he was when he first met Orla. Do you suppose she's similar to

Orla? That often happens, doesn't it; people are attracted to carbon copies of previous partners? But it's hard to imagine there being another Orla, she was pretty much a one-off, wasn't she?'

'She was,' agreed Frankie thoughtfully, a one-off who would be a very hard act to follow. But at least there weren't any children that Alastair would have to factor in to this new relationship. That was one less minefield for him to deal with. The nearest he had to that problem was with Callum, Rachel and Jenna.

'Do you think he'll really do it?' asked Danny. 'Sell up and go and live in the sun somewhere, like he said?'

'I don't know,' Frankie said. 'But would it be so bad if he did? After all, and as Alastair said, we'd be invited to stay just as we always have here.'

'It wouldn't be the same,' said Danny. 'You know it wouldn't.'

He was right; of course it wouldn't be the same. How could it be? Valentina wouldn't want a bunch of Alastair's old friends hanging about the place. The whole point of moving away was for the two of them to make a fresh start.

'I feel as if it's not just the house he's getting rid of,' murmured Danny, 'it's us; he doesn't need us anymore. We're redundant.'

'Oh, darling, don't be so melodramatic, you and Simon are his oldest and dearest friends, he's not about to forget you.'

'I wouldn't be too sure. Once this Valentina has got her hooks firmly into him, we'll be surplus to requirements. Mark my words, it'll be a case of divide and conquer.'

'Then we'll have to do all we can to ensure that doesn't happen,' said Frankie. 'Now go to sleep, it's late.'

9

Three days later and Alastair was still reflecting on how badly the weekend had gone. He had known it would be difficult, that his news would be met with equal measures of disbelief and alarm, but he hadn't expected to be left feeling the way he did.

Every night since his friends had gone home, he had tossed and turned in bed, too restless to sleep, and when he had slept it had not been for long: the haunting nightmares he'd suffered before going away had returned, wrenching from him any chance of sleeping for more than an hour at most.

For some reason last night had been particularly bad. He had been tempted to ring Valentina, had wanted to hear her voice, to be reassured that they were doing the right thing. But to have rung her, or even texted at so late an hour, would have alerted her to the truth of what she had warned him, that being back at Linston End, surrounded by his old friends, would give him pause to doubt.

He was not a doubter. Never had been. Once he made his mind up about a thing, it was as near as dammit carved in stone. He stuck at things; he was not a quitter. But the depth of his friends' shock had shaken him. Danny had managed to disguise the extent of his reaction, but Simon, never one to conceal his emotions, had made it all too clear how he felt. It was that look on Simon's face that had preoccupied him last night in bed, an expression he had never seen before and which had rendered his friend almost unrecognisable.

As the hours had slipped by in the night, and resisting the urge to contact Valentina who was visiting her mother in Moscow, Alastair had instead trawled through the hundreds of photographs on his laptop of his time away, mostly lingering over the pictures of Valentina. The ones he liked best were the photos they'd taken of themselves together, their heads touching while they posed like a couple of grinning teenagers. There was no denying the smile on his face in those pictures; he looked happier than he'd been in a very long time. Younger, too. If only his friends could understand that.

There were pivotal moments in every life. Meeting Simon and Danny had been two such pivotal moments, as had encountering Orla in his last year of university at UCL. A year older than him, she had recently graduated from Saint Martin's School of Art and was entirely different to what he'd previously regarded as his 'type' — cool blondes. At the time of meeting Orla he had recently taken up with a new girlfriend, a particularly stunning cool blonde. As far as he was concerned it was early days of their relationship, so he hadn't felt too awful about ending things with her when Orla spun into his orbit. But in one of those unpredictable twists of fate, the girl he dumped became destined to remain a part of his life: her name was Sorrel and she went on to marry his good friend, Simon.

Yet there had been no way of knowing that would happen when he met Orla. Their paths crossed at a shambles of an art exhibition off the King's Road, which he'd been talked into attending while Sorrel had been ill in bed with flu. On being introduced to Orla, she'd immediately mocked him for being an Economics student. 'Not a creative bone in your body, I'll wager,' she'd said.

'Creative enough to recognise a load of rubbish when I see it,' he'd replied, looking at the monstrosity of a picture on the wall behind them — a large canvas that looked like it had had a bucket of blood thrown at it.

'How do you know I didn't paint that?'

'I don't. But I'd still call it rubbish even if it had Picasso's name attached to it. Which I dare say makes me a Philistine in your opinion.'

'I'm sure you couldn't give a damn what my opinion is.'

Dressed in a pair of khaki dungarees splatted with paint, the legs of which were rolled up to her knees, and with her feet encased in an ugly pair of workman's boots, she was Sorrel's polar opposite. Her eyes were ringed with kohl and her hair, dyed all the shades of the rainbow, was bundled loosely on her head like a badly wrapped parcel. She made an arresting sight compared to all the other girls there, and by God she knew it! It was, he came to realise, all part of the carefully manufactured role she was playing, one that was guaranteed to gain attention.

There was something about her that intrigued

him and he'd later offered to see her home, if only to see how she'd react. 'Yeah, why not?' she said. 'Something you should know,' she then added, 'I live in a squat, so don't be thinking I'll be asking you in for coffee and After Eight mints.'

'I wouldn't have imagined you'd live anywhere but a squat,' he'd responded, amused.

'Of course it's just for effect,' she'd later said, 'slumming it is a necessary rite of passage if one is going to suffer for one's art.'

And Orla did suffer in so many ways for her art as a sculptor. Nothing she produced was ever good enough in her opinion, although to those who bought her bronze statues, they were beautiful pieces of art to be treasured. She sold well, steadily in a gallery in London as well as in Norwich and Cambridge. Ironically she hated parting with anything she'd made, regarding each statue as a child — an imperfect and vulnerable child, which needed to stay with its mother and be protected. While most of her pieces were of wildlife, she became obsessed with children, from curled newborn babies to early teens. Callum, Rachel and Jenna became her inspiration and had posed for many hours for her when they were young.

For much of their early married life, Orla had been burdened with the longing for a child of her own, but it was not to be. The fault, she was told by a less than sympathetic doctor, was down to a botched abortion she'd had when she was sixteen years old. She never spoke of the hows and the whys of that abortion, refusing point

73

blank to explain how she'd become pregnant. She even swore Alastair to secrecy, made him promise he would never breathe a word of it to his friends. He could only conclude that the experience was hugely painful for her to discuss, and that her Catholic upbringing had caused her more harm than good.

The guilt of her stain, as she sometimes referred to her inability to have a child, both fuelled her work and tore her apart. Alastair had been all for adopting a baby, but Orla had been adamantly opposed. 'What if I couldn't love that child, knowing it wasn't truly mine? What if I grew to hate it? No, no, it's too big a risk.' Alastair had pointed out that Danny had been adopted and look how successful that had proved to be for him and his adopted parents. But Orla, with her penchant for superstition and guilt, could not accept that she would be blessed in the same way. So she poured her maternal instinct into her work.

She ran classes too, wanting to pass on her passion to others. She was well respected within her field; articles had been written about her in various journals and magazines, which only added to the pressure she put herself under, always striving to do her best.

When he first got to know Orla, he would never have guessed at her deep-seated insecurities. To him, at twenty-one, she was fascinatingly different to the girls he'd previously known — she could be remote and self-contained, but also passionate and almost childlike. She would wake him in the middle of the night and say,

'Let's go for a picnic!' There by the side of the bed would be a hamper basket filled higgledy-piggledy with items of food from the fridge.

In the mistaken belief it would make a good impression on her, he had once sent her a large bouquet of roses. Orla had hated the gesture, had told him never to do anything so disgustingly ostentatious ever again.

She was an *artiste* — which was her way of justifying her every character trait, good or bad. And yes, she could be bad, extraordinarily bad — wilful, stubborn, demanding and spectacularly self-absorbed. She had loved a stormy row; the more furiously angry words exchanged, the better. On one occasion, in a fit of rage, she had thrown a glass paperweight at him, which had caught him on the side of his cheek and left a perfectly round mark for several days, just as if he'd been punched. She had been mortified, as she always was at her loss of control. Invariably the stormy rows were followed by intense make-up sex that culminated in her crying in his arms, begging his forgiveness.

He had accepted it all as another outlet for her guilt, a means to expunge the self-hate that had increasingly intensified and begun to eclipse the dazzling radiance of her personality. It was that brilliance, coupled with her childlike vulnerability, that he had fallen in love with all those years ago. He'd been bowled over by her uniqueness, and her insistence that she demanded in others only what she demanded of herself.

Her death had consumed him, haunted his every waking and sleeping moment, alternately filling and draining him of all emotion, but paramount was the feeling of anger. He had not known before her death that one could be angry and grief-stricken simultaneously.

That was why, and as unseemly as it must have appeared, coming so soon after the inquest and her funeral in October last year, he had gone away; he had needed to put as much distance between himself and Linston End, and ultimately Orla and her death. He'd grown scared that if he stayed he would go mad with guilt and grief, always fearful that he would be blamed.

Never did he think he would then experience the next pivotal moment in his life, that of meeting Valentina. Just as Orla had been dramatically different to Sorrel, so too had Valentina been different to Orla. She was refreshingly straightforward, there were no artistic or temperamental foibles at play, just a candid simplicity. He wished there was a way to explain that to his oldest friends. But they would never understand just how far to the brink Orla had pushed him.

Now, sitting at the breakfast bar absently spreading marmalade onto a piece of buttered toast, and once again mulling over the reaction of his friends, as well as that of Jenna, Callum and Rachel, a stirring of annoyance began to make itself felt. What right did they have to question how he led his life, or his desire to start afresh somewhere new? Was it because they were jealous, stuck in their ruts as they were? Lacking the imagination to do anything out of the ordinary themselves, would they deny him the right to do so himself, to grab this chance to be happy?

He stared at the piece of toast in his hand and bit into it angrily, thinking again of Simon and his accusations late on Saturday night after everyone else had gone to bed.

Simon may not have intended to question Alastair's state of mind, but that was exactly what he'd done. 'Look, mate,' he'd said, 'we know it's been a hell of a time for you, to put it mildly, and it's understandable that you would want to, well you know, get back into the saddle, so to speak, but this feels all wrong to me. And if you really thought about it, you'd see that I'm right.'

'I have *really* thought about it and it feels totally right,' Alastair had replied.

'But to sell Linston End, that can't feel right to you, surely? Trust me, I know you, and I know you wouldn't do something like that unless you'd lost the plot. That's what grief does to you, makes you behave illogically.'

'I think you'd better be quiet now and go to bed, Simon, before you annoy me.'

★ ★ ★

The next morning, Simon had apologised, acknowledging that he had been out of order. 'Too much wine,' he'd said, 'it made me shoot my big mouth off. You know what I'm like.' Naturally Alastair had pretended no offence had been taken; that Simon, along with the others, was just looking out for him.

The rest of the weekend had been a case of them all tiptoeing around him, desperate to say

77

the right thing. Never before had the atmosphere between them felt so strained or so false. Oh yes, they all asked questions about Valentina, forcing themselves, he supposed, to show interest, and so he had filled them in with all the details he felt they needed to know: that her parents were Russian and had emigrated to France where she was born and that she grew up in Paris. Her first husband, whom she'd married when she was only twenty, had been French and after no more than a couple of years of marriage he had left her for a man, finally finding the courage to admit to her, and himself, that he was gay.

Her second husband, a Russian art dealer called Ivan Petrov and many years her senior, had died three years ago. She had a stepson and a stepdaughter in their mid-thirties called Nikolai and Irina, both of whom had been educated at boarding school in England.

For many years she had worked for the UN as a translator. Her full name was Valentina Moreau-Petrov-Zima — Zima being her maiden name and to which she had reverted to make things easier. Her pragmatic approach to life appealed to Alastair enormously. 'No regrets,' she said, 'that is my golden rule in life. No matter what mistakes I make, I will not regret them.'

The details he didn't share with his friends was that Valentina had the bluest eyes he'd ever seen, that she moved with the ease and grace of a cat, that she shivered when he stroked the underside of her wrist, and that she spoke as though every word mattered. He also said nothing about the exquisite joy, and the profound release he felt

78

when making love with her. Most of all, he said nothing about the complete lack of guilt he felt that he had fallen in love so soon after Orla's death.

It had come as a relief when Sunday afternoon came and it was time for his friends to leave, all declaring themselves looking forward to meeting the amazing woman who had given him a new lease of life. Those were the exact words Sorrel had used — *this amazing woman* — and it pained him to admit that he doubted they were genuine. But then so often Sorrel wasn't genuine; it was always what she didn't say that was important.

His breakfast eaten and tidied away, and restless once again, he decided there was only one thing for it; he'd take a boat out on the river. At midday Robert Clyde from Clyde & Marshall Estate Agents was due, so he would have to be sure to be back in time to keep the appointment.

The one aspect of selling Linston End that did cause him a pang of regret was knowing that the future he had planned for the house, that of Callum, Rachel and Jenna bringing their own children here one day, would never happen now. He had always liked the idea of continuing the tradition Aunt Cora had started when she had provided him with an idyllic summer holiday on the river, but he had to think of himself, and his own future.

★ ★ ★

Down at the boathouse, he chose the simplicity of the wooden dinghy; physical exercise would help to work off the agitation he felt. Perhaps his irritable state was no more than a case of cabin fever, having spent the greater part of the last nine months outdoors. Of course his mood wasn't helped by missing Valentina. How he wished he was back in Sri Lanka with her. He didn't think he'd ever forget the way they met.

She had been assigned as his diving buddy, and as he'd joked to his friends, their eyes had met through their diving masks.

Except it hadn't happened that way at all. The truth was, and in spite of all the preparation, he hadn't been looking forward to going diving; in fact he'd very nearly dropped out after a night of terrifying dreams beforehand, but the group he'd been with had convinced him to give it a go. Perhaps that's why Valentina, with her tall, perfectly toned, slim body and mesmerising blue eyes, had been given the job of partnering him: what better distraction or inducement?

He'd been under the water for no more than a few minutes when he was stung on the leg by a jellyfish. He'd panicked, flinging his arms about like a fool and attracting the attention of another jellyfish. In his panic, his mouthpiece and regulator came adrift, and suddenly it seemed as though he'd got himself separated from the rest of the group and was surrounded by jellyfish. Try as he might he couldn't locate his mouthpiece and his breath was fast running out. All he could think of was that he was about to drown; just like Orla.

Then from nowhere came a hand and he felt the mouthpiece being put firmly in place and

Valentina was staring at him through her diving mask. While he got his breathing under control, she signalled for them to return to the surface of the water. Was his pride hurt? Damned straight it was!

Once they were back on the boat, and using a pair of tweezers from the first aid box, she proceeded to pull out the tentacles left by the jellyfish. 'You should apply a hot compress when you return to your hotel,' she advised. Her tone was brisk, and although her English was good, it was too clipped to be her first language. He had wondered before where she was from, and he wondered again as he watched her, tweezers in hand. 'Hot water will help to reduce the pain and inflammation,' she went on. 'Does it hurt very much?'

'Hardly at all,' he lied to the top of her head, admiring the way her long dark hair was plaited and lay like a thick wet rope against the side of her neck as she bent over his leg. 'I don't suppose I could repay you for coming to my rescue by buying you a drink, could I?' he asked. 'It seems the least I could do in the circumstances.'

She had looked up at him then with her extraordinary blue eyes. 'You didn't need to go to the trouble of being stung by a jellyfish to ask me to join you for a drink, I would have said yes anyway.'

What she didn't know was that it hadn't crossed his mind until that moment to suggest a drink. In fact it couldn't have been further from his thoughts. But after that evening, after a leisurely cocktail while watching the sun going down, and then dinner in a quiet fish restaurant overlooking the beach, the water lapping at the sand, he couldn't get her out of his head. It had been pretty much that way ever since.

★　★　★

He had just rowed out of the dyke and turned onto the main river when he saw a woman he didn't recognise standing in front of the mill on the other side of the water. She stood for a moment on the lawn to watch him and gave him a friendly wave. He let go of an oar and waved back, then decided to row over and say hello.

10

'You've been with me all these days and only now you're telling me you have found yourself a new husband?'

'Mama, I told you, it's much too soon to talk about marriage.'

'It's never too soon! And don't you think a third time might be lucky for you, that God is providing for you?'

At Valentina's shake of her head, Liliya Zima crossed herself with a rapid fluttering of her small wrinkled hand, her faded eyes turned heavenward, or in this case towards the high ceiling of her Moscow apartment in Ablina Street, a short walk from Kamergersky Lane, one of the oldest districts in Moscow and once upon a time, home to writers, composers and poets.

Valentina's mother had lived here in this neighbourhood as a child, when Moscow had been a very different place to the city it was now. During the 1960s her mother had been working as an assistant to a chemist called Konstantin Zima. They were secretly in love and when they were sent on a foreign trip as part of a Soviet delegation to Paris for a scientific conference, they planned a daring bid to escape the KGB agents who were travelling with the group. Their attempt was successful and they were granted political asylum. As defectors they were known from then on as *nevozvrashchentsy* — non-returnees. The

KGB tried hard to lure them home with letters claiming their parents were ill and they must travel home at once, but they had known this to be a trick.

Settled in Paris, they embarked on a new life and it was there that Valentina and her brother Sergei were born. Yet as French as the family made itself, Mother Russia flowed through her parents' DNA and so it came as no surprise to Valentina that they eventually returned home to their roots. That had been in 2000, the year in which Vladimir Putin took office as the President of the Russian Federation. A year later Valentina's father died from a stroke.

Liliya may have attended church regularly in Paris, adopting Catholicism for convenience sake, but once back in her native homeland, back into the welcoming embrace of the Orthodox church, she was once again the habitue of old, a daily worshipper at the nearby church of St Ablina, headscarf tied under her chin, a fervent kisser of icons and lighter of candles.

For all her scepticism, Valentina was not without a fondness for accompanying her elderly mother to church now and then. She had even grown fond of the icon corner Liliya had created in her apartment here. It faced east and was positioned in the hallway so that it was the first thing anyone saw when entering the apartment. With its centrally placed cross on an embroidered cloth, along with a collection of small silver icons and oil lamp, and a plethora of other sacred items, her mother kept a Commemoration Book that contained the names of family members, both living and dead, whom her mother regularly prayed for. Valentina had a whole page for herself, as did her brother Sergei, who had tragically died of meningitis when he was twelve years old. The corner contrived to create a spiritual atmosphere that in normal circumstances Valentina did not feel.

This was not her world; this reliance on another being — God or otherwise — to keep her safe, or make all her wishes come true. She preferred to do that herself. And by any means she could. But for all her fierce self-reliance, she would not refuse her mama whatever comfort her faith provided. Religion was one of the few things Communism failed to eradicate, and there had to be a reason for that.

'Tell me about this man who you say you love but don't wish to marry? Is he already married, is that the reason?'

'No, Mama, he's not married. He's widowed like me. And I didn't say I wouldn't marry him.'

'Is he rich? Tell me he's financially secure and can support you!'

'Yes, I believe he is very financially secure.'

'So why don't you marry him before he slips through your hands?'

'*Mamochka*, why on earth do you persist in this idea that I must be married?'

'I just want you to be happy. Is that so very bad?'

Valentina shook her head again, knowing that it was pointless to argue with her mother on the subject of marriage. Liliya believed that happiness was born of security and stability, love had nothing to do with it. That Valentina's first husband proved to be a homosexual did not in any way make him a bad husband in Liliya's eyes. He had treated Valentina well and had been generous to a fault; that was good enough. As for Ivan Petrov, Valentina's second husband, no matter that he was never faithful, that his mistresses were plentiful and young, and getting younger by turn. No, what upset Liliya was the inconvenience of his death, that once again her daughter, no longer in her prime, was a single woman again. What would people say? That she was so careless with her husbands that she couldn't keep them? Oh, the shame!

Adopting a mournful tone, Liliya said, 'I pray to God I shall live long enough to see the day when my little *malyshka* is happy again.'

'But I am happy, Mama. Alastair is a kind and thoughtful man. You will like him, I'm sure.'

'Then why not marry him? Or hasn't he asked you?'

'He hasn't asked me because, as I keep telling you, it's too soon.'

'Too soon, too soon, such nonsense! I married your father,' another flurry of her hand as she crossed herself, 'just three months after we were introduced.'

'It was different back then.'

'You're right, it was. In those days we had nothing. *Nothing!* Barely a rouble between us. When I think of the sacrifices your papa and I made for you and Sergei so we could give you the best start in life, and now this is how you repay us. Thank God your father is not here to witness this day.'

Valentina's patience was beginning to wane. She loved her mama, she really did, but she could be one of the most infuriating and illogical women she knew, never missing an opportunity to remind Valentina of what she owed her. When the truth was, her mother owed her an enormous debt. Had she really forgotten that it was Valentina, in times of plenty, who had persuaded Ivan to buy this apartment for her?

She went and stood at the long case window that overlooked the tree-lined street. It could be Paris, she thought with a surprising trace of nostalgia. Surprising because she had grown bored of living there, she was more than ready to live somewhere new. She was also tired of being an interpreter, even though she worked freelance so that she could pick and choose the jobs she did.

Her work, and her marriage to Ivan, had taken her to many places in the world, but nowhere really felt like home. With his children, Irina and Nikolai, at school in England, Ivan had taken her to live in St Petersburg. She had enjoyed the summers there, but the long and bitter winters had not agreed with her. She had endured it though.

After Ivan's death three years ago, which had not left her as financially secure as she'd expected, not with the risks he'd taken and the debts he'd racked up, she had wondered about moving to London to be near her stepchildren who were both living and working there. She decided that wouldn't be a good idea and returned to Paris to resume her work as an interpreter. She spoke both Russian and French fluently, and passable Italian and German. Her English was also of a high standard, but never quite perfect enough to pass herself off as an English woman.

That irked her, for it meant that like so many of her Russian compatriots, she too would be denied full acceptance by the British, who, thanks to their media, had an inherent mistrust of Russians.

Which was one of the reasons she had made it clear to Alastair that they had to live in a place where English was not the first language. She would not be put at a disadvantage. Absolutely not.

Initially Alastair was taken aback at her insistence, but then he came round to her way of thinking. People usually did. Apart from her mama, that was.

In the street below she watched a black Mercedes swing smoothly into a parking space. Its windows were tinted; such a cliche, she thought, watching the driver push open the door and step out. Why do Russians do it, make cliches of themselves? Money. It all came down to money and the flaunting of it.

She once had to act as an interpreter for a young girl from St Petersburg whose father had presented her with a credit card that was max-proofed due to the obscenely generous limit it had been given. The card, a gift for her eighteenth birthday, came with the instruction that she was to 'go and pretty herself' as a treat in Milan. Of course the girl had needed no one to help her; all she had to do was point to what she wanted, try it on and hand over her brand new card, but Valentina had accepted the job; she needed the money after all. Up and down the Via Montenapoleone they had gone, in and out of all the designer stores with a chauffeur on hand to ferry the many carrier bags back to the waiting car — a Mercedes with tinted windows, naturally. Just like the one on the street below her now, and the model Ivan had driven.

Money had become much more important to Valentina since Ivan's death. She had enough to live comfortably for the time being, but it wouldn't last forever. To remedy the situation she had taken an extended break from work to go travelling in order to find herself a new husband. She would sooner die than admit that to her mama. She had deliberately picked places where she would come across a different type of man to the sort she usually encountered. To that end, she had scored a bullseye.

Or so she hoped.

Everything Alastair had shared with her about his life in England — the death of his wife, the closeness of his friends and the emotional attachment he had to his home — might ultimately prove to be divisive. Would they be too strong a pull for him and cause him to change his mind?

She smiled at the thought of how easily he had fallen in love with her, how sweet he'd been and how gentle and romantic he was. Quite unlike the usual men she met. Ivan had not been a tender husband. The idea of spending her life with such an attractive and considerate man appealed to her greatly. She would go further than that, she would say that she loved Alastair, as much as she was capable of loving any man.

In her experience, love and happiness could be so fleeting; they were probably two of the hardest things in life to achieve. It was, she had learned, often a choice to allow oneself to be happy. But all too frequently one's head would put obstacles in the way, would over-analyse a situation and over-complicate things. Why could two people from very different worlds not fall in love and be together? What could be simpler?

The thought of being with Alastair, of making a life together in a beautiful new home, was a dream she wanted to dream. She wanted it more than anything she had wanted for a very long time. They were two grown-up people, independent and with few ties or commitments; why not build themselves a castle in the air?

For most people the fact that they had known each other for so short a time, just three months, was answer enough for why they shouldn't be contemplating what they were. How could they possibly know each other? How could they know this wasn't just a holiday romance?

For anyone else these would be sufficiently valid reasons to put a stop to their plans, or at least apply the brakes, but Valentina wasn't being led by a fickle and untrustworthy heart; it was her head that was guiding her. She knew how Alastair made her feel, and she knew that she made him happy — happier than he'd ever been, he'd said.

She wanted Alastair, and she planned to have him. That was all there was to it.

Behind her, and interrupting her thoughts, Liliya said, 'Come, let's not argue anymore. I've prepared the samovar, let's have some tea and then you can tell me some more about this English man of yours.'

That was something the Russians and the British had in common, their love of tea and its cure-all qualities. Valentina suspected she would be drinking a lot more of the stuff in the coming weeks when she flew to England to be with Alastair and when she would meet his friends. She smiled to herself, thinking that day could not come soon enough.

11

'I hate to say it,' said Simon, using that voice of his which meant he didn't hate what he was about to say at all, 'but it's what everybody is thinking, so I'm just going to say it out loud; after all, someone has to, someone has to be the voice of reason.'

Danny and Frankie looked at him, waiting for him to go on. Sorrel did the same, though with less expectation. It was the first time they had come together since the weekend with Alastair and in the intervening days, they had all doubtless come up with their own thoughts and theories.

It was early evening and the four of them were gathered in Danny and Frankie's kitchen for supper, the appetising smell of a chicken roasting in the oven and fresh mint added to a pan of new potatoes bubbling on the hob. With Danny opening a bottle of rose wine and Frankie putting the finishing touches to a green leaf salad harvested from the garden — no air-filled bags of salad from the supermarket at Walnut Tree Cottage! — it was a familiar scene, one which had taken place hundreds of times.

The kitchen here was smaller than theirs, but Sorrel had always liked it. There was a relaxing intimacy to the space, which she knew was down to Frankie's way of placing things to make the most of them, to bring out their finer qualities.

She had a knack for coming across Oriental rugs, watercolours and pottery and making them look like heirlooms that had been in the family for years. Even an uninspiring old jug found in a charity shop somehow came to life in Frankie's creative hands; she would fill it with a few flowers from the garden and it would instantly bestow a pleasing charm all of its own. In Sorrel's hands the same jug would simply look horribly out of place, like a bit of gaudy tat that nobody in their right mind would give houseroom.

The ability to bring out the best in things was something Frankie applied to people, and again it was something Sorrel knew she wasn't good at. Blessed with what Frankie down-played as nothing more than a skill for homemaking — she called herself an obsessive nester — it was nonetheless a creative talent that had bonded her to Orla in a way Sorrel had never been able to.

It hadn't bothered her unduly, but there were times when she had definitely felt left out, the gooseberry to their creative club of two. Frankie never did it deliberately — Frankie didn't have a malicious bone in her body — but Sorrel had the strongest suspicion that Orla had taken pleasure in Sorrel not quite fitting in. She'd had no problem in making someone look stupid either. She had frequently done that through her love of playing practical jokes.

She once told Rachel, when she was only four years old, that raisins and sultanas, very nearly the only things she would eat at the time, were the shrivelled up bodies of spiders. Orla's justification for her remark was to encourage

Rachel to eat something else.

Sometimes when alone with Sorrel, Orla would lapse into a lengthy silence. She was that rare thing, a woman who wasn't afraid to keep her mouth shut. But two could play at that game and Sorrel took to the challenge with relish as unspoken battle lines were drawn up between them: who would break first? Occasionally they had no choice in the matter when a third party joined them, but even then they would spin it out to see which of them could remain quiet.

Keenly attuned to the oscillating vibrations Orla gave out, Sorrel always felt that Orla could see straight through her, right to the very depths of what she really thought and believed. It was one of the reasons — apart from the very obvious one — that Sorrel had never warmed to her, why she had always been on her guard when in her presence.

Given their history with Alastair, their relationship was destined to be a complicated one, not helped in Sorrel's mind by Simon's slavish devotion towards Orla. The woman had been able to do no wrong in his eyes. He wasn't the sort to take it any further than that, though, if only because it would be a betrayal of his friendship with Alastair.

She could be wrong, of course, but generally wives weren't. Wives invariably knew if their husbands were being unfaithful, even if they refused to believe it. Denial was such a convenient mechanism to hide behind. Nobody knew that better than Sorrel, or that people lived two entirely different lives — the one others saw, and the secret one hidden from view.

'Go on, Simon,' said Danny, pouring wine into the last of the four glasses on the worktop. 'What is it we're all thinking? As if I couldn't guess.'

'That what Alastair is doing is no more than a classic case of a vulnerable widowed man imagining himself in love,' replied Simon. 'This woman he's met is merely filling a void made by his grief for Orla.'

'That may well be true,' said Frankie, hands now thrust into a pair of oven gloves, opening the oven and letting out a cloud of steam, 'but there's nothing we can do about it, is there?'

'Frankie's right,' said Danny, passing Sorrel a glass of wine. 'We may think he's making a terrible mistake, and to be honest that's what I wholeheartedly believe, but we can hardly stop him. It's his right to do exactly as he pleases.'

'But what if this story of his about Valentina saving him from a jellyfish is a fabrication, a respectable cover story? What if he found her online and can't bring himself to admit that?'

This was a new theory of Simon's and one he'd aired that morning while they'd still been in bed. It had come shortly after an attempt on Sorrel's part to initiate sex. She'd read that first thing in the morning was the best time to try when a couple had reached an age when these things took longer to accomplish. 'Sorry,' he'd said, 'I'm just not in the mood, too much going on inside my head.' His lack of sex drive had started not long after Orla's death. He claimed it was shock — shock which was later compounded by Danny's heart attack. In the early years of

95

their marriage, the thought of going longer than a couple of weeks without sex would have been unthinkable. His disinterest in her hurt, and more than she might have thought it would. Was she facing the reality that she was no longer attractive, not even to her husband?

'So what if Alastair found her online?' Sorrel said abruptly, that morning's humiliation adding sharpness to her words. 'And supposing he's not making a mistake? Maybe it's real what they feel for each other.'

'But how can it be when they've known one another for so little time?' This was from Simon.

'Yes,' agreed Danny, 'fair enough they've spent time emailing and texting each other, as well as calling each other since returning home, but essentially they've only spent a few months together.'

Easing the roasted chicken from its metal dish onto a serving platter, Frankie looked at her husband over her shoulder. 'You've always said that you knew the moment you met me that I was the girl you would marry.'

A pained expression clouded Danny's face. 'But that was different.'

'How so?' asked Frankie.

'I don't know, but it just is. We were young and — '

'Careful, Danny,' warned Frankie with a raised eyebrow, and pointing the carving knife in her hand at him, 'please don't say we were young and foolish, not when one day I want to be able to tell our grandchildren the same romantic story you've always told Jenna, that you looked into my eyes and simply *knew*.'

'Of course that was exactly how it happened,' he said, smiling brightly and going over and giving her an affectionate kiss on the mouth.

'Sweet man,' Frankie said, kissing him back. 'That's why I married you, because you know just when to say the right thing.'

He laughed. 'I do when you have a whopping great knife in your hands.'

Their cute display of devotion normally made Sorrel smile, but now, following her husband's rejection of her in bed that morning, she felt a surge of envy. Why couldn't Simon be more like Danny? Or was Danny the way he was because he'd been starved of affection as a young boy, not knowing what a caring hug was until he'd finally been given a proper home by his adopted parents? Had that experience made him value love more than the average man?

As though to prove his insensitivity by not acknowledging the tender moment passing between Danny and Frankie, Simon said, 'One way to look at it, Sorrel, is how would you feel if Rachel announced that she was upping sticks to be with someone she'd only just met? Someone we hadn't met? Like this Paul character she's been seeing?'

Sorrel rolled her eyes, took a gulp of her wine. 'For God's sake, Rachel does that practically every time a new boyfriend comes into her life.'

'But she doesn't *actually* do it, does she?' persisted Simon obstinately. He gave her a look that signalled he was far from happy that she was disagreeing with him.

'Look,' she went on, 'what's the worst that could happen if Alastair follows his heart? You'll all still be here to pick up the pieces if it goes belly up for him, won't you?'

Too late she heard the mistake she'd made, that she had set herself apart from the group — not *we'll* still be here to pick up the pieces, but *you*, as in the rest of them. How revealing was that, she thought? 'Anything I can do to help, Frankie?' she quickly asked, by way of distraction.

'If you could put some napkins on the table, that would be a help,' said Frankie, perhaps sensing she needed something to do, something that would stop her being so querulous. 'They're in the usual place in the drawer.'

Napkins in hand, Sorrel set about placing them on the table next to the discoloured bone-handled knives Frankie favoured. Sorrel had never seen the attraction in them; she preferred hygienic cutlery that could go in the dishwasher. Orla had favoured pretentiously large unwieldy pieces of cutlery, the type so heavily weighted in the handle they were forever falling off the plate. Sorrel believed you could tell a lot about a person from their cutlery, and the way in which it was held.

The task completed, she caught Simon looking at her with a frown on his face, his brows drawn, his eyes ever so slightly narrowed, his hand pressed beneath his chin. She knew what he was thinking, that she was being deliberately obtuse, refusing to accept that he was right about Alastair making a huge mistake. Sorrel was beyond caring what he thought. Perversely she was beginning to think that Valentina Zima's presence in their lives would give them all a damned good shaking up. God knew it was time they were roused from their complacent little ruts and forced to live new and different lives.

For too long Orla had controlled things, and they, like sunflowers turning to the sun, had willingly allowed her to take charge. She had done it so effortlessly, relying on nothing more than the force of her character. Sorrel had both admired and loathed Orla for having that kind of power.

She had been their guiding light; Simon liked to say, the one who made fun things happen, especially for the children. Sorrel never doubted for a moment that everything Orla had done was part and parcel of giving a stellar performance, of claiming centre stage, the spotlight permanently trained on her.

Sometimes Sorrel thought she was the only one who saw things clearly. These were the facts as she saw them.

Fact 1. Orla had not made Alastair happy.

Fact 2. Alastair's behaviour had not been that of a grief-stricken man mourning the loss of his wife.

Fact 3. They had all colluded in keeping the myth alive that their longstanding friendship was cast iron, that it was bomb-proofed against petty jealousy, rivalry and that nothing — *nothing* — would ever change it.

Fact 4. The day might well come when they would learn that the narrative by which they had lived their lives had been a lie, nothing but a conjuring trick.

The two facts yet to be established was which one of them was living the biggest lie?

And how did Orla really die?

12

How's it going in Shropshire? Have they noticed your teeth?

Rachel would have smiled at Jenna's text had she not been feeling so out of sorts.

No they haven't! She added an angry face at the end of her reply.

Told you it was a waste of money.

Not in the chuffin' mood. Go away!

Don't be like that. How was the party last night?

Gah!

Not having a good time with your future in-laws?

Oh, the greatest!

Want me to ring you?

Better not. There's a shortage of privacy.

Tell me all when you're home. Meanwhile, chin up and flash those pearly whites! X A row of smiley faces sporting big teeth then followed.

Locked inside the upstairs loo of No. 23 Calcott Close, Rachel slipped her mobile back into her pocket. Thank God for Jenna for lightening her mood, and thank God she and Paul would be leaving later that afternoon and heading back to London. Apart from sharing a bed with Paul, she'd barely spent any real time with him.

From the moment they'd stepped over the threshold of the house where Paul had grown up, he changed. It was as if he became an entirely different person to the one she knew; a stranger. His mother fussed over him as if he was a five-year-old boy incapable of tying his own shoelaces.

Rachel would be a liar if she said she didn't enjoy a bit of fussing when she went home to her parents, not that her mother was really the fussing type; Dad was more inclined to spoil her. But the way Tricia Cooper carried on, she made Paul look like some modern-day Little Lord Fauntleroy. God, it was sickening, all he needed was a pair of velvet knee-breeches and the transformation would be complete.

And boy, did Paul lap it all up! Not a trace of embarrassment did he show at being treated like a child. Both his two brothers and their partners were the same; his dad too. They sat back and let poor old Tricia run around them like a headless chuffin' chicken on speed. That was when she wasn't chasing round after the two grandchildren who were bored out of their minds and creating havoc at every turn. One of them had spilled a cup of juice over Rachel and hadn't even said sorry.

Families did things differently, Rachel knew that: every family had their own rituals and customs, but she wasn't keen on the way this family went about things. By rights Tricia should be the one with her feet up; after all it had been her birthday yesterday. But instead it was a constant refrain of 'Can I fetch anyone a drink? How about a snack for anyone? Is that light bothering you, Dean? Let me pull that curtain across so you can see the telly better.' As if Dean, Paul's twenty-nine-year-old hulk of a brother, couldn't shift himself out of his armchair to move the curtain himself!

But all this paled into insignificance compared to Rachel's real gripe — the endless mentioning of Paul's ex-girlfriend. With every reference to the wretched girl, Rachel felt her hackles rising up another notch; any higher and she'd be airborne. They had to be doing it on purpose, deliberately trying to make her feel uncomfortable, wanting her to know that she could never live up to Perfect Paula.

How cosily twee was that — Paul and Paula? It was enough to make Rachel puke up the full-English she'd struggled to force down an hour ago. Rachel was no lightweight when it came to knocking back a decent breakfast, but this wasn't any old full-English, this was an epic fry-up that could have fed every single resident of Calcott Close.

And wouldn't you just know, Perfect Paula's parents lived two doors down and were here last night for the barbecue party in the garden. For most of the evening, when Rachel wasn't trying to extricate Paul from his brothers and a rowdy group of his old neighbourhood mates who'd never moved away, Rachel could feel two pairs of beady eyes giving her the death-stare. 'Hey!' she wanted to yell at them. 'If Perfect Paula was so bloody perfect, she'd be right here, wouldn't she? She wouldn't have decided she needed space!'

'Can I do anything to help in the kitchen, Mrs Cooper?' asked Rachel, coming down the stairs now. Paul's mother was once again wearing the carpet out with her endless running backwards and forwards from the kitchen to the sitting room, where the rest of the family was watching a procession of cars follow one another round a race track.

'No need,' she said stiffly, 'I can manage. Why don't you join the others and enjoy the race?'

'I'm not really a fan,' said Rachel.

Tricia Cooper wiped her hands against her apron and shook her head. 'That's a shame, and perhaps I shouldn't say this, but Paul's previous girlfriend used to love watching a race with him. It was a shared interest for them both, you see. It's important to share things, don't you think?'

No, you shouldn't say what you've just said! Rachel thought angrily. 'Maybe I could learn to enjoy it, Mrs Cooper,' she forced herself to mutter through gritted teeth.

'Yes, maybe you should. And why don't you call me Tricia. We don't stand on ceremony here.'

No, thought Rachel, everybody sits down on their big lardy-arses and lets you wait on them hand and foot.

Paul had warned her that his family could be a tad much when they all got together, but he hadn't said what a lazy lot they were, or that they tried constantly to outdo each other with their boasting over who had the flashiest car, or the latest mobile. Was this a wake up call for her? Run, Rachel, *RUN!*

Or was she overreacting? Wouldn't Paul feel awkward with Mum and Dad politely but doggedly interrogating him?

Venturing into the sitting room where nobody bothered to tear their gaze away from the enormous TV screen to look at her, not even Paul, Rachel's heart sank a little bit further.

Until this weekend she had accepted that it was completely fine for her and Paul to have different interests, that it was even a necessary part of a healthy relationship; but now, and feeling so much of a spare wheel, a flat spare wheel at that, she wasn't so sure.

★ ★ ★

It was in the car heading back to London that she began to convince herself that she had indeed overreacted to meeting Paul's family. Alone with her, Paul was his old self.

'I know what you're thinking,' he said.

'You do?'

'You're thinking my family's a right bunch of lazy oiks and we should do more to help Mum. Am I right?'

'Well, it did cross my mind. Not the lazy oiks bit,' she added quickly, not wanting to appear too rude or critical.

'I could see it in your face the whole time we were there,' he said.

'So why don't you do more?'

'It's how it's always been. Mum runs things her way, we do as she says, it's as simple as that. She's never worked, not outside of the home. She sees taking care of the family as her job. Old-fashioned and totally non-PC, right? Bottom line is, Mum likes to feel needed.' He gave a short laugh. 'You can't change people.'

Was that true? Rachel wondered, giving him a sideways look. Wasn't he expecting her to change to fit in with his family? Surely everyone changed at some point in their lives?

With every mile they travelled away from Shropshire and the nearer they got to London, the more she found herself returning to the familiar territory of her feelings for Paul. Solid feelings she could trust, and which chased away the doubts she had experienced over the weekend. Nothing more than being out of her comfort zone and having to share him, that was all it had been. Not forgetting the constant reminders of Perfect Paula. That was enough to give any girl doubts!

As Paul drove, concentrating on the road ahead of him, his right elbow propped against the side of the door, she thought of all the future journeys they would make together. Maybe the biggest journey of all through life — marriage.

With that thought came an element of smug happiness, that as perfect as Paula might have been, Rachel was the one sitting here with Paul. Paula was in his past, just as Rachel's previous boyfriends were in her past. None of that mattered. All that counted was the present and the future. *Their* future.

And wasn't she just about the luckiest girl ever, she thought with a lightening of her heart as she took in the sexy profile of the man beside her, the strong square set of his jaw, the slightly crooked shape of his nose — broken when he'd been a child and had fallen out of a tree — and the enviable length of his gorgeous eyelashes. Then there were his arms and his big broad shoulders, the muscles all ropy and zinging with the kind of powerful energy that could lift a girl right off her feet. As a student he'd worked on building sites during the holidays, carrying bricks up and down ladders, and acquired, as he liked to joke, superhuman strength, as well as pointing him in the direction of becoming a quantity surveyor.

Jenna and Callum often teased her that she was obsessed with falling in love. She didn't see it that way. She just wanted to have that special person in her life, someone who would always be there for her.

The marriages she knew well — her parents' marriage, Frankie and Danny's, and Alastair and Orla's — epitomised for her what a loving relationship was all about. It was about sharing and supporting one another, through good and bad times. She didn't kid herself that Mum and Dad were always perfectly happy, but it was normal to bicker over the stupidest of things. Everybody did that. Well, maybe not Frankie and Danny, she thought with a small smile. But having been surrounded by those strong and loving relationships all her life, it made her want something similar, something solid and lasting.

But was Paul really the right man for her? Until this weekend she would have said yes in a heartbeat. Now her head was questioning her heart. It made her reflect on Mum and Alastair, and how for a short time, when they were young, they had been an item. Until Orla had come along and Alastair had fallen for her. Rachel couldn't remember exactly how old she'd been when Orla had told her this, but she could recall laughing at the idea, as no way could she picture Mum and Alastair as a couple. She'd even accused Orla of making it up, that it was just another of her jokes, but then Mum and Dad had said it was true.

So could she picture her and Paul as a proper long-term couple, that was the question?

'I'm sorry if you felt a bit left out,' Paul said, breaking into her thoughts, 'but I warned you that my family needs some getting used to.' He took one hand off the steering wheel and reached for hers. 'By the way, my mother thought you were great. She said what a charming smile you had, that she'd never seen such amazingly white teeth before. She was very impressed.'

Rachel smiled. 'That was nice of her. What about your dad, what did he think of me?'

Paul laughed again. 'He just needs to get over the disappointment of you not being an F1 fan like the rest of us.'

'I didn't realise you were so into it. I mean, I knew you watched it on the telly, usually when I was at the gym or seeing Jenna, but I didn't appreciate how big a thing it was for you.'

'My guilty secret,' he said, removing his hand from hers and returning it to the steering wheel, 'now you know.'

'Anything else I need to know about?' she asked. She wanted to ask specifically about Perfect Paula, but she'd sooner fling open the car door and schlep all the way back to London on foot, rather than reveal how hurt her feelings had been with his family banging on about Paula this and Paula that.

He hesitated. Then: 'There is something.'

'Go on,' she said, warily.

'Well, my mum's not the only one who thinks you're great. I do too.' He swallowed. 'Actually, and I know this isn't the best time to say it, I could choose a more romantic time and place to say it, but . . . well, the thing is,' he took his eyes off the road and shot her a sidelong glance. 'I think you're really great. So great that I think I love you. There, I've said it.'

Rachel felt her cheeks blossom with a heady rush of pleasure, and in an instant any niggling doubts she'd felt vanished. 'I love you too,' she said, the words out before she realised she was even saying them.

'Really?'

'You sound surprised.'

'I am. I thought that maybe after meeting my family you might have changed your opinion of me. I think that's why I was so reluctant to take you to meet them. And then you seemed so quiet over the weekend, I thought that was a bad sign.'

'It was hard to get a word in edgeways,' she said light-heartedly.

'Sorry about that. Like I say, we can be a bit full on.'

'I'm sure I'll get used to it.'

'So when do I get to meet *your* parents?'

13

Jenna froze with sudden alarm, her heart going from its customary steady beating speed to full-on-burst-out-of-her-chest mode. 'Callum! What are you doing here? It's not Dad, is it?'

He frowned and shook his head. 'No, I just happened to be in London and thought I'd see if you were free for lunch. But no problem if it's not convenient.'

By the time they were seated at a wobbly metal table outside a nearby sandwich bar in the full glare of the July sunshine and the fumes from the slow-moving traffic, Jenna's heart had resumed normal service and she felt she could once again breathe properly.

'It was the unexpectedness of seeing you here and me putting two and two together and coming up with the worst news imaginable,' she explained to Callum, thinking as she often did how well he looked. Hair lightened by the sun, his face tanned and making his blue eyes look even bluer, he was every inch the outdoor man he was, fit and wholesome with the casual air of someone content with his lot. He'd never been what you'd call weedy as a boy, but he'd certainly filled out in the muscle department since working at the boatyard. She had noticed a few glances turning his way while walking here, her shorter legs working to keep up with his long energetic strides. The girl who'd taken their lunch order had clearly been charmed by more than just his engaging smile, her eyes doing a less than subtle sweep over his well-honed body. To her amusement, Jenna had been as good as invisible next to him.

'I think we can safely say that if there was bad news to be delivered to you, you'd receive a phone call,' he said. 'I doubt I'd be top of the list in terms of an emergency call-out service.'

Jenna smiled. 'You'd be good at breaking bad news to me, though. Maybe that's what my subconscious leapt on. You'd certainly make a better job of it than your sister.'

He nodded his head vigorously. 'Yeah, Rachel's not known for her sensitivity. Talking of Rachel, don't tell her I was here, will you?'

'Why ever not?'

'She'll want to know why I took you out for lunch and not her.'

'Well, that is a good question, you know; why did you turn up at my office on the off-chance I'd be around?'

Their sandwiches were delivered to their table, along with their drinks. When the waitress had gone, Callum said, 'Does there have to be a special reason to see you? Or are you saying you'd rather have prior notice? If so, I apologise, it really was just a spur of the moment thing.'

Seeing the look of disappointment on his face, and realising that she had sounded ungracious, Jenna immediately apologised. 'Sorry, I didn't mean it to come out quite like that. It's been one of those mornings.'

Which wasn't strictly true, it was just the last

hour that had upended her equilibrium. On her way to the lift to go out and grab something for lunch, she had been waylaid by a voice calling to her. It had been Blake Darnell and ever since the Punch and Judy encounter with him, he had developed a habit of popping up like a Jack-in-the-box. One minute he'd been invisible to her, as though he didn't exist; now he was rarely off her radar. She'd asked around in the office to see what people thought of him, and the general opinion was that he was hot. A total hottie, if Emily, who also worked in the legacy department, was to be believed. But then as one of the few men — no, strike that, as one of the few heterosexual men in the office, perhaps that artificially upped his status amongst the heterosexual women.

Jenna knew she wasn't imagining that he just happened to be passing her office yet again, or that he had formed a strange attachment to the Punch and Judy bequest and was interested to know what would become of it. 'He doesn't give a hoot about Punch and Judy,' Emily said one day, 'it's *you* he's interested in. Trust me, I have a sixth sense for these things; he's into you in a big way. Have you noticed his dreamy eyes?'

Jenna always found her encounters with Blake fraught with some kind of undercurrent, which in turn made her uptight and on her guard. In fairness to him, he never did anything actually wrong. She knew the problem lay with her, partly because she couldn't help but wonder how she might regard him in another context, if they weren't work colleagues. But she had made that

112

vow to keep her private life completely separate from her work life, and she fully intended to keep it. She was a woman of her word, yes sir, she most certainly was.

'What are your views on relationships in the workplace, Miss Fielding?' Blake had asked her earlier when he'd stood next to her as she waited for the lift. He'd posed the question in the manner of somebody interviewing her for a job.

'Depends what your definition of relationship is?' she'd said, swatting the button to summon the lift.

'Ah yes, Lawyer Girl, I was forgetting that fine legal brain of yours, the one that requires every i dotted and every t crossed.'

'Hardly takes a fine legal brain to ask you to define something.'

'But don't forget, we on the floor above you are not blessed with common sense, or the gift of reasoning powers. No, we conduct ourselves in the dark arts of make-it-up-as-we-go-along and hope to God nobody sees through our transparency. The Emperor and his new clothes has nothing on Brand and Marketing.'

'Oh, I think you can satisfy yourselves with the knowledge that the rest of us are much too busy dotting our i's and crossing our t's to give your transparency a second thought,' she'd responded airily, giving the lift button another not so airy swipe.

'How very disappointing. I had hoped that I had made more of an impression on you. Clearly I have to up my game. By the way, just as kettles don't boil any faster for being watched, lifts never come any faster for having their buttons repeatedly thumped, no matter how bad-temperedly. *Ciao, ciao!*'

She'd watched him walk away, childishly annoyed that he always seemed to have the last word, leaving her to feel just like a whistling kettle with its lid furiously rattling and steam spurting out of the spout. *What exactly is your game, mister?* she wanted to shout at his retreating figure as he strode away, his head up, his arms swinging. As if she couldn't guess!

When the lift finally arrived and she stepped inside, she realised with annoyance that thanks to Emily, she had now noticed his eyes — their colour hovered between hazel, warm caramel and burnished copper.

Her thoughts now back on Callum, acknowledging that it was a lovely surprise to see him and knowing that he seldom came to London, she said, 'What brought you to the big old Smoke then?'

'Oh you know, the usual, an appointment with my Savile Row tailor and a trip to my hairdresser in Mayfair.'

She laughed. 'Of course, how silly of me.'

'I'm crestfallen that you don't believe me.'

'You'd be more crestfallen if I did. I know you, Callum, I know you of old, you'd no more waste money on such things than I would. We're two of a kind you and me, much too sensible for wilful extravagance.'

'Bloody hell, how dull you make us sound!'

'I didn't mean to, it's just that we're grounded in the real world, aren't we?'

'That's not what my parents said when I gave up university and took off to the Broads. They thought I was living in cloud cuckoo-land. The only ones really to respect my decision from the get-go were Alastair and Orla. Even you thought I'd lost the plot for a time, didn't you?'

'Only because I was concerned for you. But never mind all that, have you seen Alastair since that dreadful weekend? It's crazy, but nearly two weeks on and I can still feel the awful tension of that moment when he told us of his plans. I woke up the next morning hoping Alastair would say that he'd been joking, that of course he'd never sell the house.'

Callum took a sip of his coffee. 'Is that what bothers you most, no more Linston End?'

'Now you're making me sound horribly shallow. It's not just about the house, it's more a case of accepting that it's the end of an era.'

'You mean finally we have to accept we're properly grown up, that our childhood is behind us?'

Jenna gave Callum's question some thought while she chewed a mouthful of sandwich. 'Maybe you're right,' she said at length, 'and it is as simple and as selfish as that, an acceptance that it's time to put away childish things.'

'Don't take this the wrong way, but I think you've already done that.' He smiled. 'I doubt whether Rachel ever will, but I'm getting there.'

Not sure how she thought about being singled out this way, Jenna asked if he had seen Alastair in the days since they'd stayed with him.

'He was in the boatyard just the other day and,

115

I have to say, he looks much better than he did before he went away, more his old self. Given how he respected my decision to follow my heart, which proved to be the best decision I ever made, I'd feel a hypocrite if I didn't trust him to do what his heart is telling him to do. Let's face it, who the hell enjoys being told they're wrong? Not me, for sure. We all like to think we know our own mind and what we're doing.'

'You're right, of course. We have no business accusing Alastair of not knowing his own mind. So long as it is that which is guiding him,' she added.

'As opposed to his what? His man-stick?'

Jenna blushed. 'No, his heart, silly. We all know how treacherous the heart can be, especially when you've just had it torn in two by the death of the woman you've always loved.'

Callum frowned and scratched at his chin. 'Have you ever wondered about the way Orla died?'

Surprised at his question, she said, 'What do you mean?'

'Death by misadventure, it never rang true to me. Orla always knew exactly what she was doing. Even her legendary acts of spontaneity were never that spontaneous, were they? Everything she did was always carefully worked out well in advance. Like her pranks.'

Her sandwich finished, Jenna wiped her mouth and hands with a paper napkin, all the while considering Callum's comments. 'I'm not sure I fully understand what you're saying. Orla's death was an accident. She went out for one of her nocturnal meanders on the river and somehow fell in. After all, she had been drinking.'

'But why? *Why* did she fall in? That was completely unlike her. And anyway, she was a good swimmer.'

Jenna felt uneasy. 'You're not suggesting it wasn't an accident, are you?'

'I'm not suggesting anything.'

'Yes you are.'

Callum frowned, screwed his paper napkin into a tight ball and tossed it onto his empty plate. 'Forget I said anything. Like my father, I sometimes don't know when to keep my big mouth shut.'

Jenna regarded him for a moment, wondering what had prompted him to say what he had, and after all these months since Orla's death. But then she looked at her watch. 'Look at the time!' she exclaimed. 'It's nearly two-thirty, I need to get back to work.'

They were outside the front of the building where Heart-to-Heart occupied the seventh and eighth floors, and just about to say goodbye, when Jenna spotted Blake sauntering along a few yards behind them.

It was madness what she did next, but in the split second the idea came into her head, and in a rush of spontaneous certainty, it seemed the perfect solution to the problem of Blake Darnell. After this he would back off, would leave her in peace, and her vow would remain fully intact. So with the conviction she was doing absolutely the right thing, she abruptly pressed herself against Callum, and before she lost her nerve, she stood on tiptoe and kissed him smack on the mouth. She felt him start, but wanting her kiss to look as authentic and natural as possible, she kissed him again. Longer this time.

'Well,' he murmured when she let go of him, 'I wasn't expecting that.'

Out of the corner of her eye, she saw Blake push open the plate glass door to the building. He gave her an infuriatingly cheery wave as he went inside.

Her face an explosion of embarrassment, her heart beating almost as fast as it had when she'd found Callum waiting for her in the foyer, she couldn't bring herself to look at him. 'I'm sorry,' she said, staring down at her shoes, 'that was — '

'Nice,' he interrupted her with a grin. He gently tipped her chin up with his hand so that she was forced to meet his gaze. 'It was *very* nice.'

14

Timing, thought Callum. That was all that was required. The stars all to be aligned and him in the right place at the right time. Oh, and it helped that they were both single at the same time.

He still couldn't believe it; Jenna had actually kissed him. Not one of those friendly mwah-mwah cheek-brushing kisses, but a full direct hit on the mouth. What had changed? What had made her seize the moment like that? She hadn't given him any indication two weeks ago that her attitude towards him might have changed. Not that he was complaining how things had worked out, but knock him down with a feather and call him auntie Mabel, he did not see that coming!

He tried once again to wipe the grin off his face, but he couldn't. Not cool, he told himself, not cool at all to be grinning like a loon while on a train. He'd be marked out as a nutter. There again it would stop anyone taking the seat next to him.

But what did wipe the smile off his face was when a warning voice cautioned him not to get ahead of himself. Who was to say that what had happened this afternoon would lead to anything more?

Or, did she now expect him to make the next move; was that it? *Over to you, Callum Wyatt, show me whatcha got!*

And what did he have? What had he ever thought would come of pursuing a relationship with Jenna? She lived in London and he lived in Norfolk. As far as he could see she liked her life in London and he had no intention of ever leaving the Broads. Would it be a pointless exercise in following that kiss up with anything of his own devising?

But then he thought of Alastair and how changed he seemed since returning from his travels. At first hearing it sounded a case of madness what Alastair was doing, selling Linston End to be with a woman he hardly knew, and so soon after Orla's death. But fair play, was what Callum was beginning to think now, because why not grab what happiness you could when it came along? Why talk yourself out of something, or let others talk you out of it, when with a little courage you could sail off into the clichéd sunset?

Life was a gamble. A spin of the wheel here, a throw of the dice there, and who knew where you might land? And today had been one of those throws of the dice. The plan was to meet an old friend, but when Callum had arrived at Liverpool Street Station, Mike had texted to say something had come up at work and he was sorry but he couldn't get away. That was when Callum had decided he'd take his chances and surprise Jenna. The sensible thing would have been to ring her to check she was free, but sometimes a surprise was so much better.

And Jenna had certainly surprised him!

15

Danny had a reputation for being extremely easy-going; never one to let things get on top of him, but that no longer seemed to be the case.

Everything bothered him now. The poor standard of English on the radio and television; the dumbing down of language and etiquette; the lack of manners; the ruthless hacking of hedgerows and needless destruction of wildlife; the appalling standard of driving; the abundance of technology designed to outwit anyone over the age of twelve; the endless Brexit wrangling; the paucity of soft cod roes in tins which he used to love as a child — coated in a dusting of flour, gently fried in butter before placed on toast with a squeeze of lemon juice. Delicious! Now those little tins were as rare as hens' teeth. Why had supermarkets decided they were no longer worthy of shelf space? And why did people talk in terms of drilling down, unpacking, or rolling out? Why couldn't they speak plain English?

That was all for starters when it came to his long list of grumbles and gripes. He tried to make himself think positively to counteract the negative forces that were so bad for his wellbeing, but that only turned into yet another grumble — since when had he caught this disease for such psychobabble-mumbo-jumbo; when had that sneaked up on him?

Mindfulness, that was the latest buzzword to

come onto his radar. Calm yourself down with a packet of felt-tips and a colouring book. Forget that the world was going to hell in a handcart, propelled with all the force of a nuclear missile strapped to it!

Back in the day everyone had been terrified by the thought of a nuclear bomb; you were the odd one out if you didn't wear a Ban the Bomb badge. Frankie had an aunt who had actually camped at Greenham Common with all the other women protestors. What would she think of the world now, the world she had protested so vehemently to save from coming to an end.

Maybe it would all be a blessed relief not to wake up one morning, for the world to be nothing but a flattened wasteland like Hiroshima after the US had razed it to the ground with an atomic bomb. But then he'd think of Frankie and Jenna and be appalled at his cowardice, and his selfishness, that he could sink so low as to wish for the world to end just so all the gripes and grumbles he felt overwhelmed by could be gone, lifted from his shoulders. Better to fight and be alive than to be six feet under, had been Frankie's aunt's opinion.

Frankie said he cared too much. As ever, she was probably right. Just as her aunt had not been able to save the world singlehandedly, or cure it of all its ills, nor could he. But he could come and see Mrs Maudsley and keep her company for an hour or so; that much he could do.

He drove through the gates of Woodside Care Home, signed in, and was told that if he wanted to wait in the garden, Mrs Maudsley would be brought out to him shortly. Apparently she was lucid enough, and more importantly, well enough, to insist that she wanted to be taken outside.

On the terrace he passed a group of residents playing cards at a table in the shade of a large parasol. He had been sitting comfortably on a bench for some minutes when across the lawn he spotted the newest member of Woodside staff pushing a wheel-chair along the brick path. It wasn't often that Danny took a dislike to some-one, but this particular care assistant — her name was Suzie — did not pass muster with him. In his opinion, she didn't fit in with the general ethos of the care home, although with the recent change of ownership and cutbacks made, maybe the ethos was not what it used to be.

From what Danny had observed of her, Suzie Wu was too offhand and not as patient as she ought to be. If he wanted to be kind, he would say that it was because she was Chinese and English wasn't her first language, so its subtle nuances got lost in translation. But if he were being honest, he would describe the way she spoke as surly and dismissive.

He had wanted to say something to Matron, but hadn't dared for fear of being accused of being a racist. He could hear the screams of protest before he'd even opened his mouth. *Aha, so the man is a racist! How typical that the only member of staff with whom he should find fault is ethnically different.* Had she been British, Danny would not have hesitated to air his concerns.

It wasn't just the lawyer in him that made him

so fearful of the minefield of consequences, should he dare to complain. No, it was the mob of haters out there who would be only too quick to condemn the likes of him. He was white, he was middle-class, he was therefore guilty of prejudice.

All his life he had considered himself to be liberal in his outlook and in his political views, whereas Simon and Alastair were more of a Conservative persuasion, though they had briefly flirted with New Labour and Tony Blair's fresh way of doing things. But somewhere along the line, the liberal elite had hijacked what it meant to be liberal and promoted themselves to policing anyone's views that didn't exactly align with theirs. Their growing toxic intolerance made Stalin look like a pussycat and Danny didn't doubt that having claimed to be the guardians of moral decency, they would be only too keen to string him up for his intolerance towards Suzie Wu.

God help him, but he found everything about her intolerable. Even her appearance. In her late forties, it could not be said that she took a pride in her appearance. With her unkempt hair, bitten nails and shabby worn-down shoes, slovenly was nearer the mark. But who was he to judge? Perhaps she couldn't afford trips to the hairdresser or new shoes, and had a ton of worries that made her bite her nails. So long as she did her job well, that was all that mattered.

But Danny didn't think that she did, that was the trouble. Her brusqueness and lack of patience didn't sit well with him; surely patience was one of the key requisites for the job here?

Still staring across the lawn at her, anger flared within him as he watched her not paying any attention to the old lady in the wheelchair, who he now realised was Mrs Maudsley. The poor woman's head was lolling to one side and visibly bumpty-bump-bumping against the metal side of the chair as she was pushed haphazardly along the path by Suzie, who, with her mobile phone in her left hand, was too busy looking into it to give a damn about her charge.

This was the second time Danny had seen her doing a similar thing, and incensed, he was across the lawn in a flash, his legs moving before he'd even processed what he was doing, and not a thought for his straining heart.

'Why can't you take more care with Mrs Maudsley?' he demanded, the words coming out in a breathless angry rasp.

Taken by surprise, Suzie dropped the mobile phone, which hit the ground with a clatter.

'Look what you did!' she threw back at him, bending to pick up the device, its screen now cracked. 'You buy me new mobile!' She gave him a look that suggested she'd happily wring his neck if he refused.

'Rubbish!' he said. 'You should be paying more attention to what you're paid to do, not reading messages on your mobile.' He bent down in front of Mrs Maudsley and very gently moved her head to a more upright position. 'Are you all right, Mrs Maudsley?' he asked, conscious of a tightening in his chest, a deep skittering sensation that sent a tremble running through him.

The old lady's eyes flickered into focus, and as if tuning in to the correct radio station, her lips parted into a rare smile of recognition. 'Danny,' she murmured, 'how nice to see you.'

'It's nice to see you too,' he said. 'Would you like me to take you for a walk?'

'Yes please,' she said. 'But nowhere that's too bumpy, I have a terrible headache.'

He straightened up and stared grimly at Suzie. 'I'll be speaking to Matron about this.'

'So will I!'

*　★　*

It was inevitable. Suzie Wu got to Matron before he did and claimed she was being picked on, singled out by a racist bigot. She claimed she had been shouted at unfairly. She hadn't been using her mobile, merely putting it in her pocket. Mr Fielding had made everything up to get her into trouble. She wanted an apology. If not, she would find a solicitor and demand compensation for stress in the workplace. For bullying and racism too. She knew her rights. What was more, she would go to the newspapers and say what a bad man Mr Fielding was to attack her.

Oh God, thought Danny when he was driving home, his heart straining painfully against his chest. What had he done? How had he allowed this to happen? All because he cared! Because he cared that Mrs Maudsley wasn't being looked after properly. How could that be turned against him?

All at once he felt weepy with tiredness and

confusion. Confusion that he lived in a world where only the few could speak their mind; the rest of them had to shut up and jolly well lump it. Anger and misery nestled in close to his heart and squeezed it painfully.

The cardiologist who had treated him had warned him that often survivors of heart attacks suffered emotional swings, one day as high as a kite on the simple joy of being alive, and another plummeting to the depths of melancholy and depression. Was that his problem? Was he depressed?

No, he told himself firmly. All he needed was some time away and thank God that was just around the corner. Another week and they'd all be at Linston End with Alastair. Being there had always made him feel good.

But the thought didn't help. Not when he was faced with the prospect of losing his old friend to a woman they none of them knew, and on top of that they would never stay at Linston End again after this summer.

All those happy summers they had spent together. Their golden years, that's what they'd been. But not anymore. Orla was gone. He'd nearly gone, and now Alastair was abandoning them. Abandoning Danny . . . just like all those foster parents had who'd passed him around like an unwanted parcel.

The road became blurred as his eyes filled; he blinked hard, but it was no good. He slowed his speed, pulled over and switched off the engine. His heart galloping wildly, like a runaway horse, he got out and went and stood against a metal gate where a field of barley was gently swaying in the warm summer breeze.

Breathe in, he told himself.

And out.

In.

Out.

There, that was better. Was that a panic attack, he wondered? Was this something else to add to the list of things wrong with him? Something else to keep from Frankie?

Across the field of barley, way off in the distance he heard the sound of a church bell ringing. *For whom the bell tolls*, he thought, *in the midst of life, we are in death . . .*

'No, not me!' he cried out aloud, thumping the gate with his fist. 'Not yet! Not by a long chalk. Still plenty of life left in this old dog.' He just had to get a grip. That was all. No more maudlin twaddle from here on. Fighting talk was needed, not this overemotional wallowing in self-pity. If Suzie Wu wanted a fight, he'd give her one. He knew the truth of what he'd seen and he'd be damned if he apologised.

But what had he seen? Just a woman not really giving her full attention to what she should have been doing. There were worse sins she could be guilty of.

He sighed deeply. Should he take the easy way out and just apologise and say he may have overreacted? That was, after all, what the British were known for, apologising to someone who had just bumped into them.

Yes, he decided. First thing in the morning he would drive back to Woodside and apologise, and that would be an end to it. That way he wouldn't have to confess anything to Frankie and reveal what a fool he was.

16

'You should have told me! Oh Lord, what on earth were you thinking, getting yourself into a pickle like this?'

'Are you using the word 'pickle' to try and lessen the severity of the mess I've got myself into?'

Sitting across the kitchen table from him, Frankie's heart went out to Danny. 'Maybe I am, but only on a subconscious level. But, darling, nobody who knows you would believe what that woman is saying about you.'

'But what if she carries out her threat to take her story to the newspaper, claiming that I picked on her because she's foreign? She'll have me painted as some kind of right-wing, frothing at the mouth racist. Those who don't know me will be only too quick to believe every word and have me hung, drawn and quartered without ever hearing my side of it. All I was trying to do was look out for a vulnerable old lady who wasn't being given the attention she deserved.'

Frankie sighed. 'I know you were, love, I know that. But why on earth didn't you tell me you were still visiting Mrs Maudsley?'

'I thought you'd see it as a weakness in me,' he murmured.

'A weakness?' she repeated, dumbfounded.

'And maybe ban me from going, given my own health problems.'

Frankie sighed again. He was right; she probably would have seen it as an unnecessary stress and stopped him.

Without telling her where he was going, Danny had gone back to Woodside this morning to offer an apology and to admit he may have overreacted yesterday afternoon. Returning home, and visibly upset, he'd then confessed the whole sorry tale. It explained why he had been in such an odd mood last night, fidgety and unable to settle.

From what he'd told her, his apology had been accepted, with Matron suggesting he might like to curtail his visits to see Mrs Maudsley for the foreseeable future. While this infuriated Frankie — it implied that Danny was a danger to both staff and residents at Woodside — she could see that it was a sensible course of action. Especially as, according to Danny, Suzie Wu was threatening some kind of legal action if he ever approached her again, as well as taking her story to the local newspaper.

She was claiming, of all things, that Danny had been violent, that he had snatched the mobile out of her hand and deliberately thrown it on the ground, making her fearful for her life.

Frankie couldn't believe that Matron would accept that as fact, but maybe they were short-staffed at the care home and she couldn't afford to lose anyone. Whatever Matron's reasons for wanting to believe Suzie Wu's word over Danny's, with any luck, a line had now been drawn and this would be the last they heard on the subject. So long as Danny did as he'd been asked.

'Danny,' Frankie said, reaching across the

131

table to him and taking his hands in hers. 'I want you to promise me that you'll swallow your pride and keep away from Woodside. Will you do that?'

He nodded and then squeezing his eyes shut, he moved one of his hands and pressed it to his chest.

Frankie rose to her feet and went to him. This was absolutely the very last thing her poor husband needed. What she wouldn't do to protect and wrap him forever in her love.

And oh, how she hated the ghastly woman who had made these vile claims about a sweet and kind man who had visited an old lady out of the goodness of his heart. A heart that Frankie worried wasn't strong enough to cope with what he had been accused of.

17

'What are your plans for the evening? I don't suppose you'd like to hop on a plane and fly over from Moscow, would you?'

Valentina laughed at Alastair's question. 'I would love to, but don't forget we are three hours ahead of you, and with what is left of the evening I am going to enjoy a long bath and then go to bed.'

'What about tomorrow, can I tempt you to abandon your mother and come here? Speaking from a purely selfish point of view, you understand.'

Again she laughed. 'Tomorrow I'm taking my mother for lunch, and in the afternoon, while she is having her nap, I shall go to the Tretyakov.'

'What's that?'

'It's the best art gallery in the world.'

'Better than the Louvre, or the Uffizi in Florence? Or what about the Hermitage in St Petersburg?'

'Oh, much better than all of those. The Tretyakov is the home of Russian art.'

'You mean icons?'

Her tut of derision spoke volumes. 'One day I will bring you here and you will see for yourself the jewels of art that give me . . . give me geese bumps.'

He smiled. It wasn't often that she slipped up, but he steeled himself not to correct her. He must have somehow given himself away though.

'What?' she said. 'What are you thinking? Did I say something wrong?'

'No,' he lied. 'Carry on, tell me about these jewels.'

'Not until you've told me what made you pause.'

'*Goose* bumps,' he said, reluctantly, hating to correct her when his knowledge of French was at schoolboy level and he spoke not a word of Russian. 'Not geese bumps. That was all.'

'Oh,' she said. 'I will try to remember that. These colloquial words and phrases are so important. I don't want to let you down in front of your friends.'

'You could never do that. Now tell me about the art gallery and these jewels that you like so much.'

'They are not diamonds and rubies, if that is what you are thinking. I'm talking about some of the world's greatest artists that far too many are in ignorance of, such as Isaac Levitan, Vasisly Vereshchagin, Ivan Alvazovsky, Ivan Kramskoi, Ilya Repin, Konstantin Savitsky, Ivan Shishkin, Alexei Stepanov, Vasily Surikov. Impress me, Alastair, tell me you've heard of just one of those.'

He laughed. 'I'm sorry to confirm your worst opinion of me, but you have all too easily revealed my ignorance on such matters.' He was going to add that what he knew about art was mostly limited to what Orla had taught him, but thought better of saying that.

'Hah!' declared Valentina. 'In that case I shall

educate you. You will be so much more knowledge-
able by the time I have finished with you.'

I already am, he thought happily. 'How much
longer do you have to stay there in Moscow? I
want you here with me.'

'Patience, Mr Bossy Englishman, patience and
listen to something important.'

'I'm all ears.'

'*Comment?*'

'It means I'm listening.'

'Good. This is *our* story, Alastair, our very own
story, which only *we* can write. We must not
allow anyone else to try and dictate the narrative,
or the ending.'

'What are you saying?' he asked, concerned.
'That you already know how it ends between us?'

Now it was Valentina's turn to laugh. 'No one
knows that. What I am trying to say is that it
would be very easy for your friends to start
writing our story for us, particularly your part in
it. Trust me, they will not want to let me take
you away from them.'

'You're not taking me anywhere. I'm taking
myself, and willingly.'

'They will not see it that way, and you know
that in your heart. I'd like to say I won't fight
them for you, but I would be a liar. I shall fight
them every step of the way. I don't like losing
and I don't intend to lose you. I am very
determined. You should know that about me, it's
important.'

'I'm the same,' he said, 'so maybe you need to
accept that you've met your match when it
comes to stubborn determination.' And with his

135

words Orla came flooding back into his mind, together with the memory of him saying something similar to her in the early stages of their relationship. Without warning, the familiar hard lump of guilty torment wedged in his throat. He fought hard to stop himself from thinking the unthinkable, that history was repeating itself. Valentina was nothing like Orla. She was different. That was why he had fallen in love with her. She was refreshingly uncomplicated and free of artistic insecurities. With her he could relax and enjoy the simple pleasure of being happy again. Truly happy. Something he didn't think would ever be possible.

'Alastair, are you still there?'

He took a deep shaky breath. 'Yes,' he managed to say through the tightness in his throat.

'Are you all right?'

'I'm fine.'

'You don't sound it.'

'It's nothing. Just a memory that came into my head.'

'A painful memory of your wife?'

He grunted something that passed for an assertion and stared out of the window, down the length of the lawn that was sodden from the rain that had fallen that afternoon. On the other side of the river, he saw his new neighbour leaning against the wooden rail of the uppermost level of the mill. He knew from having been up there many times over the years that the view from the balcony, which wrapped itself around the mill, gave an amazing 360-degree view of the river and surrounding reed beds and marshland.

Since he had introduced himself a couple of weeks ago, the woman had become a regular sight on the balcony of the mill. Her name was Laura Manning and she was renting the mill for a few months from the owners, who were friends of friends. Similar in age to him, she gave the impression of a woman who was entirely comfortable with being alone. After all, if she craved company she would have chosen to stay somewhere more densely populated, not at Linston Mill which, given its location and limited access, had a definite sense of isolation to it. He had said that if she needed help with anything, he was just across the water. 'We tend to be quite neighbourly in these parts,' he'd explained, 'but hopefully not in an intrusive way.'

'It's okay,' Valentina said in his ear, prompting him to turn his back to the garden and river. 'You don't need to hide Orla from me. I'm not so fragile that I will fall apart at the mention of her. Of course you still have feelings for the woman who was your wife for so many years. As do I for my Ivan, even though he was not the greatest of husbands.'

My Ivan . . . Valentina's use of the possessive pronoun sounded odd to Alastair. He would never have said 'my Orla'. Whether it was no more than a subtle language difference, he knew with absolute certainty that Orla would not have countenanced ownership of herself; she would have had none of that. In contrast she had owned him, mind, body and soul.

Thinking how serious the conversation had become, in particular the manner in which

Valentina had spoken of his friends, he wondered if she was more worried than she was letting on. Did her declaration that she would fight for him stem from doubts that had crept in since they had been apart? Did she now feel the need to convince herself they were doing the right thing?

'You're not having second thoughts, are you?' he asked nervously.

'I never have second thoughts,' she said adamantly, '*never*.'

He smiled to himself, picturing perfectly the flash of her piercing blue eyes, the tilt of her chin and the set of her mouth, pursed and determined. Deciding it would be better to change the subject, and remembering the couple who were coming in the morning to view the house, he said, 'Have you had any more ideas about where we're going to live? I think we should start narrowing down our choices.'

This all-important decision had yet to be made and he had to hold firm against the dangerous thought that was beginning to make itself known — that if Valentina would only consider making Linston End her home with him, life would be so much easier.

18

'I mean, come on, your father is the last man on earth ever to attack anyone, he's as malicious as a marshmallow.' Rachel gave a short laugh. 'I'd sooner believe it of my dad, or even Mum, but never Danny. He's much too gentle in his nature.'

'Well, this awful woman is trying to make out he's a vicious bully,' said Jenna. 'And it's not right.'

'As I said before, I reckon my dad's bang on the money; this woman is a pro. Next thing she'll be claiming harassment in the workplace and hoping to grab herself a tidy bit of compensation.'

'Everything good here, ladies?'

'We're fine thank you,' said Rachel, wishing the waiters would stop butting in every five minutes. Fair enough it was nice to have some attentive service, but this was getting ridiculous. That was the trouble with these super-hip places, they tried too hard, from their steam-punk interiors and uncomfortably hard chairs straight from the school room, to the waiters who were so casually dressed in jeans and a shirt that you couldn't tell them apart from the customers. 'Anyway,' she continued, once the waiter had moved on to bother somebody else, 'we had a similar case at work, a woman accusing a co-worker of sexual harassment, but after some judicious digging we discovered she had made a similar complaint some years back with a previous employer. I bet you anything you like, the same will happen with this woman. She's nothing but an opportunist.'

'In the meantime Dad's going through hell,' Jenna said flatly. 'Mum too.'

Rachel was beginning to run out of encouraging words of comfort. She had the feeling that it wasn't only Danny on her friend's mind; there was something else making her uptight, and uncharacteristically distracted. Knowing each other as well as they did, it was always obvious when one of them was holding back.

Rachel had suggested an evening out to this recently opened brasserie on Shoreditch High Street to cheer Jenna up, but it didn't seem to be working. If anything her mood was worsening and she had barely touched her meal. For that matter, Rachel's own mood was going downhill fast.

In an effort to change the subject, and with one last valiant attempt to turn the evening around, she said, 'Thank goodness it's less than a week until we escape to Linston. And you know what we should all do? We should make Alastair change his mind about selling, not by disagreeing with him about his plans, but by having a brilliant time. That way he'll remember all the good times and — ' Her words ground to a sudden halt. 'Jenna, you're not listening to a word I'm saying, are you?'

Jenna frowned. 'I'm sorry.'

'So you should be. We're supposed to be having an enjoyable night out and you're about as much fun as a dripping tap.'

'Pardon me for worrying about my parents. How tedious that must be for you when you have something far more important to whinge about, that of Paul preferring to go away with his brothers and mates, and not you!'

Rachel's jaw dropped. 'I don't believe you've just said that, or twisted what I said. Which was that Paul can't join us at Linston because he's going to the Hungarian Grand Prix, and if I remember rightly, I only mentioned it once.'

'Three times actually,' muttered Jenna. 'And it's always good to know where a boyfriend's priorities lie,' she added.

Rachel was stunned at how bitchy Jenna sounded. 'At least I have a boyfriend!' she fired back.

'At least I'm not desperate to have one no matter how . . .'

'Go on,' Rachel said, her voice low, 'no matter how, what?'

'Forget it. Forget I said anything.'

'Oh, no you don't! You can't say something like that and leave it hanging. Obviously you have plenty more to say on the subject. Out with it.'

Jenna pursed her lips and pushed her unfinished plate away from her.

Furious, Rachel waited. And waited. She took a gulp of her wine and waited some more.

At last Jenna returned her gaze to hers. 'I just don't think he's good enough for you.'

'You've formed that opinion on meeting him just twice?'

'First impressions are important. And we've met on four occasions. You might at least be accurate.'

'Are you sure you're not jealous?'

Jenna rolled her eyes. 'Very sure. And I think if you were honest, really honest with yourself, you'd admit that I'm right. Paul isn't the one for you; he's just become a habit. He's one of those boyfriends who will never commit, and you'd rather settle for that than nothing.'

'Hah! Just goes to show what a poor judge of character you are, because Paul has told me that he loves me. And I love him. How's that for commitment?'

Jenna chewed on her lip. 'Well, that's all right then, isn't it? I'm surprised you don't look happier about it in that case.'

'How can I be happy with you being such a misery?'

'God, you can be so shallow at times.'

'And you can be so boring! To think I passed on the chance to be with Paul tonight so I could cheer you up.'

'You've done a first class job of that, haven't you? Trust me, I'd have had more fun at home cleaning the oven!'

They glared at each other across the table, their arms folded in a perfect mirror image. That was when yet again, one of the annoying waiters approached their table.

'We're fine,' hissed Rachel before he'd even opened his mouth, 'now go away and stop bothering us!'

The waiter looked at her, his eyebrows raised. 'I'm sorry?'

'I said we're fine, which means we don't need you butting in yet again. Honestly, this evening is going from bad to worse. But on second thoughts, you can bring us the bill.'

To add to her annoyance, the waiter simply grinned like a half-wit and turned to look at Jenna. 'Hiya,' he said, 'I think your friend is under the misapprehension that I'm your waiter. Pity the poor devil who is, I don't see him getting much of a tip. Bad evening?'

'You could say that,' said Jenna, her face flushed red and looking as hideously wrong-footed as Rachel was now beginning to feel.

'I'll have a word with the manager,' he said, 'who just happens to be a friend of the family.'

'No, please don't do that,' said Jenna, 'it hasn't been that bad.'

'Are you sure?' He glanced at Rachel. 'What about you, do you want to make an official complaint? Plainly something has riled you.'

Rachel shook her head, wondering who this decidedly good-looking guy was, and who apparently knew Jenna. 'I'm sorry for speaking to you the way I did. That was rude of me.'

'I've been on the receiving end of worse, I assure you.'

Was it her imagination, but did he shoot Jenna a sidelong glance as he said that, and did Jenna actually flinch? Interesting. Her curiosity roused, Rachel said, 'Are you here alone?'

His face brightened and his gaze rested on the empty chair at their table. 'As a matter of fact I am.'

'You could join us if you want,' Rachel said, warming to him, 'and then I could buy you a drink by way of apology.' To Rachel's delight,

143

Jenna's eyes widened and she looked livid.

'I thought you wanted the bill so we could go?' she said.

'I've changed my mind. Sit down,' Rachel said to the source of Jenna's obvious discomfort. 'My name's Rachel,' she added, giving him the benefit of a wide smile that showed off her immaculate whitened teeth.

'Pleased to meet you, Rachel. I'm Blake, I work at Heart-to-Heart with Jenna.'

Aha! Now it was starting to make sense. 'So you're Blake?'

'You've heard of me?'

'Oh yes, Jenna never stops talking about you.'

'Really?'

'She's exaggerating,' said Jenna, flashing Rachel a look that could fell a tree. 'She does that a lot.'

'So you're good friends, then?' he asked.

'We go way back, right to being babies,' Rachel said with a laugh. 'Our parents are old friends.'

'Ergo, you're old friends. That's nice. Continuity has a lot going for it. So how's that boyfriend of yours, Jenna?'

'What boyfriend?' asked Rachel.

'The one I saw Jenna with last week,' he responded. To Jenna, he said, 'That was quite some smooch the pair of you had going on.'

All agog, her eyebrows reaching for the rafters, Rachel looked at Jenna. This she had to hear. A boyfriend Jenna had been keeping from her? Was that why she had been behaving so weirdly?

19

Since retiring, Sorrel had dispensed with the services of their cleaner, a woman who had never done the job entirely to her satisfaction. The only reason the woman had been kept on for as long as she had was because she could be relied upon to show up every week, and a job half done on a regular basis was better than not done at all.

Now, on this wet Wednesday morning, as Sorrel waged war on the mess Simon had made after tipping the cafetière into the sink and flinging coffee grounds everywhere, Sorrel thought of Danny and the mess he'd got himself into.

She didn't believe for a minute what he'd been accused of; he simply wasn't that kind of a man. You only had to look at him to know that. With his honest and trustworthy face that radiated compassion and concern, together with his gentle manner, Sorrel had always thought he should have been a doctor. Or a doctor from a bygone era when they had time to listen to their patients and offer sympathy along with a handwritten prescription.

Danny's secret visits to Woodside Care Home had come as a surprise to Sorrel. She didn't think him capable of keeping anything from Frankie. And vice versa. She had assumed they were one of those couples who shared every detail of what they got up to, their every thought even. Clearly that wasn't the case. Or was this a recent thing of Danny's, to act so out of character by sneaking off behind Frankie's back to visit an old lady? It was all very odd.

Danny wasn't the only one to be behaving oddly. Just look at Alastair. Did he have any idea how ludicrous he was making himself look? Or how ill-timed, not to say in poor taste, it was to announce he had fallen in love so soon after Orla's death? Didn't he care what people would think? But then it wouldn't be the first time he had acted with such an appalling lack of sensitivity. Nobody knew better than Sorrel just how insensitive he could be.

She ran the tap and swished the water around the now clean sink. She rinsed the cloth under the tap, then wrung it with a strong twist of her hands to squeeze out the water. Bloody Alastair, she thought, giving the cloth another savage twist. Bloody Orla too.

After all these years it surprised her that buried deep within her, there was still a small raw spot that had never quite healed. It shouldn't bother her, not after all this time, but it did. The painful truth was, Alastair had hurt her badly — not once, but twice — and his blithe declaration, coming so out of the blue, that he'd fallen madly in love resurrected myriad memories and bitter resentments.

Last night they'd heard from Alastair that Valentina had booked her flight tickets and would definitely be joining them at Linston End. At the thought of this, Sorrel ripped off her rubber gloves. *How does it feel, Orla,* she silently taunted with a flash of malicious satisfaction, *to know that you've been replaced so quickly?* Now you know what I went through.

A better person would have felt guilty for gloating over Orla's swift replacement, but Sorrel knew, and without a trace of shame, that she wasn't that better person. Just as she knew that there was very little chance of her liking the new woman in Alastair's life, any more than the old one.

There again, she thought, a slow smile coming to her lips, how better to pay Orla back than to take an enormous liking to Valentina? 'The game's not over yet, Orla,' she murmured. 'Not by a long way.'

'You know the first sign of madness is talking to yourself, don't you?'

She spun round at the sound of Simon's voice. 'For heaven's sake, do you have to creep up on me like that? You gave me quite a start.'

'Hardly creeping,' he said, 'more like blundering around in the manner of an elephant.'

He went over to the table and plonked a large dusty cardboard box on it. He looked pleased with himself. 'So what were you muttering to yourself about?' he asked. 'Have I done something wrong, which I should know about?'

Relieved he hadn't heard what she'd said, she shook her head. 'You're off the hook. What's in the box?'

With a theatrical flourish of his hands, as if he were a magician about to pull a rabbit from a hat, he said, 'I bring you the past!'

'Meaning?'

'I've been rootling around in the loft and unearthed a collection of old photos and videos. I can't think how they ended up there in the first place.'

Sorrel could. She had hidden the box in the loft not long after moving here twenty years ago, wanting to be rid of certain memories, but not having the courage to throw away the contents of the box.

'I thought I'd sort through it all, then scan a selection to put onto a disc for when we go to stay with Alastair. We can then all enjoy a trip down memory lane.'

'Do you think that's a good idea?'

'Why ever not? It'll make for great entertainment seeing how we've all changed; the kids will love making fun of us with our dreadful clothes and hair from way back when.'

'What about Valentina?'

'What about her?'

'You don't think she'll be bored to tears if she's forced to look at a lot of old photographs of people she doesn't know?'

A resolute look came into Simon's eyes. 'What better way for her to realise how important Alastair's friends are to him, and what a crucial part of his life we are?'

Oh, Simon, thought Sorrel, with genuine sadness for him. You're going to have to let Alastair go, as painful as it will be.

20

An auction date for the sale of the Punch and Judy donation had still to be decided, and the longer it took up residence in her office, the more attached Jenna felt to it. She would miss it when it was eventually taken away to be sold. She found its brightly coloured presence a cheerful sight in her office. It made her think of happy children on a beach, of melting ice cream in the sunshine, of unfettered laughter while Mr Punch went about his slapstick business. It was a reminder of day trips to Cromer beach with Rachel and Callum while staying at Linston End, when the summer holidays stretched endlessly before them and time seemed to stand still.

She had placed her favourite pair of puppets on the shelf opposite her desk — a slightly damaged Mr Punch (his chin was chipped and an ear was missing, giving him a slightly less malevolent appearance) and Judy, his long-suffering wife next to him. Looking at the puppets, Jenna thought how universally true it was that children of all ages enjoyed the sight of somebody being hit or told off. Was it simply a case of schadenfreude, of being grateful for not being in the firing line themselves? Or was it more invidious, a desire to be the one with the big stick in their hands to do the hitting? Were they all bullies at heart with a secret desire to clout somebody over the head and not have to pay the consequences?

If Jenna could be granted that wish, she would happily take a stick to the ghastly woman who had made those fictitious claims against her father.

But Suzie Wu was not the only person to whom Jenna could happily take a big stick. Blake Darnell had easily earned himself a whack, as had Rachel for stirring the pot so enthusiastically. In reality, the person who deserved the biggest whack of all was herself. She had played a stupid game and now it had backfired on her in spectacular fashion.

At the restaurant last night, after Blake had finally left them — Jenna having lied through her teeth about some new man in her life — Rachel had turned Gestapo interrogator. She had demanded to know exactly who the secret boyfriend was and Jenna had blurted out the truth, unable to face the unappealing choice of telling yet more lies.

Rachel had been incredulous. 'You mean you used my brother to make it look like you had a boyfriend? What the hell were you thinking?'

'I wasn't thinking,' Jenna had replied, 'that was the trouble, it was a knee-jerk reaction to get Blake off my case.'

'I don't understand why you should be so keen to get him off your case,' Rachel had said, 'but more to the point, where the hell does this leave Callum?'

It was a very good question. He might have had a teeny crush on her when they were children, but that was all in the past. As adults there had never been anything other than an extremely close friendship between them. She had to admit though, his response to her kissing him had taken her by surprise, as had the expression on his face afterwards. She wasn't sure what to make of that.

He had texted her the other day to say he'd heard about the bother her father had got himself into, but not a word did he say about that kiss.

Through the open door of her office, Jenna caught sight of Blake emerging from the lift. He'd only taken a few steps when Vanessa, the intern who had started working in the legacy department this week, approached him. Furtively watching the encounter, Rachel's voice echoed in Jenna's ear — 'Has it not occurred to you that he might genuinely like you? Why else did he come over in the restaurant to say hello to you, and then join us for a drink?'

'To make me feel uncomfortable,' Jenna had retaliated. 'He enjoys making me squirm.'

Rachel's response had been to roll her eyes and do that annoying little wobble of her head she did when she thought somebody had just said something particularly stupid. 'Yeah right, the man has nothing better to do than make your life a misery,' she'd said with withering contempt.

No, thought Jenna, as she continued with her covert observation of Vanessa flirting outrageously with Blake — flicking her hair and laughing, and leaning in close with exaggerated eye contact, then moving in for the kill by patting his arm — I'm the one making a first-class job of making my life a misery. Somehow it had become a habit for her and she didn't know why. It was a habit she needed to break before, as Rachel said, her prickliness turned her into a mad and bitter old woman.

In bed last night, Jenna had vowed she would ring Callum and be completely honest with him. But what to say? 'Hey, Callum, you know when I kissed you? Well . . . ' The imaginary conversation never got any further than that; it always ran aground on the rocks of her shame and embarrassment. But then an insistent voice inside her head, sounding remarkably like Rachel, would shout: *'Tell him! Just tell him! Or I will!'* She would then try to picture herself laughing the whole thing off with Callum, dismissing the kiss as the same mistake he'd made when they were children, nothing more than an impulsive error of judgement. The trouble was Callum *knew* her. He knew that she rarely, if ever, acted impulsively — that was much more Rachel's territory. Yet she had in that instant, and it wasn't a mistake she was going to make again.

She forced her attention back to the lengthy email she had been writing before she'd been distracted by seeing Blake. Within seconds a familiar voice interrupted her flow of concentration.

'Knock knock.'

'Who's there?' she answered, knowing perfectly well who it was, and keeping her fingers moving over the keyboard, her eyes on the screen.

'Atish.'

'Atish who?' she said, playing along.

'Bless you. Okay, I can do better than that. Answer me this: Will you remember me in a month?'

'I might,' she said warily.

'That's good. Now will you remember me in a week?'

She turned to look at Blake, her fingers slowing to a stop. 'I would imagine so.'

'Knock knock.'

'Who's there?'

He slapped a hand against his forehead. 'Ouch, that hurts, you've forgotten me already.'

She chewed on her lip to stop herself from smiling; it would only encourage him. He then raised his hand to the door and rapped his knuckles against it, at the same time saying, 'Knock knock.'

'Who's there?'

'Armageddon.'

She sighed. 'Armageddon who?'

'Armageddon a little hungry, fancy some lunch?'

Prickles, she reminded herself, thinking of the habit she needed to break and the mad and bitter old woman she didn't want to become. *You can do this, Jenna Fielding. Relax.* 'Why not?' she said with a lightness that she saw took him by surprise.

★　★　★

They bought their lunch at the counter inside a deli just around the corner from Heart-to-Heart, and took it outside to eat at a table on the pavement. After the rain of yesterday, the warm summer sunshine had people in lively spirits. 'I've never eaten here before,' Jenna said by way of conversation. 'Is it a regular place for you?'

'Nope, this is my first visit. How's your charred vegetable and kale pesto wrap, is it as disgusting as it sounds?'

'I'll let you know when I've tried it,' she said. She took a bite and instantly regretted her rash decision to go for the healthy option. She chewed gamely on the foul-tasting concoction and washed it down with a mouthful of fizzy water.

'And your verdict?' he said with a smile.

'Revolting.'

He pushed his untouched BLT baguette towards her. 'I'll swap you.'

'No, there's no need, I'll get through it.'

He slid her plate away from her. 'Not on my watch you won't. Not when this place was my suggestion.'

'But it was my choice what I selected,' she said firmly, taking back her plate.

'I admire your stoicism. As erroneous as I believe it to be; but life's too short to eat stuff you don't like.' Once more he removed the plate from her, and before she could protest, he stood up and went back inside the deli, leaving her to drum her fingers on the table with irritation. How did he always do it, make her feel as though he had claimed the advantage? And why did she care so much that he did?

Minutes later he reappeared with a BLT baguette for her.

'I realise that you may well not want to eat this on principle, on account of me taking away your freedom of choice,' he said, 'but I'd feel much happier if you could forgive my impertinence so we can get on with enjoying lunch.'

She frowned, mentally still drumming her fingers on the table. 'I don't understand why you should want to enjoy lunch with me. I don't get it.'

'I like you,' he said matter of factly. 'Prickles and all.'

'But why?'

'I'm curious to know why you took such an immediate and obvious dislike to me. This may come as a surprise to you, and I say it with all due modesty, but people usually like me.'

'Maybe you need to lower the level of your charm when you come anywhere near the legacy department,' she said.

'If I did that, would you like me any more?'

'I might.'

He gave her a long and slightly unnerving stare, the burnished copper of his eyes glowing with an intensity that seemed unnatural. 'And what would your boyfriend think of that?' he asked.

Oh hell, she'd forgotten about her so-called boyfriend. 'Umm . . . he'd be happy to know that I was getting on with my work colleagues so well.'

'He's not the jealous type, then?'

'Are you saying there's anything he should be jealous about?'

'I'd say that's for you to decide.'

I'm not cut out to be a serial liar, thought Jenna miserably when they were walking back to the office. Why did she have to make life so bloody complicated for herself? She was a reasonably intelligent woman, yet she was acting like a child, digging herself a deeper and deeper hole.

They were waiting for the lift to take them up to their respective floors when, and in an effort to make things absolutely clear, she said, 'I think you should know something, I made the mistake of having a relationship with a work colleague in my last job and it didn't end well. As a consequence I promised myself I'd never make that same mistake again. I like working for Heart-to-Heart and don't want my position here to be made untenable.'

'That's a shame,' he said, after a few moments had passed, during which he seemed to give her admission his full consideration. 'A shame that things ended badly for you, I mean. So the boyfriend you now have, is he a new one?'

'He's . . . ' She swallowed, suddenly wanting — needing — to make a clean breast of things. 'He's not a boyfriend.'

He raised an eyebrow. 'What is he then; a friend with benefits?'

'No! He's an old friend who I kissed in a foolish attempt to make you stop . . . '

'To make me stop what?'

'Pestering me. I thought if you knew I was attached, you'd back off.'

He put a hand to his heart. 'Goodness, you

went to all that trouble for my sake? I'm touched.'

'And now I feel even more of an idiot than I did before.'

He nodded. 'If it makes you feel any better, I knew he wasn't your boyfriend.'

'How?'

'I asked your colleague Emily and she said you didn't have a significant other.'

'I don't believe it!'

He smiled. 'You're the worst liar I've ever met, and bumping into you last night and seeing your friend's reaction when I deliberately referred to your boyfriend only confirmed what I suspected.'

'Which was what?'

'That you'd go to extraordinary lengths to keep me at arm's distance when my only crime, as far as I could tell, was to find myself attracted to you. And I'm well aware that just by making this confession, I've now made things extremely awkward for you.'

'We could pretend you never said it,' she murmured.

'You're right, we could. As a matter of interest, what did your friend think about you suddenly kissing him the way you did? He looked pretty pleased from where I was standing.'

'I think he was shocked. Very shocked. He's Rachel's brother and we've known each other all our lives.'

'That's tricky for you both.'

'Very. What's more Rachel is furious with me for using her brother the way I did.'

The lift finally arrived and after stepping

157

inside and the door closing, Blake said, 'This is the first normal conversation we've had. We must have lunch together another time, it's been fun.'

'Fun for you maybe, I feel thoroughly humiliated.'

'You'll get over it.'

'You're actually quite nice, you know, when you're not being a total jackass.'

'Good to know. Lunch tomorrow, then? Purely as friends?'

She pursed her lips.

'As co-workers,' he said.

'Maybe.'

The lift stopped at her floor and she got out.

'See you at one o'clock tomorrow,' he said.

'Maybe,' she said over her shoulder as she walked away and the door began to close.

There, finally, she'd had the last word!

But then she heard the lift door opening again. 'I'm sorry you thought I was pestering you, that was never my intention.'

Damn, he'd done it again!

21

It was one of those perfect summer evenings, the air still and warm, the sky dramatically splashed in the west with coral and indigo as the sun began its descent.

'I could never leave here,' said Callum, watching a yacht sail silently by, while the heron that had been keeping guard from the branch of an alder tree on the other side of the river for the last twenty minutes looked on. He and Alastair were sitting on the wooden bench at the end of the garden, on the opposite side of the lawn to the pavilion. The seat was perfectly placed to give an uninterrupted view of the river, with Linston church tower in the far distance to their left, and Linston Mill to their right.

'I used to think the same,' responded Alastair.

'Sorry,' said Callum with an apologetic wave of his hand, realising how his remark might be misinterpreted, 'that was clumsy of me, as though I was saying you were doing the wrong thing.'

'No need to apologise. Life changes and the mistake we frequently make is not to recognise an opportunity when it comes our way.'

'You're right, I guess.'

'Trust me, I am. Too often we live with our heads in the sand, or become blind to what's beyond the boundaries of the world we've created for ourselves. Or worse, we become scared of taking that step into the unknown, scared of breaking free.'

At precisely the same moment, they both tipped their heads up to watch a quartet of greylag geese fly over the river in half-hearted formation, their wings flapping lazily. When they'd disappeared into the distance, and Callum had taken a long sip of his cold beer, he said, 'You sound as though you'd been wanting to change your life for some time, Alastair. Had you?'

'That's an interesting question.'

'Which you don't have to answer if you don't want to.'

This was the first time Callum had been alone with Alastair since before Orla's death. It didn't feel the way it used to. Alastair had changed. He was quieter, and more pensive. Which was understandable.

Alastair gave a shrug and scratched at a faint dirty mark on his jeans. 'Don't you think we all want to change our lives at certain times?' he replied at length. 'Or do you believe that's the prerogative of the young?'

'Not at all,' said Callum. 'I'm a great advocate of change, but I for one can't think of much I'd want to change about my life as it is now. It's pretty much perfect.'

'What if that ceased to be the case,' said Alastair, 'what if perfection bored you?'

Callum considered this while listening to the soft plop of a fish surfacing the water, and then disappearing with a flash of quicksilver. 'Then I suppose I'd do something about it,' he said.

'Exactly. That's my point.'

'So what is it about life here at Linston End that is no longer enough for you? Is it not being able to share it with . . . Orla anymore?'

Alastair twisted his head to look at Callum, but he didn't say anything.

'Hey, just tell me to keep my big mouth shut, or to bugger off for that matter,' said Callum.

'No need,' Alastair said with a small smile, before turning to look at the river again. 'But since you've set us off down this particular route, I'll go along with it. It's quite simple really. Just as you knew when you were at university that the future it offered was not for you, I left here to go travelling knowing that I was doing it to give myself a fresh perspective. Orla's death had left me . . . ' He paused. ' . . . Confused and rudderless, you could say,' he went on. 'I needed to put some distance between myself and everything that reminded me of her so that I could come to terms with what had happened, especially the way she died.'

'That makes sense,' replied Callum carefully. He badly wanted to ask more about Orla's death, to discover whether Alastair was prepared now to be honest. Because Callum knew that Alastair hadn't been entirely honest with what he'd told the police, or what he'd said at the inquest. Had he been honest with Dad and Danny, did they know the truth? Whenever Callum tried to raise the subject with his father, he lost his nerve. To suggest that Orla's death could be anything but a tragic accident was tantamount to heresy. Many times Callum had wanted to share what he knew, or what he *thought* he knew, but he didn't dare. What would it change if he did anyway? Why stir all that up again for Alastair?

'It takes courage to do what you're doing,' he said to Alastair, 'to change your life so dramatically.'

'It's been an easier decision to make than you'd imagine,' Alastair replied. 'The right decision is always easy, and this feels right. Absolutely right.'

'Do you think Orla would approve?' Callum asked, taking the potential sting out of his question by adding, 'I mean, do you think she would have done the same thing herself if, well, if she'd outlived you?'

All at once he felt Alastair's body stiffen, as though charged with an electric pulse, and turning to look at him, Callum saw a frown darkening his expression, his features disturbingly sharpened in the glow of the setting sun. For a terrible moment Callum thought he'd gone too far.

'You always did ask a lot of questions, didn't you?' Alastair said quietly. 'Even as a young boy.'

'I apologise again. I'm sorry. I don't know what's got into me.'

Seconds passed.

'My honest answer to you is, no,' said Alastair at last. 'No, I don't believe for a second that Orla would approve of what I've set in motion. Furthermore, she'd hate the idea of me loving anyone but her, and of anyone but her loving me. But that was Orla; that was what she was like, she needed the whole of a person, half measures didn't come into her thinking, as I'm

162

sure you remember. Now then,' he said in an altogether different tone of voice, and indicating with his hand the mill that was silhouetted against the setting sun, 'what do you know about Laura Manning, who's renting the mill? I've spoken with her a couple of times now, more recently in the post office in Horning yesterday, when I gave her my mobile number and email address, just in case she needs any help with anything.'

'She's renting a boat from us,' said Callum, accepting that he'd been told in no uncertain terms the previous topic of conversation was now closed. 'She seems like a very capable sort of woman. I'd say she's one of those self-contained people who's sociable on her own terms.'

Just then the still, enveloping quiet of the evening was broken by the familiar sound of loud music approaching. Less than a minute later and the *Southern Comfort*, a double-deck paddle boat that plied the river three or four times a day, now lit up with brightly coloured lights and a jazz band playing, cruised by, the party atmosphere on board spilling out across the water. During the tourist season the sight of the boat was as much a part of river life as the heron that had now flown off into the darkening sky.

★ ★ ★

Later, when it was quite dark and he was puttering home in his dinghy — a neat clinker-built wooden boat that he had restored himself — Callum mulled over some of what Alastair had said about Orla, in particular the implication that Callum knew how demanding she could be.

It was true, he could think of any number of times when Orla had offered to do something with him and always she had demanded the whole of his attention; anything less was not acceptable. On one occasion, when he'd been about eleven, and only too pleased that he'd been singled out by Orla to play a game with her, he'd unfortunately grown bored, and had begun to let her win just to get the game over with so he could go and do something more interesting, like play outside. She must have realised what he was doing, and worse, sensed that he was bored with her company, and with a single swish of her hand, she had sent the Monopoly board and pieces scattering violently across the floor. Without a word she had stood up and left the room, leaving him to pick up the pieces and put them away.

That was the thing about Orla; you never really knew where you stood with her, but for some reason you couldn't avoid being sucked into her orbit, attracted like a moth to a candle. Perhaps, and on the basis that all children like the thrill of being scared, it was the unpredictable and slightly dangerous quality about her character that he'd enjoyed as a young boy.

When he thought about it, there had been something of the child about Orla herself. He'd once heard his mother mutter to Dad about her acting like a selfish brat if she couldn't get her own way. Dad had laughed and said it was all down to Orla's artistic temperament. Dad, it had to be said, had always been quick to leap to Orla's defence, and equally quick was Mum's swiftness to criticise. But then that was hardly surprising, given that Mum had been Alastair's girlfriend before Orla came along.

He passed no other river traffic during the short journey home, the outboard motor of his dinghy the only sound to be heard. After turning into the narrow dyke that ran parallel to his small cottage, he moored up and hopped out of the dinghy. Water's Edge Cottage, a tiny two up, two down, fronted the river and was slap bang next door to Snazzell's Boatyard. Being equidistant between Linston and the village of Horning, it was handily placed to get to the shops in Horning. Linston had only a pub and a church.

So far no girlfriend had ever actually lived at Water's Edge Cottage with Callum. The last one had tried her best to move in on a permanent basis, but he had resisted Becky's frequent attempts to get more than her toothbrush over the threshold. It was this adamant refusal on his part that led to Becky giving him an ultimatum — let her move in, or their thirteen-month relationship was over. It had been an easy decision on his part, and told him all he needed to know about his feelings for Becky. Had he needed to deliberate over his response to her ultimatum, it would have proved he cared about her, but he hadn't and as brutal as that was, it proved the relationship had reached the end of the line. As Alastair had said, the right decision is always an easy one to make.

It was only now that Callum was prepared to be honest with himself, that he could admit that for many years he had been subconsciously comparing every girlfriend to Jenna. It was the natural ease of their friendship, which he had never quite replicated with a girlfriend, that he hankered for.

He let himself in at the back door, flicked on lights and set about making himself a bacon sandwich. He had the bacon under the grill and the bread buttered when he picked up his mobile and decided to give Jenna a ring.

It was more than a week since that day in London when he'd surprised her, and when she had surprised him so spectacularly. To his disappointment there had only been a reply to his text about her father. Since then there had been nothing but silence from her, certainly nothing to indicate that things had changed between them as a result of her kissing him. Had he presumed too much to think that she had instigated something? Whatever *something* was. Or if that had been her original intention, did she now regret it?

If that was the case, then perhaps it would be better not to ring her. Once again, as he'd done several times in the last few days, he put down his mobile. Better to leave things well alone.

22

'I know this is a bit unorthodox, me turning up on your doorstep, but I wanted to speak to you personally about what happened as I feel so badly about it.'

Both Danny and Frankie looked at the unexpected guest sitting across the table from them. Her name was Tess Moran and she was a volunteer at Woodside Care Home. Danny had spoken to her many times during his visits to see his mother, as well as Mrs Maudsley.

'I have no idea what it is you've come here to say, Mrs Moran,' said Danny stiffly, 'but can you tell me how Mrs Maudsley is, please?'

'Oh dear,' the woman said, 'of course, you won't have heard, will you, not actually being a relative? I'm sorry to tell you, but she died.'

A sudden squeeze on his heart sucked the breath out of Danny's lungs. 'When?' he managed to say.

'Two days ago, while I was away. Yesterday was my first day back, and that's when I heard that Suzie Wu's side of events had been believed, and not yours. You see, I witnessed what happened that day in the garden, so I know she lied. I was tidying up the sitting room and happened to look out of the window when I saw you approach her. I clearly saw her drop the mobile phone to the ground herself.'

'Then why didn't you come forward to say

that before now?' asked Frankie.

'Because when I finished my shift that afternoon, I had a few days off. I'm so sorry I didn't say anything at the time, I feel awful about that.'

'Have you told Matron what you saw?'

'Yes, of course. But by yesterday Matron knew that Suzie wasn't just a liar, she was also a thief. A number of things from the residents' rooms have disappeared. Including items of jewellery that belonged to Mrs Maudsley. And now there's no sign of her. She's vanished.'

Frankie shook her head and tutted. 'Presumably the police have been notified?'

'They most certainly have. It turns out that she's been caught for stealing before.'

'Then how on earth did she get a job at Woodside?'

'Her references weren't properly checked. It's all such a terrible shame. It would never have happened under the old management, they only employed the best staff who could be trusted one hundred per cent. I've worked at Woodside as a volunteer for many years, my daughter even helped for a few months, and never before has there been a problem like this. But lately standards have definitely slipped. It's all about money for the new owners, and how much they can keep for themselves.'

★　★　★

Later, when they had thanked Mrs Moran for coming to see them, Frankie took Danny in her

168

arms. 'I'm sorry about Mrs Maudsley,' she said.

'I'm sorry too,' he said sadly.

'But at least you don't have to worry anymore about that dreadful Suzie Wu.'

'Yes,' he agreed. But his voice lacked the conviction of his wife's.

23

Paul was late and Rachel wasn't happy. Not that she was one to talk, but this was supposed to be their big romantic night together — their last opportunity to see each other before she went up to Linston and Paul went off with his mates for his Formula One fix.

She had spent ages tidying up her small flat in readiness for a cosy night in with Paul, clearing out anything that didn't fit in with the Hygge style of wellbeing and relaxed intimacy she had wanted to create. Gone was anything of a garish colour and which jarred on the senses, along with the clutter of magazines, books and storage boxes so stuffed full their lids no longer fitted. She had got rid of the fuchsia-pink cushions she had thought so jolly, replaced them with ones the colour of stone, and covered the scruffy sofa with an eye-wateringly expensive Mongolian cashmere throw in charcoal.

Of course it would have been better if it had been autumn or winter in order to conjure up the perfect Hygge atmosphere, and to be honest the amount of tea-light candles she had burning was making her feel unbearably hot.

She ripped off her cardigan, refusing to open a window and ruin the ambiance, and went to check on the starters, which consisted of rye bread fashioned into a selection of fiddly prawn and avocado *smorrebrod*. For the main course she'd followed an online recipe of salmon fish cakes with capers, pickles, tarragon and mayonnaise and a beetroot salad to go with it. The beetroot had stained everything it had come in contact with, including a tea towel that now looked as if it had been used to clean up a massacre.

Pudding was fresh strawberries and cream and served in teacups, an idea she'd thought was cute earlier, but now she wasn't so sure about — Paul would think it was pretentious. He'd probably prefer something with a bit more stodge to it, like the steamed syrup sponge his mother had served during their visit to Shropshire. Admittedly strawberries and cream was an easy cheat, but Rachel hadn't had time to do anything more elaborate.

If she'd known this Hygge lark was such hard work, and so expensive, she wouldn't have bothered. But there again, Paul was worth it. Ever since she'd met his parents and he'd said he loved her, she had felt as though they were on course for . . . well, just on course.

Another look at the clock in the kitchen told her Paul was now forty minutes late. What was more, he hadn't responded to either of her texts. She didn't want to be cross with him, but she was fast heading that way.

He could have been involved in an accident, she told herself in an attempt to assuage her anger; he could be lying in the road somewhere, bones broken, an ambulance hurtling through the busy traffic to reach him. But then she felt guilty for wishing him harm just to stop herself from being angry.

Okay, an accident that he'd witnessed and which he'd got caught up in by offering his assistance. Yes, that was a better scenario. She could forgive him for being late if he'd been a selfless hero.

Ten minutes later, her patience and imagination exhausted, she snatched up her mobile once more.

Where on earth are you????

She added a worried face, although what she really wanted to add was a furious face with steam coming out of its ears.

When still she got no response, she decided to hit the jug of aquavit and rosemary cocktail she'd made. Unable to find any rosemary syrup, she'd cheated and added a spoonful of sugar, along with a few sprigs of rosemary and twists of orange peel. She filled her glass, added some ice cubes from the freezer, swirled it round, then swallowed a large mouthful. She shuddered and clicked her tongue against the roof of her mouth. 'Not bad,' she gasped, raising the glass again to her mouth. 'Not bad at all.'

She was well on her way to finishing the jug when finally the intercom buzzed and she heard Paul's voice. She let him up and listened to the door downstairs onto the street bang shut and then footsteps clumping up the stairs. They were not the hurried guilt-laden steps of a man who knew he was in trouble, but the slow deliberate steps of a man in no particular hurry. Which only added to her worsening mood. He could at least, after all the work she'd put in to making this evening so special, bound up the stairs as if he couldn't wait to see her.

She opened the door and stepped back to let him in, at the same time denying him the chance to kiss her. 'You're late,' she said, 'didn't you get my texts?'

'Sorry,' he said. 'Something came up and I had to . . . you've done something to the room,' he said, looking around him.

'Ten out of ten for observation,' she said sarcastically. 'I'm surprised the candles are still burning, you're so late.'

'Don't be like that. I got here as soon as I could.' He plonked his bag down on the floor by the door. 'What's that you're drinking?'

'It's an aquavit and rosemary cocktail, but there's hardly any left.'

He pulled a face. 'I'd prefer a beer anyway.'

She watched him go over to the fridge and help himself. Something in his proprietorial manner, the way he took for granted there would be his favourite beer waiting for him, added fuel to the fire.

'You've been busy,' he said, rummaging in the drawer to find the bottle opener while eyeing up the plates of food on the worktop.

'*Busy*,' she repeated, her hackles rearing up through the lagoon of aquavit she had consumed, and which had now reached her blood system and was circulating through her body with intent, causing the floor to wobble beneath her feet like a giant jelly, 'you don't know the half of it! You swan in here nearly two hours late without a word of apology, and then — '

'That's not true,' he interrupted her, 'I did say I was sorry. It was the first thing I said. And if we're going to be accurate, I'm only an hour and a half late.'

'Well, that's all right then.'

'Let's not argue. I'm not in the mood.'

'Who's arguing?'

He pointed at her with his now opened bottle of beer. 'You're giving a fair impression of somebody who's arguing.'

'Do you blame me? I've put a lot of effort into this evening. I even got off work early to make everything perfect.'

'Why?'

'What do you mean, why?'

'I mean what's different about this evening compared to any other?'

'Because I wanted it to be special!' she cried, exasperated. 'Because we're not going to be seeing each other for nearly three weeks.'

'Perhaps that's a good thing,' he said with a coldness that stopped her in her tracks.

'What's that supposed to mean?'

'I think you know exactly what it means.'

The heat of her anger cooled, was replaced with a shiver of alarm. 'What's wrong, Paul? What's going on?'

'In what sense?'

'You don't sound like your normal self, is there something you're not telling me? Has something happened at work today that's upset you?'

He looked away from her, returned his attention to the meal she'd spent so long

174

preparing. 'Shouldn't we eat?' he said. 'It's getting late and I have an early start in the morning.'

'Then I'm surprised you bothered to come at all,' she muttered, pushing him out of the way to pick up the platter of open sandwiches, which she then pointedly banged down on the table, rattling the cutlery. She had a sudden vision of behaving exactly like her mother when she was cross with Dad.

'If you're going to be like this, then maybe I should just go home.'

'Yes, Paul, why don't you?'

He put his bottle of beer on the worktop behind him. 'I'll ring you in the morning. When you've calmed down.'

Incensed by his patronising tone, she stared at him, confused. 'What the hell's happened to you, Paul? It's like you're a completely different person to the one who said he loved me.'

When he didn't say anything, she said: 'I asked you before what was wrong, and I'm asking you again. Why are you behaving this way, as though you're doing me a big favour by being here? Or rather, like you'd prefer to be anywhere but here with me?'

He blinked and let out his breath. 'Okay, I'll come clean; I was with Paula earlier. That's why I was late.'

'Paula,' Rachel repeated. 'Your ex?'

'Yes. She texted me and asked if we could meet for a drink and a chat.'

'And you agreed?'

'There seemed no reason not to.'

'Funny that; I can think of any number of reasons. So while I was here slaving away in the kitchen trying to create a perfect evening for us, you were catching up with your ex for, don't tell me, old times' sake. Is that right?'

'Do you have to be so sarky? It's very petty.'

'Oh, pardon me for not sounding deliriously happy at the thought of you and Perfect Paula having a cosy little drink together, and more to the point, that she took priority over me.'

'Please, Rachel, don't, you've had too much to drink.'

'I'll be the judge of that, thank you very much!'

He frowned. 'You're not making this any easier for me, or for yourself. And don't call her Perfect Paula, it's beneath you.'

Rachel rolled her eyes, reached for the jug of what remained of the aquavit cocktail and refilled her glass. Too much to drink? She'd show him! 'Go on,' she said, after she'd taken a large mouthful and forced a smile to her lips. 'This is me making it easy for you.'

Paul took a deep breath. 'I know this isn't what you want to hear, and I'm sorry to break it to you like this. I honestly wish there was a better way to explain it, but the thing is, Paula and I have so much shared history and . . . and we're going to give it another go.'

With one fluid movement of her arm, Rachel threw the glass in her hand at the wall and screamed at Paul to get out.

24

The following morning Frankie was at the Sewing Bee in Chelstead.

A woman who was new to the sewing class was having a classic meltdown moment. Frankie had seen it many times before, and it amazed her that people could get so het up over the simplest of things. If they could fall apart over sewing a couple of squares of cotton together, what were they like with the really important things in life? How would they cope if they were in her shoes, anxious at every turn that her husband might suffer another heart attack?

'This is hopeless!' the woman cried, yanking the fabric out from under the sewing machine needle and flinging it aside. 'If you'd explained it to me better I wouldn't be in this muddle.'

At the unfairness of the accusation, not to say the inaccuracy of it, Frankie was close to telling the rude woman to pull herself together, and that if she'd paid more attention to the instructions Frankie had so patiently given to the group, she wouldn't be in this absurd state. But no, the woman had deemed it more important to fiddle with her mobile phone throughout Frankie's sewing machine demonstration. Honestly, it never failed to surprise Frankie how many women signed up for her beginner's patchwork classes only to behave like an ill-disciplined child, or be just plain flaky and fall apart at the seams. No pun intended.

'I know it can seem a bit confusing at first,' she said, pulling up a chair to sit next to the annoying woman, 'but it just takes a little practice and you'll soon get the hang of it. Let me show you again what to do.'

An hour later, and while the class was packing away their efforts of the day, the shop door opened and Sorrel came in. 'Time for a coffee?' she asked.

'Five minutes and I'll be with you.'

★   ★   ★

Settled at a table with their drinks in the nearby coffee shop, Frankie told Sorrel about Tess Moran's visit yesterday afternoon and how relieved she was that Danny had been exonerated.

'I hope he'll receive a letter of apology,' Sorrel remarked. She took a sip of her coffee. 'Did you really have no idea that Danny was secretly visiting Woodside?'

'Goodness,' Frankie said with a frown, '*secretly* makes it sound deliberately duplicitous what he was doing, as though he was being unfaithful.'

With a small shrug, Sorrel said, 'You have to admit, it was quite odd what he was doing, sneaking off behind your back. Don't you worry what else he might be hiding from you?'

The thought had crossed Frankie's mind, but there was no way on earth she would admit that to Sorrel — not after she'd just used the words *sneaking off*, implying that Danny was up to no good. 'Of course not,' she said, pleasantly, 'his visiting Mrs Maudsley was a singular act of secrecy, and, I might say, a great kindness on his part. He just didn't want me to think he was getting too attached to the old lady.'

'But how can you be so sure there isn't anything else he's keeping from you? You've said before how he bottles things up.'

'Bottling up is different.'

'Is it?'

'What about you and Simon,' Frankie said, growing tired of Sorrel's insinuations, 'do you have secrets from each other?'

'Oh, plenty! I find it's the simplest way.'

Frankie had never really understood Simon and Sorrel's marriage, but then was it ever possible to understand another couple's relationship, even when you'd known them for so many years?

'I'd be surprised if there existed a marriage that didn't have secrets,' Sorrel said. 'Look at Orla and Alastair; they must have kept hundreds of things from each other. And from the rest of us too.'

With the feeling that Sorrel had a point she wanted to make, Frankie said, 'What sort of things?'

'I think we can safely agree that all was not well between them, but that's obvious now, isn't it?'

'What makes you say that?'

'Come on, Frankie, despite being our very own Pollyanna, you must have sussed that Orla was driving Alastair to the edge of his sanity. Another push and he'd have ended up as crazy as she was.'

'Orla wasn't crazy.'

'You can dress it up however you want, but the bottom line is, she wasn't normal. She wasn't like us.'

'Admittedly she was highly strung,' Frankie said, instinctively wanting to defend Orla, 'but she couldn't help how she — '

'Highly strung be damned!' interrupted Sorrel. 'When are we ever going to stop making excuses for her appalling behaviour? She was a calculating cat who knew exactly what she was doing at all times.'

Frankie was shocked at the vitriol coming at her across the table from Sorrel. 'I know the two of you often didn't see eye to eye with each other,' she said, choosing her words with care, 'but I didn't realise you felt so strongly about Orla.'

Her hands smoothing out a wrinkle in the gingham table-cloth, Sorrel sighed. 'To be honest, it's a relief, finally, to be able to say exactly what I think. All these years I've had to keep my mouth shut for fear of being shunned.'

'That's an odd way of putting it, *shunned.*'

'Not to me it isn't.' Then, as though warming to her subject, as if she had literally been waiting a very long time to air her innermost thoughts — her *secret* thoughts — Sorrel said, 'If I'm not right about Orla driving Alastair to the edge, why do you think he got rid of all her things?'

'How do you know he did?'

'I looked in the wardrobes in their bedroom, and the cupboards in the dressing room; there wasn't a single item of her clothing to be seen.

Not a one. There was no sign of any make-up, perfume or that ridiculously clunky jewellery she loved so much.'

'When did you look?'

'The day of the funeral.'

Getting her own back on Sorrel, Frankie said, 'You *sneaked* into their bedroom on that day of all days?'

'I didn't *sneak* anywhere. I walked in quite openly.'

'But why? What made you want to look?'

Sorrel brushed at a speck of something on the sleeve of her jacket — a speck that was invisible to the naked eye, other than Sorrel's. 'I was curious,' she said.

If Frankie was shocked before, she was lost for words now. Curiosity was one thing, but blatant suspicion was quite another.

Perhaps sensing she had gone too far, Sorrel drained her coffee cup, and when she'd settled it back into place on the saucer, turning it so that the handle was at a perfect ninety degree angle, she said, 'Well, that's quite enough about my thoughts on Orla.'

I should think so, thought Frankie. 'How's Rachel?' she asked. 'Jenna told me last night that Paul ended things with her the evening before.'

'Yes. Apparently he's gone back to his ex. I told Rachel to be grateful for a lucky escape. Better she realises now that he wasn't right for her than years later.'

Frankie could well imagine the exchange between Sorrel and Rachel, and while the advice was undoubtedly true, it probably wasn't the sympathetic response the poor girl might have hoped for. But from what Jenna had shared with Frankie, Paul had not made a great impression on her, so maybe Rachel was better off without him. A change of scene in Norfolk would probably do her the world of good.

So much seems to be happening to us all right now, thought Frankie, thinking of the many changes going on around them, not least the transformation in the woman sitting opposite her. 'Sorrel,' she said, 'you said earlier that it was a relief after all these years to say what you really thought about Orla and Alastair; what's changed for you that you now feel able to be honest?'

Once again Sorrel flicked at an invisible speck of something on her sleeve. 'I suppose it's thinking about what lies ahead for us the day after tomorrow at Linston End. It's not exactly going to be a lot of fun, is it?'

'You mean meeting Valentina?'

Sorrel nodded. 'It's going to be a huge challenge pretending we like her.'

'We might find that we do.'

'Yes, and we might find there really are fairies living at the bottom of our gardens.'

Frankie smiled. 'I still don't see how that's created this change in you.'

'It's a combination of things, I suppose. But you know how contrary I can be,' Sorrel went on. 'Well, a part of me had begun to think it would be good to have this stranger forced onto us, especially as Simon kept going on and on about her. I thought her presence might shake us up. But now, after helping Simon to go through an old box of photos of us all, nostalgia and sentiment got the better of me and stirred up the memories. Some good. Some not so good.'

'What were the not-so-good memories?'

Sorrel hesitated. 'Mostly situations when I've held my tongue, but longed to be honest. When I've wanted to admit how I really felt about something.'

'And now you plan to speak your mind?'

Sorrel gave a small laugh. It didn't have the slightest ring of warmth or humour to it. 'That will depend on what provokes me.'

Or who, thought Frankie.

25

'Remember what I said, that I'd be more than happy to come in and help while your guests are here,' Sylvia said as Alastair saw her and Neil to the door. They'd spent the day at Linston End helping to get the house and garden ready for tomorrow when everybody would be arriving. He'd broken the news to them about selling the house, but they had, of course, heard rumours already, the Broads having its own bush telegraph that worked as effectively as high speed broadband for spreading news.

'Oh yes, please let her help,' urged Neil, 'I could do with the break at home. Although God knows what I'll do when you've sold up.'

Sylvia tutted and swished her husband lightly on the shoulder. 'You mean it's the other way around, coming here has always been a way for me to escape from you!'

Alastair smiled and after they'd gone, he went back into the kitchen and opened his laptop to check his emails. For all the years he'd known Sylvia and Neil they had always exchanged pleasantries in this manner; it was pure habit, as indeed it was for most couples. What he had come to know though, was that for some people the habit became a device for disguising something far more toxic. A well-aimed snide comment was often a way to deliver a vicious or

184

vengeful punch in full sight of those around them without causing so much as a flicker of concern, let alone condemnation.

Danny and Frankie never engaged in such tactics. There was something genuinely true and honest about their affection for each other, with never a harsh or critical word exchanged; there was no doubt in Alastair's mind that they loved each other as much now as the day they married, probably more.

In contrast, Sorrel and Simon's marriage was held together by something wholly different, which, given the complicated dynamics that existed between them, he had the good sense never to explore: their marriage was their own affair. Yet whatever it was that bound them together, it could not be more complex than the ties that had bound Alastair to Orla. He was still waiting for the day when he would wake up knowing he was finally free of them.

Amongst the stream of emails in his mailbox there was one from Valentina. He kept it to read after dealing with all the others, including several from the estate agent with various viewing requests. The couple who came round a few days ago had made a derisory offer which the agent had advised against accepting, not that Alastair had been remotely inclined to do so.

He confirmed the viewing appointments with the agent, reminding him that he had house-guests for the coming weeks, then working his way through the dross, he came to an email from the woman staying in the mill — Laura

Manning. He had bumped into her in the butcher's shop in Horning yesterday, and after walking across the green to the staithe where they had both moored their boats, he mentioned that he had friends coming to stay and that she might like to join them for a meal, that's if she didn't mind a crowd.

Hello Alastair,

It was kind of you to invite me over to your house one day. As is the way of one's children, my son has just announced an unexpected intention to visit me and so perhaps I'd better decline, rather than add another guest to your already packed houseful.

With best wishes,
Laura

Alastair replied straightaway.

Hi Laura,

The more the merrier, bring your son, he's most welcome to join us. I'll be in touch to let you know exactly when.

Alastair

Next he opened Valentina's email and at once he experienced that now familiar spark of connection as he read her message.

Cher Alastair,

I am not blessed with the qualities of a saint, and so it is with great relief that I am at last leaving my mama today and flying home to Paris, before travelling to be with you. Of course I love her dearly, but she can be so very trying.

I'm afraid I have a request to make of you, one that you must not feel obliged to agree to, I will not think badly of you if you say no. My stepchildren — Irina and Nikolai — have expressed a wish to see me while I am in England, and rather than my visit them in London, I wondered if they could stay at Linston End with us? They are naturally curious to meet the man who has stolen their stepmama's heart.

It is only two days now until I see you again, I can't tell you how much I am looking forward to being with you. But we must not fool ourselves: when I cross the threshold of your home, which you have spoken of so frequently and so lovingly, we will be facing a great test of our relationship, possibly the greatest. Be brave and prepare yourself for the days ahead, just as I am!

With much love,
Valentina.

P.S. I have news to share with you regarding where we might create our new home together.

The email read, Alastair wondered if by asking to have her step-children join them here at Linston End it was a form of levelling out the playing field. Their presence would understandably provide Valentina with a degree of emotional support; equally it would mean he would be subjected to the same kind of scrutiny and judgement that she would be exposed to by his friends. To put it bluntly, it would be a case of Team Valentina versus Team Alastair.

He had no problem with that. He'd do anything to help the woman he loved feel more comfortable here, so without a second thought, or considering where the extra guests would sleep, he replied that of course they could stay.

His reply sent, he speculated as to how Jenna, Rachel and Callum would get on with Valentina's stepchildren. Never having met them, he could only hope that being of a similar age — mid thirties — that might provide sufficient common ground for them to get along.

Thinking of Callum, Alastair recalled the questions that had come up during their chat the other evening. He'd had the distinct impression that Callum had been getting at something. But what? Had there been talk about Alastair taking off so soon after the inquest? But surely if tongues had been wagging, Neil and Sylvia would have alerted him to what was being said?

Or had there been more to Callum's questions? Did he know that Alastair had deliberately lied to the police and then later when he gave evidence at the inquest? But how could Callum know? What could anyone ever know? Only two people truly knew what happened the night Orla had drowned, and one of them was dead.

⋆ ⋆ ⋆

That night he was haunted by a vortex of dreams that took him deeper and deeper into the guilt of Orla's death. As he had so many times before, he dreamt he was at the wheel of his slipper launch, *Water Lily*, secretly following behind Orla in *Swallowtail*, his Aunt Cora's old motor cruiser, its low chugging engine the only sound to be heard. It was dark, with scudding clouds passing across the moon, partially obliterating the only source of light to guide Alastair.

Orla's destination was Linston Broad. When she reached the middle, she cut the engine and let the cruiser drift. Peering into the darkness, and knowing exactly what she was about to do, he watched her balance on the prow of the boat, as though poised to jump in. He shouted to her not to do it, that he was sorry, sorry for everything, he hadn't meant what he'd said. But she merely looked straight at him, with a hatred that made him gasp, before throwing herself beneath the oily black surface of the water.

He pulled on the throttle to make the launch go faster, but the engine failed and try as he might he couldn't make it start again. In the end, and knowing it was futile, he dived in to the water and began frantically to swim. When he found Orla, her body, brightly illuminated as if by a spotlight in the water, lay motionless amongst the weeds at the bottom of the broad, almost as if she were sleeping. But then, he saw that her body was weighted down with one of her bronze statues tied around her waist. It was of a small child, its arms reaching up to Orla as though asking to be held.

With fumbling hands, his lungs bursting with the effort of holding his breath for so long under the icy water, he tried to untie the statue, and then recoiled in shock when Orla opened her eyes and suddenly began to laugh. 'It was just a prank,' she cried with sickening delight, 'to see how much you cared.'

Furious that she had played so cruel a trick on him, he left her there to die at the bottom of Linston Broad.

26

It was obvious to Simon, even to an emotional duffer like him — as Sorrel referred to his so-called inability to read a situation — that things were very different now at Linston End. The dynamics had changed. But then how could they have remained the same? It was just so disappointing to see everybody trying so hard to enjoy themselves.

Before — *before Orla's death* — enjoying themselves had come perfectly naturally, things would just happen spontaneously, or appear to do so without any real effort on anyone's part. Now it was as if they were consciously tiptoeing around Alastair, and themselves for that matter, trying to say the right thing as well as dicker about over what to do. In the twenty-four hours they'd been here — they'd arrived in various stages throughout yesterday, he and Sorrel first, then Danny and Frankie, with Jenna and Rachel the last to arrive from London — it seemed that none of them was now capable of making a decision.

Alastair in particular gave the impression of being on edge and at great pains to ensure everybody was having a good time. In turn the rest of them were acting most oddly, as if they had never stayed here before. And that was before Valentina had arrived. God help them when she did! Or maybe once she was here and

191

they'd got that part of the proceedings over with they'd settle into some kind of normal behaviour, or something close to it. He doubted it, though, and as he manoeuvred the motor cruiser out of the dyke and joined the river, he feared the unease amongst them might well be the lull before the storm.

From his position at the helm of *Swallowtail*, he turned to look over his shoulder at Alastair. *I've lost him*, he thought with miserable resignation, watching first his old friend tidy away the mooring ropes, and then Danny with his binoculars hanging from a strap around his neck. *It's just Danny and me now.* And what if Danny suffered another heart attack? A fatal one?

Death was never far from his thoughts these days and was, he knew, affecting his mood; it made him impatient and determined not to lose a moment of whatever quantity of time remained to him. Everything counted now. It was why he had taken charge after breakfast, fed up of listening to the others trying to decide what to do with the day. He'd proposed that he and Danny and Alastair would take *Swallowtail* and go to Horning to stock up on beer and wine and other essentials for the coming days. He'd seen it as probably the only chance the three of them would have to be alone together.

This was the first time they had taken *Swallowtail* out together since last year, and though nobody had said anything, it had to be on all their minds that Orla had taken this boat out the night of her tragic accident. Before that night, Simon knew that the beautiful old craft that had been repaired and renovated by Snazzell's Boatyard, long before Callum had begun working there, had been Alastair's pride and joy.

Now, and with a pang of bittersweet nostalgia, as both Alastair and Danny came alongside him, Simon said, 'Remember how we swore we'd one day go on a *Three Men in a Boat* jaunt on board *Swallowtail?*' he said. 'Why did that never happen?'

'The same reason so many things don't happen,' replied Danny, 'life gets in the way.'

'Only because we allow it to,' said Simon, steering the boat closer to the bank on the right-hand side of the river to avoid a monstrously large cruiser that was taking up more space than it needed. 'What do you think, Alastair, should we make it happen? Relive our lost youth before it's too late?'

'You may have lost yours, but I feel like I'm getting younger by the day,' said Alastair with a smile.

'Smug bastard!'

Alastair laughed. 'Guilty as charged, Simon, and I don't give a damn how annoying I sound.'

'Fair enough, but the concept surely has its appeal: a few days of just the three of us setting off together and leaving everything behind? What could be better than the three *compadres* casting their cares to the wind and taking to the river?'

'A few days of being confined in a small space with you, Simon,' said Danny with a laugh, 'I think you've just shot yourself in the foot.'

'I'd love to say yes,' said Alastair evenly, looking ahead, his eyes and expression hidden behind his sunglasses, 'but with everything that's currently going on, I really can't commit to anything.'

'It would only be for two days,' Simon pressed, 'three at most. Come on, Al, surely Valentina hasn't neutered you already, has she?'

'Give it a rest, Simon,' warned Danny.

But Simon wasn't in the mood for giving it a rest. Not now. There were things that needed to be said. Alastair needed to know that he couldn't throw their friendship aside just because he was acting like a love-sick teenager. 'A couple of days, that's all. Is that really too much to ask? We could do it next month in September, when the river's quietened down.'

Alastair turned slowly to look at him. 'Of course it's not too much to ask, and we'll do it one day, we will, just not while I'm trying to sell the house and decide where to live with Valentina. The time's not right.'

'Quick! Over there,' said Danny suddenly, a hand pointing to the bank on their left as he raised his binoculars to his eyes, 'a great crested grebe sitting on a nest.'

The conversation brought to an abrupt stop, both Simon and Alastair looked at what had been pointed out to them in the thick undergrowth, probably each knowing that, forever the truce maker, Danny had sought to reduce the tension that was building.

★ ★ ★

'You're always such a hothead,' muttered Danny when they reached Horning and had the boat moored at the staithe that was teeming with tourists. Alastair was out of earshot, having been spotted amongst the crowd by somebody he knew and gone over to have a chat. 'What the hell were you thinking putting Alastair on the spot like that?'

Simon scowled. 'What else am I supposed to do? Stand back and let him make a fool of himself? Bloody hell, did you not want to shake some sense into him when he boasted about feeling younger by the day? What next, a ponytail and a Harley Davidson on the drive? Can't you feel that everything is changing between the three of us? I don't know about you, but being here feels more like we're attending a wake than being on holiday.'

'Perhaps that's because you're not helping matters. Just try and remember what it was like for us when we first met Sorrel and Frankie; we wanted nothing but to spend our every waking moment with them. That's what Alastair's going through, so for the love of God stop acting like a jealous adolescent. Be happy for him and let him enjoy the moment, because who knows how long it will last?'

But Simon couldn't be happy for Alastair. He just couldn't. He genuinely did feel as though he was now in mourning for his old friend.

It was not the ideal thought to have in his head when making Valentina's acquaintance later that day.

27

While Alastair, Simon and Danny were out, Sorrel had seized control, something she had never done before while here at Linston End. But then there was no Orla to take charge, no Orla to instruct them on what they were to do.

Jenna had never really thought about it before, but Orla had been the axis upon which they had all revolved. They were, she now saw, adrift without that dynamic and guiding force. Funnily enough, if asked, Jenna would have said it had been Alastair who had been the driving force, but it was clear he was as adrift as the rest of them. She had never witnessed that in him before. It was strange seeing him behave so differently.

'Are you two girls going to stand there daydreaming all day, or are you going to lend a hand?'

Catching a look from her mother, who was cracking eggs, separating the whites from the yolks to make one of her famous Pavlovas, Jenna said, 'What would you like us to do?'

'For starters that pile of potatoes won't peel themselves.'

'Mum!' remonstrated Rachel who had only just surfaced from her bed and was still in her nightclothes, and helping herself to orange juice from the fridge. 'It's not even lunchtime and you're going nuts over preparing for dinner tonight. If it's okay with you, I'd like some breakfast before I do anything else.'

'You missed breakfast, that was hours ago,' replied Sorrel briskly.

'Bloody hell, it never used to be like this when Orla was alive,' muttered Rachel, which earned her a thunderous look from her mother. 'Come on, Jenna, let's go out to the garden and get some peace and quiet and enjoy the sun.'

'How about we peel the potatoes in the garden?' suggested Jenna to Sorrel.

'God, you're such a goody-two-shoes!'

'Thank you, Jenna,' said Sorrel, 'I'm glad I can rely on someone.'

'Oh give it a rest, Mum, we're on holiday and apart from anything else, you should be cosseting me as I recover from having my heart broken.'

'Maybe I would if I honestly believed you were heartbroken.'

Rachel put a hand to her chest. 'Harsh, Mum, harsh.'

'Your mother's got a point,' Jenna said, when she and Rachel had carried the large bag of potatoes, saucepan, chopping board and vegetable peelers outside to the table on the terrace. 'You don't really seem that upset about Paul dumping you. Only a few days ago you were over the moon that he said he loved you.'

Making no attempt to help Jenna, Rachel said, 'Yeah well, I got that wrong, didn't I? But I hope you're not about to say I told you so. I swore on the train yesterday that I'd chuck you in the river if you did that.'

'I wouldn't dream of it. But are you sure you're all right, you're not putting a brave face on it, are you? You know you don't have to pretend with me.'

'Nah, I'm good. I'm determined not to waste my energy on trying to figure out what happened. He's so not worth the effort.'

'Good, so I don't need to treat you with kid gloves, then? You won't bite my head off, or throw me in the river, if I say you deserve better.' Jenna knew that deep down Rachel had to be upset by what Paul had done, but she knew her friend of old; pride would not allow her to admit just how upset she was. She might not like it, but in so many ways Rachel was very like her mother. Pride and saving face were paramount to them both.

In the same way Jenna knew that she had inherited her parents' natural desire to keep the peace, to smooth the ruffled feathers of those around her; it was one of the reasons she had followed in her father's footsteps and studied law, seeing it as a way to bring calm and order to troubled lives. How naïve that seemed to her now!

'Yeah, yeah, of course I deserve better,' replied Rachel. 'So tell me about your Mr Sexy Pants, Blake Darnell.'

'Nothing to tell, and as I've told you numerous times before, he isn't *my* anything. We've established ourselves as co-working friends, nothing more.'

'Is that what they're calling it these days?' sneered Rachel. 'What about Callum, have you explained yourself to him yet?'

'I don't suppose you fancy going back to bed do you, so I can sit here without being interrogated?'

'I'm only thinking of my big bro's welfare.'

'That must be a first.'

'Having been treated the way I was by Paul, let's just say I'm sensitive about other people's feelings.'

Which was a step in the right direction, thought Jenna with a half smile.

But as Rachel closed her eyes and leant back in her chair to better enjoy the warm August sunshine, Jenna reached for another potato and pondered how she was going to tackle Callum this evening. He hadn't joined them last night, and his not being with them for the first night of their annual summer stay at Linston End had never happened before, which added to the general feeling that nothing was as it used to be.

At the sound of a boat passing at the end of the garden and children's voices singing out — they were dressed as pirates, complete with hats, stripy tops, eye-patches and armed with plastic cutlasses — she thought of all the childhood summers she had spent here with Rachel and Callum. Rarely had they allowed outsiders to infiltrate their little gang; they'd had no need for anybody else.

One summer Orla had nicknamed them The Swallowtails and the name had stuck. They had formed a club — The Swallowtail Club — much like the children in Arthur Ransome's *The Coot Club*, and had devised a code of conduct, most of which had been designed to keep adults from knowing what they were getting up to. Membership was strictly limited: once or twice a child who was visiting the sailing club in Horning would insinuate his or her way in, but on the whole it was not something they welcomed or encouraged.

Thinking how self-contained they'd been, and perhaps how unfriendly their behaviour might have seemed, Jenna knew that they would have to do better when it came to Valentina's stepchildren once they arrived.

But first they had Valentina to meet.

28

Alastair had wanted to meet Valentina in Norwich, to save her the bother of catching the train to Wroxham and Hoveton, but she had insisted there was no need for him to drive the extra distance, that she was perfectly capable of making the connection herself. 'But I'd get to see you even sooner if I drive to Norwich,' he'd said quite reasonably when they'd spoken on the phone last night. She'd laughed at that and told him what were a few extra minutes when they would be seeing each other night and day for the next couple of weeks?

She was right, of course, but he was impatient to see her. He wanted to hold her and know that she was real; that what they were doing was real. It was a phrase that frequently whirled around inside his head, as if baiting him to doubt the veracity of his feelings, to make him lose faith.

He knew perfectly well his friends were troubled about his plans to be with an unknown woman who had come into his life so soon after Orla. They had his best interests at heart, or so he wanted to believe, but a part of him was beginning to suspect that it was their own interests they were more concerned about. Perhaps that was truer of Simon than the others. He seemed quite unprepared to allow Alastair to be happy if it meant changing the status quo.

As a boy Simon had always been the more

possessive of the three of them. It would have been understandable to assume Danny would be more insecure and possessive, given the difficult years of his young childhood, but no, it was Simon with his comfortable upbringing, decent and caring parents and his extrovert manner who, deep down, was the more insecure.

But knowing this didn't make it any easier for Alastair to deal with Simon's reluctance to accept the changes that lay ahead. *He'll come round*, was the hope he hung on to, once they had all got to know Valentina and trusted the happiness she had brought into his life. Then they would relax and stop treating him as if he had lost his mind and needed certifying.

He checked his watch. The train was two minutes late, which was no big deal, it often was. He breathed in deeply, let out his breath and walked along the platform right to the end, Rachmaninoff's Piano Concerto No. 2 — the soundtrack from *Brief Encounter* — suddenly playing in his head. He smiled at the cheesiness of it, but then he thought of the film's ending when Celia Johnson and Trevor Howard accept they have no future together, and the smile was gone from his face.

He'd paced the platform a few more times before he saw the Norwich train coming into view. For a terrible moment he wondered what he'd do if Valentina wasn't on it, if she'd had a change of heart and decided a holiday romance was exactly that and had no place in the real world. The thought of having to explain that to his friends filled him with dismay. Which shocked him. Surely his first thought should have been to think how devastated he would be to lose Valentina, not about how stupid he would look to his friends, or how relieved they might be.

He looked anxiously along the platform to the now stationary train; carriage doors were opening and people were starting to appear. Holding his breath, he waited for Valentina to materialise. He knew the importance of this moment, the test of seeing each other again. Was the magic still there? Were they as they each remembered, or had they recreated each other to fit some kind of perfect ideal while being apart?

There! There she was!

She spotted him just as he raised a hand eagerly in the air and began moving towards her.

'Well then,' she said, when they were standing inches apart, her luggage at her feet, 'here we are.'

'Here we are indeed,' he said, his stomach tightening with anxiety. Simply but elegantly dressed in a pale blue silk blouse and white jeans, her glossy dark hair tied up loosely on her head, she looked spectacularly radiant, like an exotic bird of paradise in such ordinary surroundings. 'Would a kiss be in order?' he asked, glad he'd showered and changed out of the scruffy old shorts and T-shirt he'd been wearing earlier.

A slow smile appeared on her face. 'After coming all this way I would say it was compulsory, wouldn't you?'

'I certainly would,' he agreed, putting his arms around her shoulders and drawing her close. Her warm sensual lips met his, soft and parted, and the tightening in his stomach made itself felt again, but this time for a very different reason.

'I wish we didn't have to go home straight-away,' he said in a low voice, his arms still around her. Behind them the train was moving on. 'In fact I wish we could go anywhere but Linston End.'

She tilted her head back and gave him one of her ravishing smiles. 'You would deny me the fun of meeting your friends? How selfish you are.'

'Is it so wrong of me to want you entirely to myself?'

She tapped a finger against his chest. 'Very wrong.'

He sighed happily. 'God, it's good to see you again.' He picked up her luggage and guided her towards the car park where he'd left his Range Rover.

'I should warn you,' he said, when they had passed through Horning and were on the road to Linston, 'everybody is acting very oddly; they're all on edge at the prospect of meeting you.'

'I would be disappointed if they weren't on edge, it would mean they didn't care about you.'

'It might be they care a little too much.'

'Friends who care too much, how terrible.'

He glanced at her, reached for her hand and squeezed it. 'You know what I mean though, don't you?'

'I told you before that I knew what to expect, that your friends will want to protect you from me, that I will be viewed as the enemy. I am quite prepared for that.'

'I wouldn't go so far as to say it will be that bad,' he said.

'You English lie so politely,' she said with a laugh. 'We both know that nothing would please them more than for me to disappear so they can keep you to themselves.'

She was right, of course, but Alastair couldn't bring himself to admit that she was; it spoke too badly of his friends and he didn't want to cast them in a poor light. 'It'll all be fine,' he said. 'In the end.'

⋆　⋆　⋆

Valentina had primed herself that she was not here to make enemies, but then neither was she here to be walked all over. She was here to fight for her man.

As she looked up at the impressive house before her, while Alastair lifted her luggage out from the boot of the car, she wondered if she would also have to fight this home of his, this beloved Linston End which she had heard so much about. He had told her fondly of his childhood holidays here with his eccentric bird-watching aunt, how he had then inherited the house, along with what he had admitted was a sizeable portfolio of stocks and shares, and which he had never known about, not until he'd been informed of the terms of his aunt's will.

Still staring up at the house, Valentina did not underestimate how big a test of Alastair's love for her it would be to sell Linston End. But give it up he would have to if they were going to make a new life together. She had compromised too much in the past; it was not something she would do again.

The house was quainter and more charming than she had imagined, its brickwork topped off with an attractive thatched roof that hung low and deep over the windows and made her think of old-fashioned fairy tales and the large dachas of the Russian elite. The green lawn in front of the house had been recently mown, the stripes — such an English obsession — clearly visible, as though ready for Wimbledon.

She fell into step beside Alastair, half expecting a devoted and stony-faced housekeeper to open the door to them. Oh yes, she had read Daphne du Maurier's *Rebecca*. She knew that by everybody here she would be compared to Alastair's dead wife, that she could never live up to the wonderfully talented Orla, for whom they all still mourned.

But Valentina was not like that pathetic heroine from Rebecca; she was made of tough Russian stock and refused to be intimidated by a miserable housekeeper, or anyone else for that matter. Just let anyone try that and see where it got them! Besides, she knew things about Orla that they didn't. Things that Alastair had never shared with anybody else, so he'd said.

Armed with a smile and everything Alastair had made known to her about his friends, she stepped over the threshold of Linston End fully prepared for the battle ahead.

29

'I'll say this for your Uncle Al; he certainly knows how to pick 'em. He always did get the stunners.'

Callum cringed. 'Dad,' he said, 'you might want to lower your voice.'

'What?' His father said, his face all mock innocence. 'I meant it as a compliment.'

'Sure you did.'

It wasn't often his father got properly hammered, but on this occasion he was having a damned good crack at it. Odds on he'd been keeping the alcohol levels topped up since lunch-time, which was when he and Danny and Alastair had gone to Horning. Callum had seen them sitting outside the Swan Inn when he'd been passing in his dinghy on the way back to the boatyard; he'd given them a wave and they'd cheerily raised their beer glasses in return.

The much-anticipated arrival of Alastair's new woman had certainly got everyone worked up. When Callum had got here a short while before Alastair returned from the station with Valentina, he had found the household in a near state of frenzied madness. In between shouting out orders to no one in particular, Mum had been hissing at Dad to stop helping himself to the jugs of Pimm's and to do something useful, like get out of her way. Meanwhile Frankie had been fussing over the place settings on the table on the terrace, realising in alarm that she'd miscounted and laid one too few places — was that an omen? — and Rachel had been freaking out because she'd left her hair straighteners back in London.

Amidst all this, and seemingly at the sight of him when Callum had gone over to say hi, Jenna had tripped on the step leading out from the kitchen. Carrying a tray of cutlery, she had bumped into her father, who reached out to stop her falling, but in the process left dirty black marks on her dress from the barbecue coals he'd just been handling.

From the frenzied chaos of then, everyone now appeared to be alternating between tongue-tied awkwardness and sporadic bursts of inanity. Nobody was being their true self, not even Alastair who was clearly trying too hard to pretend that this was just a relaxed gathering of close friends.

Interestingly the only person who seemed to be behaving in a manner something akin to normal was the star of the show: Valentina. Of everyone here she would have been the one whom Callum would have expected to be most nervous; but no, she was as cool as the proverbial cucumber and, it had to be said, Dad was not wrong in describing her as a looker. But to be honest, Callum would have been more surprised if Alastair had fallen for anyone who didn't fit that description. Old photographs of Orla in her twenties and thirties had revealed her to be a dark-haired version of Kate Moss, all haughty, smoky-eyed defiance. Orla had hated photographs of herself, but the few that had been on show here had disappeared almost immediately after her death. Had they been too painful a reminder for Alastair?

From his vantage point in front of the barbecue, which he'd been put in charge of, and as his father ambled over to talk to Danny, Callum watched his mother surreptitiously studying Valentina as Alastair poured her a glass of Pimm's. Not for the first time Callum thought how difficult it was to read his mother's expression. She had one of the best poker faces he knew, and right now he didn't have a clue what she was thinking, or more precisely what she thought of Valentina.

'She's one of those effortlessly stylish women who make the rest of us look hideously drab, isn't she?' The remark came from his sister who had suddenly materialised at his side.

'I wouldn't say that,' he answered her.

'What would you say then?' asked Jenna, joining him on his other side.

'I'd prefer to keep my thoughts to myself if it's all the same to you two.'

Rachel rolled her eyes. 'You're no fun. Isn't that right, Jenna, he's the most boring person we both have the misfortune to know.'

'I can think of worse bores,' Jenna said with a small smile.

'Hah, talk about damned with faint praise!' replied Callum, wishing that he could get Jenna alone and clear the air between them. Clearly she regretted kissing him, because whenever he said anything to her, he sensed her closing like a clam shell. He took up the barbecue tongs and fiddled unnecessarily with the lamb chops and burgers on the grill.

'So,' said Rachel, her voice lowered, 'what's the verdict? Do we like her?'

'Nothing not to like so far,' whispered Jenna.

'Give it time,' said Rachel ominously, 'give it time.'

'I feel sorry for her,' said Callum.

'She doesn't strike me as the sort to be in need of our sympathy,' asserted Rachel. 'Far from it. It's Alastair who looks a bundle of nerves if you ask me.'

'I know what Callum's getting at,' said Jenna, 'she knows her every word and gesture is being monitored by us, one wrong move on her part and we'll all say she's not worthy to take Orla's place.'

'Could anyone be genuinely worthy of doing that?' murmured Rachel. 'Let's face it, Orla was an impossible act to follow, and trust me, that's something I know all about.'

Callum exchanged a look with his sister. He knew every minute detail of her latest break up, having had numerous long, and somewhat one-sided, conversations with her on the phone. While he wasn't entirely surprised, he was sympathetic to her being dumped in favour of an ex; it was a bitter pill to swallow for anyone.

'Now what are you three gossiping about?' asked Frankie, approaching with a tray of chicken drumsticks. 'As if I couldn't guess. Callum, these have been pre-cooked in the microwave and just need a bit of crisping up on the barbecue if there's room.'

'By crisping up, I assume you mean not blackened to within an inch of their lives?'

Frankie smiled. 'I do, and for heaven's sake you three . . . ' she looked at each of them in turn, ' . . . try not to stare at the poor woman, she must be anxious enough as it is without you three piling on the pressure so unsubtly.'

'Busted,' laughed Callum. And then: 'I'm not sure why I've been trusted to be in charge of cooking,' he said, when Frankie left them to go over and join the others grouped around Valentina.

'I think you'll find the mummies and daddies have more important things on their minds right now than standing over a hot barbecue,' said Jenna. 'There seems to be an awful lot to eat,' she added, as Callum placed the chicken drumsticks on the grill.

'That's down to Mum breaking out with the psycho routine,' said Rachel, blatantly staring at Valentina who was listening to their father with what had to be feigned interest. Nobody, in Callum's opinion, could look that interested in what a perfect stranger had to say. Especially not a stranger who'd had too much to drink. But fair play to her, she was doing a fine job of hanging on to Dad's every word, and for that she ought to be applauded.

★ ★ ★

'This is so perfectly English,' drawled Valentina, her tone to Sorrel's ears a hair's breadth from a sneer.

211

'No,' laughed Danny, pulling out a chair for their guest as they took their places at the table on the terrace, 'if this was truly an English affair it would be raining and we'd be forcing you to eat your meal under an umbrella.'

'In that case I have that to look forward to,' she said, giving him a dazzlingly bright smile. 'Now tell me, who is responsible for this beautiful flower arrangement on the table?'

'That'll be Mum,' said Jenna, indicating Frankie who was sitting directly opposite her.

'I congratulate you,' said Valentina, 'you clearly have the artistic touch.'

'It's nothing,' replied Frankie, 'just a few flowers picked from the garden here.'

'But it is the clever way you have arranged them. In my hands those flowers would look quite ordinary, but you have created a floral masterpiece. You will have to teach me how to do that.'

'I'd be happy to.'

Good Lord, thought Sorrel, could the woman lay it on any thicker? But it was a clever tactic, if a little obvious. Charming them with flattery in order to win them over was, of course, her best option, but could she keep it up, that was the question? How soon before the effort of being so irritatingly nice wore thin? Curious to see how Valentina would react, Sorrel decided it was time to liven things up.

'Frankie is very much the artistic one of us,' she said, loading on the guile, 'unlike me; I'm hopeless in that direction. But Frankie and dear Orla were two of a kind in that respect.'

There was a deliciously predictable loss of beat to the conversation, creating a pin-drop silence, during which Sorrel kept her gaze fixed firmly on Valentina so as not to see the expression on Alastair's face.

'Yes,' said Valentina, her piercing blue eyes narrowing as she returned Sorrel's stare with equal measure, 'I have heard much from Alastair about Orla's artistic gifts and what a perfectionist she was, but also how heavily that weighed upon her.'

And on us! was on the tip of Sorrel's tongue. 'Tell us about your children,' she said instead, as Frankie started passing food around the table. 'I believe we're going to have the pleasure of meeting them in the coming days.'

'My *step*children,' Valentina corrected her with steely politeness, 'and yes, Alastair has kindly agreed for Nikolai and Irina to visit.'

'Where do they live?' asked Callum, passing her a large serving dish of barbecued meat.

'In London. Nikolai works for a digital media company — please, do not ask me to explain what he does precisely, I don't have a clue — and Irina is currently employed by a firm of Knightsbridge estate agents to deal with the many Russian customers they have. Because,' she went on, while helping herself to one small chicken drumstick and passing the serving dish to Rachel, 'as you know, we Russians are buying up all your property from right beneath your noses, and oh, how you hate us for it. And now this one sitting at your table has the awful nerve to steal your very own Alastair. Where will it all

213

end, you must wonder!'

There was polite laughter around the table with Simon snorting. 'Oh, you're welcome to him, we've been trying to get rid of him for years.' And then Alastair, perhaps thinking Valentina had been interrogated enough for the time being, picked up his wineglass.

'I propose a toast,' he said, 'to the people around this table who mean the world to me, and,' his gaze settling on Valentina, 'to the future.'

She leaned towards him and kissed him on the cheek, then clinked her glass against his. 'To *our* future,' she said.

Her words left Sorrel in no doubt that Valentina planned to have Alastair all to herself. The woman had no intention of sharing him with his old friends.

30

The next morning Danny was awake early, having slept badly. He'd eaten too much and drunk too much, and stayed up much too late the night before, despite Frankie's warning him not to overdo it. His punishment was a restless night of indigestion, accompanied by the paralysing fear that it wasn't indigestion he was suffering, but his heart about to pack up. The arrival of dawn, after no more than a couple of hours' sleep, and the knowledge that he hadn't died, as absurd as that sounded, came as a huge relief.

Out of bed, carefully, so as not to disturb Frankie, he slipped on his dressing gown. In the bathroom, he looked through the window and saw a gauzy layer of mist suspended over the river. A pair of swans came into view, trailed behind by five grey cygnets. It was a beautifully tranquil sight, and one that made him glad to be alive. Thank God, he thought, somewhat melodramatically, he'd cheated death to see another day!

Downstairs he made himself a cup of tea and took it outside to the terrace, the scene of last night's gathering. It had gone better than Danny had feared it might. He'd been worried about Simon and the quantity of alcohol he'd drunk, but really Sorrel was the one who had been the loose cannon. But then Sorrel had always had a knack for causing an undercurrent of disquiet when she chose. They had lived with this habit of hers for so long they scarcely noticed it, much less challenged her over it, but last night she had made herself look cattily mischievous in pointedly dragging Orla's name into the conversation. She had done it at least three times in Danny's hearing.

He had never quite been able to put his finger on why Sorrel behaved this way, other than in this instance the possibility that Frankie's long-held suspicions were not without some element of truth: that Sorrel had never forgiven Alastair for dropping her in favour of Orla. Frankie's other theory was that Sorrel had regarded marrying Simon as accepting second best — if she couldn't have Alastair, she'd do the next best thing and have one of his closest friends. At the time Danny and Frankie were already a well-established couple, so that just left Simon.

Danny hated to think that there could be any truth in this, that Simon could be considered as second best. He loved Simon, and Alastair, as he would two brothers, or how he imagined he would love a pair of brothers had he had any. Yes, Simon had his faults, but didn't they all? He for one was no shining example of perfection, he was a nit-picker who worried over the smallest of things.

But was it possible that Sorrel still harboured feelings for Alastair; was that why she had tried to make things awkward for Valentina, had jealousy been the cause of her behaviour? And did that explain the tightrope tension that had occasionally shown itself between Sorrel and Orla? Danny had always put that down to a clash of personalities, but maybe there was more to it.

'You're such an innocent,' was the oft-made remark by Frankie about his inability to grasp the subtle nuances of behaviour that went on right under his nose. Or even the downright obvious for that matter.

'Your problem is that you expect everybody else to behave as well as you do,' was another of Frankie's comments. That was certainly true. His parents, Rosamunde and Michael, had been Quakers and had brought him up to believe in the essential goodness of every individual, and not to judge without walking a mile in another person's shoes.

As a teenager he had not taken well to sitting still for an hour during a Quaker meeting, though what child would? But now he could sit in contented silence for hour after hour if given the chance. He could certainly do that here at Linston End. The sense of calm he derived from being by the river was, he imagined, not unlike the uplifting stillness his parents must have experienced during those long silent meetings.

Frankie had been right when she'd said coming here would do them both good. Suzie Wu and her accusations had taken its toll on him. The woman may have been exposed as a liar and maybe a thief — that was yet to be fully proven — but her sudden disappearance had left him with a troubled feeling that the matter had not been brought to a proper close.

But there was nothing he could do about it, so, as Frankie would be only too quick to tell him, it was better to put it out of his mind and enjoy being back here at Linston End.

Beyond the garden the river was as smooth as glass. It was a beautifully calming sight. The mist had almost gone; just the faintest trace remained. *How could Alastair give this up?* thought Danny with sadness. Was he really making the right decision? Selfishly Danny would miss the old place; it had brought them such pleasure over the years and provided a treasure trove of happy memories. But give it up his friend must if he were to embark on a new life. Maybe he was simply haunted by Orla's presence too much to be comfortable here anymore.

'Good morning, Danny, may I join you?'

He started at the request and the sight of Valentina whose approach he hadn't heard. His surprise must have shown on his face. 'If you would prefer to sit alone,' she said, 'I will leave you in peace.'

'No, no,' he responded, rubbing self-consciously at his unshaven chin, 'please join me, but I must apologise for being in my pyjamas and dressing gown.' In contrast to his dishevelled appearance, she was already immaculately dressed in vermilion pink jeans with a white silk blouse and a strand of pearls around her neck. Draped over her shoulders was a cashmere sweater the same colour as her jeans. She looked as elegant as she had yesterday.

She waved his comment aside and sat down. 'It is a very smart dressing gown you are wearing, why should you not show it off in this lovely garden?'

'Frankie made it for me as a matter of fact.

I've had it for years.'

'Really?' Adding to his discomfort, she eyed the cream and navy-blue silk fabric that had most definitely seen better days. 'What a talented woman Frankie is. And what a lucky man you are to have her as your wife.'

'You're right, I am lucky.'

'Then that makes two of us, for I also am very lucky to have met Alastair. Do you think he was lucky to meet me?'

Taken off guard, Danny squirmed. 'Goodness,' he said, 'what a question.'

'No, it is a very simple question and requires only a very simple answer, yes or no.'

Composing himself, he said, 'The answer is yes, of course Alastair is extremely lucky to have met you. What man wouldn't be?'

She gave him a wildly disarming smile. 'You're so sweet, Danny, just like Alastair described to me. He told me also that you had a difficult time as a boy, that you were not wanted.'

Her words were like a stab to his heart. But she blithely carried on.

'That is to say, you didn't find a loving family to look after you until you were a teenager.'

'I was ten,' he said quietly, wondering why she had taken the conversation in this particular direction. He felt she was being unduly intrusive and was irritated that Alastair had divulged such personal information about him. But then why wouldn't he, when he wanted Valentina to meet his closest friends and get to know them? To know people properly, you had to understand them.

'And then your life changed for the better, no?' she continued.

'Much better,' he asserted. 'My adopted parents couldn't have been nicer, they were enormously generous-hearted and gave me the kind of loving home I'd always wanted.'

'It was as if you'd been given a second chance?' she said.

'Exactly.'

'Yes,' she said, 'and that is what Alastair has been given in meeting me, a second chance to be happy.'

Ah, so that was the purpose of her interrogation. Clever.

'May I speak freely with you?' she asked, tilting her head.

More freely than she had already? He nodded warily.

'You know that Alastair wasn't happy with Orla, don't you? Not happy in his heart. Outwardly happy, but not in his heart and soul.'

Danny hesitated, unsure what to say in response to such an outlandish claim. Was this some crafty piece of divide and conquer on her part, just as Simon had warned him would happen?

'But you knew that, surely?' she said, when he didn't comment. 'That life with Orla became unbearable for Alastair?'

'I'm afraid I know no such thing,' he said stiffly, wanting to defend Orla. She was dead for God's sake; you weren't supposed to speak ill of the dead! 'Orla was everything to Alastair,' he said assuredly. 'Yes, she could have her moments of — ' He broke off, trying to find the right word or expression.

'Rage?' suggested Valentina.

'No,' he said adamantly.

'Sulkiness? Selfishness?'

'Absolutely not.' Yet even as he heard himself assert the denial, he knew it wasn't true; Orla could be extraordinarily selfish when she chose, as well as sulk on a scale that defied all reasonable justification. On one occasion Alastair had treated himself to a new car, trading in his Jaguar for a Bentley Continental, but when he'd arrived home with it and proudly parked it on the drive, Orla had decried it as disgustingly ostentatious. 'Either that car goes, or I do!' she'd told Alastair. When Alastair declined to return it to the dealer, she refused to talk to him. When a week later the car was still on the drive, she packed a suitcase and announced she was leaving. At which point Alastair gave in and drove the car back to the showroom. Envious that they hadn't had an Aunt Cora from whom they'd inherited a house and a secret — and very generous — portfolio of investments, both Danny and Simon had privately thought Alastair had done the wrong thing, that he should have called Orla's bluff.

'Orla's artistic nature often got the better of her,' Danny said tactfully to Valentina. 'She was plagued with self-doubt as creative people so often are, and that made her unpredictable at times.'

'Yes, I have known a few neurotic artists myself,' Valentina said airily, 'and they all had one thing in common, they believed the world revolved around them.'

Again Danny wanted to refute this about Orla, but he was unnervingly conscious that Valentina was right, that for years they had turned a blind eye to the worst aspects of Orla's behaviour, in the same way they had accepted Sorrel's tendency to cause an undercurrent of disquiet. But was there anything wrong in that? True friendship was all about accommodating the good and the bad in a close friend.

His tea finished, he stood up. 'I should go and get dressed. Is Alastair awake?'

She shook her head. 'I left him sleeping. He had a bad night.'

'I'm sorry to hear that.'

Valentina gave him a disconcertingly direct look. 'He's told me before that since Orla's death he sleeps very badly here, that he suffers night terrors.'

This was news to Danny. He was beginning to think that there might be a lot more he didn't know about his old friend, things that Alastair hadn't wanted to share with either him, or Simon.

31

Ordinarily Jenna would have been the first to volunteer to go with Callum in his dinghy. But in the light of 'recent events' which she still hadn't dealt with, she hesitated at his invitation that they should follow the rest of the party together, it being too much of a squash for them all to be on board *Swallowtail*. It was catching Rachel's eye — her Judge Judy eye — that made Jenna snap out of her reluctance to be on her own with Callum. *Time to bite the bullet*, she told herself as she untied the stern line, threw it to Callum to catch, and then stepped down into his boat.

This was the first time she had actually been alone with him since arriving at Linston End two days ago, having cowardly managed to engineer things so the situation never arose. Living so close there was no need for him to stay the night with them, and anyway he had to be up early to be at the boatyard every morning. Today he'd managed to carve out some time to join them for a picnic lunch on the river. Jenna knew that to him, like her, the tradition of them all being together every summer meant something. And now it meant even more, knowing that this would be their last summer here at Linston End.

As if picking up on her thoughts, while easing the boat away from its mooring point and steering them across the river to follow behind *Swallowtail*, Callum said, 'Alastair mentioned last night that people were coming to view the house this afternoon; is that still happening?'

'Yes. He had us all tidying our rooms before we left. The agent is showing the couple round while we're out.'

Callum smiled. 'You didn't feel like sabotaging things to put the viewers off from buying?'

'Such a dirty trick didn't occur to me.'

'I bet it did to my dad. I've never seen him so rattled about anything before. Danny seems to be handling it better, but I wouldn't go so far as to say either of them are particularly pleased for Alastair.'

'It's understandable,' she said, 'it's the end of an era for them, isn't it? For us too.'

'Maybe yes, maybe no.'

She looked at him, puzzled. 'What do you mean?'

He gave her a brief look before returning his attention to the river. 'Things never go quite as we think they will, do they?' he said. 'I mean, this time last year, who'd have thought Orla would be dead and we'd be meeting a woman called Valentina? And more importantly, I never thought you'd kiss me the way you did when I saw you in London. So yeah, life has a way of throwing in curve balls just when you don't expect them. Only time will tell if this really is the end of an era for us all.'

There it was, the elephant in the room finally revealed — *Ta-daar!*

'It's okay,' Callum said, as she struggled to find the right response. 'I figured it out for myself — you've since thought better of it. Big mistake, blah, blah. It's fine. Don't look so worried, these things happen.'

'Oh Callum, I'm so sorry. I feel awful, I really do.'

'Nah, don't be sorry. But I have to say, I am a bit disappointed.'

'Disappointed in my behaviour?'

'No. That you didn't want to follow it up with a second.' He grinned. 'Or a third.'

'Really?'

'Jenna, surely it can't come as a surprise to you that I might have wanted us to be more than friends?'

'But I thought — '

'What? That I'd grown out of my childish crush on you?'

'Well, yes. You've never made any attempt to kiss me again since then, have you?'

'That's because I didn't want to ruin things. I am curious though as to why you kissed me, it did come completely out of the blue. We were standing there quite normally and suddenly you practically jumped me.'

'I did not!'

He laughed. 'You did. You totally did. Would it be so wrong on my part to know why? Or was this you getting your own back on me for kissing you all those years ago when I was an uncouth spotty teenager? As opposed to the fine specimen of manhood I am now.'

She laughed too, glad to be able to relax in his company once more; it was such a relief. She had dreaded seeing him again; in fact she had been so wired yesterday she'd actually tripped over at the sight of him.

'And for the record,' he said, 'it was a great kiss. You've obviously had a lot more practical experience than me.'

She gave his foot a playful shove. 'Behave yourself.'

'So come on, tell your old friend Callum why you kissed him. Because frankly, I'm not going to let you off this boat until you do. Why else do you think I invited you to join me?'

'Hah!' she said. 'I might have known. But if I tell you, will you promise you won't be angry with me?'

'Have I ever been angry with you?'

'Yes,' she said, 'that time I beat you in a sailing race up to Wroxham and back.'

'That was hurt pride, that's different.'

'And then another time when Rachel and I borrowed your boat and we didn't tie it properly to the mooring posts, and when we came back from the pub it had drifted off down the river.'

'Yep, got me there,' he said with a smile, nudging the tiller to swing out of the way of an oncoming picnic boat. 'I was pretty furious,' he said, waving back at the young children in their life jackets on board the other craft. They were all waving madly at them. Jenna waved as well. 'But mostly with Rachel,' Callum added. 'It was easier to be cross with her than you.'

Jenna hoped that might still be the case after she'd made her confession. She told him about Blake and how she'd seized the opportunity to make him believe she had a boyfriend. Once again she apologised. 'It was a completely spur of

226

the moment thing, maybe the craziest thing I've ever done. I just wanted Blake to accept I wasn't interested in him.'

'Did it work?' asked Callum, keeping his gaze straight ahead.

'Yes and no.' She explained that Blake hadn't been taken in by her performance, because he had already asked a work colleague if she had a boyfriend.

Callum swung his head round to look at her now, but with his eyes hidden behind sunglasses she couldn't see his expression. 'He sounds a persistent admirer, and if needs be, I'm happy to step in and play the part of boyfriend if you want. Especially,' he added with a smile, 'if it means I get to kiss you again.'

Jenna smiled too, relieved again that he seemed to be taking it so well. 'Kind of you to offer, but Blake's accepted I'm not interested in him other than as a co-worker and friend.'

'Ah, the dreaded friend-zone, I almost feel sorry for the guy. Any particular reason why you resisted his charms?'

'Don't you remember I vowed I'd never have another office relationship, not after what happened last time?'

'But where else are you likely to meet your future husband?'

'Who says I want one?'

'Partner then?'

'Maybe one day. What about you, isn't there a likely candidate here for you, or have you worked your way through the entire Broadland female population?'

'Hey, thanks for casting me as the village tart!'

'If the cap fits.'

'Says the girl who snogged me to get one over on some poor bloke who made the mistake of fancying her.'

'Ouch!'

'You started it.'

'You're never going to let me forget this, are you?'

He grinned. 'Nope! Not a chance. Here, why don't you take over for a while?' Making sure they were set on a straight course, he moved out of the way leaving her to steer the boat, which she was more than happy to do. From a young age all three children had been taught how to sail, as well as manage a motor boat. It was something Jenna loved to do, the slow meandering pace was the perfect antidote to life in London.

She could quite understand why Alastair and Orla had spent all the time they could here before making the move permanently from London a couple of years ago, and following Alastair's retirement. Of course Orla had always spent significantly more time than Alastair at Linston End, the Broads and their abundant wildlife the inspiration for most of what she sculpted or painted.

Ahead of them, to the right was the narrow opening to Linston Broad. It was where Alastair had taught Jenna, Rachel and Callum to sail, and where they picnicked and looked for dragonflies. If they were lucky, they would come across an elusive swallowtail butterfly amongst the milk parsley, both of which were a rarity. In the spring, the woodland at the far end was home to bluebells and patches of yellow celandine, the trees full of birdsong — chiffchaffs and great tits. But now the waters, a little under thirty acres, no longer welcomed them as they once did: it was here that Orla had drowned. Mum and Dad said that Alastair had never ventured again into the broad since Orla's body was found. Jenna could understand why. Was that another reason why he felt he had to leave the area, having this awful reminder so close to home?

As children, Orla had taken pleasure in telling them that Linston Broad was haunted by a young girl who'd drowned herself after her parents had died in a boating accident at the end of the nineteenth century. The story went that the orphaned girl never recovered from the shock of losing her parents and spent her nights with a lantern searching for them amongst the reed beds. Then one wintry night, when she could bear her loss no longer, she waded into the freezing water and drowned herself to join her beloved mother and father. It was said that at night her pitiful cries could be heard calling for them — '*Mama . . . Papa . . . where are you?*'

In the telling of the typically gothic Victorian tale, Orla would add her own melodramatic spin to the child's plaintive cries, and perhaps embellishing the story yet more, she would say that on some nights, when the smooth surface of the water was shrouded in a veil of mist, not only could the girl's ghostly weeping be heard, but she could be glimpsed rising out of the water, a whitish spectre draped in weeds from the bottom of the broad. Orla claimed to have seen the ghost with her own eyes.

It was heady stuff for Jenna as a child and, as is often the way for children, the scary thrill of the story only existed at night when her imagination was at its most active. During the day, when the sun was shining and they were sailing on the sparkling waters of the broad, the drowned girl and her parents were forgotten.

Now, with Orla having drowned in those same waters, how could they think of that heartbreakingly sad story, true or not, and not shudder?

'Do you ever sail in there like we used to?' she asked Callum, noticing that he was staring in the same direction as she was as they passed the broad.

'Now and then,' he answered. 'It might sound odd, but I feel I should.'

'As a mark of respect?'

He nodded. 'Something like that.'

'I'm not sure I could.'

'Are you accusing me of being ghoulish?'

'No, it just gives me shivers thinking of Orla dying that way. I was thinking of the story she used to tell us about the little girl drowning herself. Do you remember it?'

'Of course, it's part of local folklore.'

'And now Orla's death will join that folklore, and heaven only knows what will be added to her story as time goes by.'

'I'm afraid it's already being elaborated on, and with any number of macabre variations.'

'Does Alastair know?'

'I'm sure he's intelligent enough to know that

people are inventing their own truth of what happened.'

'Valentina being here so soon hardly helps matters, does it?'

Callum shrugged. 'He's moved on and I guess having her here is his way of saying he doesn't give a damn what anyone thinks.'

'He certainly seems in a hurry to put the past behind him,' she said, watching a pair of swans glide by, their beaks held high with haughty indifference.

'I agree,' said Callum. 'Some might say he's running away.'

'Is that what you think he's doing?'

'Without a doubt. Wouldn't you want to run away?'

Not answering his question, she said, 'What are people saying about Orla's death?'

'Exactly what you'd expect. That her death was no accident.'

32

Their attention caught by the sight of a traditional sailing cruiser passing by, its sail lying limply in the soft breeze, there was a natural lull in the conversation.

It was broken by Valentina. 'Alastair, you did not tell me it would be this charming.'

He smiled. 'I wanted it to be a surprise for you.'

She sighed and leaned in to kiss him. Not just a token of a kiss, but a lingering one on the mouth in the manner of a bloody great sink plunger. Simon tried not to look, but it was like gawping at a road accident, impossible to tear one's eyes away.

'It is a lovely surprise, darling,' she said, when she'd released Alastair and let him up for air, 'a picnic on the bank of the river, what could be more delightful? Thank you for sharing this place with me, I'm having a wonderful time.' She spoke with such breathy intimacy it was as if she had forgotten the rest of them were there.

Simon wished he could say the same, that he was having a wonderful time. Surely he couldn't be the only one whose stomach was churning at the embarrassing spectacle of two grown adults behaving with all the saccharine-subtlety of a cheap greeting card? He had never gone in for overt displays of affection with Sorrel, and that wasn't to say he didn't feel emotion, he most certainly did, but he reserved it for the right time and place.

They had moored the boats and had spread out two large picnic rugs on the grass in the dappled shade of an alder tree over an hour ago, and in the time since, they had eaten and drunk well. Now with his back resting against the trunk of the tree, his legs sticking out in front of him, Simon wanted to feel the mellow happiness of the day, but it just wouldn't come.

Every word and gesture from Valentina grated on him, and, if he didn't know better, he'd say that she was playing on her foreignness just a bit too much, pretending not to understand things when he suspected she understood all too well every colloquialism, every nuance. Hadn't Alastair said she spoke excellent English? Simon was convinced she was playing some kind of disingenuous game. He couldn't say what exactly, but he felt as if they were being tricked, fooled into underestimating her. Was that what a clever strategist did when going into battle?

'I know what we should do next,' she suddenly said, looking around the group, 'we should go for a swim. We should dip our skinnies!'

'I think you might mean skinny-dipping,' said Alastair with an indulgent smile.

'Although dipping our skinnies does have a certain appeal,' said Danny with a laugh.

'But nobody does that round here in broad daylight,' said Sorrel, with an undisguised moue of distaste.

'Not unless they're completely without inhibition,' said Frankie.

A slumbering memory from years ago roused itself, catching Simon unawares; it was a memory of Orla skinny-dipping in the moonlight, her body moving through the water as sleekly as an otter.

'Sorry, Valentina, but I think you'll find we're all a bit too inhibited to do something like that,' said Jenna.

'Yes,' agreed Callum. 'We're much too British, I'm afraid.'

'Then maybe you should lose your inhibitions by drinking some more wine,' said Valentina with an extravagant laugh. 'Then you will swim all the better.'

An uneasy hush fell on the group.

'I wouldn't advise it,' Simon said, when nobody responded, 'drunken swimming is never a good idea.'

His words only served to lengthen the awkward silence, until Valentina, glancing around the group, her face drawn in a frown, said, 'Have I said something wrong? Alastair?'

'It's nothing,' he said, reaching for her hand.

'But it is, I can feel it. All of a sudden everyone is so quiet. I have said something wrong, what is it? Please tell me.'

Alastair hesitated and in that moment the penny must have dropped with a heavy clang, and Valentina gasped. 'Oh, my darling, I am so very sorry, forgive me, please! Oh, how could I be so clumsy with my words when your wife died the way she did?'

He shook his head. 'It's fine, don't give it another thought.'

'No, it is not fine. I am cross with myself. How stupid you must think I am. Your friends must think the same too.'

'Of course they don't.'

Under the brim of his baseball cap, Simon rolled his eyes. He'd lay odds on her knowing exactly what she'd said. He didn't trust her. He didn't trust her one little bit. *I'm watching you*, he thought. Trouble was, he reckoned Valentina was watching him in return.

'We should play a game,' said Danny.

A sleepy groan came from Rachel where she was lying stretched out in the sun. 'Do we have to?'

'Don't be so antisocial,' her brother told her.

'What kind of a game?' asked Jenna.

'If it involves moving,' Rachel said, 'count me out.'

'How about French cricket?' suggested Danny. 'I put the old bat and ball in the locker on the boat.'

Another groan from Rachel. 'I have a better idea, how about we carry on just as we are?'

'Sounds good to me,' said Simon.

'Anything else to eat for anybody?' asked Frankie. 'If not, I'll make a start on tidying things away.'

'I'll have another pork pie if there's one going spare,' replied Callum.

'Me too,' joined in Danny. 'A pickled onion wouldn't go amiss either.'

'Help yourselves, there's plenty here.'

'Somebody pass me a sausage roll, please,' said Simon.

With everyone busying themselves around the plates and plastic boxes of food again, and all thoughts of playing a game now forgotten, for a split second it was as though nothing had changed. Here they all were just as they'd always been, enjoying a picnic on the river; but one look at Valentina, with her arm placed possessively around Alastair, and that thought turned to dust.

How had she done it? How had she wormed her way into Alastair's heart in so short a time? Had she merely seized her chance when he was vulnerable and still recovering from Orla's death? Could any woman have done that given the circumstances?

More than anything Simon wanted his old friend to be happy, but Alastair didn't look happy in his opinion; he looked permanently on edge. Frankie had said much the same earlier to Simon when they'd been alone before setting off in the boat, but always one to be fair, she had quickly justified her comment by saying that probably anyone would look anxious in Alastair's shoes right now. 'He's desperate for us to like Valentina; it's important to him.'

Watching a blue and white boat decorated with bunting puttering by, a man and a woman at the helm and a perky Jack Russell sitting on the prow, Simon finished eating the sausage roll Callum had given him. He rubbed the flakes of pastry from his hand and closed his eyes. He tried to think of something about Valentina that he liked. Just one thing would do.

His eyes didn't stay closed for long; a noisy boat was approaching with a party of *hullabaloos*

236

onboard. Simon had heard the word *hullabaloo* used a lot when he and Danny had been invited to stay at Linston End as boys. Alastair's Aunt Cora had regularly employed the expression, having adpoted it from Arthur Ransome's description of the reckless holidaymakers on the river who went too fast in their lavish motor cruisers, often with music blaring and voices raised, destroying the peace and quiet. Right now river etiquette was being blasted to hell and back by this particular boat of boisterous day-trippers — girls in bikinis were shrieking drunkenly and lads, stripped to the waist, were clowning around, pushing and shoving each other and running the risk of falling overboard. The parent in Simon wanted to chastise them for their raucous behaviour and warn them to be more careful. But they weren't his children, so he closed his eyes again and forgot them.

After dozing off for a while, he woke to hear that the conversation had turned to fate versus plain old happenstance. Valentina seemed to favour fate.

'I knew from the moment Alastair and I went diving that day in Sri Lanka that we were destined to be more than friends,' she said. 'I just knew it. Especially when he got into difficulty.'

I bet you did, thought Simon.

'But what if Alastair hadn't been stung by the jellyfish?' asked Sorrel. 'That was, after all, quite random, wasn't it? Or are you saying that was fate?'

Valentina raised an eyebrow. 'Who is to say I did not help fate *un petit peu* by making that jellyfish sting Alastair so that I could rescue him?'

Amidst the laughter, and thinking that fate had clearly had nothing to do with Alastair being ensnared by Valentina, he'd as good as had a target on his back, Simon said, 'I've always believed we should expect the unexpected, but never trust it implicitly. Human nature being what it is, we turn things into what we want them to be.'

'Valentina, you'll have to excuse Simon,' said Alastair, 'he's a boringly cynical lawyer.'

'Dad might be cynical,' said Rachel, 'but I agree with him.'

Callum scoffed. 'That must be a first.'

'No, he's right. I did that with Paul, I badly wanted him to be The One, but I can see now it was all in my head. He was on the rebound, needed an ego-boosting girlfriend after his ex dumped him, and along I came, a handy diversion to get him over Perfect Paula.' She shook her head. 'And look how well that turned out.'

'Don't be too hard on yourself, love,' Simon said kindly. 'You win some; you lose some. You did nothing wrong.'

'Other than ignore what my closest friend was saying.' She turned to Jenna. 'You kept trying to make me see sense, didn't you, but I wouldn't listen?'

'That's what friends are for, to be ignored,' said Jenna with a smile.

'It certainly is,' said Simon, catching Alastair's eye, 'but let's not forget that friendship is like

238

marriage; it's for better and for worse, till death do us part.'

Rachel looked impressed. 'Dad, that might well be the smartest thing you've ever said.'

'Oh, I'm full of smart stuff like that, it's just nobody ever listens to me.'

★ ★ ★

They were packing up to go home when Alastair approached Simon on his own. 'Are you going to be like this the whole time Valentina is with us?' he demanded, his voice low and tight.

'Like what?'

'Needling the whole time, trying to make Valentina feel uncomfortable.'

'I don't know what you mean. We've all been enjoying ourselves here this afternoon.'

'Come off it, Simon, you know full well what I'm talking about. Going on about friendship being like marriage, till death do us part, hardly subtle, was it?'

Simon felt his cheeks colour with indignation. 'It's true though, isn't it?' he retaliated. 'The three of us have been through thick and thin together. We've always been there for each other.'

'And why the hell do you think that is going to change?'

Simon sighed deeply. 'It's already changing, old buddy, you just can't see it.'

'All I can see is a jealous friend trying to offend the woman I love.' He pushed a hand through his hair and rubbed at his chin hard. 'You all want to stay the same, but I don't. I

239

want to grab hold of life and wring from it every last drop of hope, love and opportunity. So just give it a rest, will you? Leave Valentina alone. If not for my sake, then for your own.'

'My sake?'

'Yes, you're embarrassing yourself.'

Simon took a step back. 'I don't believe this, you're talking to me as if I were a child.'

'That's because you're behaving like one!'

Not since they'd been at school and fallen out over something petty and instantly forgettable had they ever had an angry exchange like this. The crushing humiliation of Alastair's rebuke felt like a punch to his gut and made Simon realise he was on a fool's errand — there was no saving Alastair from this woman. She had him hook, line and sinker. She had not come here to make friends with any of them; she was absolutely here to separate them from Alastair. And look how easily that was happening.

Not even twenty-four hours at Linston End and already she had driven a wedge between him and Alastair.

33

The next morning Rachel lay in bed listening to the noise of people downstairs getting on with the day. At Linston End she always slept in. It was one of the many pleasures of being here, she could be a carefree teenager again; free of all responsibility, her only commitment that of enjoying the long lazy days of summer.

She breathed in deeply, then exhaled a long sigh of contentment, at the same time stretching out her arms and legs like a starfish. She could honestly say she hadn't felt this good in ages and she put it down to being free of the tyranny of a relationship that had been such hard work. All that effort into trying to make it better than it really was, what an idiot she had been!

Until now she hadn't viewed it that way, but in the days since Paul had dumped her, she had gone through a whole raft of emotions, starting with the feeling that she had been hit by a truck, and then by a steamroller for good measure. Insanely bruised, battered and flattened, that's how she'd felt in the first twenty-four hours, unable to grasp that one minute Paul could tell her he loved her, and the next, he didn't. That night in her flat, surrounded by all those blasted candles she'd spent a fortune on, he'd tried to explain that he'd only said he loved her because he knew it was what she wanted to hear. After he'd gone, she'd thrown herself on the bed and sobbed; she had hated him for telling her that, because it was true. Then she had hated herself for being so pathetic, for being so desperate to be loved.

She realised now it was her ego that had taken a beating, not her heart. She'd actually had worse break-ups and the fact that she had bounced back so quickly, and could see things so clearly, proved that she had been kidding herself that she loved Paul. She'd been suffering from Desperate-Thirty-Something syndrome, fixated on finding the so-called love of her life before it was too late.

Well, to hell with too frickin' late!

And to hell with finding love!

What she needed was fun, and epic amounts of it!

And she fully intended to have exactly that while here on holiday. It was a shame poor Dad couldn't do the same; he seemed determined to have a rotten time, devoting all his energy to disliking Valentina. Mum didn't give the impression of falling over herself to like Alastair's new woman either, but then it couldn't be easy trying to shift their loyalty from Orla to her replacement.

Rachel had experienced the very same thing when she'd met Paul's family, so she wasn't without sympathy for Valentina. Following in the footsteps of an ex was no easy task. Some ex-partners had the power to make their presence felt every step of the way, even though they were invisible, but there they hovered in the wings waiting for their moment to take the stage.

Through the open bedroom window she heard music playing outside; distant music. For a few seconds she heard it more distinctly, then it stopped. Then it started again. Curious, she slipped out of bed and went to the window, expecting the source of the music to be in the garden. But the garden was empty.

Her gaze moved down the length of the lawn towards the river until it lingered on the mill opposite. There on the wooden balcony somebody — a man — was playing a violin. She listened properly now to the exquisite sound drifting across the water; it was hauntingly sad and went straight to her heart. Her elbows resting on the windowsill, she wished she had a pair of binoculars to get a better look at the violin player. Then once more the music stopped. This time it didn't resume and, disappointed, she watched the man lower the violin from his chin, turn around and go back inside the mill.

Alastair had said he'd invited his neighbour to join them for dinner that evening, along with her son who was visiting. Presumably this was the son. Interesting.

★   ★   ★

By the time she made it downstairs, everybody had decided what they would be doing with their day. Alastair was taking Valentina out on the river, just the two of them — Rachel supposed they needed to escape from the rest of them for a bit — and would return later after they'd fetched Valentina's stepchildren from the station.

Danny and Frankie were going to Ranworth Broad to the Wildlife Trust, and Mum and Dad were going to Hoveton Hall Gardens, leaving Rachel and Jenna to have the place to themselves as well as make themselves useful.

'How come we got landed with the short straw?' muttered Rachel, after everyone had gone.

'I thought you'd leap at the chance to have a day of doing practically nothing,' said Jenna.

'It's the *practically* of that sentence that worries me. How much slaving have we got to do?'

'Hardly any. Sylvia is coming in to do the bulk of the cooking, but I've volunteered us to make a chocolate mousse and a lemon syllabub.'

'And then we get to lie on a pair of sun loungers?' she asked hopefully.

'Yes, you can do whatever you want, once we've made the desserts.'

'What are we waiting for, let's get cooking!'

★　★　★

They hit their first snag when they discovered there weren't enough eggs in the fridge. 'That's that, then,' said Rachel with more than a hint of relief. 'I'll go and prepare my sun lounger.'

'You wouldn't prefer to walk down to the shops with me to buy some eggs?' suggested Jenna.

Rachel groaned. 'It's much too hot for that. Why don't we ring one of the others to tell them to fetch us some eggs, and we'll knock up the desserts later?'

'I have a better idea; let's take a boat and go the scenic way.'

But still Rachel wasn't keen and Jenna could see no amount of persuasion on her part would make Rachel change her mind. As she went outside and round to the dyke where Alastair kept his run-about dinghy, she conceded that her own stubbornness to get the desserts made was as bad as Rachel's commitment to laze the day away on a sun lounger with a book. They were two of a kind in that respect, both as strong-willed as the other.

Walking along the wooden jetty, Jenna untied the dinghy, hopped in and after making sure the shift lever was in the neutral position, she pulled out the choke on the outboard motor, and gave the starter rope a tug. It took a couple of goes, but then she was off, guiding the boat out of the boathouse. She joined the river and after pausing to admire the yellow water lilies, she picked up speed, but making sure to keep within the limit.

It was such a beautiful day she was now glad they'd run out of eggs and she had this chance to enjoy the river. She loved the freedom of being on the water like this and could quite understand Callum's passion for it. When she passed Snazzell's Boatyard she slowed her speed, but there was no sign of him. She was relieved he'd forced her into being honest with him yesterday, happy now to have their friendship back on an even keel. Seeing how fraught things were becoming between Simon and Alastair, she never wanted that to happen with her and Callum, Rachel too.

With luck on her side, she arrived in Horning just as a boat was vacating a mooring space in front of the Staithe and Willow Tea Rooms. A man who'd just finished tying up a large motor cruiser next to her offered his assistance, and Jenna graciously accepted, even though she could manage on her own. No point in looking a gift horse in the mouth, was her view.

The boat secure, she set off the short distance to the general store. The eggs bought, as well as a mint Magnum to eat on the way back, she returned to the busy staithe. She placed the eggs carefully in the small locker in the prow, put the ice cream to one side and was about to untie the boat, when she heard a voice. 'Well, of all the gin joints in all the towns in all the world, she walks into mine.'

Jenna turned around and got the surprise of her life.

'*Blake!*'

'The one and only.'

'Are you stalking me?'

'I could ask the same of you.'

She smiled. 'Seriously though, what on earth are you doing here?'

'Same as you I imagine, enjoying a well-earned holiday.'

'You never said you were going on holiday?'

'Nor did you if my memory serves correctly. Fancy a drink?' He indicated the Swan Inn behind him.

'I can't, I only nipped out to buy some eggs. Where are you staying?'

He inclined his head in the direction she'd just come. 'At Linston Mill with my mother. Do you know it?'

246

'Are you sure you're not stalking me?' she said.

He flung a hand to his chest. 'On all I hold sacred, I swear our paths have crossed quite coincidentally.' He grinned. 'Or maybe it's destiny.'

She rolled her eyes, doubting he held anything sacred. 'How are you getting back to Linston Mill?'

'The same way I came.'

'Which would be?'

He pointed further along the staithe to a small day boat. Beyond it Jenna could see the tourist double-deck paddle boat was just setting off, and not wanting to get stuck behind it, she hurriedly began untying the mooring ropes and hopped back into the dinghy. 'It was fun bumping into you,' she said, deciding to spring a surprise of her own on him. 'I'll see you around.'

'Don't rush off,' he said, 'not without giving me your mobile number so we can arrange to meet up.'

She started up the engine.

'No need, I guarantee our paths will cross again.' And sooner than you'd think, she thought with a smile as she powered up the engine and nosed the boat out into the river. She gave him a cheery wave as he stood watching her go, a bemused expression on his face. Reaching for the ice cream she'd bought, and keeping one eye on the river and the busy traffic of boats, she unwrapped it.

Of all the gin joints indeed, she thought with a laugh as she bit into the Magnum, at the same time remembering Rachel telling her about seeing somebody on the balcony of the mill playing a violin. Had that been Blake, or was there somebody else staying at the mill as well? Funny that she hadn't heard the music, maybe it had been when she was in the shower. One thing was for sure; Blake Darnell was a man of many surprises.

Well, he was in for one himself this evening.

But then she thought of Callum who would be joining them for dinner and suddenly she felt apprehensive. But why? There was nothing to be concerned about, she had resolved matters with both Callum and Blake, everyone knew where they stood; there was no ambiguity to the situation.

Yeah right, keep telling yourself that, jeered a voice inside her head.

34

'I know we've discussed this before in a hazy pie-in-the-sky sort of way, but what do you think now about leaving Suffolk to live here?'

'*Now*, meaning, as in *now you're retired?*' replied Frankie.

Danny nodded. 'Maybe also in the context of why not do it before it's too late?'

She tutted. 'Please don't talk like that.'

They were sitting on a wooden bench outside the café overlooking the staithe at Malthouse Broad. They'd driven here earlier that morning, left the car in the car park opposite the Maltsters pub — or the Malteser as Jenna had called it as a child — and taken a boat trip around Ranworth Broad nature reserve, something Danny loved to do every summer. His knowledge of Broadland wildlife was almost as extensive as the guide's who'd taken them out in the boat, a chap called Steve whom they had got to know well from their many previous visits. They'd spotted a great crested grebe, complete with its beautiful summer plumage, and a kingfisher darting across the water, but disappointingly there had been no sighting of any swallowtail butterflies. But when they'd walked back from the wildlife centre, along the boardwalk through the reedbeds and woodland, a loud and distinctive burst of song from a Cetti's warbler had made up for the disappointment.

Now, as they sat like so many others enjoying the view and the afternoon sun, Frankie considered Danny's question. It had not come entirely as a surprise, but the way he'd worded it bothered her. *Before it's too late . . .*

'I know what you're thinking,' he said. 'You're worried that if we moved here and I died, you'd be left on your own without a support network.'

She shook her head. 'That wasn't what I was thinking, but it's definitely a consideration.'

'The way I see it,' he said, 'we can live a half life worrying about tomorrow, or one to the full taking each day as it comes and as a blessing, if that doesn't sound too sentimental.'

Frankie slipped her hand into his. 'Is that how you see our lives back in Chelstead; a half life?'

'I suppose I do. You know I've always had a dream of living here one day, and how often did we say the time wasn't right to make the move? We had Jenna in school and the partnership to consider, all the usual things that keep people anchored, but now we're free of those things, we can do whatever we want and wherever we want. Doesn't that appeal to you?'

She rested her head on his shoulder. 'You know it does. But is this really the right time?'

'I don't think there'll be a better time,' he said, squeezing her hand in his. 'Would you mind very much giving up your work at the Sewing Bee?'

She raised her head and looked up at him. 'I could do the same thing here, or something similar. Maybe something better.'

'Do you mean that?'

'Danny, since when do I ever say things I don't

mean? I think it would be exciting to make a fresh start somewhere new.'

'Norfolk is hardly new to us.'

'Don't split hairs. And just so that we're clear. I know this business with Alastair and Valentina has thoroughly unsettled you and Simon, but please don't think you can trade me in for some young fancy piece to complete your fresh start.'

Danny laughed. 'God no, a younger woman would finish my poor old ticker off good and proper!'

Frankie smiled and watched a small boy toddle by in front of them. He was clutching a paper bag of bird food sold in the Information Centre and gift shop, just a few yards from where they were sitting. Doubtless catching the whiff of grain, or hearing the rustle of the paper bag, a dozen or so ducks homed in on the boy, trailing behind him as if he were the Pied Piper of Hamelin.

'Is that how you see Valentina?' asked Danny. 'As some young fancy piece?'

This was the first time they had ventured down this road. Until now, Frankie had kept her counsel, knowing that to breathe so much as a hint of criticism about Alastair would upset Danny. She had always respected their close friendship, had accepted that the bond between the three friends — Alastair, Danny and Simon — was hallowed ground. She admired them for it, having no friendship of her own that was as tightly bound, other than, of course, the relationship she had with Danny and Jenna.

'I was generalising,' she said, 'admittedly in a clumsy and clichéd fashion, but I suppose I do view Valentina in a less than favourable light.' She thought of what she had seen out of the bedroom window yesterday morning, of Valentina talking in what had struck Frankie as a very intimate manner with Danny, a manner that had seemed almost predatory in the familiarity of her body language. It had shocked Frankie. She was not the jealous type, but in that instant, she had felt more than a hint of the green-eyed monster. 'I want to like her,' she continued, 'but — '

'But you can't?'

'No. Not yet at any rate. What about you, what's your opinion of her?'

'Like you, I'm trying to keep an open mind.'

'And?'

'I can't see it lasting between her and Alastair.'

'Is that because you don't want to see it last?'

He sighed deeply. 'I don't want to see him hurt, and nothing about Valentina so far reassures me that won't happen. There's something about her that niggles at me. It's as if she's too knowing. I didn't mention this before, but she knew all about my childhood, of being fostered so many times, and it annoyed me that she knew.'

'I don't blame you. Presumably Alastair told her?'

'Yes. What bothered me was that she used that information, that very personal information that Alastair had shared with her, to . . . well, it sounds odd, but she used it to plead her own case as to why I should accept her in Alastair's life. We all deserve a second chance, was how she put it.'

'Clever.'

'Exactly what I thought.'

Moments passed.

'I suppose we just have to accept that Alastair knows what he's doing,' Frankie said. 'But if it does go pear-shaped with Valentina, we'll be there for him. Just as we were when Orla died.'

Danny smiled. 'You're right, as always.'

'I've made it a lifetime's work always to be right, darling.'

'Only a fool would dispute that.'

She smiled back at him, thinking that in that moment she was the luckiest of women to have been married so happily and for so long. 'It was a good idea of yours to suggest we all had a day doing our own thing,' she said.

'I thought Alastair and Simon needed to have some time out from each other; things were in danger of getting a bit heated between them.'

'Oh, so it wasn't about you wanting to spend time alone with me, then?'

Danny chuckled. 'Bang to rights!'

'You better believe it. Your punishment is to stand me an ice cream. Go on, off you go and buy me a Cornetto.'

He rose to his feet and bowed. 'Your wish is my command.'

'And when you're back, we'll discuss what we're going to do next about your plan for us to move here.'

He remained where he was and stared at her. 'Are you serious about considering the idea?'

'Why wouldn't I be?'

'Because it's a big step to take.'

'I prefer to think of it as an adventure.'

Danny smiled. 'That's what Alastair keeps saying about his own plans.'

'If it's good enough for him, why not for us too?'

Watching Danny walk away from her, Frankie acknowledged that her husband needed to have something new in his life, something to give him a purpose. Since suffering a heart attack and retiring, he'd lost direction and a sense of who he was; he'd lost some of his confidence too. Moving house to somewhere they both loved might give him a much-needed boost. Just so long as the stress of moving didn't make him ill. She would have to ensure that she took control of that.

She turned back to the staithe to see a Herbert Woods motor cruiser making a hash of reversing into a mooring space — mooring was stern-on here — and a flicker of anticipation stirred within her. Perhaps Danny wasn't the only one who needed a new challenge in his life; shaking things up for herself might prove to be fun also.

Over in the dyke, the traditional reedlighter — the *Helen of Ranworth*, the boat Frankie and Danny had gone out in earlier — was now setting off with another group of wildlife enthusiasts. On the staithe, the motor cruiser was still trying to negotiate the mooring spot and onlookers were doing their bit and offering advice to the man behind the wheel, none of which he seemed to be heeding.

Frankie smiled, thinking how easy it was to ignore even the most level-headed advice, to assume one always knew bettter. Certainly there

254

was no telling Alastair to be careful regarding Valentina, and why should he be careful? Why not take a risk on happiness? Just as why shouldn't she and Danny have an adventure of their own?

And what would Simon think of that, she wondered? Would it make him feel even more left behind? Because that was what Alastair's new zest for life was causing them all to feel, whether they admitted it or not.

★　★　★

'You know,' said Simon, 'I wouldn't be surprised if Alastair is actually going through some sort of breakdown. All this nonsense about being in love is nothing more than a diversion to stop him going through the pain of grieving properly for Orla.'

In the passenger seat of their Mercedes, as Simon drove them back to Linston End, Sorrel was tempted to suggest that the only person going through a breakdown was Simon. She had spent most of the day trying to distract him from what was rapidly becoming an obsession — the subject of Alastair and Valentina. In the way that Brexit was blamed for everything wrong with the country, even the weather, Valentina was being held responsible by Simon for turning his oldest friend against him.

'I'll tell you what I think,' Simon said, continuing with his monologue and drumming his fingers on the steering wheel, 'Alastair's so firmly under her control he's lost sight of what should matter most to him.'

'Which would be what exactly?' asked Sorrel. As if she didn't know.

'His friends, that's what! His friends who have been with him every step of the way, through school, college, marriage, and even death.'

Give me death any day over this purgatory, thought Sorrel, staring grimly out of the side window.

Oblivious to her mood, Simon went on. 'The three of us have been together through all the highs and lows and now, now that he's lost his head over the first woman to make a move on him in his widowed state, all that loyalty and history counts for nothing and is tossed aside.'

It was useless to say that Simon was blinded by personal bias, and that he was helping Alastair make light work of tossing him aside by his flat refusal to accept the situation. 'I've told you before,' she said calmly, 'you're exaggerating. Alastair won't turn his back on you and Danny. That's not in his nature.' It was a lie, of course, she knew from bitter experience that Alastair was more than capable of turning his back on a person.

'You weren't there, Sorrel,' said Simon, 'you didn't hear the way he spoke to me, or see the expression on his face. It was as if he was a stranger. No not a stranger, a robot being controlled by that . . . by that bloody woman!'

Sorrel closed her eyes. *Dear God, let it be over. Make him shut up.*

But Simon didn't and to her surprise, she was suddenly filled with a deep longing for a time many years ago when she and Simon had been very different people. When they had been happy. With perfect recall, she remembered the day she had told Simon that she was pregnant with their first child — Callum. He had been over the moon, had picked her up and swung her round. He lavished care and attention on her throughout the pregnancy, buying her flowers every week and pandering to her every whim, particularly her craving for cheese and onion crisps in the middle of the night. He once drove to the nearest all-night petrol station to buy her a packet. Nothing had been too much trouble for him. And when Callum was born, he was loving and patient and did more than his share of nappy changes and night-time feeds. He was the same when she was expecting Rachel.

Where had that man gone? For that matter, where had the woman she had once been disappeared to?

They were almost back at Linston, when Sorrel reached out to Simon and rested her hand on his forearm. 'Darling, you will behave this evening, won't you?'

He gave her a quick glance. 'What's that supposed to mean?'

'Try not to drink as much as you did last night. Especially as Valentina's children will be joining us.'

'*Stepchildren*,' he corrected her. 'Don't you remember how she put you right on that score?'

Sorrel remembered all too well the sting she had felt. But then she never forgot anyone who ever slighted her.

35

Back from the station, and following a relaxing day of being alone on the river with Valentina and sharing his love of the Broads with her, Alastair left her to show Nikolai and Irina upstairs to their rooms.

It was strange hearing Valentina conversing with her stepchildren in their native tongue. The challenge of learning Russian, as well as brushing up on his rusty schoolboy French, was another of the many new things Alastair planned to do. He saw his future as being as diametrically opposite to his past as was possible.

But for now he had a more pressing and potentially more difficult challenge on his hands, that of bringing about a truce with Simon. To make that happen, he was determined to do his utmost to keep things fun and light-hearted this evening. With Nikolai and Irina here, along with Laura and her son from the Mill, he hoped for a livelier and more diverse atmosphere, and less opportunity for Simon, or anyone else for that matter, to hark back with nostalgic longing to days gone by, and in the process exclude Valentina.

He'd anticipated a few hurdles to cross when introducing Valentina to his friends, but he hadn't expected the level of hostility Simon was displaying. He also hadn't expected to feel that, to a degree, they had all been living in the past, wanting to relive it at the slightest chance. Even the children had a tendency to dwell on the past. At their age shouldn't they be looking forwards to the future, not looking back? Or was he judging his friends unfairly; was there nothing wrong with a fondness for nostalgia? Surely that was one of the pleasures of their gathering here at Linston End?

Alone in the kitchen while everybody else was upstairs changing, Alastair savoured the appetising smell of lasagne cooking on a low heat in the oven, along with some kind of Moroccan vegetable bake, which Sylvia had suggested she make in case any of the guests were vegetarian. A large covered bowl of salad was on the worktop, along with some garlic bread and a selection of canapes, which he'd been instructed to put in the oven once the guests were all present. Sylvia's written instructions were Sellotaped to the fridge. It wasn't that she went out of her way to treat him as a child, or a hopeless man who didn't know his way round his own kitchen, it was just her way of being thorough. She had treated Orla in exactly the same manner and it had infuriated her, driving her to disregard any directive with deliberate wilfulness. Alastair suspected that Valentina might react similarly.

Was it overly simplistic to say that in general, women didn't like being told what to do by another woman? Or was it only a certain type of woman? Orla and Sorrel could never take an instruction from each other; they'd always had to assert themselves to get one over the other. And Sorrel had done a fair bit of asserting herself since arriving, taking charge in the kitchen and bossing everybody about, as if deliberately stepping into Orla's shoes — something which would have enraged his wife. He had to admit that it grated on him too. Especially when he'd noticed she had rearranged the cutlery drawer.

In the last few days, Alastair had quietly observed Sorrel's not so subtle manoeuvring and, concerned that she might overplay her hand with Valentina, he had enlisted Sylvia's help for this evening's dinner, thereby reducing the need for Sorrel to take charge.

Until now he'd never really considered the importance of managing one's friends, but now he could see how seamlessly Orla had somehow controlled the dynamics, ensuring that nobody could exert more power over the group than she did. She would never have allowed Simon to get out of control the way he had. But then if she were alive, Simon wouldn't be so angry with Alastair.

Orla, Orla, *Orla!* It always came back to Orla. He banged his hand down hard on the worktop. Would she never leave him? Would he never be free of her hold on him? Would he never have a thought process that didn't lead back to her?

From the fridge he opened a bottle of Cloudy Bay, poured himself a glass and took it outside. He stood on the terrace brooding, his body tense, his jaw clenched. Reminding himself that he wanted to create an evening that everybody would enjoy, himself included, he forced Orla from his thoughts and swallowed a large mouthful of wine. Then watching the boats passing at the end of the garden, he wandered down to the pavilion where Sylvia had already set the table for supper. From there he continued to watch the boats. In all the years he'd spent doing exactly this, he had never tired of the view. He would miss it without question, but he was determined to prove to Valentina that nothing mattered more to him than she did, and the life they planned together. Selling Linston End was his way of proving that to her. It was to ensure also that he would finally be free of Orla.

While out on the river today he and Valentina had settled on where they hoped to live and tonight, during dinner, Alastair planned to share the news. It was what Valentina had kept to herself since arriving, teasing him that she was waiting for the right moment before letting on what she had up her sleeve. When putting forward her proposal he had sensed that she had been anxious in case he hated the idea, but he hadn't; in fact it had put the biggest smile on his face, making him impatient to take the next step.

On the other side of the river, he spotted a young man standing on the wooden balcony of the Mill. Presumably that was his neighbour's son. He glanced at his watch. Thirty minutes and they'd be arriving. Time to get changed into something more appropriate for dinner.

Upstairs he found Valentina fresh out of the shower, a towel wrapped around her body. She was staring into the wardrobe where the clothes she'd brought with her were hanging.

'Would it be very wrong of me to suggest you wear that towel and nothing else this evening?' he remarked.

'Only if you want to shock everybody.'

'You mean more than I have already?'

'We could really shock them if you wanted to?' She dropped the towel to the floor.

He smiled and crossed the room. He took her in his arms and kissed her, then edged her towards the bed and laid her down. The warm, yielding softness of her body still surprised him. In contrast Orla's body had been hard-edged and muscular, a testament to a metabolism that had a scorched earth policy when it came to burning up energy. But then she could never sit still for long, always had to be doing something. Neurotically restless, was how he used to describe her when she would jiggle her knee, or tap her foot for no apparent reason. Sex had been one of the few things to have a calming effect on her, when afterwards she would lie completely still.

As Valentina shifted beneath him and put her hands to his face, forcing him to look into her eyes, he groaned, realising once again Orla had occupied his thoughts to the point of distraction. He rolled onto his back, staring bleakly up at the ceiling. 'I'm sorry,' he muttered.

'It's all right,' she murmured. 'I understand.'

He shook his head angrily. 'It's not all right,' he said. 'Not when it keeps happening.'

She placed a hand on his chest. 'Twice. It's happened twice, and it is inevitable, being here in the bedroom you shared with your wife.' She moved her hand and tapped his forehead. 'Orla is in there, isn't she?'

He nodded. 'I'm sorry,' he said, repeating himself.

Valentina's hand moved back to his chest and pressed it gently against his heart. 'But is Orla still there?' she asked.

He blinked. 'No. I've told you before, I stopped loving her a long time ago.' Valentina was the only person in the world to whom he had admitted the true state of his marriage, and the first time he had uttered the words aloud the relief had flooded through him like a Class A drug. But it was soon replaced by something far stronger and more addictive — guilt.

'Maybe you think you did,' Valentina said, 'but perhaps there is still a part of you that has not let go of the love you once had for Orla.'

'You're wrong,' he said firmly. 'Any feelings for Orla I once had died many years ago.' Still feeling embarrassed, he sat up. 'I'd better have a shower.'

'It will all be right in the end,' she said, when he was off the bed. 'When you leave here, you will leave Orla behind.'

That day couldn't come soon enough, he thought.

★　★　★

Valentina selected what she was going to wear for the evening and reflected on what had just happened.

Her conclusion was that Alastair was a completely different man here at Linston End to the one she had met in Sri Lanka. Different also to the happy carefree man with whom she had gone to Kenya, and where, after an exhilarating

263

day of cycling up and down steep and rocky paths that brought them to amazing views, they had collapsed into bed at night exhausted, but elated. Despite their sore bodies aching from cycling such long distances, they had found the energy and passion to make love. There she'd had the whole of Alastair, but here she had to share him with his friends and their constant distrust of her, as well as Orla's poisonous presence casting its shadow over him.

Just as Valentina had anticipated, Alastair's friends did not like her very much. If at all. But then they had nothing in common with her, apart from Alastair. She could cope with that, but the toxic force of his dead wife was another matter.

Had it, as Nikolai and Irina said, been naïve of her to imagine otherwise?

She was glad they were here; they were allies with whom, in Russian, she could talk freely and without worrying that they could be overheard. She had been surprised how happy she had been to see her stepchildren at the station, not having seen either of them for some six months or so. Maybe longer. As fond of them as she was, and they of her, they did not have the kind of relationship that required regular contact. An occasional phone call or email was quite sufficient. Besides, they had their mother, who had remarried and lived in California, to turn to for that level of emotional commitment if they so wished.

Being with Nikolai and Irina today had unexpectedly reminded Valentina of happier times with their father, when Ivan had not drunk so much, or gambled away huge amounts of money in a single game of poker. Perhaps the memories had been stirred because, as the years went by, Nikolai grew ever more handsome and ever more like his father in appearance. In addition he had the same dangerously unpredictable nature, which could make him as reckless as Ivan had been. Valentina very much hoped he would behave while he was here.

36

'I still can't believe he's here,' said Rachel, adding another layer of mascara to her already thickly coated lashes. 'It's as if it's fate.'

'You said that before, about a hundred times and I'm still not buying it,' said Jenna, wishing her friend could at least pretend to disguise her glee. Rachel had been nearly hysterical with laughter when Jenna returned with the eggs from the shop in Horning and told her whom she'd met, and that he had to be the violin-player staying at the Mill.

'And I'll probably say it again, because it's so got to be true.'

'Go on, tell me it's written in the stars.'

'Don't mock. And how do you know it isn't?'

'Because I don't believe in such things, therefore it doesn't exist. Just as I no longer believe in the Tooth Fairy or Father Christmas. Anyway, never mind Blake, what about Valentina's stepchildren? Is Nikolai the reason you're making such an effort with your appearance this evening?'

Without turning round, Rachel stared back at Jenna in the dressing table mirror. They were getting ready together for dinner, Jenna now sharing Rachel's bedroom having vacated hers so that Irina could have it.

'You've got to admit, he's worth the effort,' said Rachel with a grin.

'If you like your men arrogant with a dash of

sullen brooding thrown into the mix, and want your name added to what in all likelihood is an extensive roll call.'

Rachel laughed. 'I'm happy to risk it. And why shouldn't I have some fun after what I went through with Paul?'

Based on the short time she had spent in Nikolai's company, Jenna didn't think he knew what the concept of fun was. His sister didn't seem a barrel of laughs either. If Jenna wanted to be kind, she would say Irina was shy, and that was why she appeared so curt, but probably she was just stuck-up. They each had an air of simmering boredom about them, as though being here was a huge inconvenience. Jenna could concede that there would be plenty who would find the combination of Nikolai's laconic manner and haughty profile immensely appealing, but his hard-etched face of granite and equally hard eyes did nothing for her. She had the horrible feeling that he, along with his sister and stepmother, regarded Linston End and Alastair's friends as being beneath them, a bunch of provincial nobodies. But again, trying to be kind, Jenna reasoned it was still early days, they all needed to bed in and get used to one other.

'It's going to be an interesting evening,' she said as she pulled on her dress and then wriggled to do up the zip at her back.

Rachel snorted. 'It certainly will be. And I'll be watching you and Blake every step of the way. As will Callum, especially after you came clean about your motives for snogging him.'

Jenna rolled her eyes and tutted. 'There'll be

nothing to watch, I assure you. And it sounds like you'll be too busy throwing yourself at Nikolai to have time for anything I may or may not be doing.'

'Here's hoping!'

★　★　★

Seldom did Callum find it difficult to get on with people, but it was an uphill struggle talking to Nikolai Petrov. It was obvious they lived very different lives, but for Alastair's sake Callum was prepared to pretend there was nobody in the world he'd sooner be getting to know. All the while, however, he stole glances around the terrace looking for a lifeline, a means to bring in somebody else to the conversation, or preferably the means to escape.

There was no sign of Jenna or Rachel on the terrace where the rest of them were gathered; odds on they were hiding somewhere together, having already had their boredom thresholds crossed by Valentina's stepson.

On the other side of the terrace, Callum could see Frankie and Danny talking to the stepdaughter. Irina had the same elegant bearing that her stepmother had, and the same coolness. She was wearing some kind of pastel-coloured knitted top that was either too big for her, or was designed to be lopsided and slide off her shoulders. Her long highlighted hair was loosely tied up, and her face was what he thought of as classically Russian — wide cheekbones with almond-shaped eyes, and a determined chin. She was

268

unquestionably beautiful, but gave the impression of being untouchable. She was absolutely not his type, but even so, he found it difficult to keep from looking at her.

Meanwhile, and after much talking of his line of work, Nikolai finally, and mercifully, went quiet, as if he'd bored himself into submission. For something to say, Callum said, 'My work couldn't be more different from yours.'

'What is it that you do?'

He was tempted to say he was a male stripper, just to see what reaction he got, but instead he said, 'I run a boatyard a short distance from here, I took it over from the previous . . . ' Callum could see he'd lost his audience already. Nikolai's attention had been distracted by something behind him. Callum turned to see what he was looking at and saw Rachel and Jenna approaching.

'At last you two grace us with your presence,' he said to them, noting that his sister had pulled out all the stops on her appearance, wearing a skimpy cream dress that was as short as it was figure hugging. No guesses why that was, he thought, seeing her deploying a killer-watt smile on Nikolai, and now realising he'd been naïve in thinking Rachel would find him boring. At least Jenna looked her normal self, but then she had always had more sense than his sister.

'How about you go and find us something to drink,' Rachel said, with an imperious wave of her hand.

Under any other circumstances Callum would have told her to get her own drink, but at the chance of escaping he was happy to do her bidding. 'Your usual pint of tequila with a rum and whisky chaser?' he said.

Rachel flashed him a warning look before turning back to Nikolai. 'Brothers,' she said with an exaggerated shrug.

'Don't forget Nikolai is a brother as well,' Callum said, 'better not condemn us all.'

Rachel tutted. 'I'm sure Nikolai is a much better brother than you. I'll have a white wine, or better still, some Prosecco.'

'What about you, Jenna?' asked Callum.

'That's all right, I'll come with you.'

'Nikolai, another beer?'

'No thank you, I'll join Rachel and have some Prosecco.'

Looking far too pleased with herself, Rachel said, 'Oh, and Callum, while you're fetching our drinks, ask Jenna about our surprise guest this evening.'

'Ignore her,' muttered Jenna as they set off.

'I usually find that's the best policy, but on this occasion I'm bound to ask what she's so smug about? Who's the surprise — '

He got no further as he spotted a boat coming across the river from the Mill. 'Looks like Alastair's neighbour and son are about to arrive, shall we go and help them?'

Jenna put a hand on his arm. 'There's something you should know.'

'Yes?'

'It turns out that Laura Manning's son is Blake Darnell. You remember, he was the — '

'The one who was bothering you at work?'

270

She nodded. 'I bumped into him this morning when I called in at Horning. I couldn't have been more surprised.'

'Did he know you were staying here?'

'No. It's sheer coincidence.'

Callum frowned. 'Are you sure about that?'

'I never once mentioned to him anything about Norfolk or Linston End. It really is chance that he's here.'

'Well then,' Callum said thoughtfully, and interested to know what this Blake character was like, 'let's go and help them moor up.'

They reached the jetty just as the day boat came alongside and a voice said, 'Another gin joint and once again Lawyer Girl walks into it.'

'I think you'll find it's you walking into my gin joint,' said Jenna. 'But I told you this morning we'd bump into each other again, didn't I? Throw me that rope.'

While Jenna tied the stern line to one of the metal rings on the jetty, Callum took the other rope from Laura, then helped her out. Her son hopped out unaided. 'You could have told me this morning that you were staying directly opposite,' he said to Jenna.

'I thought I'd surprise you.'

'You have. Completely.' He turned to introduce his mother, and after she'd shaken hands with Jenna, she smiled at Callum and asked him how he was.

'You know each other already?' said Blake.

'Yes, Callum runs the boatyard where I hired the boat.'

'Is it behaving itself?' Callum enquired.

'Perfectly.' She looked at Jenna. 'Blake said he'd run into a friend from work this morning; how extraordinary that your paths should cross like this so unexpectedly.'

'I was just saying much the same thing,' said Callum. He held out his hand to Blake, wanting to establish his credentials from the get-go. 'I'm an old friend of Jenna's. She may have mentioned me to you.'

'Indeed she has,' said Blake, shaking his hand. 'I hear you go way back.'

'We do,' said Jenna quietly, two red spots colouring her cheeks.

Sensing how awkward she was finding the situation, and not wanting to make it any more difficult for her, Callum took the initiative. 'Come on up to the house and join the party,' he said cheerfully. 'Jenna and I had just been sent on a mission to fetch some drinks, so we can help you to something and then we'll find Alastair.'

He led the way and Laura fell in step beside him, leaving Jenna and Blake to follow behind. He could hear Blake explaining why his surname was different to his mother's, that after her divorce some years ago, she'd reverted to her maiden name. As he listened, Callum fought hard not to feel jealous. Jenna had made it clear that she wasn't interested in Blake, that he was just a work colleague and friend, but of course, even if she couldn't see it, there was so much more to it than that. Blake may have played it cool when he'd been consigned to the friend-zone, just as Callum had yesterday while alone with Jenna, but he'd bet his precious boatyard on Blake hoping that state of affairs would change. The look of happy surprise on Blake's face when he'd recognised Jenna on the jetty had told Callum all he needed to know.

He wondered now if he should have been honest with Jenna yesterday, laid his cards on the table once and for all and made his true feelings known. He hadn't because he'd been worried about the risk of permanently ruining their longstanding friendship. But what if he had lost his opportunity? And now he had Blake Darnell to contend with. To make matters worse, he seemed a decent guy.

★   ★   ★

They sat down for dinner in the pavilion just in time to enjoy the sight of the sun setting. Alcohol had loosened up most of them and the atmosphere was bordering on upbeat.

Alastair had insisted that he, Danny and Simon were in charge of serving dinner and had carried everything down from the house, and with the food now on the table and everyone helping themselves, Sorrel had the strongest of feelings that there was something very deliberate about the way Alastair was co-ordinating the evening.

For a start, she had been banned from the kitchen on the grounds of her having done far too much to help already. 'You're here on holiday,' Alastair had said to her, and to Frankie as well, 'just sit back and enjoy yourselves.' It felt more like a reprimand than a well-meant

273

invitation to relax, and made her sympathetic to Simon's conviction that they were all steadily, but very surely, being pushed to the sidelines. One by one Alastair was ticking them off as no longer fit for purpose as his friends, and his family. That's what they'd been to him and Orla all these years: family.

But now he had a new family — Valentina and her stepchildren. Watching the way Valentina monopolised Alastair made Sorrel sick to her stomach, made her want to do what she'd warned Simon not to do, which was to drink too much and say out loud all the unsayable things buried deep inside her.

But tarnishing Alastair's saintly reputation would never do. Nor, she realised, would she want to hurt Simon in doing that. He was hurting enough as it was. Thankfully he appeared to be heeding her advice and was behaving a lot less belligerently than before. Maybe that was why the mood around the table was less fraught than previously. Or maybe they were all behaving better because they had additional guests amongst them who had nothing whatsoever to do with the battle lines that had been drawn up since Valentina's arrival.

When everyone had helped themselves to food, Sorrel noticed Valentina giving Alastair a small nod and a smile. His response was to tap his knife against a wineglass. An immediate hush fell on the table and everybody turned to look at him. Simon groaned. 'You're not going to give a speech, are you, Al?'

'No, but I am going to make an announcement, something really important. Today Valentina and I decided where we hope to live together.'

He had their full attention now.

'Valentina,' he said, 'why don't you tell them; after all, it's thanks to you this opportunity has arisen.'

'Darling, no, this is your moment, you must tell them.'

The smile on his face widened. Sorrel's hand itched to slap it clean off his face.

'I will then,' he said. 'We've settled on the South of France. Valentina has friends who have just decided to sell their villa in Sainte Maxime, and she thinks it could be perfect for us. From what she's told me of it, and what I've seen online, I'm inclined to agree.'

Next to her Danny whistled. 'Sounds amazing.'

'Where exactly is it?' asked Jenna. 'What's it near?'

'It's not far from Saint-Tropez,' answered Irina before Alastair had a chance to reply. 'We used to stay there as children,' she added, 'the owners are old friends of our father.'

'Sounds very chic and exclusive,' said Callum.

'Yes, makes poor old Linston End sound a bit dull, doesn't it?' muttered Simon into his wine-glass.

'Not dull,' said Alastair, 'just different.'

'Will you definitely still have us all to stay?' asked Rachel.

'Of course. And my guess is you'll have a lot of fun there. The weather will be better for starters. Oh, and the villa has a swimming pool.'

'It gets better and better,' said Frankie with a smile. 'You'll be inundated with guests.'

'When do you think you'll move there?'

Alastair laughed. 'Can't get rid of me soon enough now, can you, Rachel?'

She laughed at Alastair's words, but her eyes, Sorrel noticed uneasily, were fixed firmly on Nikolai, and his on hers. Until now he had affected a manner of looking on with sardonic indifference.

'I'll help you pack if you like, Uncle Al,' Rachel said.

'I might hold you to that,' said Alastair. 'But first, Valentina is taking me to see it, so we can be sure it's right for us.'

'When will that be?'

'After your holiday here.'

Yes, thought Sorrel, get rid of us and off you go to Shangri-La.

'Well,' said Danny, 'it so happens Frankie and I also have an announcement to make. Not that it's in the same league as yours, Alastair, but we've decided after years of mulling it over to leave Suffolk and move here to the Broads.'

'Goodness!' exclaimed Jenna. 'When did you hatch this little plan?'

Frankie laughed. 'This afternoon. Your father sprang it on me, not unlike the time he proposed.'

Danny laughed too. 'Let's hope it works out just as well as that did.'

'Are you sure it's such a good idea?' asked Sorrel. It sounded completely barmy to her.

'In what way?' asked Frankie.

'Given Danny's health problems,' she said bluntly.

'Sorrel has a point,' agreed Simon. 'Is it wise to up sticks when you've only just recovered from, well, you know, it's not as if you're out of the woods and who knows what — '

'Simon, Frankie and I have discussed the point you're trying so hard to tiptoe around,' Danny interrupted him, 'but you know what, just as Alastair has come to realise we have only the one shot at life, we've also come to the conclusion that we shouldn't waste a single minute of ours.' He turned to look at the younger generation around the table. 'Don't ever pass up the chance to seize the day, not when there's no guarantee you'll have a tomorrow.'

'Oh, for God's sake, now you're just being melodramatic!' exploded Simon, reaching for the bottle of red wine in front of him.

'No, I disagree,' said Nikolai from the other end of the table, 'I think we should be greedy for life. We should experience everything before it's too late, and take as many risks as possible. And most importantly, we should never regret anything. That's my rule in life. It's what you and Papa always used to say, isn't it, Valentina?'

His stepmother nodded. 'It was a lesson I taught myself when I was a young girl. Regret is such a waste of one's energy, it's what makes so many people so very unhappy.'

'Hasn't the ability to process regret got something to do with the human psyche needing a moral compass?' suggested Jenna. 'Otherwise we'd all be selfishly running amok doing whatever we pleased, and probably at other people's expense?'

'Good point,' said Callum.

'Yes,' agreed Blake. 'Psychopaths lack the ability to experience regret, don't they?'

Next to him, his mother laughed. 'That's quite an extreme take on it,' she said, 'but I fully support the notion that regret is all too often a wasted emotion.' Her bangles sliding down from her wrists as she planted her elbows on the table, she rested her chin on her hands. 'My rule in life, and which I've tried to pass on to my son here, is to resist settling for second best, or opting for the safe option. Why do that? Why not chase the dream? It's why I'm here in Linston, because I'd always had a fancy to live in a mill on the Broads after coming here for a holiday when I was ten years old.'

'Good for you, Laura,' responded Alastair, 'we absolutely owe it to ourselves to make the most of every day we have and every opportunity that comes our way.' His gaze then moved from Laura back to Valentina, where it lingered on her with sickeningly soppy adoration, his hand reaching out for hers.

Never had Sorrel seen him look at Orla in that way. Not once.

37

It was almost two in the morning when they set off in *Swallowtail*.

It had been Nikolai's idea and put forward after the 'grown ups' — as he referred to Alastair and Valentina, and their parents — had gone to bed, and after he had helped himself to two bottles of champagne from the fridge, one of which was now empty and lay abandoned on the grass. With heaven only knows how much alcohol inside her, Rachel's response to Nikolai's suggestion had been to giggle and twirl around on the lawn in the moonlight, her shoes kicked off, her arms stretched wide either side of her. Irina and Nikolai had looked on laughing, which had made Rachel twirl even faster until she'd spun out of control and fallen over with a yelp.

Jenna had felt like an awkward social misfit at the sight of her friend's antics, and had desperately wanted to slip away quietly and go to bed. But nothing on earth would have allowed her to leave Rachel at the mercy of Nikolai and Irina, not when she had the distinct impression they were laughing *at* Rachel, not with her.

Now, and with Jenna at the helm of *Swallowtail* — she had insisted she be in charge of the boat — and their night lights switched on, she steered them along the narrow dyke and turned left onto the smooth moonlit surface of the river, the engine's speed low so as not to

279

make too much noise. She wished Callum hadn't gone home when he had, but with an early start in the morning he had left at the same time as Laura and Blake had returned to the Mill.

Going up river, and passing the Mill on their right, the solid structure loomed eerily tall in the moonlight, its white cap and sails giving off an unearthly glow against the darkness. Jenna thought she caught a glimpse of a figure at a window, and she was just trying to work out if it was Laura or Blake, when Nikolai appeared at her side. After taking a swig, he thrust the bottle of champagne towards her. 'A drink for our captain?'

She shook her head. The last thing any of them needed was more alcohol. And there she went again, a proper killjoy!

Not surprisingly there were no other boats on the move apart from them, which was a relief; it meant there was no danger of a collision in the dark. Further on, they passed the Wherry Man pub on their left, where all was quiet. Unlike Rachel and Irina, who were laughing over something they clearly found hilariously funny, their drunken high-pitched laughter ricocheting off the silent banks either side of them. 'Why don't you enjoy yourself with the other two and let me take over here?' Nikolai said.

'Have you ever been in charge of a boat before?' she replied.

He shrugged. 'No. But how difficult can it be?'

'My advice would be for you to have a go in daylight tomorrow,' she said.

He leaned in close, so close she could smell

the sourness of his warm breath. 'Are you always this dull?'

The sheer rudeness of his question incensed her, but she refused to let him see he had the ability to rattle her. 'Only when I'm around people who have had too much to drink,' she said coolly.

He gave her a long hard stare and let out a mirthless laugh. 'So you're the responsible adult of the group, are you?' He narrowed his eyes. 'Which makes you an interesting proposition.'

'No it doesn't,' she said firmly, wanting to give him a shove to make him back off, 'it makes me just as boring as you think I am.'

'Who knows, maybe you are, and maybe you're not.'

'Hey, what are you two gossiping about up there?' demanded Irina.

'Jenna is teaching me how to drive the boat,' Nikolai said smoothly. 'But I'm much more interested in hearing about the way Alastair's wife died. From what Valentina says it was near here, wasn't it, that she drowned?'

'Oooh, how ghoulish of you,' trilled Rachel.

Not to say rude and insensitive, thought Jenna.

'So which one of you is going to tell me where she drowned?'

Jenna had no intention of satisfying his morbid curiosity, but Rachel, grabbing the champagne bottle out of Nikolai's hand and drinking from it, was only too glad to provide the necessary details. 'It happened in Linston Broad,' she said, swaying on her feet and peering exaggeratedly into the darkness. 'We must be getting near the opening for it.'

'Why don't we go and look?' said Nikolai.

'What on earth for?' asked Jenna.

'Because I want to.'

Irina laughed. 'And Nikolai always gets what he wants.'

'Of course I do.'

Not if she had anything to do with it, he wouldn't, thought Jenna. 'I don't think we should go into the broad,' she said. The idea appalled her; it was too macabre for words. It was also totally disrespectful.

'Oh, come on, Jenna,' wheedled Rachel, 'don't be such a misery, it'll be fun.'

'Fun!' retorted Jenna. 'How the hell can you say that?'

'Okay, okay, wrong word, but you know what I mean.' Wobbling on her bare feet, Rachel turned to Irina. 'There's a ghost story attached to Linston Broad. A *verrry looong* time ago, a girl used to wander the reedbeds searching for her dead parents until one night — ' she paused for dramatic effect, widening her eyes — 'when she couldn't bear her grief any longer, she drowned herself, just like Alastair's wife, Orla, did.'

Jenna's jaw dropped with shock at her friend's words, but before she could speak, Irina said, 'Seriously? Are you saying Alastair's first wife committed suicide?'

'Well, maybe not exactly,' said Rachel, catching Jenna's furious gaze. 'But she might have. I mean, it was all a bit odd how it happened.'

'We were under the impression it was an

accident,' said Nikolai. 'That's what Alastair told Valentina.'

'It *was* an accident,' said Jenna, the lawyer in her roused, as well as loyalty to Alastair. She gave Rachel another stern look, urging her, just once, to keep her big mouth shut. 'The Coroner recorded an open verdict on the basis there was no evidence to suggest otherwise.'

'But an open verdict means there was something suspicious about the way she died.' This was from Nikolai.

'There was insufficient evidence to confirm exactly what happened,' asserted Jenna.

'Which only adds to the mystery,' said Rachel. Then: 'Look! There's the opening for the broad. Let's go in, Jenna, it'll look awesome in the moonlight.'

'You're not afraid we'll come across the girl's ghost, are you, Jenna?' taunted Nikolai. 'Or perhaps Orla's ghost?'

Furious with Rachel, Jenna said, 'I don't believe in ghosts.'

'Then what are we waiting for?' asked Irina.

'That's a good question,' remarked Nikolai.

'Oh, come on, Jenna,' urged Rachel, wobbling again on her feet. 'Where's the harm?'

Outnumbered, Jenna reluctantly caved in and took the turning into the broad. They'd gone some way in when she eased back the throttle and slowed the engine right down so they could better appreciate the stillness of the wide stretch of water, its black, liquid mirror-like surface perfectly reflecting the moon. An owl hooted on one side of the broad and seconds later, from the other side of the water, another owl hooted in response.

'I was right, wasn't I?' said Rachel in a low voice, as though she alone was responsible for the sight they were staring at. 'It really does look awesome.'

'It is awesome,' echoed Irina. 'Can we go further in, to the middle?'

Her every instinct told Jenna not to do as she was being asked, but she knew it was pointless to refuse, they would only gang up on her again. Grudgingly, she pushed the throttle forward and took them where they wanted to go.

'If I wanted to kill myself, this might well be where I'd do it,' said Irina.

Her brother laughed. 'I'm sure we could help you on your way if you wanted us to,' he said, grabbing her round the waist and pretending to throw her overboard. She squealed loudly and pushed him off.

'You shouldn't make jokes like that here,' snapped Jenna, 'it's in poor taste.'

'Ooh, who made you Colonel-in-chief of . . . of Joke Censorship?'

'You've had too much to drink,' Jenna hissed at her friend, and resolving not to go any further into the broad, she cut the engine dead.

Laughing at her, Rachel took a long and calculated swig from the bottle in her hand. Tipping it all the way back and finding it empty, she chucked it carelessly into the water. Something she would never have done under normal circumstances.

Her patience at breaking point, Jenna gritted

her teeth. 'What the hell's got into you, Rachel,' she muttered, 'apart from the obvious?'

'Hey, lighten up can't you?' Rachel retaliated. 'We're just having fun, or have you forgotten how to do that? But you know what, if you're so worried, I'll dive in and get the bottle so you can put it in the recycling bin when we get back.'

'Don't be ridiculous!'

'Me being ridiculous, try listening to yourself!'

'Go on, Rachel,' said Nikolai, 'I dare you to dive in and get the bottle for Jenna since it seems to mean so much to her.'

'Yeah, I'm up for that.'

'Rachel, don't!'

Ignoring Jenna, Rachel began to wriggle out of her dress, while Nikolai and Irina laughed and cheered her on. '*Do it, do it, do it!*'

'Please don't do this, Rachel,' pleaded Jenna. 'It's not safe when you've had so much to drink.'

But her words went unheeded as Rachel climbed up onto a bench seat and, rocking the boat, threw herself inelegantly into the black water. It seemed forever before she surfaced, and gasping at the coldness of the water, she looked up at Nikolai and Irina. 'Aren't you going to come in as well?'

'Try and stop us!' answered Irina, kicking off her shoes and pulling her top over her head. When she began unzipping her white jeans, she looked at her brother, who hadn't made any attempt to remove his clothes. 'If I'm going in, you're coming in too.'

Nikolai hesitated, but then he saw Jenna staring at him. 'Of course I'm coming in with you,' he said, unbuttoning his shirt and revealing a chest that was tanned and matted with hair. 'What about you, Jenna?'

'Somebody needs to stay in the boat,' she replied stiffly as Irina dived into the water.

'Can't you just throw the anchor over and live a little?' He was down to his boxer shorts now and it seemed to Jenna that he was daring her to lower her gaze from his face to below his waistline.

'This way suits me just fine, thank you,' she said, her gaze never wavering.

He shook his head. 'My word, you're a cold fish, aren't you?'

Not as cold as you'll be when you get back in the boat, she thought, watching him dive beneath the surface of the water.

With the three of them now in the water, destroying the quiet stillness of the night as they splashed each other and shrieked at the top of their voices, Jenna strained to keep Rachel within her sights. As cross as she was with her friend for acting so recklessly, Jenna didn't want her to come to any harm. But she took satisfaction in knowing that Rachel would wake in the morning with a hell of a hangover, which would serve her right.

The darkness had now consumed Rachel and the others, and with a sudden thought of Orla's body found in the northerly end of the broad amongst the reeds where they were most dense, Jenna called out to Rachel. There was no reply, only the sound of Nikolai and Irina laughing. She called again. Nothing.

It was then that Jenna realised she'd made a terrible mistake; when she switched off the engine, she should have dropped the anchor, and because she hadn't, the boat had drifted. Cursing herself for her stupidity, she checked that the stern was clear — making sure Rachel hadn't swum back without her noticing — and switched on the engine to turn the boat around and get her bearings.

She was peering into the darkness when she heard a faint but unmistakable cry. It was a cry for help and it sent a chill of fear racing through her. Oh God, she knew they shouldn't have come here.

38

'Rachel!' she shouted at the top of her voice, her eyes scanning the water. 'Where are you?'

There was no answer. She slowed the engine and called to the other two. 'Nikolai! Irina! Where's Rachel?'

From behind her she heard laughter. She spun round, surprised that the noise came from that direction. She leaned over the side of the boat and spotted Nikolai and Irina, but no sign of her friend.

'Where's Rachel?' she shouted at them.

'We thought she swam back to the boat,' answered Irina.

'She hasn't! Start looking for her!'

Knowing that Linston Broad was unique for having an undertow at various times of the year, particularly at high tide, panic caught in Jenna's throat as she shouted Rachel's name, reducing her voice to little more than a croak. She swallowed hard, fighting the fear that was in danger of paralysing her. 'Rachel!' she yelled again, cupping her hands around her mouth. 'Where are you?'

All she heard in response were the calls of Nikolai and Irina.

'Quiet!' she ordered. 'Let me listen.'

Seconds passed.

'There!' she exclaimed as she heard the faintest of cries. Her hand raised, she indicated a

288

point well beyond where Nikolai and Irina were treading water. She pushed hard on the throttle, the engine now blocking out any chance of hearing another call from Rachel. Keeping her gaze fixed on the distant point where she was convinced the cry had come from, she steered the boat directly ahead, then dropped her speed and completed a slow circle, frantically scanning the water for any sign of movement.

Sick with worry that she had misjudged it, that this wasn't where the cry had come from, she called out to her friend. A spluttering sound had her moving to the stern of the boat. 'Rachel!' she screamed into the darkness once more. 'Wave if you can see me.'

There! There was a flash of white. A hand. And then there was Rachel's face appearing ghostlike through the blackness of the water, her mouth open as if trying to call to her. But before Jenna could do anything, Rachel disappeared out of sight.

A sickness clawing at her stomach, her heart racing so fast it made her breathless, Jenna moved back to the cockpit and steered closer to where Rachel was struggling to stay afloat. Once there, she cut the engine, dropped the anchor over and rummaged in the locker for a life vest. Fumbling to get it on, she then grabbed a rope, threw it over the side of the boat, and slipping off her shoes, she jumped in.

Down she went, but the buoyancy aid meant she bobbed straight back up like a cork pulled from a bottle. Blinking the water from her eyes, adrenaline fuelling her blood, she looked around for Rachel and thankfully spotted her. With her legs kicking hard, Jenna swam over to her friend, but by the time she made it, Rachel had slipped below the surface again. It wasn't easy diving down with the buoyancy of the life vest to combat, and more difficult still to locate Rachel in the pitch-black water. Her lungs bursting as she fought against the fear that it was a hopeless task to find her friend, her eyes stinging in the opaque water, her foot brushed against something smooth and soft. She dived down further and snatched at one of Rachel's arms. Manoeuvring herself so that she could get her hands firmly under her friend's armpits, she then kicked hard propelling them to the surface.

Once there, and gasping to fill her lungs with oxygen, Jenna was tempted to remove her life vest and put it on Rachel, but she knew the risk of that, that it might endanger them both. Instead, she flipped over onto her back and kicking with all her strength, hauled the dead weight of Rachel's now motionless body towards the boat.

But the boat had moved, having dragged the anchor until it held fast to something. The weight of Rachel's body burned into her muscles, but Jenna kept on kicking her legs, turning her head every now and then to keep the boat within sight. She was a few yards from it when she heard the noise of an engine. She twisted her head round again and saw red and green lights twinkling in the darkness, as well as a sweeping and dazzlingly bright white light that momentarily blinded her.

It wasn't uncommon for a Broads Authority ranger's launch to be patrolling late at night, keeping an eye out for drunken revellers wreaking havoc, and as relief surged through her that help was at hand, her grasp on Rachel relaxed and before she could stop it, her friend's body slid out from her hands. She snatched at what she could, which was Rachel's hair and hung on to it with all her might. She then managed to get a better purchase on Rachel, gripping her hard around her ribcage.

The boat was drawing nearer and above the noise of the engine, she heard her name being called. Rachel's too.

'Over here!' she shouted, hoping her voice would carry across the water.

The arc of dazzling white light swept over her, followed by: 'There they are!'

It was only when the boat was almost on top of her and she saw Nikolai and Irina looking down at her, that Jenna saw it wasn't a patrol launch with a ranger at the helm, but her father, and leaning over to reach for her was Blake.

39

Together Blake and her father hauled Rachel's limp body out of the water and laid her on the bottom of the boat, at the same time instructing Nikolai and Irina to give them space by getting out of the way. They then helped Jenna into the boat, grabbing her hands and pulling her up. Shivering with cold, and shrugging off her life vest, her wet clothes clinging to her body, she watched Blake drop to his knees and press a hand to the side of Rachel's neck.

'We should call the emergency services,' Jenna's father said, putting his arm around her, and holding her tight. 'Blake, do you have a mobile with you?'

'No,' he said, and tilting Rachel's chin and head backwards, he pressed his cheek next to her mouth. He then pinched her nose, and breathed into her mouth. He repeated this several times, taking a deep breath in between each attempt to fill her lungs with oxygen. Jenna looked on in shocked silence, glad of her father's body to lean against. The adrenaline that had fuelled her to bring her friend to safety now gone, she felt hollowed out. She dug her nails into the fleshy pad of her palms and willed Rachel to spring back to life, for that hideous bluish colour to her skin to disappear. Near to tears, she was convinced her hope was in vain.

Changing position, Blake drew himself up so

he was leaning over Rachel, and placing his hands one on top of the other across her chest, his arms straight, he pushed down hard. Again, and again, up and down, up and down, a calm and perfect rhythm to his movements and the amount of pressure applied.

It was the policy at Heart-to-Heart for every employee to sign up for a course in CPR — a mix up over dates meant Jenna had missed the slot assigned to her — but clearly Blake had completed the course. But as much as he looked like he knew what he was doing, was he too late? Blinking back tears, she rammed her fists to her lips, pressing them against her teeth that were chattering with cold and shock. Jenna knew she would never forgive the two people responsible for causing this tragedy: Nikolai and Irina.

'I'll get us back to Linston End,' Jenna's father murmured, letting go of her. He started up the engine, shattering the deathly silence. Still on his knees, Blake stopped pressing down on Rachel's chest and reverted to pushing her head and chin back again while breathing into her open mouth. It was useless, thought Jenna miserably, her body trembling with panic and despair. Her heart was beating so hard she could feel her pulse hammering inside her head. Poor Rachel, so full of life one minute and now . . .

She gulped back a wave of sickening dread at the thought of what they would have to tell Simon and Sorrel when they returned to the house. They would be devastated; Callum too. They would never get over it. And how would Jenna ever live with knowing that she should have done more to stop Rachel? The guilt would never leave her.

She glanced briefly at Nikolai and Irina, and at the sight of them huddled pathetically together, wet and shivering, she knew real hatred. It made her want to launch herself at them, to kick, scratch and punch them until they said sorry for what they had done. But sorry would never be enough, not if Rachel was dead.

Then out of the corner of her eye, Jenna saw one of Rachel's legs twitch, followed by what looked like her body convulsing, as if an electric current had passed through it.

'She's alive!' Jenna cried. 'Oh my God, she's alive!'

Taking yet another deep breath, Blake pressed his mouth firmly against Rachel's, then drew back and rolled her onto her side, just as she seemed to take a choking breath of her own.

'We need to keep her warm,' Blake said, ripping off his own T-shirt and covering her with it. 'Danny, give me your shirt.' Jenna's father did as he was told, removed his shirt, and flung it back over his head as he pulled on the throttle and steered the boat at speed out of the broad.

'Talk to her,' Blake told Jenna, 'and rub her arms; I'll do her legs.'

Her teeth chattering even more, Jenna threw herself down onto the floor and rubbed her friend's icy cold body. Miraculously, as Jenna urged her to wake, Rachel's chest gave a great heave and she coughed and spluttered, then spewed water out of her mouth. Her eyes opening and shutting now, she began to move as if to turn herself onto her back, but Blake kept her firmly on her side, just as she vomited again, the revoltingly acrid smell of alcohol now filling Jenna's nostrils.

'It's all right, Rachel,' Jenna soothed as the poor girl began to whimper. 'You're going to be fine. Just stay where you are, don't try to move.' The tears Jenna had been trying to keep in check began now to flow freely down her cheeks and she shivered violently.

'Thank you,' she said, through chattering teeth and looking up at Blake. 'You were fantastic.'

'So were you. You're the one who found her. She owes her life to you.'

'We'll argue about that another rime,' Jenna managed to say. She looked to her side, at Nikolai and Irina. 'You're to blame for this,' she said, 'I hope you realise that.'

Irina flinched, but Nikolai stared back at Jenna, his expression defiantly impassive. His eyes devoid of emotion, he muttered something inaudible.

Jenna glared at him. 'What did you say?'

'I said nobody made her go swimming. It was her choice.'

His blatant coolness incensed Jenna. 'She'd had too much to drink and was incapable of making the right decision! And you knew that. You knew that! But you still encouraged her.'

'What about you leaving us in the water the way you did? What if I had got into difficulty?' This was from Irina.

Jenna seethed with anger. 'Then your precious brother would have saved you, if he could be bothered!'

'Jenna,' said Blake softly, his hand touching

her shoulder. 'Not the time.'

She bit her lip, knowing he was right, and forcing herself to concentrate on rubbing at Rachel's arms to try and warm her, she told her friend over and over that everything was going to be all right.

★　★　★

Downstairs in the kitchen, Frankie was frantic with worry.

She knew in her bones something was horribly wrong. If only she had thought to remind Danny to take his mobile with him she'd be able to ring him and find out what was going on. She also wished she had insisted that she had gone with him, but he wouldn't hear of it. 'It's probably just me being irrational and overreacting,' he'd said, 'but I have a bad feeling about them going out so late in *Swallowtail*. I just need to reassure myself they're okay.'

Frankie had watched him from the bedroom window take the launch from the boathouse and cruise out of the dyke. That was when she saw a shadowy figure appear on the bank in front of the Mill. It looked like Jenna's friend, Blake, and after Danny had crossed the stretch of water, he pulled in close to the bank and Blake hopped on board. They'd been gone now for nearly an hour and Frankie was growing ever more anxious. Had there been an accident? Had Danny's concern pushed his heart to breaking point?

Don't, she told herself. Stop fearing the worst.

She wrapped her hands around the mug of tea

she had made and switching off the under-light, she went and stood at the open French doors, a cool breeze blowing in. Seconds passed while her eyes adjusted to the darkness. Watching. Waiting. It was all she could do.

'Another one who can't sleep, then?'

She started at the sound of Simon's voice as he came into the kitchen behind her. 'Not much chance of that,' she said. She explained about Danny going off in the boat.

'Bloody fool going out on his own! Why didn't he wake me, I'd have gone with him.'

'He's not alone. From the upstairs window I saw him picking up Laura's son from the Mill.'

'What was Blake doing out on the river bank in the middle of the night?'

'I have no idea. But at least it gives me a degree of peace of mind knowing Danny isn't alone.'

'Did he take his mobile with him?'

She shook her head.

'Bloody fool,' Simon repeated, standing alongside her and staring into the darkness. 'And bloody fools those kids of ours going out on the river after drinking so much, and after all the lectures we've given them ever since they were teenagers. I bet it was those bloody stepkids of Valentina's leading them astray.'

'Best not to leap to conclusions.'

'Well, I'll tell you this for nothing; if he'd been here, Callum would have stopped them from going out. God, why couldn't Rachel have been born with half her brother's common sense? I'm surprised Jenna went, though, she's usually more sensible.'

That same thought had occurred to Frankie, as had the thought that Rachel had not been too subtle in her flirting with Nikolai during the evening. Would that have led her to show off and do something silly? 'Maybe Jenna went to keep an eye on them,' she said lightly.

'Yes, thank God for Jenna. She's always been the sensible one of those two girls, ever since they were little. You know, I've always been grateful for her friendship to Rachel; for the most part she's been a steadying influence.'

Frankie smiled. 'Sometimes I think Jenna's a little too level-headed for her own good; she needs to have more fun in her life.'

An owl hooted from the top of one of the trees in the garden, followed by a flap and whoosh of wings as the bird swooped the length of the lawn, before being swallowed up by the velvety blackness of the night sky.

'Are you really going to leave Suffolk and move here?' asked Simon, when seconds had passed.

'It's what Danny's always wanted to do,' Frankie said softly.

'But what about you? Is it your dream, or just Danny's?'

'I'm happy if Danny's happy. Wouldn't you do the same for Sorrel?'

'Good question.' He rubbed his face with one of his hands. 'It would depend on what it was she wanted to do.'

It was on the tip of Frankie's tongue to ask him if he had any idea what dreams and wishes Sorrel held, but she kept the question to herself.

'Look,' said Simon, staring into the darkness, 'there's a light. It's a boat. Come on, let's go and give those damned kids merry hell!'

40

'Of course we must take her to hospital!'

'But, Dad,' wailed Rachel, 'I don't want to go. I hate hospitals.'

'Rachel, just once in your life, will you do the sensible thing and do as we say? We're taking you to the hospital and that's an end to it.'

'Please don't shout,' said Sorrel, 'it's not helping; can't you see the poor girl's in shock?'

Simon blinked and told himself to count to five. He made it to three. Shock was what *he* was in and venting his feelings by raising his voice was all that was preventing him from killing Nikolai and Irina. He'd known they were bad news from the moment he set eyes on them. Valentina too. Now perhaps Alastair would wake up and realise what he'd got himself into. They were not their type of people. They were reckless. They were divisive. They were bloody great cuckoos in the nest!

When he and Frankie had gone to help Danny moor up and find out what had been going on, he'd never known an emotion so strong as the one he'd experienced in that gut-punch of a blow when he'd discovered what had happened. He couldn't believe what he was hearing, that Rachel had come so close to death. Filled with a fiercely protective love for her, he'd carried his daughter up to the house. With Sorrel's help, he'd laid her on the sofa in the sitting room, and ordered the others to fetch blankets and hot drinks, and to be damned quick about it. By then, roused by the commotion, Alastair and Valentina had appeared and not trusting himself to look at Alastair, Simon had left it to Jenna, Blake and Danny to explain. Valentina had immediately suggested she take Nikolai and Irina upstairs for a hot shower and dry clothes. 'Yes, get them out of my sight,' Simon had muttered.

He bent down beside Sorrel who was cradling their daughter in her arms as she cried, her sobs loud and choking. It was a heartbreaking sound and Simon couldn't bear to listen to it.

'I'm sorry, love,' he said, putting a hand to Rachel's cheek, a gesture he hadn't done since she was a little girl, 'but Blake seems to know what he's talking about. He says that even though you might feel okay, it would still be better to have a doctor check you out, just in case there are any repercussions. Would you do that for me, for your old dad, to put his mind at rest?'

Her shoulders heaving, her lower lip trembling, Rachel sniffed. 'If I go, Dad, I don't want to stay there. I want to come back here as soon as the doctor says there's nothing wrong with me.' Her eyes were huge and round, like those of a frightened child — *his* child, *his* very precious daughter. In a flash he recalled her as a toddler screaming as a large dog barrelled towards her and how, without a thought for his own safety, he'd put himself between her and the snarling beast. He had roared at it so convincingly, the dog had slunk away into the bushes of the park where he'd taken Rachel to play. A parent's need to protect their child knew no bounds.

Simon nodded. 'That's my girl. We'll have you tucked up in bed in no time. I promise.'

And I promise I'll have Nikolai and Irina for this, thought Simon, a lump of bitterness burning the back of his throat and threatening to erupt like steaming hot lava.

★   ★   ★

With Simon and Sorrel now taking Rachel to the hospital, Jenna was fresh out of the shower and dressed in warm dry clothes. She was outside on the terrace with Blake, each of them nursing a mug of hot tea in their hands. Mum and Dad were in the kitchen with Alastair; they were all reluctant to go to bed — or back to bed for some of them — too agitated to sleep. Valentina and her stepchildren had made themselves invisible, which was probably the right thing for them to do.

'I'm assuming you did the CPR course at work,' Jenna said to Blake. 'I've yet to do mine.'

'I'd already done one a while ago, but I did the Heart-to-Heart course as a refresher.'

'Well, it was obvious you knew what you were doing.'

'Just as you did when you found Rachel in the water.'

Jenna shook her head. 'That was different, I just swam, there was no real skill involved. I couldn't have done what you did.'

He took a long sip of his tea. 'I guarantee you will as a consequence of tonight.'

There was something about the way he spoke that made her give him a sideways glance.

'A very good friend of mine drowned in similar circumstances,' he said, in answer to her unasked question.

'I'm sorry.'

'Not as sorry as I am.'

'What happened? Or would you rather not talk about it?'

'No, I don't mind telling you. It was nearly three years ago. A group of us were away in Ibiza for my friend's stag do and we were staying in his parents' villa. The five of us, old school friends, had gone out in a boat after drinking too much. I'm sure you can picture the scene. Inevitably things got a bit silly and Robbie fell overboard. By the time we got him out of the water, it was too late. He was dead.'

He took another sip of his tea. 'I'll never forget how ashamed and worthless we all felt at Robbie's funeral, especially when confronted with his parents' grief. Robbie's fiancée and family were there too and I'm sure she blamed us. After that, I swore I'd learn how to do CPR, so that if I ever found myself in a similar situation again, I'd know exactly what to do.'

'I'm so glad that you did,' Jenna murmured, 'but I'm sorry about you losing your friend.'

Minutes passed when neither of them spoke, until Jenna said, 'It's none of my business what you were doing out on the river bank so late, but I'll always be thankful you were there and that my father stopped for you.'

'I'd seen the four of you going out in the boat

303

and, given Robbie's death, I just couldn't settle, not until I knew you'd come back.' He cleared his throat. 'And I mean *you* specifically.' Before she could say anything, he quickly went on. 'Call it a sixth sense, or whatever else you want to, but when your father appeared, and was clearly worried enough to go looking for you, I had no choice but to go too.'

She turned and looked at him. 'Right place, right time,' she said softly. *Or fate*, she imagined Rachel sniggering in her ear.

He held her gaze, then suddenly, perhaps at the thought of Rachel, a shiver ran through her at what could have happened if Blake hadn't been staying at the Mill. Or if he hadn't been so concerned about her. She squeezed her eyes shut and covered her mouth with a hand, reliving the moment when she had been convinced her friend was dead. She loved Rachel so much. She loved her for all her silliness, and for all her impulsiveness, but most of all because Rachel had always been there in her life. She also loved Rachel because she was everything Jenna could never be — she was the kind of girl who danced barefoot in the moonlight. When had Jenna ever done something like that?

Her eyes still closed, she felt Blake shift on the seat beside her, followed by his arm moving to go around her shoulder. She willingly leant against him, wanting to feel the solid assurance of him.

'It's okay,' he said quietly, 'it'll be like that for a while; the shock will creep up on you. It's quite normal.'

She opened her eyes. 'I don't think I'll ever forget this night,' she said.

'No, you probably won't.'

For the longest time they sat in companionable silence, drinking their tea and watching the sky gradually lighten with a glowing opalescence as the dawn heralded the start of a new day. A bird began to sing, followed by another, and another. Resting against Blake, Jenna was aware of a sense of energy coming off him, a sort of vibration. Or was it she who was vibrating, buzzing with some unknown force?

'You ought to get back,' she said, when she'd finished her tea, 'your mother will be wondering what's happened to you.'

'She knows I'm here, your father let me use his mobile to text her.'

'I like your mother, she's nice.'

'I'm rather fond of her myself as it happens.'

'Look,' she said, pointing to the sky in the east where the first rays of the sun were bleaching the indigo darkness of the sky.

'And with the new day comes new strength and new thoughts,' he said, leaning forward to see where she was indicating. She felt his warm breath on her cool cheek and very faintly something stirred within her. It's shock, she reasoned, shock manifesting itself in another guise. 'Did you make that up?' she asked, straightening her back so that he was forced to remove his arm from her shoulder.

'Being a lowly creative type which you clever lawyers so despise, I'll take that as a compliment, that you believe I'm sufficiently intelligent to think of it all on my own.'

She tutted and rolled her eyes. 'And just when you were doing so well, you spoil it in one small step.'

'It's actually something my mother says,' he said with a smile. 'Don't hold me to it, but I think it was Eleanor Roosevelt who originally came up with it. It's very apt though, and something I try to live by.'

Thinking how impossible it was to know what each new day would bring, and maybe it was just as well, Jenna said, 'Do you suppose Rachel will suffer any long-term ill-effects as a result of what she's gone through?'

'Do you mean after her body was deprived of oxygen for the length of time it was?'

'Yes.'

'Well, obviously the body will start to shut down when denied oxygen, but the speed of that process can vary from person to person. I'm no expert in these things, but I do know that it would happen a lot faster in a child than an adult.'

'Could it be serious? Like brain damage?'

'I don't think you need to worry about that; Rachel seemed fairly with it when we got her back here. There could be a risk of water being trapped in her lungs and that's why she should be taken to hospital, but from what I know, most people make a full recovery after nearly drowning. I'm sure Rachel will be just fine.'

'If she is, it'll be down to you.'

'No, it'll be down to the pair of us. You need to take the credit for what you did.'

He put a hand to his mouth to stifle a yawn, which had the effect of making Jenna yawn as well.

'Time for me to leave you in peace,' he said, getting to his feet. 'Try and get some sleep, won't you?'

She stood up next to him. 'You too. And thank you again.' She kissed him on the cheek and smiled shyly. 'My hero.'

He smiled. 'Don't suppose you'd give this so-called hero a lift back across the river, would you?'

'Of course.'

41

Alastair couldn't believe what had happened.

In all the years the children had spent here at Linston End, not once had they ever gone out late at night on the river after drinking. Not even Orla had encouraged an act of such reckless folly. It was the one and only house rule. 'Break that rule,' Simon had often thundered, 'and the holiday's over!'

Alone in the sitting room, everyone else having drifted back upstairs, he alternated between pacing the floor and staring out of the French windows, anxious to hear from Simon and Sorrel, but also dreading the exchange. He knew they would hold him indirectly responsible for what had happened. The accusation flung at him would be that had he not brought Valentina into their midst, along with Nikolai and Irina, Rachel would never have got herself into the situation she had. Or if the accusation wasn't made aloud, it would be what they were thinking and would become an impenetrable barrier between them. The awful thing was Alastair wouldn't blame them; in their shoes he would probably feel the same way.

He'd been staring morosely out of the window when he started at a hand pressing down on his shoulder. He spun round to see Valentina.

'Sorry,' she said, 'I didn't mean to surprise you.'

'That's all right, I was miles away.'

'Worrying, I expect,' she said.

'Yes,' he replied.

'Any news?'

He shook his head.

'I'm sure Rachel will be fine. She's young and strong.' When he didn't respond, she said, 'But that is not what is really tormenting you, is it? You're concerned more with how this will reflect on us, aren't you? Or more particularly, me.'

He wanted to lie, but he couldn't, not when he knew she was too astute to be fooled so easily. 'As a parent yourself,' he said carefully, 'you know better than me that a parent's love is ferociously protective when it comes to a child.'

'Yes,' she said with a small nod of her head, 'even to a stepmother like me. But I also know that there comes a time in a child's life when he or she has to take responsibility for themselves. Simon and Sorrel may not want to admit it, but their daughter is an adult and must therefore take responsibility for her own actions. Ah,' she said after a pause, 'I see I have shocked you with my frankness. I have yet to learn the English art of keeping quiet, of keeping to myself those things which would be better not said. I'm sorry.'

'Don't be,' he said, putting his arms around her, and breathing in the potent and reassuring smell of her perfume. He needed her certainty more than ever before. 'This will all blow over once the shock has receded,' he continued, trying to sound more upbeat. 'It's just that nothing like this has ever happened before. For the life of me I can't understand why Nikolai and Irina felt the need to go into the broad in the first place. Wanting to see where Orla died is too macabre for words.'

'But the young have no regard for such sensitivities. Death fascinates those who don't think it will ever happen to them, and the young believe they will live forever.'

After tonight they might well think differently, thought Alastair.

Tilting her head back from him, Valentina said, 'I want you to promise me something.'

'Go on.'

'I want you to promise that you will not allow Nikolai and Irina to be blamed for this. They did nothing wrong.'

'Nobody is going to be blamed for anything,' he said. 'It was an accident.'

'Of course it was,' she said, 'but I don't think your friends see it that way. I saw the way Simon looked at Nikolai and Irina, and it was not pleasant.'

'He was upset, not in full control of his emotions.'

'And you don't think they were upset by what they had witnessed? Irina was in tears when I helped her into bed. She was in shock, poor girl.'

'It's been a shock for us all,' Alastair said tactfully, and wishing that he could feel more sympathetic towards Valentina's stepdaughter. But all he could think of was how devastated Simon and Sorrel would have been if Blake hadn't been around to save Rachel's life. He let go of Valentina. 'I'm going to try ringing Simon again,' he said, 'they must have seen a doctor by now.'

★   ★   ★

In the back of the car, her mother by her side, Rachel wanted desperately to close her eyes and sleep. But each time her eyelids drooped and she felt herself slip into that dreamy state of oblivion, she was jerked violently awake by the terrifying sensation of not being able to breathe, of sinking deeper and deeper into a cold blackness.

Every time it happened, unbidden tears sprang to her eyes and she relived those last terrifying moments, the ones she could remember, when she was in the water. She had never known fear like it, the paralysing sense of utter helplessness. Of fighting for every breath and realising it was a losing battle. That no matter how hard she tried to stay afloat, her body felt weighted with concrete and her lungs ready to burst. And then, almost as if it was a mercy, she had no strength left and she gave in and let the water swallow her up, just as Orla must have done. Just as the girl with the lantern who had been searching for her parents must have done.

That was when she had thought she wasn't alone — Orla was there! And she was holding Rachel tight and dragging her down deeper, to the darkest depths of the broad. It was like being a child again, hand in hand with Orla, off on another adventure, pirate hats on, cutlasses swishing at their sides. She no longer felt cold, and the fear had passed. She was happy to be led, to be led by Orla as if flying through the air, her hair streaming behind her, her body suddenly as light and insubstantial as an early morning mist hovering over the river.

Now, after speaking to the doctor who had examined her, Rachel accepted that Orla's presence must have been nothing but a hallucination brought on by lack of oxygen to her brain. A trick designed to distract her from dying. She also knew now that the arms holding her so firmly had been those of Jenna pulling her to safety from the water.

Once again her eyes filled with tears at the thought of her friend risking her own life to rescue her. She turned to look out of the car window. How would she ever thank Jenna? And Blake too. Apparently he had been the one to give her CPR, the only one to know just what to do.

She felt totally undeserving of their efforts. She had been drunk, showing off in front of Nikolai, hoping to impress him, to prove that she was worthy of his attention. She shuddered with shame at her behaviour and then coughed, setting off a series of painful stabbing sensations deep inside her lungs. She put a hand to her aching and bruised chest, where Blake must have pressed down hard as he fought to save her life.

'Are you all right?' asked her mother, giving her hand a squeeze. 'Are you cold? Simon, turn up the heating.'

'There's no need, Dad,' Rachel said, her throat tight, 'I'm warm enough.' She met his gaze in the rear-view mirror. Never before had she seen her father so torn apart with worry; it upset her to know that she had put him through such needless pain. She knew Mum was just as upset, but she was always so much better at hiding her emotions. Rachel was more like Dad in that respect; they both wore their hearts on their sleeves.

'We'll soon be back,' Mum said beside her. 'And after you've had something to eat, we'll help you to bed and you can sleep.'

It wasn't often her mother showed this softer side of her nature and it touched Rachel. 'Thanks, Mum,' she said. 'Will you sit with me for a while when I'm in bed, like you used to when I was little?'

If her mother was surprised at the request, she didn't show it. 'Of course,' she said. 'And maybe your father might like to as well.'

Rachel's gaze once more caught her father's in the mirror. He smiled back at her. 'I'll do whatever makes you feel better,' he said.

She drifted off to sleep. When next she opened her eyes, she saw they were driving through the village of Linston, the road lined either side with the familiar sight of cottages, their gardens bright with summer flowers.

As they turned into the driveway for Linston End, she heard her mother say, 'Simon, please let's not make a bad situation any worse than it already is.'

42

The last person in the world Sorrel had wanted to encounter was Valentina, but after leaving Simon upstairs with Rachel and Jenna, she had come down to make them a drink, only to see Valentina sitting at the table outside on the terrace, calmly reading a magazine while absently spooning yoghurt into her mouth. The sight of her relaxing in the late morning sunlight without a care in the world was too much for Sorrel. She stepped onto the terrace. 'I'm glad somebody round here is enjoying themselves,' she said. 'And how kind of you to enquire how Rachel is,' she added.

Valentina looked up from the magazine in front of her. 'I'm sorry,' she said. 'I thought you were still upstairs. How is your daughter?'

'As if you care!'

Without giving Valentina the chance to reply Sorrel went back inside the kitchen. She filled the kettle and plugged it in, conscious that she was in danger of resembling a hissing cat fighting over a chicken carcass. She had asked Simon to keep his temper in check, but once more she didn't seem able to take her own advice.

Hatred for the woman Alastair professed to love now burned within her. She hated Valentina with a loathing matched only by her scorn for Alastair. How could he have turned into such a pathetically weak man who was now so blinded he couldn't see what was going on? And to think she had loved him. What a fool she'd been. All those wasted years. All those years of wanting something she couldn't have.

'I can see that you're upset, and that is why you are behaving so irrationally.'

Sorrel jumped out of her skin at the sound of Valentina's voice. It was crazy, but such was her guilt, she felt scared that the woman might have actually eavesdropped on her innermost thoughts. 'Why on earth did you sneak up on me like that?' she demanded.

'I did not sneak up on you. You simply failed to hear my approach.'

Ignoring the remark, and fighting the urge to claw Valentina's face off, Sorrel opened the cupboard above the kettle and took out four mugs. Instinctively she wanted to tidy the shelves and put everything back in order, just as she'd done a few days ago, before Alastair had practically banned her from doing anything useful in the kitchen. She slammed the cupboard door shut and yanked open the cutlery drawer. Again she had to stop herself from tidying the muddle, knives, forks and serving spoons any old how. Teaspoon in hand, she slammed the drawer shut with sufficient force to rattle the contents. Next she opened the fridge and took out a carton of milk, poured some into a small jug, then returned the carton to the fridge. All the while keeping her back resolutely turned to Valentina.

'Perhaps it would be better for us not to speak now,' Valentina said, 'not when your emotions are running so high.'

The woman's cool condescension riled Sorrel

beyond all reason. She whipped round to face Valentina. 'I can think of no better time to tell you exactly what I have to say. Because of your stepchildren my daughter very nearly died, and yet you behave as though nothing out of the ordinary has happened.' She waved her hand vaguely in the direction of the garden. 'There you were, reading your magazine and eating your yoghurt, not a thought for anybody else and the ordeal we've been through.'

'You would rather I did not eat any breakfast? Would that make you, or Rachel, feel better?'

'Don't be absurd!'

She gave Sorrel an uncomfortably sceptical look. 'Sorrel,' she said, slowly and precisely, as if she were addressing an imbecile, 'it is not me who is being absurd, and believe me, you have my sympathy for the shock you're experiencing and I know that is why you are behaving this way.'

'You have no idea how I am feeling, so don't patronise me. Where are your stepchildren, as a matter of interest?'

Valentina's eyes narrowed and she tilted her chin up. 'They're sleeping.'

'Of course they are,' muttered Valentina, 'like a couple of babies, no doubt.'

'Sorrel, let us be very clear on this point, a point I have discussed with Alastair and on which he fully supports me. I will not stand for Nikolai and Irina to be blamed for what was an accident. Do you understand me?'

'I understand you all too well.'

'I'm glad to hear that, Sorrel, because I believe for Alastair's sake it is very important there is no confusion between us.'

'Trust me, there is absolutely *no* confusion between us; I know exactly what the situation is, that you're the kind of woman to take advantage of a man when he's at his most vulnerable.'

Valentina tilted her head and gave Sorrel a superior half smile that made her grip the teaspoon in her hand so tightly it hurt.

'How strange that you should be talking about Alastair when you claim to be so upset about your daughter,' said Valentina. 'I wonder what is really more important to you. Rachel, or Alastair?'

Sorrel could have taken the teaspoon and done something unspeakable with it, but the kettle coming to the boil gave her something else to do with her hands. 'If you need to ask that question,' she said, forcing herself very calmly to put teabags into the china pot followed by water, 'then you don't understand the first thing about Alastair and the close friendship he has with us, and how we have always stood by one another.'

'And what a burden that must be for poor Alastair, weighed down by you all. Can you be surprised that he wants to be free of you at long last, and be with me?'

It was rare for Sorrel to be at a loss what to say, but the sheer venomous intent behind the honeyed tone of Valentina's words left her momentarily speechless.

'The truth always hurts, doesn't it?' Valentina remarked. 'Self-deception is such a foolish trick to play on oneself.'

'Make no mistake, self-delusion is just as foolish,' Sorrel said, finding her voice.

'I agree, which is why I never fall into that trap either.'

Taking a tray from the cupboard next to the cooker, Sorrel said, 'That remains to be seen.'

'You know, Sorrel, I suspect that you and I are not so different. Why don't you consider lowering your guard and be friends with me? Wouldn't that be less exhausting for you?'

Thinking she would sooner make friends with a rattlesnake, Sorrel prepared the tray to take upstairs. 'I would imagine,' she said at length, 'that you know that is never going to happen.'

'That is a great pity. For I make a much nicer friend than I do an adversary.'

'I don't doubt that for a second. And now, if you don't mind, I'm going back upstairs to be with my daughter.' She was at the door when she came to a stop. 'I knew it wouldn't take you long to show your true colours.'

Valentina smiled. 'The very same thought occurred to me about you. Which is another reason I think we would actually be quite good friends. You and I are two of a kind, Sorrel.'

Not trusting herself to respond to such an inaccurate, not to say wildly offensive statement, Sorrel gripped the tray in her hands and carried on through the doorway.

Hell would freeze over before she ever contemplated that odious woman worthy of her friendship. Just what did poor deluded Alastair see in her? And why was he such a bad judge of character? First Orla, now Valentina!

Yet what really irked her was the sly manner in which Valentina had dictated the terms of the conversation, deflecting it away from those who were responsible for Rachel nearly dying, and focusing it instead on Sorrel herself.

She climbed the stairs with slow careful steps. The house was unnaturally quiet. When they'd returned from the hospital in Norwich, Jenna had explained that Alastair had gone with Danny and Frankie to retrieve *Swallowtail* where it had been abandoned in the broad. It wouldn't be long before they would be back, she supposed. Then what?

She found Rachel sitting up in bed talking on her mobile phone.

'She's chatting with Callum,' Simon said, taking the tray from her and putting it on the dressing table, pushing aside the clutter of make-up, hairbrushes, tissues, jars of moisturiser, nail varnish and perfume bottles.

'Cal,' said Rachel into the mobile, 'there's no need, come as you originally planned this evening . . . No, I mean it. I'll be feeling more normal by then anyway . . . No really . . . You've got work to do . . . I know, she was a star . . . I still can't believe what she did . . . And Blake too . . . Would you like to speak to her?' Rachel nodded at Jenna, then passed her the phone. Jenna went over to the window to speak to Callum.

'Any sign of Alastair downstairs?' asked Simon.

Sorrel shook her head. 'They haven't returned yet from the broad.'

'How long does it take to find a boat and bring it back?' said Simon tightly. 'Or is he hiding from us?'

'Who knows?' said Sorrel. She began pouring

319

out the tea. 'When you've drunk this, Rachel,' she said, placing the mug on the nightstand next to the bed, 'I'll make you something to eat. What would you like? A piece of toast perhaps, with your favourite Nutella?'

Rachel hesitated. 'You know what I'd really like, Mum?' she said. 'A bacon sandwich.'

'I wouldn't mind one of those myself,' said Simon. 'Plenty of brown sauce too. Why don't I go downstairs and put some bacon under the grill?'

'There's no need; I'll do it. You stay here and drink your tea with the girls.'

He took the proffered mug. 'Sorrel, you do realise, don't you, that you can't keep me locked in here forever? I intend to have my say with Alastair and Valentina, there's no avoiding that.'

Jenna had now finished speaking to Callum and was passing the mobile back to Rachel. Sorrel gave her a mug of tea. 'There's no point, Simon,' she said, 'you won't gain anything by taking out your anger on them. I'm afraid to say Valentina has already made it very clear that she has Alastair's support, that she won't have Nikolai and Irina turned into scapegoats.'

'You've spoken to her?'

'Just now when I was making the tea. She couldn't have made her position any clearer. She's a player, Simon, a pro. She knows exactly what she's doing, and is taking great delight in outmanoeuvring us.'

'I knew it! I bloody well knew it!'

'Dad, please don't make a scene because of me, will you?'

Both Simon and Sorrel turned to look at their daughter. 'Nobody's talking about a scene, love,' said Simon. 'But there are things that have to be said.'

'But it was my fault. I told you before, I'd drunk too much and was making an idiot of myself. Just ask Jenna.'

'That may well be true,' said Sorrel, 'but from what Jenna told us before, they urged you on. That's what is so unforgivable. Darling, just think what would have happened if Jenna hadn't been there with you?'

'Maybe they would have rescued me.'

Simon guffawed loudly. 'Yeah right, from all accounts those two ninnies were about as useful as a pair of chocolate teapots.'

'But if you blame them it'll spoil everything and we'll have to leave and I don't want to. Please don't ruin the holiday because of my stupidity, especially when it's our last time here.'

Sorrel knew that Simon could refuse Rachel nothing; it had been that way ever since she was born. He looked at her, then back at Sorrel, his dilemma plain to see. What was more important to him — Rachel's happiness to let things go, or his need for retribution?

43

Out on the terrace Valentina was finishing her coffee which she had been drinking before Sorrel had appeared. She was savouring her victory over a woman who had obviously seen herself as the guardian of Alastair's wellbeing since his wife's death. It was foolish of Sorrel to think she could intimidate Valentina, not when her every word and gesture revealed her to be pettily vindictive and laughably jealous.

The last of her coffee now drunk, she went back inside the kitchen, placed the cup and saucer, along with the spoon, in the dishwasher and, flouting any attempt at recycling, dropped the yoghurt pot into the bin. She then opened the cupboard where yesterday she had noticed a collection of labelled keys hanging on a row of hooks. She selected the one that interested her most, and seizing her opportunity, she went out to the garden, following the path to the left of the house. Hidden behind a tall beech hedge, she kept on going until the winding path brought her to a small secluded clearing.

Before her, and framed by a canopy of leaves shimmering in the sunshine, stood a green painted one-storey cottage with pretty white trim to the eaves and windows. There was a sense of magical isolation to it. If Linston End had reminded Valentina of the lavish *dachas* of the Russian elite, this put her in mind of the humble wooden clapboard *dacha* in the summer village of Peredelkino near Moscow, where her mother holidayed with her cousins.

When alone on the river yesterday with Alastair, Valentina had glimpsed what looked like a romantic hideaway through the trees, and on asking who it belonged to, he'd said it was his, or more precisely it had been his wife's. 'We bought the land many years ago so Orla could have a proper studio,' he'd explained. 'It was where she liked to think and be alone,' he'd added, but without inviting further comment.

Valentina inserted the key she'd taken from the kitchen into the lock and turned the handle. Initially the door refused to budge, but after jiggling the handle and pushing hard against it, the door creaked open.

She stepped into the cool interior, brushing away a cobweb and wrinkling her nose at the fusty smell of dust. The interior wasn't at all what she expected. There was no narrow hallway leading to a couple of cramped rooms stuffed with tables, chairs, chests and cabinets filled with china and samovars, as in the *dacha* her mother frequented, but instead there was one large open and airy space.

The floor was of white painted boards and at one end was a scruffy rug, a small log-burning stove, an empty log basket, a wooden table with a mixed assortment of chairs around it, a tall larder cupboard, a sink beneath the window, and a two-ring gas stove on which stood a battered metal kettle. There was a daybed against one of the walls and opposite it, several easels, and a functional bench on which stood a number of statues of birds, otters and hares.

Above the bench was a noticeboard with sketches pinned to it, some detailed, some no more than a swift and fluid stroke of a brush or a pencil capturing the flight of a bird. The sketches of a heron launching itself into the air, and seen from three differing angles, caught Valentina's attention and she leaned over the bench to take a closer look. Grudgingly she had to admit Orla had had an enviably deft touch. The sculptured works, which she knew Orla was known for, impressed Valentina less. To her taste, they seemed generic in comparison to the sketches. Why had the woman squandered her talent on churning out these spiritless sculptures when it was quite evident her real talent lay in the uncomplicatedness of a brush and pencil in her hand?

Had that been the source of what Alastair described as his wife's perpetual sense of failure, the frustration that she could not portray through the medium of clay or bronze that which she could so effortlessly put on paper?

Valentina didn't know whether to condemn the woman for that futile persistence, or admire her for it. It struck Valentina that maybe she was facing something similar — the battle to prise Alastair away from his previous life and have him entirely for herself, or admit defeat and accept she could never have him heart, body and soul.

Alastair had not lived a nomadic life as she had as an adult, where home was merely where she happened to lay her head. Linston End was very much his home; it was a part of his being, she now understood.

But she was confident that once she got him to the south of France, and they saw the house in Sainte Maxime together, things would change. In the meantime, she would fight Linston End, and his friends, to possess him. Her father used to say that once she was set on a course of action she was like an extreme force of nature, capable of sweeping aside all those who were foolish enough to try to stop her.

Turning away from the sketches, she looked at the daybed against the wall. A cream cotton throw with tassels at the corners covered the mattress, and a pile of cushions lay at one end. Had Alastair lain on that with Orla? Had they made love on it? Or had this been a strictly private retreat for Orla, a sacred place designed to keep the world out, even Alastair?

She went over and sat on the edge of the mattress, and looked at the river through the window. Her lips twitched with a smile. To hell with this being a sacred place! The first opportunity she had in the coming days, she would find a purpose to come here with Alastair and they would make love on this daybed. It would be a satisfying way for Valentina to make her mark on this place, and to banish Orla further from Alastair's mind.

Or would it?

So far their lovemaking had not been entirely successful here at Linston End. She blamed the house, the connection it had to Orla. It was obvious that Orla was present at every turn and that was another reason she had to get Alastair away.

Through the window she could see a boat passing on the river, followed by another. Realising that it was Alastair with Danny and Frankie returning from fetching the motor cruiser left in the broad last night, she got quickly to her feet, locked up and retraced her steps along the path towards the house. What happened next would be crucial in determining just where Alastair's loyalty lay. With the past, or the future.

To some Valentina may have appeared unmoved by Rachel's near-drowning, but that was just her way. She was not the sort to fall into the trap of becoming hysterical. And anyway, it was not her child who had nearly died; she scarcely knew the girl, so why would she be overly upset? Her nature was to be wholly pragmatic. A cool head was of far more use in a crisis than one full of panic and melodrama.

It was a very cool head she had employed earlier when dealing with Nikolai and Irina. Very quietly, and while everybody else was downstairs, she had taken them to task, particularly Nikolai. 'You are too much like your father,' she had said, 'you drink too much and get yourself, and others, into trouble. You cannot go through life doing this! What if that silly, simpering girl who couldn't take her eyes off you all evening had died?'

As he so often had in the past, Nikolai made a fulsome apology and swore he had learnt his lesson. And just as she had so many times before, including that time a week after his father's death when he had borrowed her car in Paris without asking her and crashed it, she absolved him. Because that's what a parent does. Even a step-parent. And that meant she would fight like a tiger to ensure the finger of blame was not pointed at him, or Irina. Loyalty and family pride meant as much to her as it did to Alastair and his friends, and she would not tolerate any criticism levelled at her stepchildren.

Irina had wanted to pack up her things and leave immediately, but that was not Valentina's way; running away was the act of a coward and, in this instance, it would insinuate guilt. She had been adamant that they stay out of the way under the pretence of sleeping off their hangovers, and then present a united front, before leaving tomorrow as originally intended.

It was annoying that this turn of events had occurred, but she would not let it derail her campaign to win Alastair.

Only when she was back up at the house did she realise that she'd left the key for Orla's studio in the door. Oh well, no matter, nobody would think it was she who had gone there.

44

It had been hard for Alastair to revisit Linston Broad. Not since Orla's body had been found there had he returned. He simply hadn't had the courage.

Danny had proposed he and Frankie should do the job of fetching *Swallowtail*, but Alastair had known he had to face his demons and brave the waters that had claimed the life of his wife, and very nearly Rachel's. He had also needed something to do, something that stopped him thinking of the barrage of unthinkable what ifs . . .

What if Rachel had drowned?

What if Jenna had drowned in her attempt to rescue her friend?

What if his friends had lost both their daughters and blamed him?

The way Simon had looked at him when he'd put Rachel in the car to take her to the hospital had rocked him, had left him in no doubt that Simon would want retribution for nearly losing Rachel.

Taking the launch out with Danny and Frankie had been a distraction from the awful waiting for news about Rachel. He had left numerous messages on Simon and Sorrel's mobiles, but had heard nothing back from them. He was convinced they were deliberately ignoring him. Danny had tried to reassure him that he shouldn't read too much into the prolonged silence; neither he nor Frankie had heard anything either. But what if the silence was because the news was the worst kind to deliver, that Rachel had suffered permanent and maybe life-threatening side-effects as a result of nearly drowning?

It was while entering the broad, and with Alastair consciously trying to think of anything but Orla and the nightmares he suffered so frequently — of his ineffectual attempts to save her, and those taunting words of hers, that it had been nothing but a prank on her part — that Frankie had received a text from Jenna saying Rachel was now home and appeared to be okay.

Relief had made Alastair want to reach for his own mobile and ring Simon, but he'd decided to wait until he could speak to him face-to-face. The relief of hearing the good news had served to make him momentarily forget Orla.

Now, as he and Danny finished securing the boats in the dyke, he could only hope the worst of Simon's anger had cooled, that relief would make him understand that no one was to blame; it was an accident. He also hoped that Valentina had not minded him leaving her alone. He hadn't wanted her anywhere near him when he was in the broad where Orla had drowned.

Walking up the garden towards the house with Danny and Frankie either side of him, he suddenly felt like he was carrying the weight of the world on his shoulders. Nothing was as he thought it would be. Returning from his time away, so full of hope and renewed energy, the prospect of a new life spent with Valentina had seemed so wonderfully uncomplicated. And so right. As though his whole life had been leading to meeting this extraordinary woman.

Was it nothing but a sharp dose of reality he was now experiencing? Had he been a fool to think it could be as easy as he'd imagined, that two very different lives could be brought together without a few hitches along the way?

He came to an abrupt stop. 'Do you think I'm making a mistake?' he said.

Danny and Frankie stopped walking and looked at him, both visibly startled at his candour.

'Tell me honestly,' he said, when neither replied, but glanced briefly at one another. 'Why do I get the feeling it's all turning to shit?'

'It's not,' said Frankie, putting a hand on his forearm. 'And perhaps now isn't the time to question things. Let's go and see the others.'

'Of course,' he said with a shake of his head, 'I'm being selfish, thinking of myself.'

'You're not being selfish,' said Frankie. 'It's understandable that you should have doubts when you're on the verge of taking such a massive step.'

'It's not doubts exactly,' Alastair said, 'it's disappointment. I thought you'd all be happy for me.'

'Look,' said Danny with surprising firmness, 'we've all had a hell of a shock in the last twelve hours, and Frankie's right, now isn't the time for this conversation, or for you to question things.'

Again Alastair shook his head. 'You always

were the wise one of the three of us.'

Danny smiled. 'Not difficult, given who I'm up against.'

'Cheeky sod.'

'An exceptionally wise cheeky sod, I think you'll find.'

They'd only walked on a few yards when Alastair said, 'Do you believe Nikolai and Irina are to blame?'

It was Frankie who answered him. 'It was an accident, Alastair, they may have been reckless, but it wouldn't be fair to heap the blame on them.'

'Would you say that if it had been Jenna who nearly drowned?'

'I'd like to think so.'

Alastair wasn't convinced. 'But we know that if they hadn't suggested going out in the boat the accident wouldn't have happened. They were the catalyst. Good God,' he said with a weary shake of his head, 'when I think how Orla and I drummed it into the three children when you entrusted them to stay with us every summer, never *ever* to take unnecessary risks when out on the water. What the hell went wrong?'

'It was a bad judgement call on Rachel's part,' answered Frankie, 'and carelessness on Nikolai and Irina's, but not vindictiveness. They did not come here with the intention of hurting anybody; it would be madness to suggest they did.'

'But what the hell made them want to go and see where Orla drowned?'

'Morbid curiosity I expect,' said Danny with a

shrug. 'Wouldn't we have done the same at their age after an evening of drinking?'

These were all points he must put to Simon, Alastair thought, as once again they continued towards the house. But would Simon listen? He was such a hothead, would he listen to logic, or would he be led by his heart?

But then who was he to accuse Simon of being led by his heart, hadn't he done exactly that when he met Valentina? Hadn't he always done it? First Orla, then Valentina?

But not Sorrel. Poor Sorrel. She was the exception. She had had nothing to do with his heart. Had she ever forgiven him? Or was that arrogant of him to assume she still gave a thought to his cruelty? And he had been cruel. Unconscionably cruel. To an extent he could clear his conscience with regard to his first act of unkindness, on the grounds that had he not cast her aside in favour of Orla, she wouldn't have married Simon and there would be no Callum and Rachel. His second act of callousness, and his most regrettable, was not so easy to dismiss.

'Things always work out in the end for the best,' Valentina had said only last night when they'd gone to bed, oblivious to the drama about to unfold. He hoped to God that was true, because at this precise moment nothing felt right. He wasn't given to bouts of defeatism, but he felt as though everything was stacked against him, that the life he'd set his heart on with Valentina was fast slipping out of his grasp.

From nowhere he heard Orla laughing at him. Laughing at his naïve belief that he could have imagined she would let him go so easily.

'*You're mine . . . you've always been mine, and you'll always be mine . . .* '

Those were the words they used to exchange with each other with such loving passion. They were the last words she said to him before she drowned, but they had not been uttered with loving passion. Far from it.

45

As he followed Frankie and Alastair through the open doors of the conservatory, Danny braced himself for what lay ahead.

Never keen on confrontation, having spent too much of his childhood exposed to it while being shunted around children's homes and foster families, he was determined to ensure that the tension which had been steadily building was not about to explode into a situation that could never be recovered from.

Danny couldn't honestly say he had taken a great liking to Valentina, but for the sake of Alastair's happiness he knew he had to make more of an effort to think well of her. After that exchange in the garden just now, Danny sensed the first chink in Alastair's certainty. Had Simon been there, he would have jumped on it, but Danny knew better; a softly-softly approach was by far the more effective course of action.

God knows he wanted his old friend to be happy, to find love again and start afresh, but not at the expense of everything else he'd previously held dear. Or was that a presumption on Danny's part, that what used to be important to Alastair, was still?

Wasn't starting afresh something he wanted to do in moving here to the Broads? Why was it acceptable for him and Frankie to up sticks, but not for Alastair? Because bluntly, it didn't feel right what Alastair was doing, it was too much too soon. He was a man still grieving, a man still coming to terms with the death of his wife and in such tragic circumstances. Danny had seen how he had reacted when they'd entered the broad where Orla had drowned — the whiteness of his knuckles as he clenched his fists, and the ghastly look of foreboding on his face. He'd looked haunted, almost as if he was terrified they might come across Orla's dead body floating in the water. Even if it had been an irrational fear, it had felt real enough for Danny to be aware of it.

How could anyone be trusted to make a life-changing decision when clearly still in the grip of such a tragic loss?

There was nobody about on the ground floor of the house, just the appetising smell coming from the kitchen of bacon having recently been cooked, and so, taking Alastair's lead, they ventured upstairs. They'd made it to the top of the stairs when a door to their right opened and Valentina appeared, followed by Nikolai and Irina. As the two of them took up a position either side of their stepmother, it felt weirdly like a stand-off with all six of them facing each other.

It was Irina who spoke first. 'Alastair,' she said, her voice low and husky, her expression pained, 'how is Rachel? You must have all been so upset and concerned. Is there anything we can do? We feel just awful over what happened.'

She was either a very good actress, or she meant what she said, and she and her brother were genuinely contrite. Danny's opinion made a sharp U-turn though when Nikolai spoke.

'If I'd known how drunk Rachel was,' he said, 'I would never have allowed her to get into the boat. Or to go swimming.' His affected smooth tone left Danny in no doubt that he didn't give a damn about Rachel; he was only interested in exonerating himself and shifting the blame entirely onto her.

'If you'd rather we left,' said Irina, 'please say and we'll go.'

'Yes,' drawled Nikolai, 'we would hate to make anyone feel uncomfortable, as I believe we have already.'

'I'm sure there's no need for that,' said Valentina, her gaze on Alastair, 'isn't that so, darling?'

'Of course not,' he said.

'There,' said Valentina to her stepchildren, 'I told you there was no need to overreact. Now why don't you come downstairs with me and I'll make you some coffee? Is that all right with you, Alastair?'

'Of course,' he said. 'As I said before, you must make yourselves at home here. I'll join you in a bit; first I want to see Rachel.'

'Please tell her we were asking after her,' said Irina.

All very cleverly stage-managed, was what Danny thought of their performance, as did Frankie, judging from the inscrutable expression on her face. But at least they were playing at being conciliatory, which was something.

Alastair led the way along the landing, his glance straying fleetingly over his shoulder to watch Valentina and the others go downstairs. It was anybody's guess what he was thinking.

Sorrel opened the door to them after Alastair gave it a discreet knock. They crowded in and Danny was particularly pleased to see Rachel sitting up in bed looking better than he expected her to.

Alastair went straight over and crouched down beside the bed. 'How are you feeling?'

'How the hell do you think she feels?' snapped Simon.

'Dad, remember what I said. No blaming anyone else, it was my fault. And I couldn't be more embarrassed, or ashamed. I'm sorry for all the trouble I've caused.'

'Don't apologise,' said Alastair. 'We're just all so relieved you're okay. So how do you feel?'

'Wrecked. Like my chest has been kicked in and my lungs stripped out with bleach. But apart from that, just fine. I know I was lucky, Uncle Al. Maybe luckier than I deserve.'

Behind Alastair, Sorrel tutted. 'Don't say that, Rachel. Not ever.'

'Your mother's right,' Alastair agreed. He looked across to the other bed, to where Jenna was sitting. 'You did well, Jenna, that was incredibly brave what you did.'

'I just did what I had to,' she said. 'And Dad needs to take his share of the credit, if he hadn't come to see what we were doing, and picked up Blake on the way, well . . . ' her voice trailed off and she pursed her lips, then chewed on a thumbnail.

'You're right,' Alastair said. 'Danny's instinct to go out looking for you was spot on, and I think we should find a way to thank your friend Blake properly.'

Rachel smirked. 'Best way to do that would be to let him perform CPR on Jenna.'

Alastair smiled. 'Oh, it's like that, is it?'

Jenna glared at Rachel. 'No it isn't! And I think the lack of oxygen must have got to a certain person's brain.'

Rachel sniggered, causing Danny to look askance at his wife. This was news to him that there might be something going on between Blake and their daughter. But then that was typical Jenna; she rarely gave away more information than she considered necessary. Frankie gave him a small shake of her head. Plainly she didn't know anything either.

'I think Rachel should have some proper rest now,' said Sorrel.

'Do I have to, Mum?'

'Yes. And that's my final word on the subject.'

They were all making a move towards the door, when Alastair said, 'Irina and Nikolai wanted you to know they were asking after you; they're both very upset by what happened.'

'I bet they are,' muttered Simon darkly, throwing Alastair a murderous look.

'Dad,' warned Rachel. 'I thought you'd promised to play nicely.'

'Just a slip of the tongue, that was all. Take no notice of me.' He went back and kissed her on the cheek. 'Now go to sleep and your mother and I will check on you later.'

He loves her so much, thought Danny, was it any wonder he'd wanted to lash out at the nearest person he could to blame? And wouldn't Danny do the same if it were Jenna?

His arm around his daughter's shoulders, he said, 'So tell me about this Blake character, then?'

'Dad, not you as well!'

He smiled. 'At least we'd know you were in good hands.'

'Stop it.'

'Yes,' agreed Frankie, 'stop meddling, Daniel.'

'Uh-oh, I know I'm in trouble when she calls me Daniel.'

'And rightly so. You know jolly well it's my job to meddle in such matters, not yours.'

Jenna shook her head. 'Honestly, you two are as bad as one another.'

'Always happy to take a compliment,' smiled Danny. 'Happy to eat something too. Breakfast seems a long time ago. Alastair, what's the plan for lunch?'

He gave Danny a bewildered look. 'I'm afraid I haven't thought that far ahead.'

'How about Simon and I go to the shops and get what we need for a barbecue, something easy, burgers and sausages, and maybe some steaks?'

'Yes, and your poor old heart will just love that, won't it?' said Frankie.

He groaned. 'Please don't suggest a salad. I need more than that. Simon, come on, help me out here. Back me up.'

They were at the top of the stairs and Danny was working hard to inject some levity into the proceedings. Trouble was, everyone else knew exactly what he was doing and the false note of his cheerful banter was clanging with all the subtlety of a fire alarm. Help came from an unexpected source.

'Why don't you three go off together?' said Sorrel. 'Frankie, Jenna and I can get things organised here.'

'Somebody should be with Rachel.'

'Simon,' she said tiredly, 'go and get some fresh air. I'll put my head round Rachel's door every fifteen minutes to check on her.'

He grunted and started off down the stairs.

'Perhaps you could ask Valentina to help you all?' said Alastair, standing back to let Sorrel go ahead of him. 'You know, as a way to make her feel more included.'

Sorrel stared at him as if he'd just handed her a plate of dog excrement. 'As if she hasn't done enough to help already,' she said sourly, following Simon and leaving Alastair to look awkwardly at Danny and Frankie.

'Well then,' said Danny, suddenly catching his breath, when they were downstairs, 'shall we drive or take a boat?' He fought the urge to clutch a hand to his chest, feeling the pressure building inside his ribcage, reminding him of the old pressure cooker he and Frankie were given as a wedding present. For twenty years it worked perfectly, never gave them a moment's trouble, then one day, without warning, it exploded, sending a lamb casserole flying into the air. This tension wasn't doing him any good, he thought. Frankie was right; he had to stop caring so much. It wasn't his job to solve everyone else's problems.

340

'Simon?' asked Alastair. 'What would you like to do?'

'Your house, your rules, you decide. It's not as if you'd take any notice of what I say anyway.'

Alastair sighed like a man at the end of his tether. Or a man counting to ten to keep his patience in check.

'Let's take *Swallowtail*,' suggested Danny. 'It might have a calming effect on us all.'

★ ★ ★

They were cruising towards Horning when they spotted Callum coming out from the boatyard. They each slowed their boats, easing back the throttle and slipping into neutral.

'I know I only spoke to her a short while ago,' said Callum, 'but I have a spare hour, so thought I'd go and see Rachel. Where are you off to?'

'The butcher's,' said Alastair. 'Danny's idea is to have a barbecue for a late lunch, can you join us?'

'I'm afraid not, I have to go to Norwich. I wondered if maybe Jenna might like to come with me for a change of scene. That's if she doesn't mind leaving Rachel.'

'You can but ask,' said Danny.

They'd only gone a short distance along the river when they saw Blake and his mother coming towards them. Once again they slowed their speed and idled the engine.

'How's Rachel?' asked Laura. 'Blake heard from Jenna that she was back from the hospital.'

'She's in bed resting,' replied Simon. He

shoved his hands into his pockets and looked at Blake. 'Thank you for what you did. You saved our daughter's life and my wife and I will always be grateful to you for that.'

Blake gave an embarrassed shrug of his shoulders, but his mother smiled, and not without justifiable pride, in Danny's opinion. 'I was wondering,' she said, her gaze now on Alastair, 'and when Rachel is feeling up to it, if you'd all like to come over to the Mill for a drink some time.'

'We'd be happy to,' replied Alastair, 'if our party isn't too much for you.' He looked at Simon, as if seeking his approval.

Simon clamped his jaw shut and studiously avoided his gaze, at the same time thrusting his hands deeper still into his pockets; any deeper and he'd be touching his kneecaps.

When they were once more on their way, Danny couldn't help but think that if it had been a woman like Laura Manning who had come into Alastair's life, things would be very different.

46

Rachel lay in bed trying to sleep. Her body was exhausted and craved the kind of oblivion only the deepest of sleeps would bring. But her mind just wouldn't untangle itself; it was like a jumble of wire coat-hangers that refused to come apart and just kept on clanging noisily inside her head.

In an attempt to stop her parents worrying, she had made light of the pain she was in; but lying here alone, all she could think of was how awful she felt. Her lungs and throat felt as if they had been rubbed raw with sandpaper and every time she coughed, it was as if a knife was being thrust between her ribs. She had been told at the hospital that ribs were often cracked when CPR was carried out.

Yet perhaps what caused her the most pain was the knowledge of what she had put her parents through, and Jenna too. And all because she had been so intent on flirting with Nikolai; of trying to impress him. Was it to be her role in life, always to be the pathetic airhead of the group? Why couldn't she be more like Jenna, or her brother?

She had a sense of this being the turning point in her life, when finally she realised it was time to grow up: no more playing the giddy goat, as her father used to describe her.

There was a soft knock at the door and hoping

it might be Jenna defying her parents' instructions that she should be left to rest, she said, 'Come in, I'm not asleep.'

But it wasn't Jenna; it was Callum.

'Tell me to go away if you'd rather,' he said, hovering in the doorway.

Only too happy to see him, Rachel eased herself into a sitting position. 'No, no, come in, please. And then cheer me up.'

'Not before I tell you what a bloody idiot you've been.' He shook his head. 'I know you never like to do things by halves, Rachel, but this was definitely a step too far. And worse still, you endangered Jenna's life into the bargain. What if she'd drowned?'

It was a refreshing change for somebody to be brutally honest with her, to treat her normally and without kid gloves. 'There's nothing you can say that will make me feel any stupider, or more guilty than I already feel,' she said.

He sat on the edge of her bed and regarded her severely.

'Well, that's a move in the right direction,' he said, 'I'm pleased to hear it. So stern words over, I gather it wasn't entirely your fault, that you were egged on by Nikolai and Irina.'

'I'm not going to use them as an excuse, Cal. Drunk or not, it was absolutely my fault. Poor Jenna, she tried to stop me, but I wouldn't listen. I was actually quite nasty to her.'

'She's forgiven you, I'm sure.'

'But do I deserve her forgiveness? I mean, like you just said, I put her life at risk too. What if we'd both drowned?' Tears filled her eyes. 'I'm such a failure, Cal; I get everything wrong. Why can't I be more like you?'

He passed her a tissue from the box on the bedside table. 'One massive error of judgement does not constitute you being written off as a failure. And frankly,' he added with a grin, 'you could never hope to attain my level of perfection, not in a million years.'

She sniffed and smiled back at him. 'Pig.'

'That's more like it. Now then, how soon before you'll be up and annoying us all again?'

'I'm not staying here in bed any longer than I have to. But the thing is, and don't you dare breathe a word of this to Mum or Dad, my chest hurts like hell, inside and out. If Blake hadn't saved my life, I'd have him for assault, I'm black and blue.'

'Better a few bruises than the alternative. From what I hear, it was pretty impressive what he did.'

'Yeah well, I had no idea what was going on, but what I'm told is that I wouldn't be here now if he hadn't known what to do.'

Callum suddenly looked serious. 'What was it like?'

'What was what like?'

'I'm trying to be sensitive here. What was it like coming so close to, well, you know . . . ' His voice trailed away.

'Death?'

He nodded.

'Tunnels and white lights, you mean?'

'Were there any?'

She shook her head. 'Not that I was aware of.

345

It was just darkness. But before that, I could have sworn Orla was there with me. Except she wasn't saving me, she was taking me further down into the water, as though she wanted me to be with her.'

'You were probably hallucinating, or something close to it.'

'Jenna reckons it was when she had grabbed hold of me and my brain was all over the place with lack of oxygen.'

'Sounds eminently feasible, and just as likely that you would associate drowning with Orla.'

Rachel scrunched the tissue she'd just used into a small hard ball. 'It's a horrific way to die, Cal,' she said. 'I keep thinking of Orla and how awful it must have been for her.'

'I don't think that's something you should dwell on,' he said, 'not after what you've been through.' He took the screwed up tissue from her and tossed it into the wastepaper basket.

'But that's just the point. After what I've gone through it's hard not to think of Orla. I keep wondering if her death really was an accident? Do you suppose Alastair asks himself the same thing?'

Callum got to his feet and went over to the window. With his back to her, he said, 'Orla was always an up and down sort of person, for all we know she might have hit a particularly low point and wasn't thinking straight.'

'So you *do* think she could have committed suicide?'

He turned around. 'I didn't say that, and really what's the point in going over it? Intentional or

346

not, she's dead and that's an end to it. Let's talk about something else. After all, you did want me to cheer you up.'

Rachel glanced towards the door, which Callum had left ajar when he came in.

'Do you want me to close it?' he asked.

'Yes.'

When he had, and he was sitting on the bed again, she said, 'I want to talk to you about Jenna.'

She saw a flash of wariness in his eyes. 'Oh yes,' he said lightly, 'anything in particular about her?'

'Yes. You need to be proactive.'

'In what respect?'

'Don't be obtuse,' Rachel said, noting how his body had stiffened at her words. 'I've seen the way you've been looking at her.'

The colour flooded his cheeks. 'Where's all this come from?'

'I know I'm not considered the bright one of the two of us, but I've never been slow in saying what I think, and I reckon you need to be honest with Jenna before it's too late.'

'Are you talking about our friend over at the Mill?' he said.

'You know perfectly well I am.'

'What about Jenna? How does she feel about Blake?'

'She keeps going on about him being a work colleague and therefore out of bounds, but I'm not convinced.'

His brows drawn, Callum said, 'What gave me away?'

'I'm your sister. I know that look that comes into your eyes when you're interested in a girl.

I've seen it a few times in the last few days. You've been looking at Jenna differently to how you used to.'

'That's as maybe, but I've already hinted that I'd like to be more than that and she didn't leap at the suggestion.'

'Perhaps she needs more encouragement from you. Something more tangible than merely a hint?'

He looked doubtful. 'Even if that's true, I always come back to the same sticking point, that it would turn everything weird between Jenna and me if we changed gears and became a couple.'

Rachel stared at him. 'Does it feel weird at the moment?'

He smiled. 'Coming so close to dying has sharpened your perspective, I'd say.'

'Yeah, I'm reborn.' She suddenly yawned, then grimaced at the pain it caused in her chest.

'You're tired,' he said, 'I should leave you to sleep.' When she didn't dispute this, he stood up. 'Thanks for the chat, little sis.'

She snuggled down into the bed, overcome with weariness, her eyelids already closing. 'My pleasure. And think hard about what I've said.'

Her last thought before succumbing to sleep was that she did feel strangely reborn. Knowing that life could suddenly be snatched away so easily had given her the ability to see things through different eyes. Clearer eyes.

★ ★ ★

There had been no sign of Jenna when he'd arrived, but now Callum found her alone in the garden sitting on the wooden bench overlooking the river. Was it his imagination, or was she staring out across the water at the Mill? Was she thinking of Blake? He could hardly blame her if she was. The guy had saved her best friend's life after all.

By rights Callum should be jealous of the man, but he wasn't. The truth was, he liked Blake and could easily imagine them enjoying a drink together.

But was Rachel, not ordinarily known for her wisdom and discernment, right to say he should be proactive? And how could he, after the chat he and Jenna had had two days ago? A line had been drawn and surely there was no crossing back over it? It seemed to him that their roles had been defined a long time ago and to step out of character now was just too risky.

Look at what was happening amongst their parents as a result of Alastair behaving out of character — Dad was all over the place, Mum was claiming Valentina was the devil incarnate, Frankie and Danny were suddenly planning to leave Suffolk to move here to the Broads, and his sister had very nearly got herself drowned!

He ran a hand through his hair. Was it any wonder people preferred to stay in their safe little ruts, living their safe little lives the way they always had?

So no, he thought with conviction, as he approached Jenna, he wouldn't do as his sister advised. He'd continue just as before.

Unless Jenna herself chose to change the status quo.

She turned, as though alerted by some sixth sense that he was there. 'Hi, Callum,' she said, 'have you been to see Rachel?'

'Yes. I left her nodding off, having thoroughly exhausted her with catching up on all that's been going on. I don't know, I leave you for a few hours, and look what happens.'

She gave him a small, sad smile. 'Time to sit and chat for a while?'

'Just for a few minutes. I have to go to Norwich; don't suppose you fancy coming along for the ride?'

He saw the hesitation in her face. 'That's okay,' he said hurriedly. 'It was only a thought.'

'I'm not sure I'd be very good company right now.'

'Jenna, you're always good company.'

She smiled properly now. 'You know what I mean. I'm whacked, not having slept. Oh look, there's Alastair and the others back from Horning. We're having a barbecue by way of a late lunch, are you sure you can't stay?'

He watched Alastair expertly swing *Swallowtail* into the dyke that ran parallel with the length of the garden, and where a group of Greylag geese were pecking at the grass. 'No, I'd better get on. Lots to do.'

'Are you joining us this evening?' she asked.

'I expect so, somebody has to keep an eye on Rachel after all.'

She looked affronted. 'I did my best last night.'

'Hey, I'm sorry. That came out all wrong. I was being flippant.' He instantly plonked himself down on the bench next to her. 'Jenna, you did a fantastic job last night; I know that. As does everyone else. I also know that if it weren't for you and Blake, Rachel wouldn't be here now with us.'

'What would you have done had you been here last night? I keep thinking I should have been firmer with them all, that I should have stopped them from wanting to go out on the river. I certainly shouldn't have let them talk me into taking them into the broad. I knew it was madness, but they ganged up on me, which makes me sound woefully feeble.'

'There's nothing feeble about you. As for what I would have done,' he said thoughtfully, 'it's a good question. I'd probably have punched Nikolai's smug face and laid him out cold, but that's the thug in me.'

'You're no thug, Callum.'

'Trust me, when riled I can be pretty thuggish. You've never seen me in full flow when handling a boat of lads who've been on the pop for forty-eight hours.'

'Really? Now I'm beginning to see you in a new light.'

He smiled. 'Nah, same old me, just tapping into some of Dad's temper, which I've inherited and fall back on when it's needed. Anyway, if you've forgiven me for my crass comment, I'd better get on. Sure you don't want a break from the madhouse?'

'Another time maybe,' she said with a smile, 'if the offer is repeated, or something similar?'

'Of course.'

He was halfway up the lawn when he spotted

Nikolai and Irina coming out of the house with Valentina. Knowing he had nothing good to say to them, he made for his boat, passing his father and the others as he did so.

'Gotta dash,' he said cheerfully. 'I'll see you all later this evening.'

'You couldn't persuade Jenna to go with you, then?' enquired Danny.

'No,' said Callum, 'I think she's in need of some quiet time after last night.'

Steering his boat out of the dyke, he waved goodbye to Jenna. She looked such a forlorn figure sitting there on her own, he was suddenly consumed with the desire to turn around and go back to her. And to hell with some imaginary line!

47

They had only been sitting down for a short while to eat when the first fat drops of rain began to fall.

The clouds had been steadily gathering, large and ominous, but in true British fashion they had stuck it out. Now, and like scurrying mice, they fled the garden, carrying their plates of food and glasses of wine with them. By the time they had made it to the shelter of the house, the rain was coming down with sufficient force as to resemble a tropical monsoon.

In the kitchen, a cacophony of crockery and cutlery being clattered onto the table competed with the noise of the downpour, along with breathless gasps and rain being shaken from hair and clothes. It was a few moments before everyone was seated and they resumed eating.

Before, when they had been sitting at the table in the garden, Jenna had been uncomfortably aware of the tension hanging over the group, much like a thundery cloud. She was sure she wasn't alone in wanting to point the finger of blame at the strangers amongst them — *Until you came, we never had anything like this happen to us!*

But their sudden run for cover had cut through the tension and now the atmosphere was less charged, as though they had left some of their resentment out in the garden. But would it last? Or would it take just one wrong word or gesture to ignite them into an explosion of saying what they all really thought of each other.

She for one could not look at Nikolai and Irina without thinking of their utter indifference to the near tragedy they were responsible for setting in motion. Neither of them had spoken to her directly, but then she had not gone out of her way to invite conversation. Sitting here with them made her feel uncomfortable, made her wish she could be upstairs with Rachel, watching over her as she slept.

'This reminds me of that time when we were caught in the rain in the garden and Orla refused to come in,' said Sorrel. 'Do you remember, Alastair, she danced on the lawn? We'd been celebrating something, hadn't we? What was it?'

The mood around the table changed in an instant.

'I'm not sure I remember,' Alastair replied without looking up.

'I can picture Orla now,' Sorrel continued, 'she was spinning around like a Whirling Dervish.'

'I know what we were celebrating,' said Simon. 'It was Alastair and Orla's silver wedding anniversary.'

'That's right,' said Sorrel. 'It had been a year of us all celebrating twenty-five years of marriage.'

'If you're trying to make a point, why don't you just come right out and say it?'

This was from Nikolai, his dark eyes fixed on Sorrel across the table.

'I'm not making any kind of a point,' she said.

'I'm merely reminiscing. Or is that something else we're to be denied?'

'Sorrel, please, you're being deliberately provocative.'

She stared at Alastair. 'Am I?'

'You know you are.'

'I'm intrigued to know more,' said Valentina, entering the fray. 'What in particular is it you feel you're being denied, Sorrel?'

Before she could answer, there was a loud ring of the front doorbell. As if startled out of his seat, Alastair jumped up. 'Can I suggest this conversation is curtailed as of now?'

Nobody responded, but once he was gone, Danny said, 'Alastair's right, we're all uptight from last night, and while emotions are still running high, let's not say anything we'll come to regret.'

'I'd say it's a bit late for that, isn't it?' remarked Nikolai. 'I'd go so far as to say that you should all have the decency to say what you're really feeling, which is mostly resentment towards my stepmother being here.'

'Darling,' said Valentina, her voice low, 'there's no need to rush to my defence.'

'I disagree,' he replied. 'Strikes me that somebody has to stick up for you with this lot.'

'Niki's right,' said his sister. 'And it's not just you, Valentina, who they resent, it's us as well. And we've done nothing wrong.'

'Nothing wrong,' said Simon, who until now had been strangely quiet. 'You have to be kidding me.'

'Please don't argue,' murmured Jenna. 'It

won't help matters.' Much as she'd wanted Nikolai and Irina held to account, she didn't think this was the right way to go about it. But then what would be the right way?

'I think you have a nerve to sit there and claim to be victims,' said Sorrel, ignoring Jenna's plea. 'Because of you, my daughter is lying upstairs in bed lucky to be alive.'

'At last, the finger has been pointed,' said Nikolai with a satisfied sneer. 'The wonder is it's taken this long for somebody to come right out and blame us.'

'Please,' said Frankie, echoing Jenna's plea, 'none of this should be said.'

'No, it really shouldn't,' agreed Danny. 'Let's just eat our lunch.'

Valentina shook her head. 'I disagree, I think everyone should be honest and air their thoughts, and maybe then we can get beyond the friction which my relationship with Alastair is causing you. And which is perfectly understandable, given your history together.'

Jenna cringed. The reasonableness of the woman made the rest of them seem so embarrassingly rude and petty. 'This isn't who we are,' Jenna said, looking around the table, notably at Sorrel. 'We don't fight like this. We just don't!' Her voice had taken on an embarrassingly shrill tone and she realised she was irrationally near to tears.

Her father looked at her with concern, as did her mother.

'No, we don't fight,' said Sorrel, 'we do something far worse; we push things under the rug and pretend they don't exist. It's what we've

356

always done. Maybe Nikolai is right and it's time for some honesty amongst us. God knows it would make me feel better.'

Jenna didn't know what Sorrel was getting at, but judging from the expression on Alastair's face as he came back into the room, he did.

'Do you have something specific to say, Sorrel?' asked Valentina.

'Sorrel, I'd advise you to stop right now.'

'No, Alastair, I won't. It's time things were said. Orla never made you happy. And this woman' — she pointed at Valentina — 'won't either.'

'Simon, Sorrel is obviously still upset about Rachel, please take her upstairs and — '

'And what, Alastair?' demanded Sorrel, springing to her feet. 'What precisely do you want Simon to do? Carry on living in ignorance of how we've betrayed him? Is that what you want?'

'You're talking rubbish, Sorrel. You're upset and over-wrought. For the sake of everybody else, just stop.'

Her face set like a mask, her hands balled into fists at her sides, her knuckles white, she squared up to Alastair. Jenna didn't think she had ever seen Sorrel look so formidable. 'And what if I don't?' she said. 'What if after all this time, Alastair, I want to be honest?'

'Well, this is interesting,' drawled Nikolai with insufferable insouciance. 'Who knew lunch today would turn out to be this much fun?'

'I really wouldn't,' said Simon in a low growl. 'If you had any manners, you'd keep quiet.'

Nikolai laughed. It was a horribly patronising laugh and Jenna expected it to send Simon into a fury. But he barely reacted. He just sat there staring at Sorrel, and then Alastair.

Jenna tried to make sense of what Sorrel had just said. What betrayal? How could she and Alastair have betrayed Simon? There seemed only one answer to the question, but she couldn't bring herself to accept it.

'We'll deal with this later,' said Alastair in a shockingly grim tone of voice. 'For now, I have people in the hall who have come to view the house. I forgot about the appointment, so if you'd just go and make sure your rooms are relatively tidy, I'll show them round down here. Will you do that for me, please?'

Given the precarious atmosphere Sorrel had created, his request felt bizarrely surreal, and weirder still when Simon rose from his chair and said, 'They can't go in Rachel's bedroom.'

'I'll tidy the kitchen,' offered Jenna, now that everybody was on their feet.

'There's no need,' said Valentina, already reaching for plates and effectively forcing Jenna to step out of the way, 'I shall do that with Nikolai and Irina's help.'

Made to feel that she had no right to be there, Jenna climbed the stairs behind her parents with a heavy heart. Simon and Sorrel were ahead of them and muttering furiously at each other.

Back down in the hall, Jenna heard Alastair apologising to the couple for keeping them waiting, then suggesting they might like to see the sitting room first.

'No need to apologise,' said the woman. 'Oh, darling, just look at the view of the river. And there's a windmill too. Goodness, how could you possibly move from here?'

Jenna would have liked to hear Alastair's reply, but she kept moving forwards until she was outside the room she shared with Rachel, and where Sorrel was now looking in. Simon had disappeared inside the room he and Sorrel always stayed in.

'She's still asleep,' Sorrel said. 'Better you don't go in and disturb her.'

'I promise I'll be quiet,' said Jenna, determined to be with her friend. She was suddenly tired of people telling others what they could and could not do, and anyway, where else was she going to go while Alastair was showing the potential buyers around the house?

Sorrel looked far from pleased, as though recognising she was being challenged, but after a split second of hesitation, she stepped back to allow Jenna to pass. 'Come and get me if she wakes.'

Once inside, Jenna closed the door and went and hovered over Rachel to make sure she was all right. She then sat on her bed and checked her mobile, which she'd left charging and switched to silent mode. Blake had texted. *How's it going over there?*

She tapped in her response. *Pretty bad.*

Almost instantly he replied. *With Rachel?*

No. She's sleeping. It's everyone else that's the problem.

Sorry to hear that. Anything I can do to help?

If only it were that easy, thought Jenna. *It's complicated,'* she wrote.

Do you fancy escaping? The rain's easing off now. I could come over for you.

Jenna hesitated. She really didn't want to leave Rachel, but since her friend was fast asleep, and since she didn't want to get caught up in any more unpleasantness, or think how Sorrel and Alastair might have betrayed Simon, she decided to accept Blake's invitation.

Give me ten minutes and I'll be down at the entrance to the dyke.

Excellent!

48

Sorrel had seen Blake picking Jenna up in the dyke and soon after, Frankie and Danny had announced that since the rain had stopped, they would go into Wroxham and see what the estate agents there had to offer.

Their sudden departure, along with Jenna's, had seemed to be carried out with indecent haste, as though the three of them couldn't get away fast enough. But perhaps she couldn't blame them after the scene she had caused in the kitchen. She hadn't intended to say what she had, but once provoked there had been no going back. Years of anger and resentment had spilled out of her and she hadn't cared one iota about the consequences. And it had felt so good to see the look of abject horror on Alastair's face.

She had no idea where Simon was, but Valentina was still in the kitchen with Nikolai and Irina.

From her position at the top of the stairs, standing back so she couldn't be seen, Sorrel could hear Alastair down in the hall charming the couple viewing the house into buying it. He was labouring the point that it had been the most idyllic of homes, but after the tragic loss of his wife, it was time for him to start afresh somewhere new. It seemed an unnecessary amount of information to impart to strangers, but she supposed it was a mark of his keenness to escape his old life.

He could run, thought Sorrel, as she turned to go and check on her daughter, but he would never be able to forget. Just as she would never forget, or forgive him for the way he'd treated her. For the way he had used her.

Observing Rachel sleeping on her side like a contented baby, something the poor girl had never actually been — sleep had been anathema to her until she was nearly three years old — Sorrel's heart contracted with love for her daughter. And guilty regret that she had not been able to protect Rachel when she'd most needed protection.

It was a fact that mothers are wired to feel guilty about anything and everything to do with their children, even when it's not their fault, but until now, Sorrel had never felt such a crucifying sense of blame for failing her child. Why hadn't she predicted the trouble Rachel was going to get herself into? Why had it been Danny who had had a feeling that something might happen? How could she have slept when her daughter was drowning?

She pressed her hands to her mouth to try and stifle the involuntary cry that escaped her lips. Her darling daughter, always the one to get herself into a scrape, whether it was tumbling down the stairs when she was little, or flooding the bathroom as a teenager when she'd left the taps running, or falling in love at the drop of a hat. Poor hapless Rachel, searching for that elusive great love of her life.

With a weary sigh, she sat down heavily on

Jenna's bed and, suddenly consumed with tiredness, she lay back on top of the duvet. She was mentally exhausted, and not just with worry for Rachel. She was tired of all the lies and the pretence. And the guilt.

★　★　★

It began with a drink in a bar during a skiing holiday in Meribel. She had been there with her parents, her brother, his then girlfriend and her mother's sister and her family who owned a chalet in the resort. On this particular evening they had been at a typical Alpine bar where loud music was playing and the après ski was in full swing. It had been Sorrel's twentieth birthday and her parents had organised a cake, complete with candles, which they'd presented to her amidst the chaos of the packed bar. The place had erupted with a spontaneous and rowdy rendition of Happy Birthday and when she blew out the candles, she noticed a trio of men at the bar watching her. But it was the attractive man in the middle of the trio, with his stylish blue and white ski jacket that really caught her eye, that and the way he was so obviously sizing her up.

A knife was produced for her to cut the cake, plates passed around, more champagne poured and all the while the man in the blue and white jacket continued to watch. Emboldened, and very much liking the look of him, Sorrel took three plates of cake over to the bar. 'You look hungry,' she said, making it obvious which of them she was addressing. The other two laughed.

The darker-haired man of the group said, 'Take no notice, he always looks like that.'

'And it's not food that makes him hungry,' the other remarked with a guffaw of laughter.

'Ignore them,' the object of her interest said. 'I've never met them before in my life.'

'If only that were true,' said the one who'd laughed.

'Thank you for the cake,' the attractive man said. 'Can I buy you a drink? A birthday drink for the birthday girl?'

'Maybe later,' she said, turning to go, confident that he would make the effort to look out for her, if not later tonight, then tomorrow.

The following evening she and her brother and two cousins found themselves a table in the crowded bar, and sure enough within ten minutes, the trio from the previous evening made their appearance. There was no attempt from the attractive man to pretend their meeting had happened by chance: there was no pretence on her part either. Back then, deception had never been a part of her make up; she was honest and direct, bluntly so at times.

They spent several afternoons skiing together, and when it was time to return home to England and get back to college, Sorrel was in no doubt, given that he had asked for her telephone number, that she would hear from Alastair again. He rang her two days later and they met for dinner in London where they were both studying — she was reading English at King's College and he was an economics student at UCL. They spent the night together, just as Sorrel had known they would. He was not her first, just as she was certainly not his first.

For several months there wasn't a day when they didn't see each other, and Sorrel grew convinced that this was the man she would marry. She loved everything about him, his pitch-perfect manners, his strong athletic body which he put to good use, both in bed and out, running every morning and regularly playing squash. She admired his ambition to be the best at whatever he applied himself to. But her feelings of admiration very quickly turned to love, an all-consuming love that roused in her a passion she hadn't believed herself capable of feeling. No boyfriend had ever made her feel the way he did, as though she were walking on air, her every sense keenly alive to the astonishing beauty of the day. When apart from Alastair she longed for him, counting the hours until she would see him again. He made her world sing and those around her noticed the dramatic change in her, teasing her that she was high on love.

But then completely out of the blue, he dropped her for a girl with hideously dyed hair who went around in overalls and ugly workman's boots. Sorrel couldn't believe it and to her shame she begged Alastair to reconsider. 'I thought you loved me as much as I loved you,' she said. 'I thought we were perfect together.'

He'd shaken his head and said he'd never actually loved her, and that it was best just to accept things and part on good terms.

'Best for you, no doubt,' she'd cried, choking

back tears of humiliation.

'Don't be like that. It was good while it lasted, wasn't it?'

His casual indifference was hard to take. Being dumped was a new experience for her — never before had she been so ruthlessly discarded; it was always the other way round, she was the one who called the shots. Her final words to him were to say she hoped his new girlfriend made his life a living hell, and that one day he would realise the mistake he'd made and regret it.

The name of Alastair's new girlfriend was Orla Malone and it turned out that from that day on she had the upper hand when it came to Alastair's emotions. As for Sorrel's emotions, she now knew the misery of having fallen headlong in love only then to have her heart broken. She vowed never again to allow herself to feel that depth of passion, or to feel so vulnerable again.

It was some months later that their paths crossed at a ball in Nottingham where Sorrel's brother was coming to the end of his first year of studying law. Between girlfriends, Rafe invited Sorrel to go with him, and no sooner had they arrived when she saw Alastair propping up the bar, along with his two friends she'd met in Meribel. There was no sign of a girl hanging off his arm and with a flash of spite she hoped he'd had a taste of his own medicine. More likely he had simply dumped her just as he had Sorrel, and was here to find a replacement.

She was helping herself to a plate of food from the buffet when she was tapped on the shoulder. She turned around expecting to see her brother back from the bar, but found herself being smiled at by one of Alastair's friends. It was Simon.

'I thought it was you,' he said. 'How are you?'

'Fine,' she said guardedly.

'I was sorry to hear that things didn't work out between you and Alastair.' He smiled. 'Well, if I'm honest, I'm not sorry at all; he can be a bit of a bugger when it comes to the girls. You'd be better off with somebody like me, solid, reliable, and very loyal.'

She regarded him with a raised eyebrow. 'Is that so? And do you make a habit of helping yourself to Alastair's unwanted girlfriends?'

He looked pained at the question. 'Absolutely not! And for the record, had Alastair not been around that evening in Meribel, I would most certainly have bought you a birthday drink myself. Would you like to dance?' He eyed her plate of food. 'When you've finished eating, that is.'

He wasn't really her sort, not athletic enough in his appearance, not quite smooth enough. He was probably one of those bull-in-a-china-shop types, blundering around without thinking before speaking. But she could do worse than agree to dance with him, especially if it had the added benefit of getting Alastair's back up.

'I'd be happy to,' she replied. 'Come and find me in about half an hour.'

'Or I could stay and eat with you?' he suggested.

Pushy, she thought, but with no sign of her brother now, she agreed anyway.

She wasn't at all surprised when, at the end of the night, Simon asked if he could see her again. She wanted to say no, but there was something about his boyish eagerness that appealed. And what better way to show Alastair that she had moved on by going out with one of his closest friends?

That night of the ball, she had feigned an air of being very much over Alastair. She put on such a good act of cordiality she almost convinced herself she meant it.

But as time went on, and she slipped into a relationship with Simon, she realised that she really did enjoy his company. He made her laugh in a way Alastair never did, and he never let her down or took her for granted. She also enjoyed Danny's company, and that of his girlfriend, Frankie, an attractive brunette. Before too long, she found herself drawn in closer to the group of friends, until one day she realised that she wasn't on the outside looking in anymore, but was a fully participating member of the club.

During this time Alastair's initial awkwardness around her gave way and eventually he apologised for the way he'd treated her; he claimed that he had done a lot of growing up in the past few months. Sorrel strongly suspected his apology was of Danny and Frankie's doing — they both had a natural desire to smooth any feathers in danger of being ruffled — but she accepted it all the same.

The only fly in the ointment was Orla. Sorrel found it difficult to foster any real affection for her, and she had no cause to doubt that the feeling was mutual. But they made a reasonable pretence of liking each other.

Danny and Frankie were the first to marry, followed swiftly by Alastair and Orla, and then, as if not to be left out, Sorrel agreed to marry Simon. But that was also because she discovered she was pregnant and the thought of having a child out of wedlock would have appalled her parents, not to say herself. So there they all were, married, not just to their partners, but to one another.

There's a theory that the intensity of one's first true love can never be replicated, and although Sorrel loved Simon, it was not in the same way she had loved Alastair. Occasionally she would fall prey to the nagging doubt that she had made do with second best in marrying Simon, but perhaps he had too in marrying her, because it became increasingly obvious to Sorrel that he was in awe of Orla. He was dazzled by her unconventional demeanour, her effortless ability to radiate an unfathomable allure that made everyone gather around her. The more Sorrel saw that attraction develop, the more she disliked and resented Orla.

It didn't stop with her husband. Callum and Rachel also came under Orla's spell and would often say things like, 'Auntie Orla lets us do that, why don't you?' And 'Auntie Orla is always so much fun, she never minds us making a mess.' And the one that hurt the most: 'You're so boring, Mum, why can't you be more like Auntie Orla?'

Bloody Auntie Orla! was all Sorrel could

think. The woman was Mary bloody Poppins incarnate!

Except with the passing of more years, and as the children became more independent and less malleable, Orla's appeal had its limits. There were times when she lost her temper for no real reason. She could also be downright cruel. She once told Rachel that she was getting podgy and that she should watch what she ate. Sorrel was furious, but Orla merely shrugged her scrawny shoulders. She said she stood by her remark, and that if Sorrel was doing her job properly as a concerned mother, she would be honest with her daughter and nip the problem in the bud before it was too late. Rachel was only seven at the time.

Life was so very black and white for Orla; there was no room for diplomacy or tact in her thinking. Expecting Simon to support her, he had shocked Sorrel by taking Orla's side, that maybe Rachel had put on more than just puppy fat. Simon never criticised his daughter, and to hear him do so felt like the worst of betrayals. It hardened Sorrel's heart, and it was shortly after this incident that she betrayed her husband in the worst possible way.

A knock at the door had her opening her eyes and at the sight of Simon peering in, she hauled herself back from the past to the here and now. She knew she had to face the consequences of what she'd said in the kitchen, but she wasn't ready.

49

Mindful of his sleeping daughter, Simon kept his voice low. 'Sorrel,' he said, 'I want to talk to you.'

'Not now,' she whispered back at him.

'But we need to,' he said more urgently.

'Please, not now,' she repeated. 'You'll wake Rachel.'

'When, then?'

She sighed and closed her eyes, as though shutting him out. 'Later. We'll talk later.'

With great reluctance, he closed the door and went downstairs. He was at a loss what to do. Mostly because he couldn't be sure just what was going on. Or was that a lie? Had a part of him always wondered, but had steadfastly chosen to ignore it?

All he'd ever wanted was an uncomplicated life. He wasn't a greedy man, or a particularly ambitious one. For him what counted was his family, his friends, and a fulfilling job. It wasn't much to ask for. But suddenly it felt like it was all being taken from him.

The couple who had come to view the house had gone, and as he stood at the foot of the stairs, he tried to discern where Alastair and the others were. He was tempted to have it out with Alastair, but the coward in him wasn't ready to confront him. Not yet. Suspecting and knowing were two entirely different things.

He crossed the hall where weak sunlight was

371

filtering through the open doorways, and peered into the conservatory. Finding it empty, he entered the room, pushed open the double doors and went outside. After the rain, the air was markedly fresher now. He headed down the length of sodden lawn towards the pavilion, breathing in the coolness, wanting it to clear the confusion in his head.

But the sight of Valentina sitting in the pavilion brought him to a stop. Here was the cause of everything that was crumbling to dust around him.

'Don't run away because I am here,' she called to him, just when he turned with the intention of going anywhere but to the pavilion. 'Sit with me and let's talk. It is time, don't you think?'

'That rather depends on what it is you have in mind to talk about,' he said tersely.

'We both know what needs to be discussed.' She patted the seat nearest her. 'Come, sit with me.'

Despite every fibre of his being telling him to put as much distance as he possibly could between the two of them, he did as she instructed. Was that her secret, making people do what they didn't want to? Was that how she had ensnared Alastair? 'Where are Nikolai and Irina?' he asked.

'They've gone. Alastair has taken them to the station.'

'Without saying goodbye? I'm heartbroken.'

She looked at him with a gaze that was as steely as any Sorrel was capable of giving. 'I'm sure you are,' she said.

'Why didn't you accompany them to the station; why leave it to Alastair? Or were you too ashamed to be in their company for a moment more than you had to?'

She raised her chin defiantly. 'I am not ashamed of my stepchildren. But if you want to know, I stayed here because I wanted to have the opportunity to talk to you alone.'

'And sitting out here all on your lonesome was going to make that happen?'

'You're here now, aren't you? And to be honest with you, I knew you'd stop hiding in your room and eventually come outside. You don't like to be . . . ' she hesitated, 'what is the word I am searching for? Ah yes, to be *cooped* up. You are a man of action, never one to let the lawn grow under your feet.'

'Grass,' he corrected her automatically. 'Never one to let the *grass* grow under one's feet.'

The corners of her mouth curled into a half smile and her eyes gleamed, making him feel that he had walked straight into a trap. 'There,' she said, 'now I have given you the chance to feel superior over me. That is how you like things to be, isn't it?'

'I take great offence at such a suggestion!'

'And there you go with your magnificent display of outrage. In the short time I have known you, I have come to know that you do this so wonderfully well.'

'Is there a point to this interesting examination of my character?'

'Yes. I would like to hear why you dislike me so much.'

Where to start! he thought.

'Let me help you,' she said. 'You dislike me because I have come from nowhere and am disrupting your well-ordered lives. I am the outsider, the villain of the drama, the one the audience is meant to hate. You hated me before I had even set foot on the stage of this little drama of ours. Was that fair, do you suppose?'

He rolled his eyes. 'You don't think you're being overly dramatic?'

'But I am foreign,' she replied with a shrug. 'That is how I am supposed to behave in your eyes.'

He shook his head, wondering if she wasn't a little bit mad. 'You keep telling me how I see things, but you have no idea what I really feel or believe. How could you, when you hardly know me? When you know nothing about us as a group of friends, or the real Alastair for that matter and what we mean to him?'

'Oh, poor lonely frightened Simon; it is you who knows nothing. I know everything. Alastair has told me all.'

He scoffed. 'I doubt that very much.'

'I know that when you were fourteen years old, you and Danny hero-worshipped Alastair, and that you would do anything he said, so when he dared you both to steal with him from a record shop during your summer holiday, you didn't hesitate. I know that when you three were caught with the hand red by the owner, he made you give back the records you had taken, as well as make you work for free in the shop, instead of taking you to the police station.

'I know that Callum and Rachel mean the world to you. I know that Sorrel has never truly forgiven Alastair for choosing Orla over her, and that you have turned the blind eye to her still being in love with him. But that is because you wanted your wife to love Alastair as much as you do. How am I doing when it comes to knowing you, and knowing that you are behaving in the manner of a jealous lover?'

Simon rose slowly to his feet. 'I don't know where you've got this pack of . . . of lies from, but I'd advise you to keep your poisonous thoughts to yourself.'

'But it is from Alastair I have heard these things. Straight from the pony's mouth.'

'Horse!' Simon bellowed, his self-control suddenly gone. 'Straight from the *horse's* bloody mouth!'

She laughed. 'How peculiar it is that my English is not so good when I am around you. You must make me nervous.'

'Oh, I doubt that very much. You know exactly what you're doing and saying. Every word you utter is precisely thought out, designed to manipulate whoever is on the receiving end. Don't think for one minute you can fool me, or make me believe that Alastair confided in you willingly.'

'Why wouldn't he?'

'Because he wouldn't! Because friends don't do that to each other!'

'Poor Simon, you so badly want to believe that, don't you? Does it seem like a betrayal to you to accept that Alastair would confide in me?

And is that how you see his love for me, a betrayal of your love for him?'

Simon stared in disgust at this woman whom Alastair had somehow convinced himself he loved. What did he see in her? There was no good in her. None whatsoever.

'You have no idea what kind of an enemy you have just made in me,' he said, his voice low and tight as he willed himself to keep a lid on his anger.

'You were already my enemy, Simon. Nothing has changed.'

'Oh, but it has. When I tell Alastair of this conversation, he'll see you for what you are.'

'What would that be exactly?'

But before he could reply, from across the water came the haunting sound of a violin playing. He recognised the music; it was the theme from *Schindler's List*. It was the only piece of music that had ever had the power to move him to tears. He remembered being in the cinema watching the film and feeling as though his heart was being torn out from his chest. Sorrel had sat beside him completely dry-eyed, while he had blubbed like a baby.

Perhaps it was a reflection of the highly emotional state he was in, but damn it, he could feel the backs of his eyes pricking. His breath ragged, and needing to escape, he marched back up the garden, then took the path to Orla's studio, where he knew he could be alone.

★ ★ ★

376

Jenna couldn't take her eyes off Blake.

She was mesmerised, not just by the heartbreakingly poignant sound he was producing, but by the level of his concentration. His feet apart, and the violin placed on his left shoulder, his chin on the chin-rest, there was something incredibly sensual about the way he held the bow so lightly with his fingers while stroking it across the strings. With his eyes closed as he swayed with the music, he seemed completely lost in what he was doing.

Jenna was glad she was sitting down, because as ridiculous as it felt, her legs had turned to cotton wool. With each exquisite note vibrating through her, she found herself lost in the music too, her throat tightening with an emotion she was unable to put into words. More worryingly, she was fighting the thought of what it might be like to be loved by someone who was capable of feeling such a depth of passion.

In that moment, just as the pale sun broke free from a cloud, light streamed in through the open door and a halo appeared to form over Blake's head, turning his hair to amber. It made Jenna think he was quite beautiful. Never in her life had she previously thought such a thing of a man. What was happening to her?

When he had played the last note, he stood perfectly still for a very long time, before lowering the violin and bow, and opening his eyes.

'What were you thinking while you played?' she asked quietly, afraid to speak too loudly for fear of breaking the spell he had cast.

'The same as I always do when I play that particular piece. What did John Williams have to give of his heart and soul to be able to write such deeply moving music?'

'Do you believe that's what great musicians have to do in order to create at that level?'

Blake nodded, and put the violin back in its case on the table behind him. 'I do as a matter of fact. I think it's true of all great artists, whether they be writers, painters or musicians. It's why I know I could never be any more than average in my playing, I don't want to make that kind of sacrifice.'

'I don't think there was anything average in the way you just played.'

He smiled. 'You're being kind.'

'I'm being honest. And thank you for playing for me.'

'Perhaps I should have chosen something more upbeat.'

'No. It was perfect what you chose.'

He held her gaze. Then with a tilt of his head, he indicated they should go outside on the balcony.

Standing next to him, their shoulders almost touching, she stared across the river towards Linston End. It was funny seeing it from this perspective. It looked larger, more imposing, but then it was one of the finest properties on the river. There was nobody in the garden, as far as she could see. The only sign of life was a heron; it was as still as a statue and reminded Jenna of the many bronze pieces Orla had created. She had once said that each and every one of her statues was a part of herself that she gave away. Maybe Blake was right when he said those of an artistic persuasion had to chip away at their souls in order to produce their finest work.

'It's a beautiful house,' Blake said.

'Yes,' she agreed, 'it is. I've known it all my life; I can't quite believe that this will be my last summer here. It's like losing a best friend.'

'Change isn't necessarily a bad thing,' he said, resting his hands on the rail and leaning forwards.

To their left, a motor cruiser came into view, rounding the curve in the river, the children on board waving happily up at Jenna and Blake. They waved back, which encouraged the children to wave even more, eliciting smiles from their parents. When they'd passed, Blake said, 'I've been thinking about making some changes.'

'Really? What kind?'

'I've been considering a change of work scene.'

She turned to look at him, surprised. Surprised too at her immediate reaction, that she would miss him. 'I thought you liked it at Heart-to-Heart?'

'I do.'

'So why leave?'

He stared at her, then rubbed his fingers along the wooden rail, back and forth, reminding her of the way he'd played his violin with such intensity. 'A new job somewhere else might open up other avenues for me,' he said finally.

'A better job, bigger salary?'

'That wasn't exactly what I was thinking.'

'What then?'

'Oh, Jenna,' he said, his gaze back on hers again and with considerable force. 'Don't give me that bemused look of yours, you ought to know by now how it drives me crazy.'

She felt the colour rush to her face. 'I don't know what you mean.'

He shook his head. 'Come on, Lawyer Girl, surely you can figure this one out?'

She frowned, and then it dawned on her what he was saying. 'You can't be serious?'

'I've never been more serious.'

'But — '

'But what?' he cut in when she hesitated. 'There'd be no point? Is that what you're about to say? If so, don't. Not straightaway. Give yourself time to consider what I've said, and then let me know what you think.'

50

'Wasn't that Alastair?' remarked Danny. He and Frankie were standing on the pavement outside the last one of the estate agents they had wanted to visit.

'It certainly looked like his Range Rover,' Frankie said, staring at the charcoal-coloured vehicle disappearing into the distance. 'Maybe he felt the need to escape like we did. I'm beginning to feel sorry for him; our coming here has been nothing short of a disaster.'

'It wouldn't be so bad if we could muster the smallest grain of approval for Valentina,' Danny said as they crossed the road in the direction of where they'd left their car in the car park at the back of Roys.

'I feel the same way. I came here badly wanting to be happy for Alastair, but all I feel is an awful sense of dread.'

'And you know what not one of us has had the courage to ask, and it's none of our business, I know, but how is this new life Alastair is planning going to be funded? Is he footing the entire bill, hence the hurry to sell Linston End, or is Valentina pitching in?'

'You mean, is she a blatant gold-digger?'

'Yes. Exactly that. I just wish I didn't keep getting the feeling that she's playing some kind of game.'

'You're beginning to sound like Simon.

Perhaps we simply have to accept that it's no more complicated than she loves him and he loves her, irrespective of how financially well off the other is. For all we know, she might be as rich as Croesus.'

'But of all the women in the world, why her? Surely Alastair can see that she just doesn't fit in with his old life?'

'That might be the very reason he's so attracted to Valentina. He wants to be rid of his old life, and all those painful memories of Orla. It's perfectly understandable.'

Danny shook his head. 'But it's not possible to treat the memory in that way. It's not like wiping clean the memory of an old computer or mobile phone.'

'True. But what if Alastair finds our connection to the past, in particular our connection to Orla, too much to bear?'

'If I died, would you want to cut all ties with Alastair and Simon and Sorrel? Did that thought go through your head when I was in hospital?'

Frankie came to a stop just yards from their car. 'Danny, all I could think about when you were in hospital was willing you back to full health. And if you don't mind, I'd rather you didn't speak so flippantly about you dying. It upsets me.'

'I'm sorry, love.'

Danny drove out of the car park in silence. He was cross with himself for upsetting Frankie. But then these days they all seemed to be upsetting each other. That scene around the table in the kitchen earlier had been excruciating. What had got into Sorrel?

It had been a golden rule between Danny and Frankie that they would never gossip about their friends. It was something Danny felt strongly about, and was a trait he'd learned from his parents — do unto others as you would have them do unto you. But now he was going to break that rule.

'Do you think Sorrel and Alastair have had an affair?'

Frankie stopped flicking through the haul of property brochures they'd gathered while trawling the agents. 'A relationship other than the one they had before Orla came on the scene?' she asked.

'Yes.'

'Are you sure this is something we should discuss, after all — '

'Yes. Just this once I think we need to.'

'Well,' she said, while keeping her gaze fixed on the car in front of them, 'I've always believed there was an unresolved issue between the two of them, and with — '

'Why do you think that?'

'Are you going to keep on interrupting me?'

'Sorry. Carry on.'

'I'll try to, if you give me half a chance. I've always suspected that Sorrel still had feelings for Alastair, and that the way he dropped her when Orla showed up hurt her profoundly.'

'And you believe — '

Frankie raised a hand. 'No interrupting!'

'Sorry.'

'I think the pain she experienced all those years ago never left her and she would have leapt at the chance to get her own back on Orla by sleeping with Alastair again. After what we witnessed at lunchtime, I think it's highly likely they did have an affair, but maybe only very briefly. Maybe just a one-off fling.'

Danny could see the sense in what Frankie had said. 'Permission to speak?' he asked.

'Granted.'

'When do you think that might have happened?'

'Orla had her ups and downs, we all know that, particularly when she suffered yet another miscarriage. I'd hazard a guess that Alastair may well have sought a distraction during one of those episodes. Not that I'm condoning it. But then I'm not judging either.'

'Have you always thought this about Alastair?'

'In my subconscious, perhaps so. It was never something I consciously articulated though.'

'And you were never once tempted to share this with me?'

'Again perhaps subconsciously I didn't want to say the words out loud for fear of making it true. I know how important the stability of your relationship with Alastair and Simon is to you, and to suggest that Sorrel was betraying one of your closest friends by sleeping with the other, was not a Pandora's box I wanted to open. But when you think about it, can you honestly say you believe Sorrel has been truly happy all these years?'

'I don't know what to think. I suppose I just accepted Sorrel for being, well, Sorrel; not entirely capable of expressing joy. She's not one of life's naturally spontaneous people, is she?' Before giving Frankie the chance to respond, he said, 'Do you think Simon may have had the same thought as you?'

'I wouldn't like to say.'

Danny drove on in silence, mulling over all that Frankie had said. Then: 'Have you ever . . . ' his voice trailed away with embarrassment.

'Have I ever what? Wanted to go to bed with another man? Specifically Alastair?'

Danny swallowed. 'Yes.'

'No. Hand on heart, I can assure you one hundred per cent I have never entertained that thought, or desire. Shame on you for asking me.'

'You're right; I am ashamed. But everything seems so up in the air suddenly, as though anything's possible.'

'I'll tell you what's not possible, and that's for me to love any man but you.'

'You don't know that, not for sure.'

'I do!'

'But what if I died? I'd hate to think of you spending the rest of your life alone. I wouldn't object to you marrying again, you know. I'd want you to be happy.'

Frankie let out a long exasperated sigh. 'Just stop, will you! I won't have you talking this way. How would you like it if I kept going on about my demise?'

Danny knew he'd gone too far. 'Ignore me. I'm not myself.'

'No, you're not. The man I married would never have allowed himself to become so maudlin. Now cheer up, that's an order!'

Danny forced himself to smile and reached out for her hand. 'Message received loud and clear.'

Some minutes later, and as he turned right at the junction to take the Linston Road, he said, 'Do you suppose Orla would have wanted Alastair to marry again?'

'Good Lord no!' Frankie replied with a short laugh. 'Orla didn't mind sharing him with us, but Alastair belonged to her. He was her property.'

★ ★ ★

After he'd dropped off Nikolai and Irina at the station in Hoveton, Alastair had wanted time to be alone. So when he'd arrived back at Linston End, he had skirted round the side of the house on foot, and despite knowing he wasn't being fair to Valentina by leaving her on her own for so long, he'd untied *Water Lily* and set off up river.

In the past, whenever Orla was going through one of her low periods, and when he couldn't console her, or do anything right, he had spent hours on the water. It was all that had enabled him to keep a hold of his sanity.

It was during one of these low periods that he had made a colossal error of judgement, a mistake which he had never been able to erase, or atone for. How could he? How could he confess to Simon and expect to be forgiven? It was unforgivable what he'd done, and he feared the worst now. Now that Sorrel seemed intent on ruining everything.

If marriage to Orla had taught him anything, it was that you cannot, under any circumstances, negotiate with a madwoman, particularly a madwoman hungry for revenge.

A woman scorned was perhaps the most dangerous species alive, and it was a miracle Sorrel had kept quiet for as long as she had. He had always hoped that she would have believed she had too much to lose by opening her mouth. But he'd been a fool to think that one day she wouldn't find some reason to seek retribution. Valentina was clearly sufficient reason.

Rarely, if ever, was revenge rooted in logic; it was the basest of needs, the desire to inflict the maximum amount of pain to exact the powerful urge for vengeance. In this instance, it would all be for a mistake that should never have happened. A sordid and regrettable mistake, which Alastair had not shared with Valentina, unlike so much else of his life.

'I want you to know everything about me,' he'd told her. Except that wasn't entirely true. Had anyone ever uttered those words and genuinely meant what they said? We only ever give the version of ourselves we want to project, and the one he'd selected for Valentina was of a grieving husband who'd been to hell, not only in the aftermath of his wife's death, but also during his marriage; a man pushed to the edge of endurance.

All of which had been true.

Up ahead, he could see a pair of traditional wherries coming towards him, their sails catching what little breeze there was. They were the finest-looking craft on the river and allowing them plenty of room to pass, Alastair steered *Water Lily* closer to the bank. Just a few yards later, and once again he was confronted with the entrance to Linston Broad. But unlike this morning when he had had no choice but to enter the broad to retrieve *Swallowtail*, he turned his back on it — and Orla — and pressed on up river.

Untimely.

Unexpected.

Tragic.

Unforeseen.

A ghastly waste.

Heart-breaking.

These were all words that had been uttered at Orla's funeral, none of which had rung true for Alastair. Her death had been a merciful release. For them both.

As his mood darkened, and a small nondescript cruiser passed by on his left, he wondered what the middle-aged couple on board would think if they knew they had just smiled into the face of a man who was responsible for his wife's death.

51

Sorrel woke from a deep sleep and a dream in which she was begging Alastair to realise that she was the only woman worthy of his love. She was telling him that he'd pretended for too long it wasn't true, but it was time now to stop denying themselves their right to be together.

Lying on Jenna's bed, Sorrel recoiled from the raw humiliating pain of the dream. Her body as rigid as a board, she could not recall a time when she felt more full of hatred. It was a hatred directed at herself. She had learnt to live with jealousy, one of the most destructive of emotions, but its close companion, self-loathing, had now joined forces and was cruelly taunting her for her pathetic blindness.

How could she have lived this long the way she had? And for what? The hope that somehow Alastair might admit that he had made a mistake and married the wrong woman?

Had she really believed he would do that? And what if he had? What had she really hoped for?

Definitely not this. Not him running straight off into the arms of a stranger once he was free of Orla. Not the pain of having his newfound happiness shoved in her face by bringing the new love of his life here so he could show her off.

Could he have been any more heartless? But then she supposed anyone caught up in the initial rapture of what they think is love enters a state of near madness, of seeing the world as they want to see it. Nothing that has gone before is of any importance; it's all about the moment. Certainly that was how she was when she fell in love with Alastair.

It was how she had felt again when Alastair turned to her in his hour of need, when life with Orla proved too much for him. Later, when he'd had his fill of Sorrel, he had excused himself, blamed what he'd done on a temporary loss of control.

'Loss of control?' she'd repeated. 'We've been sleeping together for the last four weeks, how is that a temporary loss of control?'

'You know what I mean.'

Oh, she knew full well what he meant. She'd served her purpose and now it was to be business as usual.

That was twenty-five years ago, when Orla was facing the reality that if she didn't conceive soon, it was game over for her when it came to motherhood. After yet another miscarriage, Alastair had been at his wits' end trying to console her — a fool's errand if ever there was one; Orla was not the consoling kind.

But Alastair was in need of consolation and Sorrel had played her part beautifully, offering him a ready shoulder on which to cry. Not that it was her shoulder he was interested in; his needs were far more basic than that. He had wanted her body, and sex that wasn't done to order. He wanted honest-to-God, uncomplicated sex without the burden of expectation hanging over him. And Sorrel willingly provided the means for that to happen.

At the time, she wasn't working and while the children were at school she could easily slip down to London on the train to meet him. With Orla up at Linston End throwing her inconsolable anger and frustration into her art, Sorrel met Alastair at their house in Fulham. Lying in bed she relished knowing that she was the one he had turned to, the one whom he could rely upon to make him happy. She had almost hoped that she would end up pregnant by him, if only to flaunt her fertility in Orla's face, but Alastair was meticulously careful in that respect.

Following their lovemaking she would take the train home feeling on top of the world one minute, then wracked with guilt the next. What sort of a woman was she that could do this to her husband, and with his best friend? But then she would recall Simon siding with Orla over poor Rachel gaining more weight than was good for her, and her vengeful heart would harden.

When Alastair decided that 'things' had gone on for long enough, that what they were doing wasn't fair to Orla and Simon, Sorrel felt her heart being cracked in two all over again. How had she allowed this to happen? Did she really think so little of herself that she had given herself to Alastair only to be cast aside when his conscience got the better of him?

Ashamed of her weakness, she had readily promised Alastair that she would keep the affair secret. She didn't want anyone to know that she had been used. But as time went by, she saw that her promise to Alastair gave her an irrevocable tie to him. It gave her power too, a power that she knew she could wield as and when she chose.

Alastair had always assumed she had too much at stake to risk telling Orla of their affair, that the consequences would bring her world tumbling down around her. He had made the assumption that her loyalty to Simon and their children was his trump card over her, and for many years it had been; but now she was consumed with the need to disabuse him of that arrogant certainty and to hell with the consequences.

It was the way he had looked and spoken to her in the kitchen during lunch that had been the final straw. But then he had asked them all to leave to ensure their rooms were fit to be viewed by the couple waiting in the hall. And in what now seemed like an act of astonishing compliance on her part, she had obeyed. That's how it had always been for her, she supposed.

But now she wanted everyone to know what a shallow two-faced bastard he was, how he had used her, and how he was the worst friend anyone could have. If that meant she went down with his sinking ship, so be it. It was no more than they both deserved.

That was what self-loathing did for a person, it made every ounce of guilt you had suppressed rise to the surface. In Sorrel's case it had opened her eyes to the truth of what she had allowed herself to become, and it needed to end.

52

For the first time since arriving at Linston End, Valentina was beginning to have her doubts. Something she rarely did.

From her vantage point of sitting alone in the pavilion, and nursing a headache that had come on while tidying up the kitchen after lunch, she had seen Alastair going off on his own in one of his boats. She had very nearly called out to him to take her with him, but the very fact that he had not sought her company made her think twice. For Alastair to do that — for him not even to come looking for her on his return from the station — implied he wanted to be alone. And then Simon had appeared, and she had swept aside any nagging concerns and focused her energy on showing Simon that she was not some silly woman he could push around. She knew his type of old, full of hot air and with no sense of how absurd he was.

But the moment he had left her, she had felt herself deflate, and wondered why she hadn't taunted him about his wife's performance at lunch. It really wasn't like Valentina to let an opportunity slip past her. Was she losing her touch? Or was it simply that she had been momentarily wrong-footed by Alastair's behaviour?

She texted Irina to ask if anything had been said in the car when Alastair had driven them to the station. Seconds later her stepdaughter replied.

It was very awkward, Alastair hardly spoke to us.

In the circumstances, perhaps that was to be expected, thought Valentina. She regretted now that she hadn't gone with them to the station, but she had felt as if her skull was having a hole drilled through it.

She hadn't wanted Nikolai and Irina to leave, not when it gave the impression that they felt responsible for that wretched girl nearly drowning and were cowardly running away, but Nikolai had been adamant. 'We've hardly been made to feel welcome here,' he had said, 'and after that scene during lunch, I'm surprised you don't want to get the hell out as well.'

Naturally whatever Nikolai said, Irina agreed with, because that was how they were; she always followed her brother. Nikolai was as headstrong as their father had been, so Valentina had known it was futile to expect them to change their minds and leave tomorrow morning, as originally planned.

Valentina had seen the relief on Alastair's face that they were leaving and that had irked her. Worse than that, it had disappointed her. But she'd be damned if she let anyone see that, or showed less than her full support for her stepchildren. Her mother had brought her up to believe that family loyalty was all; it came with being Russian. Russian blood, so her mama said, was thicker than any other type. It was nonsense, of course, blood was blood, whoever's veins it ran through.

Yet as much as Valentina believed in family

loyalty and held it closer to her heart than almost anything else, she was starting to appreciate that Alastair and his friends had a loyalty to each other that she had severely underestimated.

Similarly, she had miscalculated having Nikolai and Irina here with her; their presence had backfired badly. If only Nikolai hadn't flirted with Rachel, but then he never could resist leading a girl on. His father had been the same. At a restaurant, or a party, his eye had always wandered. He would do it because he knew the effect he would have on the recipient; he enjoyed the power it gave him. Nikolai was the same. Valentina had never objected to the games Ivan had played; she had known that if he strayed he would come back to her.

Infidelity was nothing to get worked up over in her opinion. She too had strayed while married to Ivan, and she now suspected that Alastair had too. With none other than Sorrel. Now that did surprise her. She guessed it would be a surprise to Simon also.

It was another disappointment to Valentina that Alastair hadn't been honest with her. She had believed him when he'd said he didn't want there to be any secrets between them, and she understood now that she had wanted that to be truer than she realised. She had wanted to believe that Alastair was different from other men, that she had found somebody special. But he wasn't. He was just like any other ordinary man. The surprise to her was that it bothered her so much.

But what did Sorrel hope to gain by outing

Alastair and revealing their guilty secret? Did she think that would alter things between Valentina and Alastair? Or was Sorrel so full of bitterness that she was prepared to sacrifice her marriage, as well as the respect of her friends and children, for the sake of shaming Alastair? Did she care so little for her husband's feelings that she would do all that? And what of her own self-respect?

But if Sorrel went ahead with exposing Alastair as an adulterer who had betrayed one of his best friends by sleeping with his wife, then it would have the satisfying effect of driving a very large wedge between the group of friends, and would push Alastair further into her arms. As if they weren't doing that already with their constant bickering amongst themselves, and their ridiculous attempts to remind him of the good old days. Did they really think they could compete with the life Valentina was offering him?

Mulling this over, she felt the tension in her head dissolve and her old courage and confidence return. Alastair was hers. Nothing was going to stop her taking him away from this dreary backwater to the dazzling future that awaited them both. She would not be thwarted! She would not have all her carefully made plans destroyed. She planned to marry him and nothing would stop her from making that happen.

53

Simon had found the key in the lock of the door for Orla's studio, which surprised him. Had Alastair left it there? Had he been here to feel closer to Orla in some way? To check in with his wife and reflect on the mess he was making of his life without her, as well as contemplate the other lives he was wrecking into the bargain? Probably not. More likely he'd brought that couple who had viewed the house earlier to see the studio.

Once inside, Simon closed the door, as if needing to cocoon himself in this quiet oasis of calm where nothing could touch him. He sat on the daybed, his shoulders slumped, his head bent. What the hell had happened to them? How had they reached this state of acrimony?

If only Orla hadn't died. If she were still here, nothing would have changed; they'd be the same people jogging along quite happily, pushing whatever they didn't want to confront discreetly under the rug, just as they always had. Just as everyone did.

Orla's death had been the catalyst for where they now found themselves, with Simon feeling he was pitched in battle with Alastair and Valentina, and now Sorrel who was refusing to speak to him, as though he were to blame for everything!

Was he? Was that what she thought, that it was

somehow his fault that their daughter had very nearly drowned? As if he were to blame for —

He cut himself short. He could not say the words, even inside his head. He simply could not bring himself to admit what Sorrel had been on the verge of saying in the kitchen earlier.

But the truth was, he *was* to blame. He'd been a fool to think his actions would not have consequences, that Sorrel wouldn't retaliate and pay him back. He'd kidded himself all these years that she hadn't known, that he'd got away with it, but he hadn't. He knew now with a gut-churning certainty that his drunken fumble with Orla, on this very daybed, had inevitably come back to haunt him.

It had only happened once, about fifteen years ago, when they were both sloshed. Thank God, and just in the nick of time, they had come to their relative senses, but only because he'd killed the moment by falling over while trying to rip off his trousers. Orla had clutched her sides, roaring with laughter at the unedifying spectacle of him scrabbling about on the floor in his underpants. He had been appalled at what they'd almost done and had begged Orla not to tell Alastair. His disloyalty to his best friend was immense, and he hated himself for what he'd done. To his shame, it was his loyalty to Alastair, and not Sorrel, that had concerned him first.

'You're so funny,' Orla had said, when he'd said how profoundly sorry he was, 'of course I won't tell Alastair. Besides, there's nothing to tell. Just two pie-eyed old friends acting like a couple of randy teenagers.'

But had Orla told Sorrel? Perhaps even taking delight in doing so? After all, there had never been much love between them, despite the pretence.

If so, was that what had led Sorrel to exact her revenge, a case of two can play at that game? It was logical and wholly rational that she would, especially as she and Alastair had a shared history. How better to get back at Simon than to sleep with Alastair?

There. He'd said it. At last. That was the ugly truth of what Sorrel had come so close to saying at lunch; a truth which had been lurking all this time — like the perilous weeds at the bottom of Linston Broad where Orla had drowned — just waiting to ensnare and drag them down.

Simon had no idea when Sorrel and Alastair may have slept together, but he'd lay odds on it happening after his drunken escapade with Orla. What he did know for sure was that ever since, he had collaborated in the lies they'd told each other. Anything rather than rock the boat.

For the first time ever, he gave himself permission to consider the possibility that Orla had found out about Sorrel and Alastair. Given how possessive she was of him, had she been unable to live with his betrayal, and gone out that night in *Swallowtail* with the sole intention of ending her life?

Suicide.

It was such a desperately tragic thing for anyone to do, to believe that life wasn't worth living. If only Orla had confided in him. *If only . . . If only . . .*

But this was why he had doggedly clung to the belief that it had been a tragic accident, because to accept the truth was much too painful. Better to believe that in a confused and emotional state from drinking too much, Orla had inadvertently fallen overboard. Going out alone at night in a boat was not an unusual occurrence for her; she liked the darkness and the solitude. So really, death by misadventure was highly plausible.

But equally, so was suicide.

Now that he was being brutally honest with himself, Simon had to face up to the possibility that he might well be indirectly responsible for Orla's death, for he had played his part by driving his wife to even out the score.

And why the hell was he so damned calm about Sorrel's infidelity? Perhaps it was because his own indiscretion precluded him from having the right to judge or be angry with her.

In truth, he was guilty of so much more than that one moment of drunken behaviour with Orla. He couldn't remember when it started, but for some years he had secretly fantasised about sex with her. He had convinced himself that it didn't count as adultery, that so long as he never crossed the line, a harmless daydream had no repercussions. It had been easy to fool himself into believing that it didn't hurt Sorrel when he imagined it was Orla in bed with him, and not her. It was a cruel deceit on his part and ironically ended after that sloppy fumble with Orla, and when subsequently he lost all his respect for himself.

He'd read once that all men are adulterers at

heart, that this natural instinct to stray was constrained only by a sense of honour and conscience, both of which were as flimsy as tissue paper. But was the same true of women?

It really was shocking the level of pain married couples could inflict on themselves with their lies, and their selfish disregard for the consequences of their actions. As guilty of doing this as the next person, who was Simon to condemn Sorrel for what she had done? Or Alastair? That was what he had wanted to tell Sorrel when he'd knocked on Rachel's door. He had wanted to put his arms around her and say he understood. Moreover, he had wanted to urge her not to say anything else. He couldn't bear the thought of Rachel and Callum knowing their shameful secrets.

He shuddered, closed his eyes, lay down, and to his horror began to cry. Something he hadn't done in a very long time. As the tears flowed freely down his cheeks, he acknowledged that the changes Alastair was hell-bent on making, and which Simon had been fighting so hard to resist, was all part of a greater concern. What he'd really been fighting was the sad truth about his friendship with Alastair and how it had become a sham of its former self, riddled with deceit, which they had willingly lived with.

How he envied Danny and Frankie with the contented simplicity of their marriage, both wanting only the best for each other. It wasn't that they were perfect; nobody was, but they lived in enviable harmony.

Yet try as they might, Simon and Sorrel had

never achieved the same level of accord during their marriage. There had, in more recent years, been a sense of swimming against the tide, or of struggling not to go under.

It was an analogy that shook him out of his weepy self-pity.

Rachel! He must pull himself together and go back up to the house to be with her. Surely she must be awake by now. He must also talk to Sorrel; there was so much to be said.

54

Rachel was dreaming.

She was dancing with Paul, but not very well. He kept treading on the hem of her dress, which was trailing the floor and getting dirtier by the second. She was becoming angry with him. Didn't he know how much her wedding dress had cost? It was the dress she had always dreamed of wearing for her Big Day, and she felt beautiful in it. But here was Paul in his muddy shoes trampling all over the ivory-coloured silk. He was doing it deliberately. Of course he was. And why hadn't he polished his shoes before marrying her?

Over his shoulder, she suddenly saw Nikolai. He was with Irina and they were laughing at her. Laughing at her ruined dress, which she now realised had a rip all the way up the front. She looked a mess. A hideous mess and Paul was to blame! She wrenched herself out of his grasp and marched off, except she couldn't march, the dress was twisting itself around her legs, binding them together so that she couldn't move.

Next thing, she was falling down a hole; a dark hole that went on and on. Like Alice in Wonderland, she tumbled down and down, caught in a vortex of nothingness until she realised she was under water and could no longer breathe. She tried to call for help, but nothing came out of her mouth, only a stream of bubbles. And then she heard laughter again. It was Nikolai and Irina. They were peering down through the shadowy darkness from a distant point way above her head, their faces blurred, but their mocking laughter all too clear.

She wanted to escape their laughter, so forced herself to sink further down into the cold water. But their voices followed her. They were calling her name, getting nearer. She thrashed her legs to get away from them, but it was no good, their voices were growing louder, and nearer. Frightened, she began to cry. Great gulping sobs that shook through her body. She was a child again wanting her mother and father to save her. She cried out to them and in an instant, she was being held, hands holding her tight. She heard a voice. A soothing gentle voice.

'Rachel . . . wake up, Rachel.'

She opened her eyes with a start. 'Dad?'

'You were dreaming, sweetheart,' he said in a hushed voice.

She took a moment to orientate herself, rubbed her eyes and swallowed back the grainy dryness in her mouth. On Jenna's bed she could see her mother was fast asleep. 'What time is it?' she asked quietly.

'Nearly six o'clock,' her father whispered back.

'Really? I've been asleep for ages then.'

'You obviously needed to.'

She frowned. 'I was having such a horrible dream. Nikolai and Irina were in it.' She shuddered. 'It felt so real.'

'If it makes you feel any better, they've gone. Alastair took them to the station.'

'Did he make them go?'

Her father shook his head. 'I don't know the ins and outs, but I'm glad they didn't stick around.'

'I'm sorry for all the trouble I've caused. Alastair must be so annoyed. Everything's gone wrong for him since we arrived, hasn't it?'

'Hey, don't you dare apologise. And if things haven't gone exactly the way Alastair hoped they would, it's not your fault. Got that?'

She nodded and stretched her arms above her head. 'I should get up,' she said, forgetting to whisper. Over on Jenna's bed, her mother's right foot jerked, as if she was kicking something.

'Are you sure you feel well enough?' her father asked in a low voice.

'I'm not an invalid, Dad,' she said quietly, pushing back the duvet. 'A shower followed by something to eat and I'll be as right as rain. Where's Jenna?'

'No idea.'

'She went across to the Mill to see Blake.'

This was from Mum who had now turned over and was raising herself into a sitting position. The skin around her eyes looked red and puffy from sleep. Or had she been crying?

'Sorry if we woke you,' Dad said.

Ignoring him, Mum straightened her clothes and came over to Rachel. 'How are you feeling?' she asked.

'Pretty good, all things considered,' Rachel said brightly, not wanting to add to the worry she had already put her parents through. They

405

both looked like they'd been to hell and back, and she felt guilty for being the cause.

★　★　★

The shower was hot and powerful and as much as she appreciated the sensation of being revived and cleansed, Rachel could not bring herself to put her face under the jets of water. Was this something she would now have to live with, a fear of being under water? Was she also destined to suffer nightmares like the one she'd just had?

It was strange that Paul had featured in the dream. Why had her subconscious connected him to her nearly drowning? She would ask Jenna about that. Jenna was always good at figuring things out. Had she figured her dilemma out regarding Blake and Callum, Rachel wondered? Was that why she was over at the Mill?

When she had finished showering and crossed the landing back to her bedroom, Dad had gone, but Mum was there and laying clean clothes on the bed, just as she used to when Rachel and Callum were little.

'Thanks, Mum,' she said, touched by her thoughtfulness, 'you're the best.'

The reaction to her words was not what she expected. Her mother's lips trembled and her eyes filled. Rarely had Rachel seen her mother in less than full composure mode and it was alarming to see her so unlike her usual cool and undemonstrative self. 'Oh, Mum,' she said, 'I'm sorry for being such an idiot and putting you through so much worry.'

Her mother's face froze and then it crumpled. Her heart full of tender love, Rachel put her arms around her mother and hugged her tight, and for the first time in her life she felt that she was no longer a child, but an adult.

★　★　★

Downstairs on the terrace in the garden, Frankie and Danny were struggling to make polite conversation with Valentina.

For something to do, Frankie had fetched her bag of quilting, which she never travelled without, and needle in hand, was applying herself to the patchwork quilt she was making for Jenna. Next to her, Danny was engrossed in the estate agent's particulars they'd brought back from Wroxham.

Valentina was lying languidly on a teak steam chair with a glass of wine on the small table at her elbow, both of which Danny had rounded up for her, dutifully playing host in Alastair's absence. She gave the impression of being a woman without a care in the world, but Frankie had noticed the occasional jiggling of her right foot, like a cat's tail twitching when it was annoyed.

'Life moves at a slow pace here, doesn't it?' Valentina commented as they watched a sailing boat pass by at the end of the garden.

'That's its charm,' said Frankie. 'A slower pace of life. It's good for the soul.'

'I suppose it could be,' said Valentina, 'if one did not die of boredom first.'

'Oh dear, do you hate it very much?'

'Hate is too strong a word. Let us just say, I would soon tire of its charms.'

'That's a great shame,' said Danny, putting down the brochure in his hands, and joining in with the conversation.

Valentina swivelled her head to look at him through her sunglasses. 'Why do you say that? Am I not allowed to have a different view?'

Frankie could see the bluntness of her question threw Danny, but only momentarily. He cleared his throat. 'Well,' he said, 'it's something to share with Alastair, isn't it, a mutual love of something?'

She shrugged. 'But this house is in the past for Alastair, and the past cannot be shared if it has not been experienced together, not really. But the future can be shared, and I see that as being more important.'

'That's certainly one way of looking at it,' replied Danny evenly, 'but I suppose, and loving Linston End the way I do, it's difficult for me to understand how anybody could not enjoy being here.'

'Yes, I can see that that would be a problem for you. But tell me, Danny, and you too, Frankie, do you both believe that if only I would declare myself in love with Linston End, then Alastair would not want to leave?'

Danny turned to Frankie, a hint of desperation in his eyes. 'It's a possibility,' said Frankie, deciding she'd had quite enough from this blunt-speaking woman; it was time for her to swallow a dose of her own medicine. 'Undoubtedly it would be less expensive for you and Alastair to live here than in the South of France, or are you one of the lucky ones in this world who doesn't have to worry about money?'

Valentina let out a small laugh. 'How very un-English of you to talk about money, Frankie. I would not have expected that of you.'

I bet you wouldn't, thought Frankie with a fixed smile. 'Are you one of those lucky people, then?' she pressed.

'I would say that is my business, wouldn't you?'

Frankie widened her smile, and taking up a pair of sharp pointed scissors, she snipped off a length of cotton thread, while at the end of the garden a fleet of motor cruisers passed by, engines chugging, happy voices carrying across the water.

'You do know, don't you,' said Valentina when the river was quiet again, 'that Alastair had decided to sell Linston End before he met me?'

'Really?' said Frankie.

'It's true,' said Valentina, sipping her wine. 'He told me that when we met. He said he was bored with his old life, tired especially of living in a house that constantly reminded him of Orla. You can understand that, can't you?'

'Of course. But we all thought that with time Orla's shadow would pass.'

'Obviously I never knew the woman, but I know enough about her to know that her shadow will never pass from here. She haunts poor Alastair, torments him at night by keeping him awake with terrifying nightmares. I'm surprised you haven't heard him crying out in the night.'

Frankie glanced at Danny. She could tell from his expression that this was news to him, as it was to her. 'I'm sorry to hear that,' she said.

'When we were together in Sri Lanka, and then Kenya,' Valentina continued, 'he did not have nightmares; it's only here it happens. That is why he must leave. You see that, don't you? It's for his sanity he has to move away and leave Orla behind. I will make him whole again.'

So where is Alastair now? thought Frankie. Why has he gone off on his own? Why isn't he here, being made whole by this woman who sees herself as his saviour?

55

A hundred yards from the ancient church of St Peter, Alastair left *Water Lily* and set off on foot along the overgrown path that led directly to where Orla was buried.

It had surprised him that she hadn't wanted to be cremated, her ashes scattered at a meaningful landmark, or if not that, her body laid to rest in the heart of a forest in a biodegradable coffin made of willow, or even disposed of in a cardboard box. Certainly she had flirted with those options, but then out of the blue she had declared her wish that, when the day came, she was to be buried with all the bells and whistles of a traditional ceremony. She wanted a lavish casket lined with crimson silk and ivory lace, the sort seen in old horror movies, and from which Christopher Lee would rear up, fangs bared — her words — and a burial plot of her choosing at St Peter's.

'A room with a view,' she had said of where she wanted to be laid to rest, 'I want a view I can enjoy for eternity, not shoved at the back of the graveyard with only a crumbling wall to look at.'

He hadn't really taken her seriously, but on her death he discovered she had secretly arranged everything and selected a prime spot.

Location, location, location, even in death, Alastair thought grimly as he stood looking down at where Orla now lay, her feet pointing towards the river. There was an empty space next to her, which, he'd also discovered on her death, was meant for him. A companion plot . . . bound to each other even in death.

'Sorry to disappoint you, Orla,' he murmured, crouching down on the wet grass, the smell of damp earth rising up to him, 'but I have no intention of ending my days here. Not now.'

This was his first visit to her grave since the funeral. He had expected there to be more weeds encroaching, but there were very few — perhaps only the bravest had had the audacity to take root amongst the stone chippings within the raised granite plinth. He began picking at one, tossing it aside, then wondered why he was bothering; the weeds would only return and he wouldn't be here to halt their advance.

But then for that matter, why was he here at all? Was it to taunt Orla with his plans for the future? *To hell with your bloody companion plot, I'm off to pastures new with a beautiful woman who doesn't have a neurotic bone in her beautiful body! A woman who is giving me the chance to live a life of freedom and endless new possibilities!*

Or was it a subliminal need to ask for Orla's forgiveness?

All he really knew was that he'd come here because he needed to be alone, or more precisely away from everybody at Linston End. He'd never felt so claustrophobic there before, but the last twenty-four hours had closed in on him.

The irony was not lost on him that, of all the places to which he could have escaped, he'd ended up crouched over Orla's grave. It was as if she had lured him here, tugged on that invisible thread between them and forced him — as good as on his knees — to be with her.

His hands once again pulling absently at a weed, he tried to shake off the feeling that he was here to confront his sins, that Orla was demanding it of him. *Why else have you come?* he imagined her saying.

'Because I want to be free of you, once and for all,' was his answer.

You'll never be free of me, came back her reply, quick as a flash in his head. *Not after what you drove me to!*

There it was, the stark ugly truth of his conscience, the recognition that this was his punishment: he was to be permanently shackled to Orla, and the past.

You can run all you like, he heard Orla say, *but you can't hide.*

He clenched his hands into tight angry balls. He *could* run! He could run and run! Wasn't it the case that when he left Linston and he was travelling, he was free of the burden Orla had placed on him? That's why he had to get away, he had to leave all this behind him. He had to be free!

Me? came Orla's accusatory voice again. *Don't you mean the burden you placed on yourself by not saving me?*

'I was tired of saving you!' he fired back, startling a nearby blackbird in the bushes at the loudness of his words. More quietly, he muttered, 'I kept on saving you, Orla; again and again.'

As if suddenly realising what he was doing, and ignoring the wetness of the ground, he plonked himself down on it and clasped his head between his hands. Was he going mad, talking to his wife's rotting corpse, imagining her responses and justifying himself? Was this what she had driven him to?

Purgatory. This was his fate until the day he died, to be forever punished for failing to save Orla . . . to save her from herself.

He still couldn't make sense of why he had stayed as long as he had in the marriage, when so much of it had been a lie, when repeatedly he hoped things would change. But seldom do relationships make sense, and he had loved her so much in the beginning, had never believed that he would ever feel differently. Her outrageous sense of fun and her energy had been intoxicating, and he had thrived on her unpredictable nature, the storm force of her magnetism. Their sexual dynamism was at the core of their relationship; the extreme fierceness of it drove them deeper into each other's hearts. There was tenderness too, that was all the more poignant for its rarity.

But then the axis of their love changed when Orla's unfulfilled desire for a child impacted on their relationship. It was the first time in her life when she had been unable to have her own way over something, and it drove her to the edge of reason. His role then, as she became increasingly unable to cope with the internal forces that drove her to extremes, was that of protector and keeper of the worst of her emotions. For the most part he didn't mind — for better and for worse; that was what he had signed up for.

Orla made him promise that he wouldn't share the full extent of her misery with his friends. And just as he had always respected her wish that he never spoke of the abortion she'd undergone as a young girl, he kept his promise. If you loved somebody, you respected their wishes, that was what he believed.

But what she didn't appreciate was that he too had suffered heartache over their inability to have a family, and desperately in need of emotional support himself, he had turned to the one person he should not: Sorrel. He couldn't deny that it was a shamefully pathetic cliche that when he sank to his own emotional low, he turned to another woman to assuage his sorrow.

Not just any woman, but the wife of one of his closest friends. Sex with Sorrel had been so easy and uncomplicated — no temperatures taken, no strict timetable of optimum moments to adhere to, when sperm and egg might collide, and no pressure to perform to order, just the basic animal instinct to lose himself in a yielding woman.

The worst of it was Orla must have suspected. She never said anything directly, but she had to have noticed the perceptible change in Sorrel's manner, the glances that lingered on him for too long, the hand that rested on his arm unnecessarily, but most of all, the air of possession Sorrel began to display, as if she were confident of usurping Orla's position.

If he could turn back time and not make the

mistake he'd made of turning to Sorrel for comfort, he would do so in a heartbeat. It was a mistake he paid for dearly, when, and out of the blue fifteen years ago, Orla forced him to admit that he had slept with Sorrel. He had no idea what triggered her suspicion, but she had been triumphant in extracting the admission from him. He'd made it in the hope that once it was out in the open between the two of them, he would feel less guilty about it. He was tired of living in the shadow of his deceit; he wanted to be free of it.

He'd misjudged Orla's reaction. Her moment of triumph that she had been proved right was quickly surpassed by the need to punish him, to make him atone for his betrayal. Such was his remorse that whatever she demanded of him, he complied, hoping each time she would exonerate him. She never did. This then became the new reality of what marriage to Orla meant. And the crazy thing was, there were times when they were genuinely happy, when he still loved her. She could look at him in a certain way and he felt just as he had the day they met.

Yet more and more it crossed his mind to leave her, and whenever she recognised she had pushed him too far, she would cede him some small measure of respite and behave as though they were the happiest couple alive. It never lasted. Always there was the threat that she would tell Simon what he and Sorrel had done. It was a threat he had no wish for her to carry out and he did all he could to ensure she didn't.

But when last year he finally realised that he

couldn't keep up the pretence that their marriage resembled anything remotely normal or happy, he told her straight that enough was enough. 'I can no longer be your punchbag,' he said. 'The price you want me to pay for my one small mistake is too much.'

'It might seem a small mistake to you,' she'd countered, 'but to me it was the greatest act of betrayal. For which,' she'd added, 'you will have to pay the greatest price if you leave me.'

'You'll tell Simon?'

'Of course.'

'But why? Why after all this time would you want to do that to him? And to Sorrel, and Callum and Rachel as well. You'll deliberately hurt them all. Why?'

'I don't care about them; it's you I care about.'

'If that's true, you have an odd way of showing it.'

'I love you, Alastair. I love you in a way you've never understood. I need you for me to be able to function. I always have. Your love has always given me breath. Without it, I can't live.'

Summoning his courage, he'd said, 'But your love is choking me, Orla. You're slowly suffocating me with your desire to make me pay for hurting you. Wouldn't it be better for us to part and breathe air that hasn't turned toxic?'

She'd looked as if he'd slapped her. 'You can't leave me!' she'd cried. 'You can't! I won't let you!'

'Your threats won't make me stay,' he'd said, 'not now; it's gone beyond that.'

'But I need you! And you need me; you know

you do. We've always needed each other.'

He'd shaken his head. 'The only thing I need from you now is my freedom.'

She had turned manic at that. 'I'll kill myself if you leave me. I swear it, I'll kill myself and you'll have my death on your conscience for the rest of your life. You'll never be free of me!'

His patience pushed to the limit, he'd laughed. God help him, he'd laughed at her. 'Go ahead,' he'd shouted. 'Kill yourself and put us both out of our misery! I'm sick of your threats!'

Eighteen hours later, her body was found amongst the reeds in Linston Broad.

So yes, when he'd watched from an upstairs window and seen her take out the boat at two in the morning, when he knew she had been drinking and was in a highly emotional state, and had done nothing to stop her, he'd as good as put his hands around her neck and killed her.

But then they'd effectively been doing that to one another for years, slowly but surely squeezing the life out of each other.

The worst of it was, as she'd steered the boat out of the dyke in the moonlight, she had turned to look back up at the house and seen him in the window. She thinks I'll take a boat out and follow her, he'd thought, that I'll be there to save her from carrying out her threat.

He hadn't done that. He'd turned away from the window and had gone to bed not caring in the slightest if she tried to drown herself, almost wishing that she would.

★   ★   ★

418

The back of his neck twitched and he looked up, half expecting to see Orla standing over him. But it wasn't Orla; it was Sylvia. 'Are you all right, Alastair?' she asked.

He dashed away the wetness that he realised now covered his face, and heaved himself to his feet. 'Sorry,' he said, embarrassed to be found in such a way.

'There's no need to apologise,' Sylvia said. 'If a grieving husband can't cry over his wife's grave, I don't know when he can.'

He let her think whatever seemed plausible to her. 'What brings you here?' he asked.

'Neil and I come every few weeks to keep the grave neat and tidy. We started doing it when you went away. I hope you don't mind.'

That explained how few weeds there were, he thought, pushing a hand through his hair. 'Of course not,' he forced himself to say, 'I'm grateful.'

A short while later he retraced his steps to where he'd left *Water Lily* and headed for whatever it was that awaited him at Linston End. It was time to sort things out once and for all.

56

'Do you think we'll all have to leave now?'

Jenna slid her gaze from the Mill across the smooth surface of the water and looked at Rachel in the chair beside her. They were sitting in the pavilion at the end of the garden. 'Do you want to leave?'

'There doesn't seem much point in staying, does there?' Rachel said. 'Although you might want to stay because of your fiddle-playing lover-boy.' She tilted her head to where Jenna had just been staring.

'Stop fishing.'

'I'm an invalid, it's my right to fish.'

Jenna smiled. 'You're going to milk your near-death experience for all it's worth, aren't you?'

'Damned straight. Tell me again about you and Blake cosying up over at the Mill. Have you kissed him?'

'I wouldn't tell you if I had.'

'You have! You've kissed him! And while I was fighting for my life.'

'While you were sleeping, don't you mean?'

Rachel pounced. 'Aha, so you admit it, you have kissed him!'

'I thought you said you were feeling all worldly-wise and grown up as a consequence of nearly dying? Seems to me you're your usual daft self.'

Rachel offered her a pitiful smile. 'And you're your usual prickly self, batting away my questions. For your interest, I'm only enquiring about who you may or may not have snogged because I want to know where you stand with my brother. I don't want you upsetting him. That's my very grown-up self speaking.'

'I stand in exactly the same position as I always have with Callum. He's made it very clear that we're just friends. As I believe I informed you before.'

Rachel snorted. Nobody could invest more disdain or disbelief into such a simple gesture. 'Whatever Callum told you it would have been said to gauge your reaction, to see whether you agreed with him. Did you agree, one hundred per cent? Or did you feel a teeny flicker of disappointment?'

Jenna thought about this. The truth was, afterwards she had. But wouldn't that be true of anyone being friend-zoned, the door being firmly shut? Was that the fickleness of the human heart, never to be entirely satisfied?

'I'll take your silence as a yes,' remarked Rachel, 'that you were disappointed.'

'It's not as straightforward as that. Haven't you ever been in a situation where your head and heart are giving out confusing messages?'

'All the time; that's why I keep on picking the wrong boyfriend. So who has your heart and who has your head, that's the million dollar question?' Rachel wagged her finger. 'The truth and nothing but the truth. Imagine I have a gun pointing at your head and you have two seconds

421

to reply, or it's curtains for you.'

Jenna smiled. 'What if I snatched the gun out of your hands and coshed you over the head with it instead? Which is quite tempting right now.'

'Then I'd never speak to you ever, ever again! Honestly, why can't you play fairly?'

'It's my speciality. As a lawyer I'm trained never to answer a question with a simple yes or no.'

Rachel puffed out her cheeks. 'Well, for what it's worth, I know for a fact that Callum is very much interested in you. He told me so himself.'

Jenna was shocked. 'When?'

'Earlier.'

Which meant, surmised Jenna, that when he came out to the garden and chatted to her, he'd already had this conversation with Rachel. Yet he'd given no hint of how he felt.

In contrast Blake had made his feelings all too clear. She still couldn't believe what he was prepared to do, that he would leave Heart-to-Heart so they could be more than friends. Was it just a wild and hollow gesture on his part, or was he serious? A few days ago, she might have said he wasn't capable of being serious. But she had changed her view dramatically in the last twenty-four hours, having seen a more sensitive and mature side to him.

Never would she have guessed that Blake could make her feel the way he had while playing that exquisite piece of music for her. She thought now of his hands holding the bow of his violin, and the extraordinary intensity of his concentration. She had wanted to believe it was the poignancy of the music she had responded to, and not him, but she knew that was a lie. She had found the experience of watching and listening to him play powerfully erotic. And yes, she had been more than tempted to kiss him, but she hadn't.

None of this was she prepared to share with Rachel. Not yet. Not until she had fully processed what she felt for Blake, and whether or not she could trust these fledgling feelings for him. From the far reaches of her memory came the words of so many of her old school reports — *'Jenna is highly methodical . . . Jenna's reasoning is consistently sound . . . Jenna needs to learn to trust her own judgement more when confronted with a complex challenge.'*

'Hello? I'm still here you know.' said Rachel, nudging Jenna with her elbow.

'As if I could forget that when you're determined to interrogate me.'

'I've told you before; it's what good friends do. So back to what I was saying a few minutes ago — '

Jenna groaned.

'Calm down, I'm putting you and Blake, and Callum, to one side for now. I want to know your thoughts on Alastair. Do you think he would prefer us to leave?'

Grateful that Rachel had changed tack, Jenna said, 'I'd like to believe he doesn't, but what with all the tension and negative vibes everybody's giving off, I can't imagine he's enjoying us being here. Perhaps that's why he's disappeared.'

'Tell me again what was said, while you were

having lunch, and this time don't edit like you did before.'

'I wasn't editing,' Jenna lied.

'Yes you were. I know you, Jenna, I know when you're holding back.'

Jenna tutted. 'I'm beginning to regret helping to save you last night. Any chance I can throw you back into the broad?'

'That's harsh.'

And so was the conclusion Jenna had reached based on what she had witnessed in the kitchen. It was the last thing on earth to share with Rachel, but in a way she wanted to repeat every single word that had been said, so that her friend could judge for herself, and hopefully say it was all nonsense, that of course her mother couldn't have had an affair with Alastair!

As much as she didn't want to believe it was true, it was hard to read any other meaning into what Jenna had witnessed, especially Alastair's reaction and his attempt to shut Sorrel up. If they had had an affair, did Jenna's parents know about it? Or was this one of those secrets that friends, even the best of friends, kept from each other?

'Jenna?' prompted Rachel, 'I can practically hear the cogs working inside your head. What is it you're not telling me?'

'I'm not sure I should tell you,' she said, at length. 'I might have got the wrong end of the stick.'

'That's about as likely as me becoming prime minister. Now spit it out, and let me decide which end of the stick you've got hold of.'

And so Jenna did, but reluctantly. When she'd finished, adding that really people were saying extraordinary things at the time, Rachel pursed her lips. 'Mum and Alastair. Bloody hell! When?'

'I don't know, and please, Rachel, I could be wrong.'

Rachel frowned, as if still taking it in. 'Poor Dad,' she said finally, 'how the hell could Mum do that to him? And poor Orla. Hey, what if that was why Orla topped herself?'

'There's no evidence to suggest that she did. None at all.'

'But you have to admit, an affair changes everything. Now suicide doesn't look so out of the question, does it?'

Jenna recalled that day in London with Callum when he had hinted that maybe Orla's death wasn't quite the accident it had been made out to be. 'I think your brother knows more than he's ever let on,' she said.

'Why do you say that?'

Jenna explained. And then she said, 'You don't seem overly shocked that your mother might have had an affair.'

Rachel shook her head. 'I'm not sure that my brain is fully functioning yet, maybe shock will come later when I've had more time to think about it.'

'Do you suppose it's inevitable when a group of friends have lived their lives so closely linked that the lines become blurred and — '

'They end up in one another's beds?'

Jenna winced. 'That's one way of putting it, yes.'

'If it's true, then I want you to swear here and now that you'll never sleep with the man I marry. That's if I ever do marry.'

'I'd never do that,' said Jenna, 'not in a million years.'

'Swear it. Swear it on your mum and dad's lives.'

'I swear it on Mum and Dad's lives. And you need to promise me that you won't say anything of what I've told you to your parents. Just pretend we've never had this conversation.'

Rachel nodded, but she didn't promise. Instead she said, 'It just goes to show that you never really know your parents, do you?'

'Maybe that's because we see them only as parents and not fallible like us.'

'Parents are supposed to have it all sussed. They're not meant to make mistakes. That's our job.'

Thinking that she would be utterly devastated if her own parents decided to separate, Jenna said, 'What would you do if your parents divorced over this?'

'I'd stop them. I'd do everything I could to make them stay together.'

'Even if it makes them unhappy?'

'Bloody hell, are you trying to break up my family?'

'No!'

'Sounds like it.'

'Honestly I'm not, quite the contrary. I hate the way so much has changed in the last year. I want everything to be the way it used to be.'

'Up until yesterday, I would have agreed with

you, but now I'm beginning to see things differently. Perhaps Alastair has the right idea in wanting to start a new life somewhere else. Although God knows why he thinks Valentina is the person to do it with. I wish I knew what it was that he sees in her. She's a Class A bitch.'

'He loves me because I make a refreshing change to his dead wife and judgemental friends,' said a firm and very clear voice.

At the sight of Valentina appearing from nowhere at the side of the pavilion, Jenna all but sprang out of her chair. But Rachel didn't flicker. Perhaps coming so close to death really had desensitised her to shock.

'Didn't anyone ever tell you that it's rude to eavesdrop on a private conversation?' Rachel said with an imperious coolness that reminded Jenna of Sorrel. Not a trace of embarrassment did she show that they had been caught talking about Valentina so unflatteringly.

'I couldn't help but hear you, you were hardly being discreet,' the woman said.

'Was there anything you actually wanted?' asked Rachel.

'I came to ask how you were feeling.'

'As you can see, I've made a good recovery, considering what happened to me.'

'I'm very glad to hear that.'

'I'm sure you are,' muttered Jenna sarcastically. 'For Nikolai and Irina's sake, no doubt.'

Valentina stared hard at Jenna. 'I find it very strange what you were saying before, that you don't want life to change, especially given how young you are. Life has to change. It *must* change. If it doesn't, one becomes nothing but a rotting vegetable.'

'How long were you listening in on our conversation?' demanded Rachel.

'Long enough. But I shall leave you now so you can return to your spiteful gossiping.'

'You might think you can fool Alastair, but you can't fool the rest of us,' Rachel called out after her.

Valentina turned, an expression of bitter amusement on her face. 'But I'm not interested in fooling any of you, or what any of you think of me. It is only Alastair's opinion that matters.'

'If I were you I wouldn't be so sure that you have that squarely in the bag as you believe. I mean, where is he right now?' Rachel made a play of looking around her. 'You know what, I'd put money on him hiding from you because he's beginning to have doubts.'

The woman tried to hide it, but Jenna saw the flicker of emotion pass across her face. A nerve had been touched and, cruelly, Jenna was glad that Rachel was being so direct.

But then Valentina snatched back the advantage. 'If I were you,' she said, 'I would be much more concerned about your mother's behaviour, than my relationship with Alastair.'

Jenna put out a hand to restrain Rachel from rising to the bait, and in a pulsating silence thrumming with tension between them, they watched Valentina walk away.

'She's a piece of work, isn't she?' Jenna said at length. 'How can Alastair be so blind to what she's really like?'

'He's welcome to her,' Rachel said angrily, jumping to her feet. 'And you know what, if he's the kind of man who can sleep with his best friend's wife, then he can go to hell for all I care. And I'm going to say that to his face the minute he gets back from wherever he's gone. Then I'm going to pack my case and leave. Everything feels tainted here now, like nothing was ever as I thought it was. It was all a lie!'

As though the shock of what Jenna had shared with her had now finally hit home, Rachel's eyes filled with tears.

57

Callum had just arrived back at the boatyard when his mobile pinged with a text. It was from his sister. *Don't ask why, but can I come and stay with you?*

What now? What new drama was his sister at the centre of? Instead of replying straightaway, he texted Jenna to get the low-down. Unlike Rachel, Jenna could be relied upon one hundred per cent for an objective overview.

When he didn't get a response, he slipped the mobile back into the pocket of his jeans, deciding to defer replying to his sister until he was in full possession of the facts. As fond of Rachel as he was, being cooped up with her at Water's Edge Cottage would be a trial of monumental proportions.

He went to check on the 1930s cruiser Kyle and Ian were working on. It was a lengthy renovation project, a labour of love that was costing the client an eye-watering amount of money, but the end result would be worth every penny.

He found Ian on his own, changing out of his overalls. He was Callum's most experienced worker, a man who'd spent all his life working in boatyards. There wasn't anything he didn't know and Callum lived in dread of him wanting to retire. Thankfully he showed no obvious desire to do so any time soon, but being well into his sixties, Callum was selfishly making the most of the man's talents while he could. Such was Ian's dedication to his craft; he was a keen advocate of training up younger lads, just as he had with Callum. It still felt odd to him that he was now Ian's boss.

'Kyle asked if he could get off home early,' Ian said as Callum went over to inspect the hull of the boat. 'I hope you don't mind, but I said he could.'

'Of course I don't mind. Nothing serious, I hope?' said Callum, running his hand over the satisfyingly smooth wood of the craft above his head.

'His fiancée wasn't feeling so good and Kyle was anxious.'

'I've lost track of when the baby is due.'

'Not for another two months.'

'Did Kyle think he'd be in tomorrow?'

'I don't rightly know. It'll depend on what the problem is with Vicky, I suppose.'

'If he needs more time off that's fine by me, but let me know and I'll give you a hand with this.' Callum tapped the side of the boat. 'I want us to deliver on time, the client's had to wait long enough as it is.'

After Ian and the others had gone, Callum sat at the cluttered desk in his cramped and untidy office, and contemplated the meeting he'd had in Norwich at the bank that afternoon. It had gone surprisingly well, better than he'd hoped for. If all went to plan, he would be able to borrow enough money to extend the boat rental side of the business. Another change to add to the many currently going on.

He scrolled through his emails, dealt with

those that needed his immediate attention, and was about to switch off the computer when his mobile pinged. Then pinged again.

The first message was from Rachel asking him where the hell he was and why hadn't he replied to her earlier text.

The second was from Jenna. *All getting a bit weird here, will try to explain this evening if you're joining us for dinner. That's if we make it to dinner, chances are we won't!*

He didn't think twice. He rang Jenna. She answered after two rings.

'Okay,' he said, 'what's going on now? More to the point, why does Rachel suddenly want to come and stay with me?'

'I didn't know that she did.'

'Apparently she does.'

'It might be because we had a bit of a run-in with Valentina.'

'Over what? Those bloody obnoxious stepkids of hers?'

There was a pause in his ear. Thinking the signal had cut out, he said, 'Jenna, are you still there?'

'Yes.'

'Why are you hesitating?'

'Perhaps you should speak directly to Rachel.'

'Why?'

'I . . . I just think you should.'

'Is that my brother?' Callum heard Rachel demand in the background. There was a muffled response from Jenna and then his sister's voice blasted in his ear. 'Why didn't you reply to my texts?'

432

'I was just about to,' he lied. 'I was busy earlier.'

'So can I come and stay with you?'

'What's brought this on?'

'If I don't come to you I'll head back to London,' she said without answering him.

'I wouldn't advise going back to London on your own, not after what you've just been through, and if you come to my place, not only will it be a bit cramped, but you'll be on your own while I'm working. Is that what you really want?'

'Anything would be better than staying here with that vicious-tongued Valentina. Honestly, Cal, you wouldn't believe how vile she is. And worse still, it looks like Mum and Alastair have had an affair.'

'*What!*'

'Oh God, I didn't mean to tell you that. Jenna said I shouldn't mention it to anyone until we knew for sure.'

'Rachel, stop babbling and tell me what the hell you're going on about? Of course Mum and Alastair have never had an affair, don't be ridiculous!'

'There's no need to shout, Cal.'

'Yes there is when your mouth is out of control and you're not making any sense. Now take a deep breath and start from the beginning by explaining what is going on, or what you think is going on, because I'll tell you straight, there's no way Mum would have cheated on Dad, and with Alastair of all people. It's madness.'

'Is it? Then maybe you'd better speak to Jenna, she was the one who was present when all this kicked off. I'll hand you over to her and you can — '

'No,' he interrupted, 'don't bother; I'll come up there.'

★ ★ ★

Alastair still hadn't made it back to the house. He'd spotted Laura sitting alone at a table near the water's edge in the garden of the Wherryman, and after she'd spotted him and waved, he'd changed course and moored up.

He'd ordered a cold beer at the bar and was sitting opposite Laura when he felt a settling of his mood. There was something about her company that he found oddly calming. There was no hurry to her, no quickness of movement or speech. She was measured and thoughtful and her low-pitched voice, together with a level gaze, had the effect of quietly drawing more out of him than he might otherwise want to share.

Or was that a lie on his part? Had he deliberately decided to stop and have a drink with her for the sole purpose of clearing his head of the clamour that was building there? But why did he think she would have the ability to do that?

'You look troubled,' she said as he watched an elegantly regal swan gliding by with half a dozen cygnets following closely behind. 'Would I be right?'

'Whatever gives you that impression?' he said, his hands wiping at the condensation on his beer glass.

'I thought it the other night and I'm thinking

it now because you have a house full of guests, but here you are having a drink with a stranger.'

'You're not a stranger.'

'But neither am I part of your circle of close friends. Which perhaps gives me an advantage over them, in that I see you through unblinkered eyes. I have no preconceived ideas about you. Therefore, I see what I see.'

'And what do you see?'

She smiled. 'Are you sure you want to know?'

Curious, he nodded. 'I'll risk it.'

'In that case, I see a worried man who finds himself backed into a corner wondering how on earth he got there.'

He smiled back at her, tried to keep his voice light. 'Do you see an escape route for this allegedly worried man?'

'Is that what you want to do: escape?'

'Don't we all at some stage in our lives?'

'Oh yes. I've done it myself. After my marriage ended with Blake's father five years ago, I sold my house and went to live in Greece. It was the barmiest thing I ever did, like running away to join the circus, but Lord it was fun!'

This was the most she'd ever given away of herself, Alastair realised. 'And now here you are on the Broads, staying at the Mill,' he said, 'where you probably hoped to enjoy some peace and quiet, but instead find yourself opposite a house of mayhem. For which I can only apologise.'

She smiled again. Such a knowing smile, he found himself thinking as he watched her drink her wine.

'But the question still stands,' she pressed, 'are you in need of escape? If so, what is it you want to run away from?'

'Running away sounds such a cowardly act.'

'Depends what one is running from. It might be the bravest thing one ever does.'

He drummed his fingers over the rough wood of the bench table they were sitting at. 'Everyone thought I was being so incredibly brave after Orla's death; now I suspect they think my actions are that of a fool. A misguided fool.'

'Falling in love can make even the most rational of people behave quite out of character.'

'Do I seem rational to you?' he asked, while a large motor cruiser manoeuvred into a mooring place in front of the pub. 'Personally, I'm beginning to have doubts about my ability to think straight.'

'I'd say you're as rational as the next person who's still going through a painful grieving process,' she answered him.

'What if I said you were wrong, that I'm not grieving. Not anymore. My marriage was like one long grieving process. Towards the end, it was a car crash of a marriage.'

She lowered her wineglass to the table and fixed him with a direct gaze. 'Even the loss of something that caused such pain still needs to be grieved for,' she said quietly.

When he didn't respond, she said, 'You stayed married for all that time. Why? You had no children, no real ties.'

How strange it was to be able to talk so openly with this woman he barely knew. But then as she'd said, she viewed him through objective eyes; she had no expectations of him. Unlike Simon and Danny, and all the others, who expected him to behave in a certain way and to be the man he'd always been. Even Valentina now had expectations of him. When they'd met, he'd presented himself with a clean slate — he could be whoever he wanted to be. Had that been the attraction? And was it ever possible to wipe the slate clean, effectively reinvent oneself and start afresh?

'Orla and I were tied to each other in ways that I don't think anyone else would understand,' he murmured.

Laura looked at him sceptically. 'I'm not buying that, Alastair; you could have walked away any time you chose. What really made you stay? Was it Orla's dependency on you? That can be a very powerful bond between a couple, much like a drug.'

He wondered how Laura had made such a leap of thought, and then suddenly realised why he felt so comfortable in her company — she reminded him of Aunt Cora, a woman who had the most insightful and analytical approach to any problem. Nothing had fazed her. Laura seemed the same. He said, 'Orla's dependency on me was certainly part of the problem, but strange as it sounds, after what I've admitted, I did love her. I really did.' As he said the words, a great well of emotion rose up within him and suddenly scared he might lose control of his emotions, like he had at Orla's graveside, he looked away, over to the other side of the river where a great crested grebe was nosing in and out of the bank. When he trusted himself to be able to speak again, he turned back to face Laura. 'You're a very intriguing woman, aren't you?'

She raised her eyebrows. 'Am I?'

'I think you know you are. It's part of your charm. And funnily enough, you remind me of someone for whom I had the utmost respect.'

She smiled. 'I'll take that as a compliment, in that case, thank you. But if I could be permitted to give you one small piece of advice, it's this. We mostly choose what we want to remember, and sometimes it doesn't always give the complete picture.'

'Biased selective memory, you mean?'

'We all do it, and maybe it might help you to be more at peace with yourself if you don't dwell on those memories, perhaps even learn to distrust them. That way the confusion and pain might lessen for you.'

For some moments he contemplated whether there was any truth in what she said, then he abruptly drained the last of his beer. 'I ought to be getting back, everybody will be wondering where I am.'

'Have you been out for long?'

'Long enough to raise some concern, I should think. I switched off my mobile, which again will only have added to the concern. I needed time to think.'

'And have you been able to do that?'

'It's confirmed the sensation that's been creeping up on me, that I'm at the wheel of a speeding car that has no brakes, and I'm heading downhill towards a cliff edge.'

'You do realise you can stop the car whenever you want. You just switch off the engine.'

On his feet now, he said, 'Is life always that simple to you?'

'I've come to know that we're more in charge than we give ourselves credit for; it's just a matter of knowing exactly what it is we want. Do you want to be with Valentina more than anything else in the world? If so, run off with her and take the risk that you may or may not live happily ever after.'

'And the alternative?'

'Good heavens, Alastair, do I really need to spell it out for you?'

'I'm interested to know what you think the alternative is.'

'You confront what it is you're really running away from.'

58

'Sorrel, we can't go on like this.'

'Like what?' she asked, listlessly.

'You've been avoiding me. We have to talk.'

'You're right, Simon,' she said, 'we do.'

She turned around from the open window to face her husband. For what felt like an eternity she had been rooted to the spot in their bedroom, just staring — unseeingly — down at the garden, her mind blank, her body as still as a statue. She felt dead inside, impervious to anything that might touch her.

'Why have you been hiding from me?' he asked, closing the door behind him.

'We've been hiding from each other since forever.'

He shook his head, gave her one of his bewildered-out-of-his-depth looks. 'Sorrel, I'm a simple straightforward man, don't give me this cryptic crap.'

'There's nothing cryptic in what I'm saying, Simon, but you need to ask yourself whether you really want this conversation to go any further. Do you? Because once the genie is out of the bottle, there'll be no going back, no pretending in the way we have for most of our marriage.'

'Have you ever thought that that was half our problem, the pretence?'

Surprised at his question, at his apparent insight, Sorrel went over to the dressing table and moved her bottle of Chanel No.5 so that it lined up precisely with the rest of her cosmetics. Order. That's what she had busied herself with all her life, keeping the external world in order, because her internal world was a mess. Bringing order to chaos, that was her speciality.

'Sorrel?'

Without answering him, she raised her hand and swept away the neat orderliness of the dressing table. What she missed, she swiped at yet again, clearing every last inconsequential item.

She stared at the mess now strewn across the cream carpet, wanting to crush everything under foot, to grind the contents of those pots, tubes and bottles into the soft woollen pile, to smear the carpet thoroughly with the ugly greasiness and symbolic artifice of it all.

Destruction. That was the course she was now set on.

In the frozen silence, she looked at Simon and saw the disbelief on his face. 'I slept with Alastair,' she said.

He swallowed. 'Yes,' he said simply.

She faltered at his response, feeling perversely cheated that he wasn't angrier. Did he care so little for her? 'It wasn't a one-off thing,' she said. 'It happened many times.'

Simon's jaw tightened. 'How often?'

'I can't remember exactly,' she replied, 'I didn't keep a log-book on our affair.' Which was a lie. She could recall every encounter, every time she had lain in bed with Alastair. Each coming together of their bodies was etched on her memory. Now with painful shame.

'When?'

'Does it matter?'

'Yes.'

She sighed. 'It was years ago.'

'How many years ago? I want to know when.'

Annoyed by what she saw as the triviality of his question, she said, 'Twenty-five years ago, when Orla miscarried for the last time. When Alastair was at his wits' end coping with her.'

She saw genuine surprise flicker in his expression, as though she had given him the wrong answer. Then: 'What? You slept with Alastair to comfort him? Is that your justification?'

'I'm not trying to justify what I did. You wanted to talk, so I'm talking to you. I had an affair with your best friend. What else is there to say?' Her words slowly crashed down like bricks, one after another, demolishing once and for all the faulty foundations of their marriage.

'How can you be so indifferent to what you're admitting to?' he asked. At his sides his fists were clenched and his pulse was ticking at his right temple.

'Because it's not news to me; I've lived with the knowledge for a long time.'

'Are you even going to say sorry?'

'Would it change anything?'

He blinked. 'Have I been such a poor husband to you?'

'Are you trying to make me feel guiltier than I already do?'

He shook his head. 'I'm trying to understand you.'

'I wouldn't bother. I'm beyond understanding.

But if it helps, I am sorry.'

He breathed in deeply. 'The irony is that I wanted to say I could forgive you, that I always knew that Alastair was special to you. After that scene at lunch today, I had no choice but to force myself to accept that maybe once, or even twice, you had slept with him, and that you regretted it.'

'How very generous of you to say you could forgive me.'

He frowned at her sarcasm. 'Not generous at all. I saw it as a way to atone for my own guilt, for very nearly doing the same with Orla.'

'*Very nearly?*' she echoed. 'What does that mean?'

'There was a night. Here. We'd had too much to drink. We were in her studio and . . . ' his words trailed away and he went over to lean against the windowsill, carefully stepping over the mess she'd made on the carpet.

Her husband's sickening and dogged devotion to Orla had always irritated Sorrel, and now morbid curiosity compelled her to want to know more. Had he tried his luck with the Queen Bee herself and been turned down? 'Don't be coy, Simon,' she said, 'spit it out.'

He turned around. 'We could have had sex, but I didn't go through with it. I couldn't. I couldn't do that to you, or the children. Or Alastair.'

'How very virtuous of you. How did that go down with Orla?'

'As so much did with her; she laughed it off, just regarded it as a drunken moment best forgotten.'

'And based on that drunken moment, you feel

you can forgive me my sins?'

He hesitated, shoved his hands into his trouser pockets. 'I thought I could, but now I'm not so sure. Now I'm not sure I can bear to be in the same room as you.'

'I don't blame you; I feel much the same way about myself.'

He stared at her.

'I mean it, Simon. Whatever anger you have towards me is nothing compared to the self-loathing I now have to live with.'

'Now?' he repeated. 'Why now and not before? What's changed?'

'Everything's changed. Just as you kept saying.'

'You mean now that Alastair has Valentina and you've been forced to accept he'll never love you? Is that it?'

His voice resonated with bitterness, and was no less than she deserved. 'I've been forced to accept that I've been a fool. So where does this leave us?'

'Apart from me wanting to beat the hell out of Alastair?'

'How reassuringly macho of you.'

He crashed his fist down on the windowsill. 'What the hell is wrong with you, Sorrel? I'm doing my best to be civil here and you appear to be determined to — '

'Determined to do what?' she cut in. 'To be honest for the first time in our marriage?'

He inhaled deeply, then out. 'Answer my question then, where do we now stand as a couple?'

'Given that you feel you can't bear to be in the same room as me, I'd have thought it was obvious.'

'Are you saying you want a divorce?'

'Don't you?'

He slumped like a ragdoll before her, his hands covering his face.

From the garden Sorrel heard voices; they were raised voices. Moving to the open window, she looked down to see Callum emerge from the pavilion with Jenna and Rachel in tow. He was marching towards Alastair who was in the process of mooring *Water Lily*.

* * *

Danny was first on the scene to pull Callum off Alastair, but it wasn't easy, the boy was throwing punches like a thing possessed. Frankie and the girls were yelling at Callum to stop, but he was deaf to their cries. It was only when Sorrel and Simon appeared with Valentina close behind that he seemed to come to his senses. But then he turned on his mother.

'How could you! How could you do it? And with all people, Dad's best friend?'

White-faced, her eyes wide, Sorrel flinched at her son's words. 'Who told you?' she asked breathlessly.

'You practically announced it yourself at lunch today, so I'm told. And Alastair's just confirmed it to me.'

They all turned to stare at Alastair who was now being fussed over by Valentina. 'You see, my darling,' she was saying, 'this is why you have to get away from here, there is too much history here, too much animosity amongst your so-called friends for you. Only now are you seeing the situation as it really is.'

He seemed far from grateful for her attention. 'I'm okay,' he told her roughly, batting her hands away with some force. She looked at him, stung.

'I'm sorry, Simon,' Alastair then said, wiping the blood that was coming from his mouth. 'Believe me, if I could go back and erase what I did, I would. It was a terrible mistake. It should never have happened.'

'A terrible mistake you kept on repeating, I'm reliably informed by my wife. She's just told me it happened so frequently she can't recall how many times the two of you betrayed Orla and me.'

Alastair levelled his gaze on Sorrel. 'Could you not have spared him?'

'It serves you right,' she said, 'for tossing me aside when you'd had your fun. One way or another, you were always going to have to pay for that. This is retribution.'

At Danny's side, Rachel let out a small gasp, and as if suddenly remembering their presence, Sorrel said, 'I'm sorry, Rachel and Callum, that you had to find out this way.'

'As am I,' said Alastair.

'You're not sorry!' roared Simon, and without warning, he whipped round and slammed his fist into Alastair's jaw, sending him sprawling to the ground. 'Violence never solved anything,' he said, rubbing the knuckles of his hand, 'but it

446

sure as hell feels the right thing to do.'

Staggering to his feet, Alastair said, 'Go on then, hit me again if it makes you feel better, but it won't change anything.'

Simon took him at his word and suddenly the two men were brawling like a couple of drunks, winding back their arms to land a punch, then grabbing hold of each other, grunting and groaning.

'Stop it!' shouted Rachel, when the two men thumped onto the ground with Alastair on top of Simon. 'Just stop it!'

Danny was about to try and pull them apart when he heard a mobile phone ringing. He instinctively patted his pockets, but then saw Frankie reaching into hers. He could tell from her face when she listened to who was calling that something bad had happened. Something far worse than what was going on here. If that were possible.

59

In numb and muted shock, with the acrid stench of smoke filling their nostrils and permeating their clothes, maybe even their skin, and the drip, drip, drip of water beating like a drum in their ears, Frankie stared around at the blackened and sodden wreckage of their beloved home.

What hadn't gone up in flames in the blaze had been ruined by water. It was strange what had survived the flames — blackened skeletal wooden remains of armchairs, the upholstery burnt away; the two pottery jugs on the charred windowsill; the ceramic tiles and metal surround to the fireplace and companion set. Even the drenched rug beneath their feet — bought while on a long weekend to Istanbul many years ago — was only partially blackened.

It was inconceivable that anyone could have deliberately done this, that sweet-natured Danny, of all people, had been targeted so sadistically and so personally. It was a wicked and malicious violation. But thank God their neighbours had been so quick off the mark to call the fire brigade. Thank God also that Jim across the road had been looking out from an upstairs window and seen with his own eyes what the deranged woman was doing — pouring petrol and shoving lighted rags through the letterbox, and in broad daylight too.

'It could have been a lot worse,' Frankie said in defiance of what her heart was telling her, 'we should at least be grateful that the fire never really had a chance to take hold and destroy the entire house.'

Danny looked at her, his eyes wretchedly glazed with shock, his face grey, his lips pale. 'It's my fault,' he said. 'I'm sorry. I've brought this on us.'

She slipped her hand through his, squeezed it hard, knowing that, like never before, he needed her solid reassurance. 'This was *not* your fault.'

'How can you say that? If I hadn't interfered at Woodside Suzie Wu wouldn't have done this. It's nothing short of a vendetta and all because I opened my mouth.'

'A vendetta it might be, but it's come from a dangerously twisted mind.'

Danny put his hands to his face and shook his head. 'I keep thinking what would have happened if we'd been here . . . if we hadn't been at Linston End, if that crazy woman had done this at night when we'd been asleep in bed and the fire had — '

'No!' said Frankie firmly. 'You're not to say that. We weren't here, so let's be thankful nobody was hurt, and that it was only the hall and the two rooms at the front of the house that have been ruined.'

'But the smoke damage,' he began to say, 'it's — '

'No buts,' she interrupted him. 'We can put it right. It will take time, but we can do it.' She wrapped her arms around his sagging shoulders.

'We'll do it together. Yes?'

Before he could reply, and from behind them, they heard footsteps crunching on broken glass.

'The police say they've caught Suzie Wu,' said Jenna, indicating the phone in her hand. 'What's more, they have CCTV footage of her at a petrol station filling a container with petrol as well as buying a lighter.'

'That and Jim's video of her running off down the road has her pretty much bang to rights,' said Simon.

'Meanwhile,' said Alastair, 'the house needs to be made secure. I've arranged for somebody to come and board up the windows and front door. The man I spoke to said he'd be here within the hour.'

'We also need, given the legal responsibility involved, to get a surveyor in asap to ensure the building is safe, and an electrician as well.' This was from Simon.

'I've already notified the insurance company,' said Jenna. 'You'll need to decide whether or not you want to appoint a loss assessor. In the morning, when it's light, I'd recommend we come back and take as many photographs of the damage as we can, as evidence.'

'Goodness,' murmured Frankie, reeling at the information coming at her, 'you've all been so busy.'

'That's what friends are for,' said Simon staunchly. 'As we speak, Sorrel and Rachel are back at home making up the spare room for you. You can stay for as long as you need.'

'You can also use Linston End if necessary,'

said Alastair. 'It's yours for the asking.'

Frankie pursed her lips, suddenly frightened she was going to cry. One minute Simon and Alastair had been grappling with each other on the ground like a pair of mauling bears, now they were pulling together to help her and Danny.

After she had answered her mobile back at Linston End and had taken in what the police officer had said, that there'd been a fire at their house, a possible arson attack, Simon and Alastair had let go of each other and everyone had leapt into action. It was as if the surreal events of the afternoon — of the last few days — had never happened. Callum and Valentina were the only ones to remain behind. Frankie had overheard Alastair explaining to her that there was no need for her to come as well. Valentina's face had darkened with petulance and she had muttered something Frankie couldn't hear. It had not had the ring of a sweet endearment to it and caused Frankie to wonder if the woman would still be there when Alastair later returned to Norfolk.

Whether she would be or not was of no consequence to Frankie; her priority was dealing with this mess and keeping Danny calm in the process. All the way here in the car — she had insisted on driving — she had willed his heart to stay strong, that the shock and strain of what lay ahead would not be too much for him. Never had she been more aware that he was a heartbeat away from death. She had been glad to have Jenna with them in the car, knowing that she would share the job of watching over her father.

451

★ ★ ★

It was nearly midnight when Jenna drove her parents to Ashleigh House, where Simon and Sorrel lived.

Every time she caught sight of her father's bleak expression in the passenger seat next to her, Jenna's throat tightened with fear and sadness; he looked almost as ill as he had after his heart attack. She was worried for her mother too, there was going to be so much to do in the coming days and weeks. Everyone was being so helpful, but Jenna was worried that wouldn't last for long, not when Simon and Sorrel had cataclysmic troubles of their own to deal with, and Alastair was planning to leave — he was probably in an even greater hurry to get away now.

With everything changing so fast, Jenna didn't dare think what might happen next. Even on a personal level, that was true. When she thought back to that day when Blake had come across her playing with the Punch and Judy puppets in her office, her life had been comparatively straightforward. Ever since though, he had unsettled her equilibrium. He still did.

There had been no time to explain to Blake that she was leaving Linston End, not until she was in the car with her parents and on their way to Suffolk. He'd replied to her text immediately, saying that if he could do anything to help, she only had to say.

His surprise announcement that he was contemplating leaving Heart-to-Heart, and the significance of what lay behind his decision, still stood between them. But now it seemed more likely that Jenna might be the one to leave the charity in order to help her parents sort out the mess here. Or perhaps she could take a leave of absence.

At Ashleigh House, she parked on the drive alongside Simon's car. She wondered with trepidation what the atmosphere inside the house would be like. Would Simon and Sorrel manage to keep the apparent truce of earlier in place for while they were there? She hoped so. Selfishly she didn't want to be caught up in any more animosity or drama; all she wanted was a quick bite to eat followed by a hot shower to get rid of the awful stench of smoke that now clung to her, and to go to bed.

Switching off the engine, the car was suddenly filled with a bright light. She turned around in her seat and saw that a familiar Range Rover had pulled in behind them. 'You won't believe it,' she said, 'but Alastair's here with us.'

Her parents also turned around in their seats. 'I thought he was driving back to Linston,' remarked Frankie.

'Maybe he's changed his mind and is hoping to stay the night.'

'I don't see that being very likely, Dad,' said Jenna.

'What about Valentina,' her father said, 'what's she going to say if he doesn't go back to her tonight?'

'To be honest, I don't care,' said Frankie. 'We have more important things to think about.'

As one, they pushed open the car doors and stepped out. Alastair was already waiting for them, his hands fiddling with his keys. It was a nervous gesture, and one that Jenna had never seen him do before. With sadness she now knew that the Alastair she knew of old — Uncle Al — no longer existed, that this man before her — the man who had had an affair with Sorrel — was as good as a stranger. But a stranger who had been only too ready to help her parents, she reminded herself. That counted for something.

The four of them fell silently in step and approached the house. The front door opened and Simon was there to greet them. For a split second it was as though everything was perfectly normal — and this was just another visit, when a warm welcome was guaranteed and Rachel would drag Jenna upstairs to her bedroom, leaving the boring grown-ups to their wine and chatter. But that illusion was shattered when, in the light cast from the coach lamp above the front door, Jenna saw Simon's expression alter at the sight of Alastair. It was a look of pure hatred.

★ ★ ★

Back at Linston End, Valentina was filled with an abundance of restless energy that she could put to no use, other than to pace back and forth across the terrace, occasionally venturing down the lawn to the river, guided only by an intermittent moon bursting through the clouds in the midnight sky. In her hand was a large glass of red wine — the near-empty bottle was on the kitchen table, along with her mobile.

Her temper barely under control, she had switched off her phone after Alastair had finally deigned to ring her. She had ended the call before he had had a chance to say goodbye. His wheedling tone asking for her patience and understanding had disgusted her.

Oh, she understood the situation all too well! She counted for nothing when it came to a choice between her and his friends. They would win every time.

Was this really the man she wanted to be with? A man who wasn't prepared to put her first? A man, who, with one whistle from his leech-like friends was happy to abandon her and go off to be by their side. He was no better than a pathetic little lapdog!

To be with him meant she would have to settle for being second best. Just as she had with Ivan. Was that what she wanted?

No! No it wasn't!

She drank deeply from the wineglass and sinking down into a chair on the terrace, she closed her eyes, and forced herself to remember how she had felt when she first met Alastair. The attraction had been instant, on both sides. Oh, how she had wanted him! And in those weeks of getting to know him, she had realised he had something to offer her which she had not known before in a man — complete and utter adoration. She had wanted to wrap herself in his adoration, to bask in it and know that he was hers. *All* hers.

She had had enough of sharing in the past — of sharing Ivan with his other women, his dubious business contacts, and Nikolai and Irina. For once in her life, she wanted something all to herself. Was that really too much to ask?

It had seemed so perfect, the two of them together — *Valentina and Alastair, Alastair and Valentina*. He had not just merely wanted her — he had *needed* her, to make him whole again. That's what he had told her two days before they parted for him to fly home to England, when they had been full of plans for their bright new future, and the glorious opportunities in store for them.

Had that been a lie — his need of her? Was it just another lie to add to the many it now transpired Alastair had told?

And to think she had believed him to be so refreshingly different.

But no, he was as bad as the rest of them.

Her initial reaction to the revelation that he had had an affair with his best friend's wife had been one of casual acceptance; after all, it was in the past and Orla had been such a difficult woman to live with.

But now, after a good deal of wine, Valentina had cause to question all that she knew about Orla. Or what she thought she knew. Had the woman been such a terrible wife? What if everything Alastair had shared with her about Orla was nothing but a stream of lies, a reinvention of the truth to suit the narrative he wanted to portray of himself?

'Never trust an Englishman,' her dearest Papa used to say. 'Beneath their superior act of gentility they don't play fairly, or honestly.'

Did anyone? And so what if Alastair had lied to her? She was not entirely innocent of that crime herself. Everybody lied, and for all manner of motives. She had lied to Alastair about her financial situation, or rather she had allowed him to think she was better off than she really was, encouraging him to believe that most of her money was tied up in various trusts and investments, which she couldn't touch for some years for tax reasons. Not once had he questioned her on the subject. In time, just as soon as she had Alastair securely committed to her, she had planned to make out that she had been swindled by a charlatan of a financial adviser who had disappeared off the face of the earth, taking all her investments with him.

In the deathly silence of the garden, the hoot of an owl close by startled her into opening her eyes. She raised her face to the moon, which had once again burst through the clouds. She breathed in the chill of the dank night air, thinking how it could not compare with the warm, lavender-scented air that she was offering Alastair in the south of France. There they could delight in the sweet fragrance of lemon and orange-tree blossom, along with mimosa and jasmine. Oh, how she yearned to leave this miserably parochial backwater and be some-where more cosmopolitan, where there were bars and restaurant and shops. And culture. Oh, how she craved that!

On the other side of the inky-black, brooding surface of the river, which to her looked menacingly sinister, she saw a light glowing in one of the windows of the Mill. As her gaze took in the garden and the looming shadows of the trees and bushes, she thought of the unedifying spectacle of Alastair and Simon thrashing around on the lawn, and before that, Callum brawling with Alastair. What had shocked her most about the incident was not the violence, but Alastair pushing her hands away so forcibly, and the harshness in his voice telling her not to fuss. In that split second, she could have happily slapped his face and walked away, all the way back to Paris. What had stopped her was the thought of how triumphant his friends would have been.

'I feel as though I've known you all my life,' Alastair had said to her only a few weeks after meeting.

Obviously it was only now that they were getting to know each other properly. The question was, did she like what she was getting to know? Could she readjust her thinking and accept that Alastair was not the perfect man she had wanted to believe he was?

60

Alastair was dog-tired. It had been a long day, and it wasn't over yet.

Torn between wanting to drive home to Linston End at breakneck speed, or to take it slowly because tiredness inevitably meant his reactions weren't as sharp as they should be, he was being sensible and sticking rigidly to the speed limits.

He was full of regret for the way things had turned out that day. He'd give anything to undo the harm he'd caused. He had badly wanted to talk to Simon, that was why he had changed his mind about driving back to Norfolk straight-away, and instead had driven to Ashleigh House to try and make amends in some way.

But Simon was in no mood for reconciliation. Alastair couldn't blame him. It had been okay when it had been a case of all hands on deck to help Danny and Frankie, but quite another matter when Alastair had begged to talk to him alone. Simon had been adamant as they faced each other on the doorstep that it would be better if he left.

With little traffic on the roads, the journey was proving soporific and Alastair was beginning to find it hard to stay awake. He knew he should pull over and rest, but he couldn't, he felt compelled to push on. To keep moving. It wasn't even as though he was in a hurry to get home, which appalled him. Only a few days ago, all he could think about was being with Valentina. Now there was a part of him that wanted to avoid her. Just as he had that afternoon when he'd gone out on the river.

'I have to help Danny and Frankie,' he'd explained when he was saying goodbye to her, before setting off for Suffolk with the others. 'Surely you see that?'

The coldness in her face told him she didn't. 'I understand that your friends will always come first,' she'd said.

'That's not true,' he'd replied, 'and it's twisting the situation. This is an emergency.'

'But it's not *your* emergency. It's Danny and Frankie's. Let them sort it out.'

'I can't do that,' he'd said.

She had shrugged and turned away to go back inside the house. He'd watched her go, shocked that she could be so callous. Could she really expect him to abandon his friends when they needed him most? What kind of a woman was she that she could be so heartless? All the way to Suffolk he was consumed by the worry that only now Valentina was showing her true colours. If this was the real Valentina, then it changed everything.

Not wanting to believe this, he'd phoned her as soon as he'd left Ashleigh House to say he was on his way home. He hung on to the hope that she would have calmed down and realised she had been unnecessarily petty. If she apologised, he told himself, he would be able to forgive her. But she didn't.

'I'm surprised you're bothering to come back,' she'd said. 'Why not stay there with your precious friends, who clearly mean so much more to you than I do.'

'Valentina,' he'd said patiently, 'I know the last few days have been difficult for you, but please don't take it out on me.'

'Why shouldn't I when you've lied to me?'

'When have I lied to you?'

'You didn't tell me you'd had an affair with Sorrel. You said you didn't want any secrets between us.'

She had a point. 'I'm sorry I kept that from you,' he'd said, 'but in my defence I didn't want you to think badly of me.'

'Well I do think badly of you! What kind of a man sleeps with his best friend's wife? How do I know you won't do it again with somebody else?'

'I promise you it's not something I've made a habit of doing. You have to believe me.'

His words were met with a silence. 'Look,' he said, 'we're both tired. After a good night's sleep, we can talk about this in the morning and — '

That was when he realised Valentina wasn't at the other end of the line anymore. Thinking the signal must have cut out, he rang her again, only to get her voicemail. He didn't leave a message. There was nothing he felt able to say. Better to wait until he was home.

With a bolt of adrenaline-pumping shock, he snapped his eyes open. How long had they been closed? One second? Ten seconds? More?

He opened the car window and gulped in the cool night air. Next he switched on the radio,

461

then changed his mind and found his old friend Stan Getz on the music system. After a few minutes, and deciding he was wide awake now, he closed the window, the better to hear the exquisite tone of the saxophone playing.

Orla had never shared his love of jazz, and had often teased him for his 'old man' taste in music. He had taken her to Ronnie Scott's on a date not long after they'd met, and it had amused her greatly to see how absorbed he became in the music.

'I might as well not be here,' she'd said, leaning in close and running a finger across his lower lip. As seductive moves went, it had the desired effect on him. They'd got happily drunk and later tumbled into a cab and, back at his student digs, they had enjoyed breathless and unprotected sex.

'If I'm pregnant now,' she'd said in the morning, 'you'll just have to do the decent thing and marry me.'

'I'll marry you even if you're not pregnant,' he'd happily declared.

'I may hold you to that.'

'Do!'

Funny, he thought now, that after all this time, and after everything that had happened, he should think of a good memory associated with Orla. And there had been so many good times, it was just that they had been eclipsed by the darkness that had slowly but surely obscured Orla's world.

Laura's words at the Wherryman that afternoon came back to him about choosing what we want to remember. He saw now that she was right and that the mind was capable of doing all sorts of strange things.

Had his played a trick on him, he wondered, thinking of Valentina. What if it had all been an illusion? A trick of the heart, as well as the mind?

If so, how had he been taken in? He liked to think that he was not a stupid man — that he was actually gifted with an above-average level of intelligence — yet somehow, through believing himself to be in love, he had managed to destroy everything that had mattered to him — the love and respect of his friends, and now the future he had imagined.

Believing himself to be in love . . .

The significance of what he'd just said hit him so forcibly he could have wept. He saw now that he should have listened to his friends. But he hadn't wanted to. He'd wanted so much to believe in Valentina and everything she represented. But none of it had been real. His behaviour had been that of a desperate man, clinging to the foolish hope he knew what he was doing.

How he wished now that he had never left Linston End and set himself on this disastrous path. A path that had led to Sorrel breaking her promise, and jeopardising her marriage to Simon. Poor Simon, how would he recover from this? Would he ever speak to Alastair again? Would Rachel and Callum?

He was just thinking of Callum's understandable rage that afternoon, when from nowhere he felt an explosive thud that ripped through him.

The sound of metal crunching and glass splintering filled his ears, and then he was being repeatedly and violently hurled against something hard.

Not knowing if time had stood still, or if minutes, or hours had passed, he struggled to make sense of what had happened. But when he tried to move, he found he couldn't, he was pinned against something, and he couldn't feel his arms and legs.

He gave up trying to move, vaguely aware that the world — having seemingly spun off its axis — had now gone black and eerily quiet. It was then that he realised he was barely able to breathe, that his chest felt crushed. Was he suffocating?

Or was he drowning?

Was this how Orla had felt when she was drowning? Had her lungs overridden her desire to end her life and fought desperately for a life-saving breath?

Alastair!

How strange. Somebody was calling to him. He strained to hear who it was. The voice was too far away for him to make it out though. Or had he imagined it?

He forced air into his lungs, and heard a strange bubbling sound like a drain emptying, followed by a wave of agonising pain. He cried out, but that just made the pain worse. He was conscious now of his throat constricting and liquid filling his mouth. Blood. It tasted of salt and metal, and was now seeping out through his lips.

Alastair!

There it was again. And he knew that voice. Knew it with every fibre of his being. It was Orla.

What was she doing here?

But then where was he?

This is death, Alastair. Didn't I tell you we'd never be parted?

To his surprise, he felt a great surge of emotion rise up within him at the clarity of her voice. It was love for the woman who had been so impossible to live with, but who had been such a vital and vibrant part of his life. Life would have been immensely dull without her.

'Orla,' he murmured, 'is that really you?'

Who else would it be?

He found he wanted to believe it. But was this another trick of his treacherous heart and mind?

He willed his lungs to fight for breath, before finally the pain and effort became too much and he gave up the struggle. With relief, he let go and slipped into the dark and unknown abyss.

And where, he knew, Orla was waiting for him.

61

Simon woke with a jolt. Squinting his eyes in the dark, he looked at his mobile and saw that he'd been asleep for less than an hour. Something — a sudden noise — had woken him from a dream that had felt disturbingly real.

He'd been dreaming of Alastair, of the two of them as boys. They'd been climbing a tree, each daring the other to go higher and higher. Simon had spotted a branch that didn't look as strong as the ones they'd already climbed, but he dared Alastair to pull himself up on to it. He then watched his friend — no longer a boy, but a grown man — tumble in slow motion to the ground, his arms and legs flailing wildly, his cry for help barely audible as the ground opened up beneath him, and he plummeted into the blackness of what looked like a well.

From the very tallest branch of the tree, and with grim satisfaction, Simon watched his friend disappear from sight. But then he realised that he couldn't climb down, he needed Alastair's help. Full of remorse, he called to his friend. But there was no answer. Only silence, an awful silence that told him he'd lost Alastair forever. But then he heard a noise. In the silence it had sounded as loud as a gunshot going off.

Now that he was fully awake, Simon recognised the noise as a creak of a door opening. He pushed away the duvet that covered him on the sofa and saw that there was a light coming from the direction of the kitchen.

He found Danny there in his pyjamas waiting for the kettle to boil.

'Sorry if I woke you.'

'You did me a favour,' Simon replied, helping himself to another mug from the cupboard and a teabag. 'You woke me from a gruesome dream in which I pushed Alastair to his death.'

Danny winced. 'Not surprising in the circumstances, but a bit extreme.'

They made their drinks and sat at the kitchen table. 'What the hell's happened to us, Danny?' Simon asked with a deep sigh. 'At this time in our lives we should have it all licked and be enjoying ourselves.'

Danny stared back at him over the rim of his mug. 'I wish I had an answer, but I'm afraid I'm as bewildered as you.'

'I doubt that,' Simon said with feeling.

'It's good of you to have us here,' Danny said after a pause, 'but with everything you and Sorrel have got to work out, we'll gladly make other arrangements.'

Simon shook his head. 'If I'm honest, having you here acts as a buffer, it keeps Sorrel and me from making any decisions.'

'As a friend I'd urge you not to do anything hasty. You and Sorrel have been married for so long. You have such a wealth of shared history, including Callum and Rachel, isn't that worth fighting for?'

'How would you feel if it was Frankie who'd had an affair with Alastair?'

'I would like to think that once I had recovered from the shock and anger, I'd want to know why.'

Simon puffed out his cheeks. 'I think we all know why Sorrel did it. Alastair was her first love. I could never compete. Not really.'

'Has the affair really come as such a big surprise to you, then?'

Seconds passed while Simon wrestled with his conscience. 'You're right,' he said at length. 'I always wondered if something might happen between them, but the thing is, I ignored it on the basis that I couldn't claim any moral high ground. There was always something about Orla that . . . well . . . you know, she was such an extraordinary woman. But I didn't pursue what I felt for her. Even though there was a moment when I could have. And that's not a confession I ever thought I'd have to make to you.'

He went on to explain that he'd shared this admission with Sorrel, in the hope that she would realise he was prepared to forgive her, because he knew all about temptation himself. 'What shocked me most, was that their affair happened long before my . . . my transgression.'

'When exactly?'

'Twenty-five years ago.'

'Does that make a difference to you?'

'I know what you're getting at, but in my mind, forgiveness hung on the fact that Sorrel had paid me back for what I had so nearly done, and that was fifteen years ago.'

'You thought she knew, so it was quits? Is that what you mean?'

468

Simon nodded. 'It occurred to me that Orla might have said something, or hinted at what we'd done, just to taunt Sorrel. She could be mischievous like that, couldn't she?'

Danny smiled. 'Oh yes, she loved playing games.'

In spite of everything, Simon smiled too. 'Didn't she just?' he murmured.

'Do you think it might help if Frankie or I spoke to Sorrel?'

'What, play at being mediators?'

'Yes. Would it do any harm?'

'Probably not, but the bigger question is what do I want? Do I want to be with a wife who maybe has never truly loved me, because that's the way it's looking.'

'We all love in different ways, Simon. Don't you think Sorrel would have left you already if she didn't love you?'

'Oh, Danny, you're such a tireless advocate of seeing the good in people, aren't you?'

'It's better than always seeing the bad. But can you really imagine a life without Sorrel?'

Simon shook his head. 'No,' he said sadly. 'No I can't. But it's more a case of what she wants.'

'There's always a way back, if it's what two people want. Maybe all that was needed was for the truth to come out, no matter how painful, because only then can things be put right.'

'Danny, I applaud you for being so positive.'

'Don't applaud me too much, it's easier to think about another person's problems than one's own.'

Simon put down his mug and slumped back in

his chair. 'I still can't believe what that madwoman did to your house. I guess this will put your plans to move to the Broads on hold now?'

'It will, yes. But perhaps that was nothing but a dream. The sensible thing would be to fix the house and stay here in Suffolk.'

'Who the hell wants to be sensible, Danny? If you have a dream, bloody well follow it, and while you still can!'

Danny smiled. 'That was Alastair's attitude.'

At the mention of their friend's name, the memory of the dream Danny had woken him from came back to Simon. He'd never been one for analysing dreams, but this one really didn't require much figuring out. What disturbed him was the sensation it had left him with, that despite everything — the betrayal and lies — he was mourning the loss of his closest friend.

It then struck him with a chill that Danny had put Alastair in the past tense.

That *was* Alastair's attitude.

★　★　★

They were just finishing their drinks when there was a ring at the doorbell.

'Who the hell can that be?' said Simon, glancing up at the clock. It was half past three in the morning.

With Danny alongside him, he went through to the hall and cautiously opened the front door.

Two police officers stared back at him. 'Mr Simon Wyatt?' one asked.

'Yes,' he replied apprehensively.

'May we come in, please?'

'What's this about?' he said, when they were all standing in the kitchen. 'Is it to do with the woman who set fire to my friend's house?' He indicated Danny at his side.

The officer who had spoken before looked confused. 'No, sir, it's nothing to do with that. I'm afraid there's been a serious road accident involving a Mr Alastair Lucas.'

62

Two months on, and following a police investigation as to the cause of the accident, a post-mortem and finally the coroner giving permission for the burial to go ahead, it still didn't feel possible. Alastair dead. His once handsome and virile athletic body soon to be laid to rest alongside Orla's. Just as Orla had wanted, Alastair having left no specific instructions as to how he wanted to be disposed of.

That was how Sorrel kept picturing him, as the young man she had first known. Was it an unconscious desire on her part to turn back the clock to a time when they believed themselves to be immune from something as commonplace as growing old, or immune even from death itself?

She watched Simon approach the lectern, his head bowed, his shoulders drooping. Danny had just given a reading, now it was Simon's turn to give the tribute. Sorrel had no idea what he planned to say, and she found herself holding her breath when Simon raised his head and gazed out at the congregation seated in the pews of the medieval church of St Peter's.

He began by honouring the friend he and Danny had known since childhood, saying how they had taken an instant liking to each other. 'We formed a triumvirate,' he explained, 'to which we swore undying loyalty.' He paused to clear his throat, and even at this distance, Sorrel could see his hands were shaking. 'I'm sure Danny would say the same,' he went on, 'that the three of us were as close as brothers. Somebody a lot smarter than me once said that we have as many personalities as we have friends, and I'd like to give Alastair the credit for shaping my personality, for without him, I would not be half the man I am — ' his voice cracked and he lowered his head again, his hands gripping the sides of the lectern.

It was a while before he could continue, and in those long agonising seconds, Sorrel couldn't bear to look at him. His sorrow was destroying him, taking him apart bit by bit, just as her own grief had been dismantling the protective armour with which she had equipped herself for far too long.

In the days and weeks after they had received the news that Alastair's Range Rover had skidded off the road on the A11 and hit a tree head on, Sorrel had moved through each day as if in slow motion. She had so many regrets. So much for which she blamed herself.

Had Alastair lost concentration behind the wheel of his car because he had been so upset by her cruel desire to expose him as a liar and a cheat?

Had the accident happened because he was devastated by Simon's refusal to let him in, and for which she was responsible?

Had he crashed because Sorrel had destroyed his relationship with Simon and Rachel and Callum?

These were the questions that kept her awake

at night. And then there were the if onlys that spun around inside her head.

If only Orla hadn't died.

If only Alastair had never met Valentina and invited her to stay at Linston End.

If only Sorrel's jealousy had not turned her into a monster hell-bent on revenge.

If only Sorrel had not broken her promise about their affair.

This was her punishment. Knowing that she had been instrumental in causing Alastair's death. Knowing too that Simon must blame her. How could he not?

For years she had fed the ravenous beast that was her jealousy, and only now did she realise the effort and energy she had put into keeping it under control, and what a bitter and petty woman it had turned her into. It had coloured her every thought, her every action.

It had not always been her intention to wreak havoc like some power-crazed avenging god. In the immediate aftermath of her affair with Alastair, she had been too humiliated by his casual ending of things with her to want to add further pain to her bruised emotions by admitting to anyone what they had done. She had felt emotionally defiled, reduced to wanting to pretend it had never happened. But gradually, oh, so gradually, the need for revenge, to put right the wrong he had committed, had grown within her, and then Valentina had arrived at Linston End, and had ripped open the unhealed wound of Sorrel's profoundly hurt pride.

Roused from her thoughts, she realised Simon

had resumed speaking, and he had put away the piece of paper he had been reading from.

'Alastair was not perfect,' he was saying, 'and he'd be the first to say that of himself; after all none of us is. But he was damned near as perfect a man as I had the good fortune to call my friend. I just wish that the last time I saw him, it could have been different, that we had not — '

At that, Simon's words broke off once more and he almost fell against the lectern, knocking it over. It was clear he could not carry on, and with the backs of her eyes pricking with the threat of tears, Sorrel watched Callum and Danny step forward to help him back to his seat in the pew next to her. Her heart, which she had believed now to be incapable of emotion, was full of compassion for him, and she tentatively reached out to take his hand, not knowing how he would respond. There had been so little contact between them since that awful day that had led to Alastair's death.

There had been no talk of divorce since they'd been informed by the police that Alastair was dead. It was as if they had no appetite for discussing their future, as though now it was irrelevant. And maybe it was.

With Danny and Frankie living with them while the lengthy process of sorting out their cottage dragged on, they somehow managed to be civil. They slept apart — Simon sleeping in Rachel's old room — and circled around each other guardedly.

Her eyes now blurred with tears, she felt Simon's warm hand wrap around hers. And in that moment she knew that despite it all, despite every accusation, every petty grumble, grievance and resentment, every jealous thought, or spiteful word, she did love Simon. It was just that she had loved Alastair too.

★ ★ ★

Just as his father regretted he had not had the chance to apologise to Alastair, so too did Callum. It weighed heavily on his conscience and he'd give anything to change things, but it was a wish he would never be granted.

He was still shocked by the revelation that Mum and Alastair had had an affair, and whenever the image of the two of them together came into his mind, he had to rid himself of it fast, before it could gain a proper footing and poison every good memory he'd ever had of his parents, and of Alastair.

Their affair had made him question so much about his parents' marriage, but as Danny had said to him, no one knows the truth behind a marriage except the husband and wife, especially not the children. Frankie had tried to explain that all marriages have their strengths and weaknesses, and their honest and their dishonest parts.

'Even yours?' Callum had asked.

'Oh yes,' she'd said, 'Danny and I each lie to one another in our different ways. I hide from him just how much I worry about him and his heart, and he lies about his own fears for the future. And look how he was visiting that care home without telling me, and then the mess he got himself into with Suzie Wu.'

Callum could see that she was right, but whatever lies people told in their relationships, and having seen the tragic results of his mother's feelings for Alastair, he vowed that he would never fall into the same trap with Jenna. He would banish all thoughts he'd ever contemplated about there being the potential for something more than friendship between them. He would not turn himself into a pathetic third wheel admiring Jenna from afar. He would not allow himself to be jealous of the man with whom she chose to spend her life. History would not repeat itself.

He had no idea if Jenna and Blake had established themselves as something more than 'just friends', but Blake was here today for the funeral, along with his mother, Laura. In fact the small church was full, mostly with people Callum recognised as local Broadland folk. The vast majority were here because they had been genuinely fond of Alastair.

However, there was one notable absence: Valentina. She had disappeared like a puff of smoke, as though she had never existed. Except she had existed and she had left a trail of devastation behind her. Rachel had sworn that if Valentina did show up for the funeral and made a showy tearful entrance, maybe even with her stepchildren in tow, she would personally bury the three of them in the graveyard. Thankfully there was no sign of the woman. Had she really loved Alastair? It was hard to believe that she had.

To Callum's left, his father was pressing a handkerchief to his eyes, his head bowed. His other hand, Callum noticed, was wrapped around Mum's. It gave him hope that his parents might somehow find a way to deal with what had gone wrong between them. He didn't want them to part. He wanted them to find a reason to stay together. As did Rachel. Was that selfish of them?

His sister was seated next to him on his right, and with her head resting against his shoulder, she was studying the order of service on her lap, the front page of which featured a photo of Alastair smiling happily on board *Swallowtail*. Dad had taken the picture a couple of years ago during one of their many days out on the river. Long before any of them had any idea their lives would be so thoroughly disrupted.

Mum and Dad had both lost weight since the accident, each blaming themselves for Alastair's death. The post-mortem had found traces of alcohol in Alastair's blood, and consumed much earlier in the day, it put him well under the limit and was not considered to be a contributing factor to his death. The probable cause of death was simply Alastair had fallen asleep at the wheel of his car. Even so, questions had been asked about the state of his mind that day. But just as it had been claimed that Orla had been her usual self the night she drowned, so it was with Alastair. Nobody had wanted to cast him in a poor light — to create a scandal. The truth, it seemed, was best kept to themselves. And maybe that was only right.

But Callum could not help wondering if once

again suicide was the real cause of death. Had Alastair deliberately driven off the A11, wanting to bring about an end to his life? Had it all got too much for him?

As it had so many times before, especially so in the last two months, the memory replayed itself in Callum's head of that night, very nearly a year ago, when he'd overheard the row between Alastair and Orla. He was on his way home in his dinghy after an evening spent at the Wherryman, and thinking he'd call in to let Alastair know he could collect *Water Lily*, that the engine problem he'd been experiencing had been fixed, he had left his boat in the dyke and approached the house. Lights were on in several rooms, including the conservatory where a door was open, and through which he could hear raised voices.

At first he thought it was something on the television, but then he realised it was Orla and Alastair shouting at each other. He had occasionally heard them argue, much in the same way Mum and Dad did, but this was altogether different, this was real hammer and tongs stuff, with Orla raging hysterically at Alastair, and he in turn retaliating with equal ferocity.

Callum had stood on the lawn transfixed, shamelessly curious to know what they were arguing about. Drawing closer, he heard Orla say, 'I'll kill myself if you leave me. I swear it, I'll kill myself and you'll have my death on your conscience for the rest of your life. You'll never be free of me!'

He'd heard what sounded like laughter

479

coming from Alastair — not amused laughter, but taunting laughter — and then the words: 'Go ahead. Kill yourself and put us both out of our misery!'

Shocked at what he was hearing, and not wanting to hear any more, Callum stole quietly away into the shadows. For all he knew rows like this were a regular occurrence between Alastair and Orla when they were alone, and were not to be taken seriously; they were just part and parcel of Orla's highly-strung nature.

When the news broke the following day that her body had been found in Linston Broad, and the assumption was instantly made that her death was a tragic accident, Callum waited for Alastair to say something about the argument they'd had the night before, and Orla's threat to kill herself. But Alastair never said a word, and so Callum kept his counsel. He didn't tell a soul, probably out of a sense of loyalty to a man he'd always respected and admired. What good would it serve anyway, to say what he knew? It wouldn't bring Orla back, would it?

His thoughts now strayed to the evening not so long ago, which he had spent with Alastair. When it had been just the two of them enjoying a beer, and when Callum had deliberately steered the conversation towards discussing Orla's death. He could still recall the sudden change in Alastair's manner in response to Callum's questions, and the abrupt darkening of his mood. There had been instant wariness in his expression, and a very obvious refusal to discuss the matter any further. Callum had been stupid to think that Alastair might want to confide in him, and admit that he had lied to the police, as well as in the evidence he had given at the inquest.

But just as he had kept quiet last year about what he knew, Callum would do so now. He saw no reason to stir things up any more than they had been already. Dad and Danny needed to hang on to what was left of their friend's memory, and Orla's too. Even if it meant papering over the cracks, or reinventing the past as they wanted it to be. Besides, in view of the extraordinary generosity of Alastair's will, Callum would feel as if he were betraying the man to divulge what he knew.

★ ★ ★

The service was now coming to an end and nudging his father, Callum got to his feet. Together with Danny, the three of them were helping to carry Alastair's coffin out of the church, and to one of his favourite pieces of music by Stan Getz. It was 'Autumn Leaves' and could not be more fitting, now that it was early October, and summer was far behind them.

63

After the last of the guests had left Linston End, having had their fill of wine, canapes and small talk, Simon could still feel the impression of Alastair's coffin on his shoulder. He never wanted to lose the sensation of carrying his old friend, of doing one last thing for him.

It wasn't a particularly cold October day, but he had decided, if only for something to do, to light the fire in the sitting room. It was probably where they would all gravitate to, once they'd eaten supper. As he struck a match and watched the flames lick greedily at the balls of newspaper and kindling in the grate, he thought of all the times he, Danny and Alastair had made campfires out in the garden when Aunt Cora had allowed them to sleep in an old army surplus canvas tent she'd had knocking around. At the time they had believed they were blissfully unsupervised, free to do as they liked, but Aunt Cora had been a wily old bird and had, of course, kept a surreptitious eye on them. That was what had always been so great about staying here at Linston End; for them as youngsters, and then for Rachel, Callum and Jenna, it had offered the kind of freedom a child seldom experiences in their own home.

And now the magical house, with its myriad memories, belonged to the children. In a move that had taken them all by surprise, Alastair had written a new will a few weeks before he'd gone travelling last year, leaving the house to the next generation, as he put it. Appreciating that they would never be able to afford the costs involved at their young age, he had also arranged a trust fund for them, which was to be used solely for the upkeep and running of the property. His hope, so his will stated, was that in time their own children would one day benefit from spending holidays here, that it would be as transforming for them as it had been for him.

When Simon learned of the contents of Alastair's will — obviously written before he'd met Valentina and decided to sell up — any last residue of anger he had harboured towards his old friend for his betrayal in sleeping with Sorrel was swept away. He could not remain angry with Alastair. Yes, lines had been crossed, and in the worst possible way, but there was nothing to be gained in dwelling on their mistakes; better to accept they had each played their part.

'You all right, Dad?'

Still crouching in front of the fire, the box of matches in his hand, Simon glanced over his shoulder to see Rachel. 'I'm fine,' he said. 'Well, as fine as can be expected in the circumstances.'

She came and knelt on the hearthrug with him. 'It's been a bloody awful day, hasn't it?'

He sighed. 'Yep, bloody awful just about covers it.'

'Danny's suggesting we have a fish and chip supper, what do you think?'

'As ever, I think Danny's right.'

'He's also suggested that we look at all those

old photos you unearthed from way back when. We never got the chance to see them when we were here in August, did we? It seems a fitting tribute to Orla and Alastair.'

'Yes,' he said, 'it does.'

She took the box of matches from his hands and hugged him. 'I love you, Dad, you do know that don't you?'

'Don't,' he said, but not meaning it, 'you'll set me off blubbing again, and I've done quite enough of that today.'

'You're allowed to cry, you know. No matter what Mum and Alastair did, he was still your best friend.'

He held her roughly to his chest, suddenly remembering how he'd felt the night she'd nearly drowned, and how it had brought home to him just how dear she was to him. 'Where is your mother?' he asked, when he let her go.

'She and Frankie are upstairs making a start on bagging up Alastair's things.'

'And the others?'

'Danny and Callum are putting the last of the glasses into the dishwasher, and Sylvia and Neil have gone home.'

'What about Jenna?'

'Ah, she's gone over to the Mill to see Blake.'

'Don't they see enough of each other at work?'

'He stopped working at Heart-to-Heart a few weeks ago and is with an ad agency now. He did it to give Jenna space.'

'Why? What does she need space for?'

Rachel wobbled her head about, just as she had as a child. 'Oh, the silly girl made a ridiculous vow not to date a co-worker, so he's removed that particular obstacle.'

'He's a determined fellow, then.'

'He is. And Jenna's too cautious for her own good. As I never stop telling her. Some risks are worth taking.'

The fire having really got going now, and feeling too hot, Simon stood up and moved away to stand at the window. 'Caution isn't a bad thing, Rachel,' he said. 'Look where risk-taking took Alastair, with his rushing headlong into a relationship with . . . with that dreadful woman. And need I remind you — '

'Need you remind me that I risked my life by nearly drowning because I wanted to impress Nikolai?' she cut in. 'Risk, risk, risk, blah, blah, blah, I do it all the time. But, Dad, endless procrastination is bad for you. It means you never do anything.' She came and joined him at the window. 'Have you and Mum talked yet? And I mean talked properly?'

He shook his head. 'Not yet.'

'Don't you think you should?'

'We both need time.'

'That's an excuse, Dad. You're scared to talk to Mum, aren't you?'

'With good reason. I might not like what she says.'

'Have you thought that maybe she's scared as well? But unless you stop hiding from each other, you'll never know what the other is thinking.'

He thought of Sorrel's hand reaching for his in the church that afternoon. Had that been a sign

485

that she was willing for them to stay together after all? Or had it been pity for him? Either way, he was grateful to his daughter for trying to reassure him. 'When did you get to be so wise?' he asked.

'I'm not. But I know when something is glaringly obvious. Promise me, Dad, talk to Mum. Do it for me. And for Callum. We can't bear the thought of the two of you separating. I know it's not easy, but please try to forgive her for what she did.'

He could deny Rachel nothing, and he'd give anything to grant the wish she so desperately wanted, but in this he feared he would fail her. 'It's not as simple as saying I forgive her, sweetheart,' he murmured, 'it's what your mother wants. And if she doesn't want to stay married, there's not a lot I can do about it.'

'Perhaps you should try asking me what it is I do want?'

It was Sorrel herself, standing in the doorway, a bulging black bin bag in each hand.

Before Simon could speak, Rachel had moved across the room so that she was equidistant from them. 'You know I love you both,' she said, 'and because of that I want the pair of you to be happy. Let's face it, you'd be completely miserable without the other. Dad, think how you'd miss Mum, and all her nagging you to pick up your smelly old socks from the bedroom floor, and her funny way of always straightening things and keeping you on your toes. And, Mum, think how you'd miss Dad's dreadful jokes, and having somebody to tut at. And yes, I'm quite aware these don't sound like the most romantic or exciting of reasons to stay with somebody, but it's who you both are, who you've always been. Surely that means something, doesn't it?'

She looked from one to the other, her expression heartbreakingly earnest as she implored them to do as she asked. It forced Simon to be brave, to stop procrastinating, just as Rachel had accused him of doing. He loved Sorrel, he really did. He didn't want to lose her. It was time to let her know that. Time too, to remember the very last words Alastair uttered to Simon before he set off on that fateful drive home to Linston End. *'Don't let me be the reason that you and Sorrel part. I'm not worth it.'*

He swallowed his fear and met his wife's gaze head on. 'Well, Sorrel,' he said, 'what *do* you want?'

'I'd like you to put these bags in the garage ready for when we have a full car-load to take to the charity shop, and then . . . ' she paused as the expression on her face softened imperceptibly and the corners of her mouth lifted into the faintest of smiles, ' . . . and then I want us to put our children and friends out of their misery. We've tortured them for long enough. Ourselves too.'

'Does that mean you don't want a divorce?' blurted out Rachel, and again before Simon could speak.

'That's exactly what I mean,' Sorrel replied. 'Is that what you want, Simon? Can you forgive me for what I did?'

He went to her, fumbled awkwardly for a

moment to remove the heavy bags from her hands, then took her in his arms, gently at first, almost scared that she might push him away, but she didn't, so he crushed her to him. 'Of course I forgive you,' he said hoarsely, burying his face into her hair and breathing in the beautiful familiarity of her. When he finally released her, they looked about the room and realised they were alone. Rachel had gone.

'That must be the first discreet thing our daughter has ever done, disappearing like that,' remarked Sorrel. She then tipped her head back to look at Simon, and he knew she was going to say something serious, something that forced him to hold his relief in check.

'I can't unsay all those unkind things I said to you, Simon, but I want you to know, it wasn't really about you; it was me I was trying to lash out at. I hated myself for being so weak, for loving Alastair the way I did, for being blinded by what now seems like an obsession. Can you really forgive me when you know that I've spent the greater part of our marriage living a lie?'

'We've both lied, Sorrel; I told you that before.

'Yes, I know, but often the greatest lies are those which aren't actually said aloud, they're hidden out of sight and cause the worst damage.'

'That might be true, but we can't keep saying sorry to each other forever. We have to let go of it all.'

Once more a flicker of a smile softened her expression. 'It's a shame we're not Catholics and we could make a one-time confession and have done with it.'

'As far as I'm concerned, we've made our confession, and forgiveness has been given. So let's wipe the slate clean and start anew. I'll even throw in the promise to pick up my socks, and to stop whatever else it is that I do that annoys you. Perhaps you could make a list?'

'If only life could be that simple,' she said with a small shake of her head.

'Life is as complicated as we want to make it.'

'That sounds like something Danny would say.'

'Yes,' he said, 'I suppose it does. Now then, about these bin bags.'

★   ★   ★

It was when he was in the garage, putting the bags of Alastair's things on the spotless floor — Alastair always did like his garage to be as neat as a pin — that all over again, he felt the loss of his friend. It hit him like this at least a dozen times a day. Alastair gone. Dead. No more.

He looked at the bags Sorrel had given him and opened one. On the top was a charcoal grey cashmere sweater. He pictured Sorrel carefully folding it and adding it to the pile destined for the charity shop. Was that the sum total of a man's life, his possessions bagged up for the likes of Age Concern and Heart-to-Heart? He thought again of Sorrel folding the sweater. Had she done it lovingly? Had she pressed it to her face so that she could breathe in the smell of Alastair . . . *her lover . . . ?*

No!

He had forgiven Sorrel. He was not to torment himself this way. It was over. Hadn't he just said that to her?

What they both needed was time. Time to recover and to heal, and to learn to trust one another again. He'd be a fool to think it would be easy, but who said love would ever be easy? And what was the alternative? Whatever it was, he didn't want it. He wanted Sorrel and his family. They were his world.

★ ★ ★

On her way back upstairs to rejoin Frankie, Sorrel paused when she reached the top step. She was thinking of the naked vulnerability in Simon's face just now when he had asked her what she wanted. His eyes had been those of a frightened boy who feared he was about to be severely punished. And she was the one who was entirely responsible for reducing him to that. Suddenly she couldn't breathe and she gripped the banister hard, acutely aware of a rising sense of panic at all that she had done. All that she *hadn't done*, and all that she *hadn't been*.

For years she had secretly blamed Simon for failing to be the man — the husband — she had wanted him to be, but the reality was, she had not been the wife he had wanted.

But had she left it too late to undo the harm she had caused? Was it too late for them to put things right and be the people they were supposed to be? And could she really somehow wipe the slate clean as Simon wanted and learn to love the whole of him in the way he deserved? Because he did deserve more than she had given him. So much more. He was a good man and a loyal one who was prepared to forgive her. Not many men would be capable of doing that. Or was it merely laziness on his part? Was he afraid to be on his own and so it was better to stay with the she-devil he knew? Was it fear and laziness on her part too, to remain with him?

She blinked hard and took a deep breath, letting the air fill her lungs to the point of bursting. She needed to stop questioning everything. She needed to learn how to . . . what precisely?

To be happy again. That was what she needed to learn, to appreciate what she had and not hunger for something that did not exist. Everything Alastair had been to her had been a figment of her imagination, an unattainable object of desire that had blinded her. Even their affair, in all its physical intimacy, had not brought her genuine happiness. It certainly hadn't brought them closer. In the long run it had made her miserable and unable to appreciate what she had already.

She had to change. Change, or stay the same and be miserable. It was an easy choice. So she straightened her back, took the final step of the stairs and went to find Frankie.

64

In Moscow it was night time already and the weather had dropped to an unseasonably cold temperature.

Standing at the long case window of her mother's apartment, Valentina could feel a draught whistling through a gap in the wooden frame. It felt like only yesterday when she had stood here being chastised by her mama for not rushing to marry Alastair. It had been a recurring theme in their conversations since Valentina had arrived two days ago, and it never varied from the script. They were running through it again now, as though her mama believed the more times she gave her opinion and advice, the more chance there was of Valentina heeding it.

'Did I not warn you that he would slip through your fingers if you did not marry him?'

'Mama, he did not slip through my fingers. He died!'

'Tsk, tsk, there is no need to shout. All I am saying is that you need to choose your husbands with more care. At least select a man who is likely to live. First Ivan, now this Alexander.'

'His name was Alastair. As I've told you many times before.'

'What does it matter what his name was?' Liliya said with an indifferent shrug. 'He's gone, and now you must find somebody new to support you. Why not try a Russian again? A handsome man moved in to the penthouse apartment a few weeks ago, and he drives a beautiful car. I believe he travels a lot, so he wouldn't be any trouble to you? And wouldn't it be perfect, if you lived right here in the same apartment block with me?'

Valentina could think of nothing worse.

Oh yes, she could. Being stuck in dreary old England with Alastair's boring, shallow-minded friends, that would be so much worse!

It pained her to admit it, but she had misjudged Alastair and his commitment to her. And more importantly, she had misjudged her plan to win him for herself through a process of divide and conquer. By alienating his friends — by having them gang up on her — she had assumed Alastair would take her side and see that they did not truly have his happiness at heart, only their own.

Happiness . . . it was so elusive, like trying to catch a butterfly. For a short time she had been wildly happy. That was when she had first met Alastair, when she had come to his rescue. She smiled at the memory, remembering how much she had enjoyed herself in those early days of getting to know this charming Englishman. How simple it had all been, the two of them spending their days on the beach, and before too long, their nights in bed together.

With his engaging vulnerability — he wore his widowhood lightly, but it was there all the same, an underlying note of unhappiness that occasionally made itself known — she had taken him under her wing with ease.

For that brief time, when she knew he was in thrall to her, she had been a completely different person, freer and full of dreams. She had loved him for that, for giving her that gift.

But that gift had been snatched away from her, along with all her dreams. No more south of France. No more dreaming of castles in the air.

Her forehead resting against the cool glass of the window, she sighed. Her plan had so very nearly worked, but then Nikolai and Irina had ruined everything. She should never have encouraged them to visit.

And now she was back to square one, having resumed work as an interpreter in Paris, on the pretext that she needed to be occupied after losing the man she loved. The reality was, she needed the money.

Down on the street below, she saw the headlamps of a large, shiny black car sweep into a space directly in front of the apartment block. In the light cast from the street lamp, she could see the car was a Bentley. The driver pushed open the door and stepped onto the pavement, a mobile phone pressed to his left ear. At this distance, four floors up, she couldn't get a good look at his face, but his silvery hair was thick and wavy. Tastefully dressed in a dark suit and a smart overcoat, he approached the entrance to the apartment block with a purposeful stride, coupled with an unmistakable air of possession. Here was a man who knew what he was about.

'What car does the new owner of the penthouse drive, Mama?' she asked, now that the man had disappeared from view.

Her mother came and joined her at the window. She looked down on to the street. 'That car,' she said, pointing with her well-manicured forefinger. 'That is the one he drives. And now, my little *malyshka*, I suppose you would like me to invite him in for tea one day? Or maybe an aperitif?'

'I see no reason not to be a good neighbour,' Valentina said, absently.

'No reason at all,' agreed Liliya, pulling the curtains across. 'Leave it to me.'

As one door closes, another always opens. That was what Alastair had often said to her. It was Valentina's avowed belief too.

65

'You've just missed my mother,' Blake said as he passed Jenna a mug of tea, 'apparently she had something urgent she had to rush out and do.'

'Why *apparently?*'

'I think she thought we'd want some time alone.'

'Did she indeed? Or was it you who suggested she went out?' Jenna asked.

'Why, Lawyer Girl, what a suspicious mind you have.'

She smiled. 'With you, Blake, I find that's the best way to be.'

He smiled too, and then pointed towards the sofa across the kitchen. 'Shall we?'

'Would you mind if we went out on the balcony instead? I love the view from up there.'

'Are you sure you won't be too cold?'

'I'll put my fleece back on.' She picked it up from the chair, where Blake had put it when she'd arrived. They had both swapped their formal funeral clothes for jeans and, weirdly, the navy-blue boyfriend-cardigan she was wearing was very like the one he had on.

He led the way from the quirkily designed kitchen that had been built to fit the circular shape of the mill, and took her up the two flights of narrow stairs.

Outside, the late afternoon light was fading and wispy strands of indigo and violet cloud stretched across the opalescent sky, all of which was reflected perfectly in the glassy surface of the river. It was a magnificent sight and one Jenna would never tire of. Now, thanks to Alastair's generosity, she was part owner of Linston End with Callum and Rachel, and would be able to visit as often as she wanted. It really didn't seem possible. But then so much that had happened this summer didn't seem possible.

Including Blake — her fiddle-playing lover-boy, as Rachel annoyingly still referred to him. From nowhere he had come spinning into her orbit, and ever since had made her feel dizzily disorientated. Nobody had ever had the same effect on her before. And just as he had said he would, he had left Heart-to-Heart two weeks ago, having resigned and worked his notice. She had felt guilty at the decision he'd taken, but he had reassured her that he had intended to move on anyway.

The office had seemed very dull without him, and despite the sad circumstances of their meeting today, Jenna had been looking forward to seeing him again. She had longed to turn around during the funeral service to locate him in the pews behind her, but reminding herself of the reason she was there, she had refrained from doing so.

Not until they were gathered around the grave was she able to steal a proper glance at Blake. Dressed in a suit, shirt and tie, he had looked uncharacteristically sombre and even more youthful than he usually did, like a sixth-former on his way for an interview. At the sight of him, especially when he'd caught her eye and nodded, her heart had done that absurd jumpy thing it had started doing recently whenever she thought of him. It was doing it now. *Jumpety-jump-jump, jumpety-jump-jump.*

'It was good of you and your mother to come to Alastair's funeral,' she said, trying to still her out-of-control-heart. She turned her head to look at Blake and realised he'd been staring at her, and not the view as she had. 'You really shouldn't do that,' she said, her stomach now performing back-flips and somersaults.

'What?' he said. 'I was breathing, that was all.'

She tutted. 'If only that was all you ever did.'

He smiled. 'What's the latest on your parents' house? Has work started yet on putting it right?'

'We were warned by the insurance company that the process would be slow, but it looks like we're finally getting somewhere. The builders start work next week.'

'Fingers crossed it's plain sailing from then on,' he said. 'How's your father doing?'

'He's behaving himself and not overdoing it, much to Mum's relief, and mine, so that's good. I was so worried about him before. But then Rachel reckons I worry far too much.'

'Better to care than not at all.'

'That's what Dad says when Mum tells him he cares too much.'

'So you're a chip off the old block, are you?'

'I suppose I am.'

'And I suppose that's what I like about you. The fact that you don't trivialise things.'

Her heart suddenly lurched at his words, and

the intense way he looked at her. Before she could say anything, he said, 'Would I be pushing my luck to ask if you've missed having me around at work?'

'Funnily enough, I have,' she said, attempting to play it cool. 'So how's the new job going?'

He laughed. 'Oh, no you don't! You're not changing the subject just as it gets interesting. Tell me, and be truthful, on a scale of one to ten, how much have you missed me?'

Another sip of her tea. Another attempt to play it cool. 'Goodness, who knew you could be so needy?'

'Answer the question, Lawyer Girl.'

She drew her brows together and pressed a finger to her lower lip as though giving the question her greatest consideration. 'Oh, about five, I'd say.'

'Only five,' he repeated, 'and after I've tried so hard? I mean, come on, I'm good for a seven, surely? An eight if you were feeling benevolent?'

'I'm kidding,' she said with a small smile. 'Ten. Maybe even eleven.'

He whistled. 'As high as that? I'm honoured. And if you're interested, I've missed you ten to the power of ten. Which begs the question; where does that leave us? Given that I'm not a work colleague anymore? And by us . . . ' He paused to take her mug of tea and place it, along with his, on the floor behind him. He then put his hands on her shoulders, ' . . . And by *us*, I mean you and me.'

After two months of being frantically busy with work, as well as helping her parents sort out the mess of Walnut Tree Cottage, it was time now to be bold. Time now to stop pretending she didn't feel the way she did. 'I think it's high time we kissed. Don't you?'

She saw a glimmer of surprise in his face, and then, moving a hand from her shoulder, he placed it deftly on the nape of her neck. Instinctively she leaned towards him, closing the gap between them. With her mouth a tantalising few inches from his, and drawing the moment out, she looked up into the beguiling caramel warmth of his eyes. All summer, she thought, it's taken me all summer, right through to autumn, to allow myself to do this.

'Shall we jump?' he asked.

'Jump where?' she murmured.

He leaned in and brushed his lips against hers, sending first a tingle up and down her spine, and then a shock-wave of exhilarating desire through her body. 'Into the unknown,' he said, 'the two of us together.'

Without another word exchanged, she kissed him, and she kept on kissing him, hurling herself headlong into the unknown.

'Would it be ungallant of me to say that was worth the wait?' he asked, when at last they parted so they could catch their breath.

'Oh, horribly ungallant.'

'In that case,' he said, wrapping his arms around her. 'I'd better not tell you that you had me at 'That's the way to do it.''

She laughed at his Mr Punch voice. 'You're joking.'

'I'm not. The moment I saw you playing with

those puppets, I wanted to know everything about you. And I mean *everything*.'

She pulled a face. 'I hope that doesn't mean you have some sort of peculiar thing going on for Mr Punch.'

'I assure you I don't. The only thing I have going on is my total susceptibility when it comes to you.' He kissed her lightly on the lips. And again.

It felt so natural between them, his kissing her and standing here in his embrace. It was as if they were already an established couple.

'When can I see you again?' he asked, trailing a finger along the length of her jaw, all the way to her ear, and setting off a seismic reaction deep inside her.

'Hopefully very soon,' she murmured.

He smiled at that. 'Tomorrow?'

'Tomorrow evening Rachel and I are going back to London, what about you?'

'I leave first thing in the morning. I have a client meeting at three o'clock, and being the new boy, I need to toe the line. Are you free the day after when you've finished work?'

'Busy, I'm afraid.'

His brow creased with a frown. 'Oh.'

She smiled at the disappointment in his voice and tapped his chest with a finger. 'Busy seeing you for dinner, I hope.'

His face instantly brightened. 'Brilliant! I'll let you decide where we eat. Hey, I nearly forgot. You'll never believe it, but my mother's thinking of buying the Mill.'

'Really? How wonderful!'

'Well, she's made an offer to the owners, which they're considering. So if all goes to plan, it'll mean I'll have the chance to visit here a lot more often. And maybe,' he added with a tilt of his head, 'when you just happen to be here.'

'I think that's likely to happen quite frequently,' she said happily. She kissed him once more before sliding round within the circle of his embrace to look across the river to the house she'd loved all her life — Linston End. Who knew what the future held for it, and for herself?

Maybe Blake would be a part of that future, or maybe he wouldn't. But for now, with his arms around her, his chin resting on the top of her head, she was content to enjoy the moment, to let it be whatever it was destined to be.

66

They felt it was the right thing to do late that night, and before going their separate ways tomorrow.

It was nearly midnight and they were in the pavilion at the end of the garden; all around them flickering candles caused shadows to dance on the wooden walls. On the table were seven champagne flutes and a bottle of Alastair's prized Dom Perignon from his wine cellar. Danny didn't like to think how much it had cost, but he was sure Alastair wouldn't begrudge them drinking it.

With the greatest of care, Danny began pouring out the champagne, while Frankie passed the glasses round in the subdued silence. He had wondered whether to suggest to Jenna that Blake and his mother should join them, seeing as she had returned from the Mill with a definite spring in her step, and a radiant sparkle in her eyes, the like of which he couldn't recall seeing before. But he'd decided not to. There would be plenty of occasions in the future when they could do that. In fairness to Alastair, this was his night.

And in fairness to the woman Alastair had loved, Danny had contacted Valentina to let her know when and where the funeral would take place. When he'd known the details himself, Danny had driven over to Norfolk and using his key — years ago Alastair had given both him and Simon keys for Linston End — he had accessed Alastair's laptop. Knowing of old the password — Getz1927 — he'd found Valentina's email address and had switched off the computer straightaway. Not for anything would he have invaded his friend's privacy by reading any of the emails that had been exchanged between the lovers.

That evening, and back at Simon and Sorrel's, where he and Frankie were still staying, he had emailed Valentina. He received a reply the next morning, the terseness of which bristled with formality and brevity. She thanked him for contacting her, but she would not be attending the funeral.

And that was it. No reason given. No clue as to what she felt about Alastair's death. Nothing. That Alastair had fallen for such a cold-hearted woman was beyond Danny. But then there was so much he had discovered about his old friend this summer that was beyond him. It just went to prove the adage that you never really know a person, even when you would swear on your life that you did.

But here they were preparing to bid a final farewell to their beloved friend. To Danny's right was Sorrel, and on the other side of her was Simon. It was good to see them looking a lot less hostile towards each other. The harsh downward slope of Sorrel's mouth had been replaced with a softer, more benign expression, and Simon was less tense.

When Rachel had earlier burst into the kitchen

where Danny and Callum were still clearing up, and had eagerly shared the news that their parents weren't going to split up after all, Danny had been delighted. Inwardly though, he didn't underestimate the challenge it was going to be for Simon and Sorrel to put the events of the summer behind them.

It was much the same for him and Frankie with the lengthy process they had ahead of them in restoring Walnut Tree Cottage. Yesterday, and after much thought and discussion, they had taken the decision that as soon as the house was as good as new, they would put it on the market and resume their search for somewhere to live near Linston End. They had yet to tell Jenna, or anyone else, of their plans, preferring to wait until after today. It gave them both a sense of hope with something new and exciting to look forward to.

With all the evidence the police had, Suzie Wu had been held on remand since being charged with damaging property and intent to endanger life. A trial date was set for next month. Much to his and Frankie's relief, bail had been denied on the grounds that there was a strong possibility the woman would reoffend. She was also considered a threat to others and a flight risk.

Despite being a lawyer, or maybe because he had a legal background, Danny dreaded the court case. He didn't want to have to relive what the woman had put them through. He just wanted to put it behind him and get on with their lives. Moreover, he knew that Frankie would worry about him, or more specifically, worry about the strain his heart would be under while the case was being heard.

But for now, that wasn't important. Saying farewell to Alastair was the immediate priority, and with everyone holding a glass in their hand, he looked around the table at those who were so dear to him — Frankie, Jenna, Rachel, Callum, Sorrel and Simon. 'Who wants to do the honours?' he asked.

'I will,' said Simon. He cleared his throat and took a moment to think. 'To our very great friend,' he began, 'to whom we owe so much. Without him, we wouldn't be here, not one of us, and we wouldn't be the people we are. Here's to you, Alastair. And to you, Orla. Farewell dear friends.'

He raised his glass, indicating that that was all he was going to say. And really, it was all that needed to be said.

'Farewell dear friends,' everyone echoed, their wineglasses touching across the table, their eyes glistening in the candlelight as they acknowledged the great love they'd had, not just for Alastair and Orla, but also for the magical place that was Linston End.

Acknowledgements

I must give thanks to all I met on the Norfolk Broads who, whether they realised it or not at the time, helped me while I was researching this book.

Special thanks must also go to Adrienne Seddon and her husband who run the post office in wonderful Horning, and where I stayed several times while working on this novel. Thank you, Adrienne, for sharing your local knowledge with me.

Thank you to my god-daughter, Millie, for guiding me through the process of creating Heart-to-Heart.

More thanks go to Clever Trevor — he knows why!

Inspiration can come at the most unexpected times and the idea for *Swallowtail Summer* and the friends who would gather at Linston End came to me after a conversation in Norway last year. The person I was chatting to shall remain anonymous, but I'm most grateful for the conversation we had while he drove me around Oslo. I knew straightaway that, inadvertently, he had just given me the idea for my twenty-second novel. Although, of course, my story bears no relationship to what he told me. That's fiction for you!

The Inspiration for *Swallowtail Summer*

One of the things I love about writing is the tingly feeling I get when the perfect idea for a novel drops out of the ether and lands in my lap. It happened to me last spring when I was in Oslo promoting a book, and it was something somebody told me, about a group of close lifelong friends who had known each other since their school days. In their sixties, these friends were all still married to the women they had met when young, still lived in more or less the same area they always had, and every year they planned a holiday together.

Firstly, I was struck how amazing this was, but also how remarkable, comparing it to my own immediate circle of friends and how career changes, divorce, and death had fractured the dynamics of the friendships formed so many years ago. My next thought was to imagine this enviably close-knit group of friends and wonder *what if* . . . What if, and for whatever reason, one of them broke rank from this cosy world of best-friends-forever? What would be the consequences? Would cracks appear in what they had believed were their rock-sure foundations? Would the ties of loyalty that had bound them together for so long come unravelled? Would years of suppressed resentments and petty jealousies reveal just how flawed their friendship really was?

It might seem cruel the way my mind took hold of this group of devoted friends and turned their world upside down, but in my defence, it is the job of an author to wreak havoc at the heartless swish of a pen, or the vicious tap of the keyboard. After all, one has to break a few eggs to make an omelette.

While I was metaphorically cracking eggs, I was also finishing *Coming Home to Island House*, and when that was done I decided to treat myself to a couple of days away exploring an area of the country I'd never been to before — the Norfolk Broads. The moment I caught my first glimpse of Horning and the river Bure, I knew without a shadow of doubt I'd just found the setting for my next book. It was that tingling feeling all over again. I've said it many times before, that having grown up by the sea, water is in my DNA and it invariably finds its way into my stories, whether it be a lake, a pond, the sea, or a river. So it felt right to set a book on the river and create my own idyllic village called Linston, and an equally idyllic house called Linston End with its toes dipping into the water's edge. It would be where I would mentally spend the next twelve months while writing the book, and the prospect couldn't have pleased me more. Even better, (for research purposes, you understand) I stayed on the Broads both in the summer and the autumn and absolutely fell in love with the slow pace of life on the river. If I hadn't had a book to write, I could have happily stared out of the window for hours at a time watching the wildlife quietly going about its business and the boats passing by.

I hope that in reading this latest book of mine — my twenty-second — you might also be tempted to visit this unique and very beautiful part of the country.

reveal just how flawed their friendship really was?

It might seem cruel the way my mind took hold of this group of devoted friends and turned their world upside down, but in my defence, it is the job of an author to wreak havoc at the heartless swish of a pen, or the vicious tap of the keyboard. After all, one has to break a few eggs to make an omelette.

While I was metaphorically cracking eggs, I was also finishing *Coming Home to Island House*, and when that was done I decided to treat myself to a couple of days away exploring an area of the country I'd never been to before — the Norfolk Broads. The moment I caught my first glimpse of Horning and the river Bure, I knew without a shadow of doubt I'd just found the setting for my next book. It was that tingling feeling all over again. I've said it many times before, that having grown up by the sea, water is in my DNA and it invariably finds its way into my stories, whether it be a lake, a pond, the sea, or a river. So it felt right to set a book on the river and create my own idyllic village called Linston, and an equally idyllic house called Linston End with its toes dipping into the water's edge. It would be where I would mentally spend the next twelve months while writing the book, and the prospect couldn't have pleased me more. Even better, (for research purposes, you understand) I stayed on the Broads both in the summer and the autumn and absolutely fell in love with the slow pace of life on the river. If I hadn't had a book to write, I could have happily stared out of the window for hours at a time watching the wildlife quietly going about its business and the boats passing by.

I hope that in reading this latest book of mine — my twenty-second — you might also be tempted to visit this unique and very beautiful part of the country.

We do hope that you have enjoyed reading this large print book.

Did you know that all of our titles are available for purchase?

We publish a wide range of high quality large print books including:
Romances, Mysteries, Classics
General Fiction
Non Fiction and Westerns

Special interest titles available in large print are:
The Little Oxford Dictionary
Music Book
Song Book
Hymn Book
Service Book

Also available from us courtesy of Oxford University Press:
Young Readers' Dictionary
(large print edition)
Young Readers' Thesaurus
(large print edition)

For further information or a free brochure, please contact us at:
Ulverscroft Large Print Books Ltd.,
The Green, Bradgate Road, Anstey,
Leicester, LE7 7FU, England.
Tel: (00 44) 0116 236 4325
Fax: (00 44) 0116 234 0205

Other titles published by Ulverscroft:

SONG OF THE SKYLARK

Erica James

Lizzie has always had an unfortunate knack of attracting bad luck, but this time she's hit the jackpot. Losing her heart to her boss leads to losing her job, and with no money in the bank, she finds herself forced to move back home with her parents. When she reluctantly takes another job, she meets Mrs Dallimore, a seemingly ordinary elderly woman with an astonishing past . . . Now in her nineties, Mrs Dallimore is also coming to terms with her situation. Old age is finally catching up with her. Embarking upon an unexpected friendship with Lizzie, she tells the story of a young girl who left America before the outbreak of World War Two and, in crossing an ocean, found herself beginning a new life she could never have imagined . . .